FINDING
FAITH

FINDING FAITH

A Novel

Kami Abrell

Kami Abrell
Pendleton, IN
kamiabrell@gmail.com

ISBN 979-8-378-04044-5

Dedicated to the girls finding their way. Faith over fear.

December 22nd

"GET AWAY! MOVE! HURRY! MOVE AWAY!"

The words are muffled and barely audible against the ringing in my ears. My brain continues to scream orders at my body, but my movements are slow and sloppy, much like the movements of a wobbly infant. My leggings prove to be no match for the shards of glass on the wet pavement, slicing through the material. I feel each prick of glass on the skin at my knees; my palms are scraped and bloody.

"GET AWAY! YOU NEED TO GET AWAY FROM THE CAR!" The voice is deeper than my own and I realize the words are not mine. The voice is getting louder as are the footsteps coming toward me. There is a shrill, piercing sound of a siren off in the distance and I can still feel the waves of heat. I look up to see who is racing toward me, but all is see is the halo of the streetlight outlining a tall, dark figure.

"You need to get you away from the car!" I feel myself being lifted off the wet asphalt. My feet try to keep up, but I hear the scraping of my leather boots on the pavement. "Faith..." I croak, my throat raw. I look over my shoulder trying to see her through the cloud of smoke. I stumble slightly as the giant carrying me whispers, "I got you," and I notice my boots aren't scrapping the concrete anymore. We must have made it to the other side of the road the strangers lowers me to back to the ground. Just then my legs give our and I am face down on the ice-covered grass. The roaring flames grow louder as a pungent smoke fills the crisp night air.

"I see something!" I barely hear over the roaring fire and screaming sirens, but I can tell the voice is different than the one talking to me. "Over here! We've got another one!" Thank God, they found her! I'm vaguely aware of the heat at my back in contrast to the cool wetness on my face from the snow. And then, darkness…

Before

There is no right or wrong way to treat someone when their life is turned upside down. It's not like there is a manual for anyone to follow. And there isn't anything anyone can do or say to help, but that doesn't stop people from trying. Some anyway. Others try to avoid the conversation all together, like that will fix it. But what no one seems to realize is nothing will ever be the same. At least not for the four of us.

Who are we? We are sisters…Faith and me, Fiona, and our two BFF's. It's been us four since Lyla and I became friends in sixth grade. Long before Faith and Ella had their driver's licenses, and we rode our bikes everywhere. But that didn't last long. Faith and Ella are three years older, and Faith got her license when Lyla and I were in seventh grade. We ditched our bikes and proudly took our spots in the backseat of Faith's Camaro and became the envy of every seventh grader in Brookston.

Faith and I live less than a mile from downtown Brookston, a small country town in Southeastern Indiana, less than a thirty-minute drive to Cincinnati, Ohio. Brookston has the fastest growing population in Delmont County. Manly due to the proximity of Cincinnati and the

Greater Cincinnati Airport, but for natives of Brookston, like Faith, Lyla, and me, it's a sense of pride with us that we were born and raised here. As for Ella, she moved here in first grade and Faith determined it's "close enough" for Ella to be a native Brookstonian. Basically, if you moved to Brookston after sixth grade started, you are a transplant. Still accepted, but...we save this title for students whose families relocated with the main purpose of moving to the hilly countryside to "get out of the city."

"Turn toward Hamilton Heights at the four-way, Faith," I instruct as we pull up to the one and only flashing light in Brookston.

I reach for the button on the radio and turn the volume down. Normally, I am all for Cardi B, but I just can't right now. Plus, I know my sister, she's not going to let this slide without an interrogation.

"I thought we were picking up Lyla?" Faith turns to me with eyebrows raised as she waits for the car in front of us to go, but I hear the blinker come on and I sink back into my seat. "This doesn't have anything to do with the party at SWU over fall break, does it?" Faith tilts her head slightly and looks at me out of the corner of her eye with a disapproving pout.

Faith knows how to play me. She knows I don't like to share my feelings and will shut down if I'm not ready to talk. So, she waits until the right time to ask me about the SWU party. And apparently that's now. I'm sure she heard about it from Ella or Lyla.

"No. Don't be ridiculous." I pick at a scab on my arm from where my cat scratched me and feel the heat rise in my cheeks.

"Fi, Lyla is allowed to have other friends—"

"I know that," I snap and I hear myself scoff and add an eye roll I know Faith can't see since her eyes are on the road.

"Then what's the problem?" Faith lets out a laugh knowing full well she's hit a nerve. The engine of the V6 Camaro roars as Faith presses the gas pedal and turns left. I watch out the window as we take the first curve and begin the descent down the hill; lifeless tree branches flash by the window. Beyond the trees, the clouds hang dark over the barren hillside. The dead brown grass would be so much prettier covered in a layer of snow.

"Fi?" Faith's voice snaps my attention back to the unavoidable conversation about my best friend.

"Ugh." I throw my head back on the head rest and close my eyes. "You're gonna think I'm being extra." I lean forward and reach in the glove box for a napkin to put on the scratch I have bleeding again.

Gross, Fiona. I scrunch my nose in disgust, thankful it's just us.

"Oh! I am sure of that." Faith throws her head back with laughter. "But seriously, Fiona, if you can't be real with me, who is there? I'm

5

your sister. And I might just understand." Faith glances over at me then sits quietly, waiting as she turns the wheel to adjust to the curves carved in the hill side.

I pull the napkin back, it's still bleeding so I cover the scratch again, placing pressure on the napkin.

"Fine," I sigh. "You remember Sara who hangs out with us sometimes?" I look to Faith as we cross over the bridge and into Hamilton Heights, Ohio.

"Yeah, she has long brown hair, right? And she made the JV squad this year," Faith says. I nod without looking in her direction. "Why did I always think her name was Sadie?" Faith's brow furrows and I see a frown at the corner of her mouth.

I let out a laugh. "She said her mom wanted to name her Sadie, but her dad wanted Sara after his aunt, so Sara it was. But her last name is Hawkins so her Instagram is SadieHawkins. She thought it was *so* clever." I giggle at the memory of us trying to come up with the best names in middle school for our social media accounts. All I could come up with was FionaRenee. *Very creative.*

"That's right. That's what made me think her name was Sadie." Faith giggles as she takes another turn and crosses the narrow bridges over the creek. "You kept calling her Sara last year and I couldn't figure out who you and Lyla were talking about. But then, every once in a while, you called her Sadie Hawkins."

"I wondered why you always looked so confused around Sara." I shake my head and let out a laugh remembering the look on Faith's face when Lyla and I used "Sara" and "Sadie Hawkins" interchangeably in a conversation. "Why didn't you just ask me?"

"Ugh, I was trying to keep my confusion lowkey." Faith rolls her eyes and throws her hand into the air before dropping it into her lap.

"So, you played it off like she is just a freshman so who cares what her name is?" I glance at Faith. I know her too.

"Well, it worked." Faith shrugs and we both giggle. "Okay, so Sara and Sadie Hawkins are the same person and you have been hanging out with her more."

"Yes. I guess it just kind of happened since you and Ella left for college. So anyway, Lyla and Sara were hanging out the night Ella texted Lyla and said she should find a ride and come to Cincy for a house party." I bite my lip knowing how petty this sounds.

"And you feel like Ella should have texted you too?" Faith asks, and she side eyes me with a smirk, but I know she is making a statement, not asking.

"Well, yeah. Or at least Lyla should have texted me." I pout. "I had to listen to Lyla and Sara for a week bragging about how great that party was. They are my friends and they all left me out."

"You don't think they did it on purpose, do you?" Faith frowns, keeping her eyes on me and cracks her window to let in fresh air. I shiver but not so much from the cool air.

"I'm not sure." I think back on the night my best friends excluded me. "Maybe..."

"Why do you think that?" Faith snaps. "Are you and Lyla having issues? She never said anything to me when she called last week."

"She called you?" My heart pinches as I look to Faith. "I mean, I know you two talk all the time just like we do, but she never said anything about it." I clench my fist and look out the front window wondering why this bothers me so much. Lyla always tells me when she talks to Faith.

"Wait, so Sara and Lyla didn't invite you to the party and you think they may have planned it. Now you're upset that Lyla didn't tell you about our call. Do you tell her everything?"

"I used to, but—"

"But what? When did it change?" Faith realizes what I am getting at.

"I don't know. Maybe the last few months." I shrug my shoulders.

"Are you sure you're not imagining this?" Faith's voice is shrill. "Have you talked to her about this?" I look to my lap and shake my head no. "Fiona, she can't read your mind. What did she say when you told her you and Sam broke up?"

"I-I didn't tell her." My voice trails off.

"What? Why?" Faith asks. Again, I shrug not wanting to admit that telling Lyla would have made it real. Telling Lyla would have let my biggest fear out. My fear that I am not good enough. I don't want anyone to see it.

After a few moments of silence, Faith continues.

"So, if you didn't tell her, how did she find out?"

I shrug, not sure if Faith sees me. "I guess the next day at school when everyone else found out." I lift my chin and look out the window while avoiding Faith.

"So, you're upset that she is not telling you everything or including you in things, but you didn't turn to her with one of your biggest heartbreaks ever. You didn't even turn to me, Fiona! I had to learn about it from Mom. What the hell?" Faith slams on her breaks as the light turns red. The seat belt cuts into my chest and slams me back into my seat.

I remain silent not wanting to discuss this anymore. I think back to how Faith and Ella being away at school and me and Sam always hanging out pushed Lyla to become closer with Sara. It's my own fault Lyla and I are drifting apart. But how could I tell her, tell anyone, that Sam didn't want me?

Lost in my own thoughts, Faith's voice startles me.

"Don't you think you should at least let her know we aren't coming to get her?" Faith asks gently.

"What am I going to say?" I toss my hands in the air.

"Just tell her we had a change of plans. We want a sister day." Faith nods. I pull up Lyla's last message and start to text. Then Faith interrupts my thoughts.

"So, what were you doing?" Faith asks.

"What? When?" I drop my phone in my lap and lift my eyes up to the window tossing her question around in my head.

"I mean, the night Sara and Lyla went to the campus party at SWU?" Faith asks.

I frown, trying to understand her question, but then I realize what she is implying when I see the eyebrows raise.

"Faith!" I sit up in my seat and turn to her to show my disapproval, my eyes huge.

"Well!" Faith giggles. "It seems to me that you probably would have been with Lyla and Sara if you weren't doing anything. What were you doing that night?" Faith glances at me as she makes another

10

turn. "Let me guess. Does it start with S and end with M?" Faith sing-songs as I swallow the lump in my throat. Hearing his name feels like a dagger in the heart. It's only been two weeks.

"We-we were supposed to go to a party, but Sam said he would rather stay home and watch a movie, so that's what we did." I look under the napkin and see the bleeding has finally stopped so I drop the napkin as I turn to the passenger's window. I close my eyes trying to block out the memory.

"Uh-hu and what were you doing during the movie?" Faith is enjoying this too much. I ball the bloody napkin up in my fist and squeeze until my nails dig into my palm.

"Nothing Gawd! Sam wanted too but I said no. Okay?" I rub my palms on my black leggins to fight off the chill of this damp December day and let out a sigh. My fluffy socks look warm, but my feet are still cold in my black military boots. I should have worn my UGGs, but Faith said they didn't look right with my outfit.

I turn my head slightly toward Faith, blonde curls shielding my face, but when I see her, she is still. No smile, no expression, staring straight ahead at the interstate as she drives.

"What are you thinking, Fay?" My voice raspy.

"Why did he break things off Fiona? You never told me." Faith's voice is light, but she doesn't look at me.

11

"He said I didn't love him since I wasn't ready to have sex." I swallow hard and watch the trees roll by on the other side of the guard rail.

"You didn't tell him?" Faith glances at me, then back to the road and I shake my head no with a shiver. I look down at the black Weather Tech floormats Dad bought Faith to protect the carpet from damage.

"About Terrace Grove?" I whisper and turn slightly to look at Faith.

"We are the only two in the car, Fiona, you don't need to whisper."

"No, I-I just couldn't. You, Ella, and Lyla are the only ones that know what happened. Well, and Mom." I roll my eyes. "Besides, it was two summers ago, Faith, shouldn't I be able to forget about it?" I turn in my seat toward Faith, hoping she has the answer.

"Fiona, that is not something you forget. You—you...I don't know. You learn how to deal with it, you get stronger I think but you never forget. You learn from it."

"Is it bad that I let it get in the way of Sam and me?" I watch for Faith's reaction, but she keeps her composure. So, I turn to the road in front of us.

"No. Not at all. I think it means you're stronger. But it still sucks it happened." Faith looks to me and takes my hand. "I should have never taken you to that party. You were only in eighth grade. What was I thinking—"

12

"I was going to be a freshman," I object. "Besides, I begged you, remember? Lyla and I listened to you and Ella talk about how much fun the Terrace Grove Campground end of the school year bash was since your sophomore year. We wanted to go more than anything. That's not your fault."

"Maybe, but me letting you out of my sight at a party that size was my fault. Parties are a lot of fun, but you have to watch your back and look out for your friends."

"Let's drop Sam and Terrace Grove. This is supposed to be a fun day." I clear my throat and fight back my tears and the threatening memories from that night two years ago.

I take a deep breath and exhale heavily, pushing the memories away and smashing my emotions deep inside where they need to stay.

"Well, when you make Winter Court this year, Sam will be so jelly, and he will come running back." Faith nods. "Would you take him back?"

"Yes! That's all I've wanted the past two weeks. I just don't understand why he doesn't want me. I just want things to go back the way they were." I clasp my hands in my lap and squeeze my fingers together. I look out the window and see a tear rolling down my check in my reflection.

"When was the last time you talked to him?" Faith asks and I let out a sigh.

"Last night. I called him and asked if we could work things out." The flush in my checks gives away my embarrassment. I haven't told anyone we still talk every night. He never calls me, but I can't seem to help it. I always call him.

"Well? What did you talk about?" Faith prods and looks in my direction.

"The usual." I throw my head back onto the headrest and look to the felt covered roof of her car. "That I hurt him. That he feels I am keeping something from him, or I would be okay with having sex. That he thinks we were too serious, whatever the hell that means." I swallow back tears and continue. "He thinks we need to see other people, but he swears he isn't dating anyone. But then he calls when he is hanging with his friends on the weekend and asks me if I want to come over. But at school he won't talk to me."

Faith takes a breath and starts to say something but stops. She keeps her eyes focused on the road.

"Anyway." I shake my head. "Maybe if I make Winter Court, Mom will get off my back at least." I roll my eyes knowing Faith will understand.

14

"Ugh, I can only imagine." Faith shakes her head and sighs. "She's one of the reasons I avoided dating in high school. Let me guess, Sam breaking up with you looks bad on you and in turn, looks bad on her?"

"Yep. 'Well, just why did he break up with you, Fiona? He comes from a good family so you must have done something wrong. He must have found out about your past.'"

"She. Did. Not." Faith's mouth agape. "Oh my God! What is wrong with her?"

"Yep, in that accusing voice and all." I throw my hands in the air and look to Faith for an answer.

"Mom is so extra. But that was savage. Just wait till you make Winter Court. That will shut her up for a while." Faith shakes her head. "Ugh, she pisses me off."

I bite my lower lip to keep from saying anything, releasing it only when it starts to hurt. I don't want to admit how much I want to make Winter Court. I have to keep it lowkey in case I don't make it.

Chapter 1

After

January 12th

"Bradbury wrote this novel in 1953. What similarities do we see in the novel and the world we live in today, Miss DeWitt? Miss DeWitt…Miss. DeWitt."

And with that I snap out of my head and back to a giggling classroom. I squirm in my seat and flip the page before glancing around the room to see all eyes on me. I sink down in my seat and look up over the page to see a scowling Mr. Jones.

"Umm, can…can you repeat the question?" I ask, laughter rings in my ears. Mr. Jones is not laughing. His pudgy face burning red, the vein on his forehead has surfaced and I swear his nostrils flare, which usually only happens when Kyan Meeks gets under his skin. But the weight of his glare is on me, smashing me down in my seat.

"Again, the novel we are reading was written in 1953, seventy years ago. What are the similarities we can see in Bradbury's world and our world today? Enlighten us, Miss DeWitt." Ol' man Jones' sarcastic tone brings out a few more giggles.

"Well…umm…I think—"

"I take it you didn't read the assignment?" Mr. Jones stands up from the stool he is perched on during class discussions, walks down the row I'm in and turns to stand over me.

Don't look up, I remind myself. *And DO NOT answer that. It's not a question but a statement meant to shame me.*

I bite my lip as I think back to last night.

I tried to focus on the chapter but the beep, beep, beep of the machines in Faith's hospital room kept distracting me. I tried rereading the chapter again when I got home but I kept hearing the beeping.

In the end, I couldn't recall any of it. But I can't admit that to the class. That would show weakness.

You hear people say that everyone has weaknesses, but somehow, theirs don't seem to be noticeable.

Well, except for Faith. Faith has no weaknesses. She is a genius. And just like everyone knows she is a genius; everyone knows I'm not.

"You are not stupid." I can hear Faith's voice now. I never had to talk about this with her. She just knew and knew it bothered me. I know I'm not stupid, but I work hard for my grades and still get the occasional B. I don't think Faith ever had a grade lower than an A+ in her life, including her first semester at college.

It seems easier to let Mr. Jones think I didn't read the assignment than admitting I did, twice, but can't recall any of it.

"I'm sorry—" The bell rings, signaling an end to this torture.

Laughter and chatter surround me as students gather their books and begin exiting the class. With a sigh of relief, I conveniently take my time, check my phone so I'm one of the last ones out of the room.

I lower my head as I walk past Mr. Jones' desk when I hear a calmer voice beckon me.

"May I have a minute?" Again, not really a question. I wrap my arms around my iPad and book like a shield in front of my body and look up only slightly to see Mr. Jones now sitting behind his wood desk.

"Yes, sir?"

"I expect more out of you, Dewitt." Mr. Jones takes a drink of his coffee. I can't take my eyes off the ring left on his desk from the bottom of his mug.

I fight the urge to scream, "I am not Faith!"

"Look, I understand that things seem crazy for you right now," Mr. Jones continues.

I close my eyes to avoid rolling them at the absurdity of his statement and give a polite nod.

"You worked really hard last semester and I saw great strides in your work. I don't want you taking a backward slide and I feel I have been too easy on you since we've been back. I realize now that I have not done you any justice." He pauses just long enough to let that sink in but I'm not really paying attention; I just want out of here.

"In times of tragedy," he continues, "we must find our strength. You need to find yours."

"Ah, thank you." I force a smile and turn to leave.

"Oh. Miss DeWitt. I almost forgot." His outstretched hand holds an envelope with my name on it. "I was asked to give you this."

Can't you just call me Fiona like everyone else? But my courage slinks away before the words are audible. At the beginning of the year, I thought he just couldn't remember which one I was, Fiona or Faith. But Mom said she thinks it's his way of reminding me of my potential.

I think it is his way of putting me in my place by reminding me who I am not.

I take the envelope and turn to leave, sliding the envelope in my folder to read later.

The classroom spills into the freshman locker bay. As I step into the hall, I'm swallowed up by the loud, obnoxious ninth graders slamming

19

their lockers and yelling from one bay to the next. All the sounds I used to love hearing at school. The excitement of all the possibilities in front of me reminding me that I am in the center of it all. But lately I find myself feeling agitated and overwhelmed by the very things I used to love.

Lyla. I need my bestie like a child needs her security blanket.

I stand on my tippy toes trying to peer through the crowded hall of students, who all seem to be taller than me, in hopes of seeing Lyla rushing toward me. But when the crowd parts, Lyla is nowhere to be found.

I take out my phone, hoping it makes me look busy, not desperate, and I send Lyla a text.

"where r u? Remind me to call Officer Quincy after school to check on Ella's case"

I wait a few seconds but no response.

Lyla and I were assigned to the same cheer squad for 6th grade boys' basketball. I remember the eye rolls and whispers when I was assigned to her squad by the other girls, but not Lyla. I always found it odd that Lyla befriended me that year. She was part of the popular squad. The ones with cool clothes and hair styles someone helped them with, the ones all the boys liked, and the girls envied.

For some reason Lyla ignored all the popular girls' dislike for me and asked me to go shopping with her after a Saturday afternoon game. Of course, I said yes, but wondered if this was some kind of prank. Faith suggested I give Lyla the benefit of the doubt, so I did.

Lyla and I cried in each other's arms when we didn't make the seventh-grade cheer squad and then again when our crushes didn't acknowledge us. We spent the rest of our seventh-grade year and that summer at the gym working on cheerleading. I changed my focus from gymnastics to tumbling and stunts to help me get ready for eighth-grade tryouts. When we weren't at the gym, we were watching the best squads on TikTok, making up our own cheers and routines and practicing in the backyard. And of course, we had to figure out what to do with my hair.

When eighth grade started, I looked like a new person. We walked into school that first day of eighth grade, and with Lyla by my side, I knew it was my time. We took our place on the throne and on the eighth-grade cheer squad.

But now, Lyla is nowhere to be found. We always meet up and walk back to our lockers together, but this is the third time in the past two weeks that she's abandoned me.

I know she is still bothered that Faith and I did not pick her up on our way to go shopping. But with everything that happened that night, thank God she wasn't there. But Lyla's feelings are hurt, and I didn't address it when I should have. Now, I'm afraid to bring it up so I stuff it back down inside like I always do and pray I never have to address it with her. I hate conflict almost as much as I hate thousand legged insects. I shiver at the thought of both.

"Hey, did you hear what she did?" I hear a girl to my left whisper. I glance in her direction to see a group of freshman girls huddled together looking at me.

This would have never bothered me before, especially when Lyla is with me. But suddenly, I am very aware that I am alone.

You are not the dorky girl anymore, I assure myself, but it feels like I'm right back in sixth grade.

I breathe a sigh of relief as I reach the edge of the locker bay. Then I see my locker. My stomach flips as I read the word *BITCH* in big black letters.

I glance over my shoulder, there are several pairs of eyes quickly darting away. I swallow hard and I turn back to my locker. I let my long curls fall forward covering the red in my face as I work on the combination, but the whispers continue.

"Hey…" the girl whose locker is next to mine trails off as her eyes go wide. She looks away from me and I can sense her pity for me and the relief she feels that it's not her locker. Maybe the culprit wrote on my locker by mistake, thinking it was someone else's.

"OMG, Fi!"

I close my eyes at the excitement in Lyla's voice. I should be relieved that she came to find me, but I know she will be so extra about this. She sees my locker before I can beg her to stay quiet, her eyes grow wide, and she throws her free hand in the air pointing to the graffiti.

"Who the hell did that?" Lyla demands and I cringe at the volume of her voice. But the golf ball sized lump in my throat prevents me from responding. I dig in my locker for my folder for next period and wish my locker would swallow me up. I keep my face turned toward my locker but when I slam my locker shut, I turn to find Lyla. Her hands on her hips, eyebrows knitted together and mouth agape.

I look down at the iPad in my hand and shrug my shoulders as I fight the burning sensation at the back of my eyes. I scurry past her without checking to see if she is following me because I know she is.

I shove the office door open harder than I intend which causes everyone in the office to look at me.

"Can I help you?" The school secretary asks.

Out of the corner of my eye, I see a few student office workers look my way.

23

"Someone wrote something on my locker," I say in a low voice.

The secretary looks at me quizzically for a few moments waiting to see if I provide any more information, but I don't. Then I realize Lyla didn't follow me as I thought because if she had, she would have taken over the conversation when I couldn't speak.

"What's your locker number?" Maybe it was the tears sitting in my eyes or my flushed skin, but the secretary realizes I'm unable to elaborate on the situation and pushes a piece of paper and pencil toward me.

"I will call the custodian to have him clean it off; let me get you a pass to class."

"Thank you." I don't recognize my own grumbly voice. I grab the pass, immediately reaching up to free my hair from behind my ear so it covers my face and turn away from the students eager to get a glimpse of me. I tilt my head, creating a curtain of blonde hair to hide behind, and leave the office.

My hand starts trembling and I feel the tears begin to spill from my eyes, so I duck into the bathroom before anyone sees me and hope the stall farthest from the entrance is open for privacy. It is. The restroom is empty.

I lean back against the cool, concrete block recounting the events of today; the stares, the giggles, the murmurs when people realized whose locker it was. A wave of nausea rushes through me. A familiar sensation I know all too well.

Just like that day in early December, the confusion and rejection are back.

Hearing the words from Sam's mouth, "I want to break up," shocked me to my core. I hadn't seen it coming.

Unable to sleep that night for the crying and the nightmares that woke me when I did finally sleep, I felt like a zombie walking through school that next day. I didn't talk to anyone. Didn't tell anyone. I wanted to curl up and die. And my stomach was in knots.

In the stall, I rest my hands on my knees and close my eyes hoping to push away the tears. "Not here, Fiona," I whisper to myself. "Not at school." Nausea rolls through my stomach, and I feel the sting of tears leaking from the corner of my eyes.

"Who would do this to me?" I whisper to myself.

I think back over the past week and remember Saturday night.

I went to the party after the game but couldn't stand seeing Sam flirt with a freshman volleyball player, so I made sure Lyla and Sara had a ride and I left. When they asked why I was leaving, I told them I wanted to go see Faith.

Around midnight, I heard a knock on my window and "Fiona" whispered through my bedroom window. I looked up to find Sam at my window like I had so many times before. My heart skipped a beat or three.

I pulled off the covers and slide open the window.

"What?" I whispered so my parents didn't wake up.

"Let me in. It's freezing out here." Sam shivered and shoved his hands in his coat pockets. I could smell the hint of beer on his breath.

I opened the clasps on the window and removed the screen and Sam crawled through.

"Why did you leave the party so early?" Sam was fighting to get his legs through the window.

"I wanted to see Faith," I whispered as I helped him through the window, so he didn't crash to the floor. "But it was too late, so I went to bed when I got home."

"My mom asked me about you tonight. And Faith." Sam crawled on the floor and stood up enough to sit on the edge of my bed as I closed the window.

"How is your mom? And dad?" I added, knowing the answer.

"Dad is Dad. He was drunk when I left for the game tonight, again. I asked Mom if she wanted me to stay home, but she insisted that I go. 'It'll be ok. Hopefully he will pass out and sleep it off,' she said." Sam had his elbows on his knees and ran his hands through his hair and

looked away so I couldn't see his face. I know him well enough to know he was fighting tears that he wouldn't let me see.

I wrapped my arm around his waist and put my head on his shoulder. It felt so right. Him. Me. There together like we should be.

"I've missed you, Fi," Sam admitted. He took my chin in his hand, turned my lips to his. The kiss deepened and he wrapped an arm around my waist and pulled me backward on top of him. I ran my fingers through his hair and felt his cold hand run up my thigh.

My heart raced and Sam rolled me over on my back as his lips found my throat.

"Sam," I whispered, my eyes flutter closed. I struggled to remember what I need to say.

"Mmm…" he mumbled as his lips continued along my chin.

"Sam…" His lips found mine again and I fell deeper into the kiss, then remembered what I need to say. I pulled my head back and pushed my hands against his chest. "I love you, but you know I'm not ready."

Sam froze then dropped his forehead to mine.

"Fi, you know how much I love you," Sam whispered. His heartbeat thumped in his chest.

"Then why are we still broken up?" I pushed myself up on my elbows and looked at his face in the light of the moon. My heart skipped a beat as he stared into my eyes.

27

"Fi, you know why."

"No, I don't." I shook my head as my face contorted into a grimace. *"How can you love me and not want to be my boyfriend?"*

"I-I...don't want to hurt you." Sam pushed himself off my bed, stood up and opened the window, and crawled out like he came in.

"Bye, Fi," Sam whispered. He turned his back to me and jogged through the yards toward the cul-de-sac where he parked.

I take a deep breath, exhaling the painful memory. I pull myself upright as I wipe the corner of my eyes and open the stall door. The mirror above the sink reassures me that the little makeup I do wear is still in place but of course my skin is flushed. A trait that always frustrates me. My eyes are glassy, but no tears.

I take another look in the mirror as I run my fingers through the underside of my hair, breaking up the clumps of curls. I notice just how much the blonde has grown out and I'm not sure the color is working since I have lost my summer tan. I snap a selfie and send to Lyla with the caption: "need hair help"

One last look in the mirror, I check to see if the red rims of my eyes have gone away, and the pink of my skin has subsided. My phone beeps and I look at my text from Lyla.

"who the hell wrote that on your locker?"

I type back. "idk...thoughts?"

I stand frozen, running scenarios through my mind.

My phone beeps again. Lyla texts: "sam obvs have you talked to him since last sat? coulda been Leigha heard she is jelly and a bit salty"

I twist a piece of my hair around my fingers as I think it through. I reply. "y? sam is d46 with her. we talked wed night"

I wait a few seconds but don't get a response back, so I grab my things and head to fourth period.

The afternoon is excruciating. By the end of the last lunch, the entire sophomore class knows about the graffiti and doesn't mind speculating about the artist.

My phone is blowing up with Instagram and Snapchat notifications about my locker. And of course, several students took pictures before the custodian had a chance to clean it off. Most of the comments were in my support with hashtags like #heartFiona but there were a few hashtags for the other team like #karma and #getwhatyoudeserve.

My jaw clenches and eyes narrow as the last few hashtags reach out and slap me across my face. First the graffiti, then the hashtags.

I squint as I look at the names of the last few hash tags. I don't even know who bellaj313 or kjread08 are.

A text message pops up as my phone beeps. It's Jace Wells, a fellow classmate I've had a crush on since kindergarten. Not that I would ever tell him though, especially since we're good friends. That didn't happen until I was in the third grade.

Faith wanted to learn to snowboard, and a classmate agreed to teach her. Dad took us to Brooks with the first snow that November. I had never snowboarded before and spent most of that first hour on my butt or face in the snow. But when some older kids started picking on me for my lack of snowboarding prowess, Jace appeared out of nowhere. He skated in front of me, blocking me from the bullies, and told them to get lost. Jace turned to me, helped me off the ground and spent the rest of his time at Brooks that day teaching me how to snowboard. I was lost in those blue eyes and hung onto everything he said.

Another beep on my phone brings me back. I ignore the notification and open Jace's text. "hey fiona, been looking for u. u ok?"

I let out a sigh, roll my eyes and type: "yeah, i'm fine ty"

I hit the power off button on my phone and slide it in the back pocket of Mom's old Calvin Klein wide-leg jeans she wore in the 90's. Lyla and I were in heaven when she dug out an old box in the basement filled with the vintage version of today's latest fashion trends.

Whispers and the occasional sh's swirl around me, but at least no one is saying anything to my face, which I feel is a relief somehow.

The dismissal bell rings at the end of the longest seventh period ever. I want to run out the door and find solace in my Jeep, but team rules say I have to be at practice tonight in order to cheer at the game Saturday.

Just then, Lyla swoops in, wrapping her arm through mine and pulls me down the hall with excitement in her fast pace.

"OMG. You are not going to believe who just talked to me." The words are pouring from her lips faster than I can't keep up. Typical Lyla.

"Umm, I have no—"

"Marcus Johnson," she interrupts. "Marcus Johnson! OMG I am dying here." Lyla was practically screaming. Marcus has been Lyla's crush since she first laid eyes on him during the varsity basketball game last year. Marcus was a junior and not aware that any of us freshman even existed, or at least he acted like he didn't. But every once in a while, I would receive the latest update, "MJ said 'Hi' today." or "Guess who I saw after Geometry? MJ!" But that was as far as it went. Today was the first time he actually said more than "Hey."

"I was walking out of chem and I ran right into him," Lyla squeaked. "He was texting someone, so he didn't see me, and I was talking to Sara, so I wasn't paying any attention." Lyla waves her hand in the air. "He almost knocked me down. He had to wrap his arms

31

around me to keep me from falling. Once I got my balance back, he asked if I was okay. I think I said 'yeah' but hell, I don't know. Then as he started to walk away, he looked back and said 'Lyla, right?' Can you believe it?"

"Yes, I ca—"

"He knows my name!" Lyla gushes and keeps going. "Maybe he will ask me to the Winter Formal..." and she finally stops to get verification from me, but my brain is trying to catch up to her spot in our conversation.

"I heard he likes Tarin," I spit out and I cringe as soon as I realize what I said. The whole thing happened so fast, it's the first thing my brain told my mouth to say.

Lyla blinks as she takes in the words and her bottom lip trembles.

"Shit Ly, I am so—"

Lyla lets out a huff, her eyes narrow while turning on her heels and she storms off down the hall without looking back.

"Damn it, Fiona. Really?" I whisper with an eye roll. I slam my locker and I turn trying to catch Lyla, but she is gone. Lyla has four inches on me with her long, muscular legs. When she is on a mission, I practically have to run to keep up with her.

I push my way through my classmates hoping to catch up to Lyla in the locker room and apologize. This is normally one of my favorite times of the day. Lyla and I making our way to the other end of the building, arm in arm just as we had a few minutes before, laughing about the silly events of the day.

When I get to the locker room, Lyla isn't there. I quickly change and make my way to the cafeteria hallway where we practice. Most of the squad is already seated on the ground and huddled around our captain. I take a seat in the back and on the other side of Lyla and Sara.

At the beginning of practice, we have a quick team meeting about the basketball schedule. The reminder that there is no game tomorrow night, so we have Friday night off. The game is at 7:30 Saturday evening, so our captain covers the time we need to arrive at school, and what uniform we are wearing.

The team captain also adds that with sectionals being a little over a month away, she wants to work up a few new cheers. This announcement should excite me as I love making up new cheers, but my heart isn't in it right now. I glance at Lyla and hope for a sign that we're okay, but she ghosts me.

No one says a word about my locker during practice, and Lyla and Sara don't acknowledge me. She rides home with me after practice since she doesn't have her license yet and her house is on my way home. I hope Sara doesn't need a ride tonight so we can talk.

When Takiesha, our cheer captain, dismisses practice, I start to call Lyla's name, but Takiesha stops me.

"Hey Fiona. I just want to run this by you before I announce it to everyone. I want you to be a flier in our next stunt I am putting together, okay?"

"Ah, sure. I guess. But I've always been a base."

"I know but I think it would be good for you to grow into a new role." Takiesha shrugs her shoulders and nods her head to the side.

"Okay, yeah if you think so." Deep down I always wanted to be a flier and I should be ecstatic about this new development. But I am worried this will piss Lyla off even more.

"Great. We will start working on it soon." Takiesha flashes her megawatt smile and turns to another girl.

I turn back to where Lyla was sitting, but she is out of sight. I grab my bag and jog to the locker room once again hoping to catch her, but as I round the corner to the locker room corridor, I see Lyla with another cheerleader huddled up and giggling as they rush out of the building with Sara in tow. Shelby Walker is the only junior on the JV squad, and let's just say, she was not happy that Lyla and I made varsity.

"Lyla!" I call, stopping in my tracks. But the navy-blue door at the other end swings shut and the corridor is hauntingly quiet.

Chapter 2

"Fiona. Hey, wait up." Avery bounds up beside me as I make my way out of the locker room. "I was just texting you. What are you doing tonight?" She slides her phone in her back pocket.

Before I can answer, she continues.

"Remember the guy I told you about on Monday during health? You know, I met him at the basketball game last Saturday when we played Barrington?"

"Oh, yeah. Have you heard from him?" I try focusing on Avery's words, but I keep running the conversation I had with Lyla through my mind. It's not fair to Avery so I shake the thought out of my head and refocus on her and notice she has purple in her long braids. *How did I not notice this earlier?*

"He called Tuesday and asked me to the movies tonight, of course I said yes. But today he texted and asked if I have a friend that would like to go. His friend wants me to set him up." I hear the hope in Avery's voice and my mouth goes taught.

"Ahh...I don't think so, Avery. I just finished practice and I plan to see Faith tonight."

I go visit Faith every night, usually with Lyla. I share the events of my day with Faith; it helps me keep her close. And Lyla loves to share the latest gossip. By the time we get Faith caught up on the latest news, Mom and Dad arrive and we work on our homework there. If Lyla is with me, we leave early, and I finish my homework at home or Lyla's house.

"I just worry about you. I don't see the same Fiona that I came to love. I miss her." Avery pouts for effect and I try to understand what she is implying. "Look Fiona, I understand you worry about your sister, but she wouldn't expect you to stop living your life. One night away isn't going to hurt anything. Your parents would understand," Avery insists.

"I'm not sure about that," I add with a sarcastic laugh. "They have been so distant the last few weeks. They swear they aren't mad at me, but I can't shake the feeling that they blame me for everything. Especially Mom."

"You're being too hard on yourself. They love you and are worried just like you. You didn't see them taking turns between your hospital room and Faith's over Christmas break, Fiona." Avery places her hand on my arm and stops walking. "They were praying, crying, sharing stories with visitors and begging the doctors for information about both your conditions," Avery says, and I turn to see her face. "They know you are out of the hospital and safe, so they've turned their focus to Faith. It's not that they feel differently for you, they are consumed in their own grief right now. They need you as much as you need them."

"I never thought of it like that." I look down at the ground and think about Avery's words. And that is why I have grown to value Avery's friendship. She tells you what you need to hear, calls you out when necessary but supports you all at the same time.

"It's not always easy when you're in the middle of it. Just don't assume that they blame you. Gurl, talk to them." Avery throws her arm around my shoulder as we start moving down the athletic hallway toward the door.

"Thanks. I'm going to pass on the movie though, not 'cause I didn't hear you, but because I did and need to see my family tonight." Avery doesn't need to hear that I'm still heartbroken over my breakup with Sam. In Avery's mind, that would be why I need to go with her.

Avery and I have known each other since seventh grade when our elementary schools came together in middle school. But it wasn't until last fall that we became friends when our teacher gave us assigned seats next to each other in finance. This semester we have health together and chose to sit by each other, to the teacher's dismay. We stop talking when we get the look. That's when the texting starts.

Avery's carefree spirit and her honesty is sometimes hurtful but needed. Some people don't know how to take her and say she's a bitch, but I don't see it that way. Her honesty is refreshing and the fact that she doesn't care what others think is amazing to me. I wish I had that quality.

In Avery fashion, she asks the first thing that pops into her mind.

"So, you really don't remember anything that happened the night of the accident?"

"No." I shake my head and feel my face scrunch up at my own words.

"What's the last thing you do remember?" When most people ask me this question, I know they are being nosy, but Avery has a concerned, quizzical nature. She is asking the questions wanting to put the puzzle pieces together in hopes to help relieve my suffering.

I think back to the day of the accident. Faith and I were telling Mom our plans for the day.

Dad walked in the kitchen in the middle of the conversation and started talking to Mom about a house he was building. They both completely shut us out even though we weren't finished, something they do often. I looked to Faith, and she started giggling and continued

38

telling them our plans even though they weren't listening to a word we were saying.

"Yeah, then we are going to hook up with these older guys Ella knows and have an all-nighter with 'em," Faith teased. I laughed at Faith's words.

"They are going to buy us beer and I'm sure there will be drugs involved," I added. We just couldn't help ourselves; we were on a roll.

Faith stopped laughing long enough and added, "I bet there's going to be sex, lots of sex. And unprotected!"

To which I concluded, "We'll probably end up in jail before the night's over."

At the exact same moment, Mom and Dad stopped talking, turned to us and said, "Have fun kids."

Then Mom added, "Be safe. Love you."

They hadn't paid attention to anything we said.

"Love you too," we said at the same time and giggled all the way to Faith's car.

"I thought for sure me saying 'we'll go to jail' would get their attention," I said to Faith over the top of the car as I fell laughing into the passenger's seat.

Unaware of the smile that has spread across my face at the memory, I jump at Avery's words.

"What's so funny?" Avery asks and I look up at the navy blue and gold strips along the white concrete block walls with the giant Eagle painted in between the girls' and boys' locker rooms.

"Ah, nothing. Just something that happened that day. Ah, I remember telling my mom our plans, saying bye to them, Faith and I leaving to go shopping and that's it. Next thing I know, I wake up in the hospital and Ella's mom is there asking if I had heard from Ella."

"So, you don't remember any of the accident at all?" Avery turns to look at me as we walk past the vending machines that are only turned on after school. I shrug and shake my head no and suck in a deep breath as I push open the heavy blue door that leads us out into the cold January air.

I'm not aware that Jessica Brindle is walking behind us as we exit the building. When we get to my Jeep, Avery gives me a hug.

"I am so sorry, Fiona. For you and Faith." Avery releases me and steps back. Her gray jeggins matching the snow clouds in the sky. She pulls up the hood on her long mauve puffer jacket and wraps her arms around her body to fight off the cold air.

"It's okay, I don't care—" My voice catches in my throat as I fight back tears, but a few manage to escape.

"Do you want me to stay with you?" Avery asks.

"No. Thanks though," I sigh. "I'll be okay.

"Call if you need to chat. Okay?" Avery turns toward Tarin's car in the scarce parking lot.

"Thanks," I call and reach for my door handle and stiffen at the sound of my name.

"Fiona."

I cringe at the recognition of the voice behind me and force myself to acknowledge her.

"Hey Jessica." I turn back to my Jeep as I put my bag in the passenger's seat, purposely trying to look busy hoping Jessica will go away.

Jessica is a classmate who is in our squad and is friends with Sara. She was part of our sixth-grade cheer squad who didn't like me being there and made sure I knew it. Even today, her biggest attribute is spilling tea and not the fun, uplifting tea Lyla shares.

"Where's Lyla?" Jessica asks. The last thing I need is for Jessica to hear about our fight before I can talk to Lyla. When I don't respond, she continues.

"Are you okay?" She places her hand on my forearm. "You know with everything going on and the locker and all?"

I feel a lump in my throat at Jessica's words, but when I look at her, I notice Jessica's head is tilted and leaning toward me, thirsty for anything I give her. I feel my brow furrow and eyes narrow on her.

41

"Yeah, I'm good," I mutter with a wave of my hand, hoping to remove her arm off mine.

I turn toward my Jeep to get in, but before I can, Jessica reaches out for my arm again and stops me. I close my eyes trying to calm myself before turning to her, so I don't lose my shit and find myself viral on TikTok. When I do, a tear escapes the corner of my eye. Dammit!

"But you're crying..." Jessica is almost begging.

I pull my arm away. "Yeah, I don't care." And step into my Jeep and close my door, leaving Jessica standing alone in the parking lot.

Instinctively I reach in my cheer bag for my phone and hit Lyla's number on my favs list. We will have a good laugh over the real reason for Jessica's questions. Jessica is searching for tea.

Lyla's voice on her voice mail startles me, and I start to leave a message.

"You're not gonna believe—" Then it hit's me, what I said to piss her off. I guess she isn't over it yet. If she was over it, she would be with me right now.

"Shit!" I hit the end call button and drop my phone into the cup holder on my console with a thud.

I run through a local fast-food joint and order food.

Mom and Dad are already at vigil over Faith when I arrive, and barely acknowledge my presence in the room.

Faith was air lifted to SWU Hospital the night of the accident. SWU has the only level trauma center in the city. I rode in a regular ambulance, but I don't remember it.

I look at Faith hoping to see some sign of change but my heart sinks at the unrecognizable site of my beautiful sister. The bruises and swelling on her face that came after the second reconstructive surgery last week are still significant. This surgery was to reconstruct her broken jaw. The only resemblance I see of the sister I love is her naturally blond hair spilling big ringlets around the bandages on her face and head.

That beautiful blond hair reminds me of our differences. Even though our bone structure is very similar—oval-shaped face with defined cheekbones—we look nothing alike. Faith has natural white-blonde hair that looks like she spends every waking minute at the beach and sky-blue eyes just like Mom's. And in spite of her light hair and eyes, she tans very well. I take after Dad with my strawberry blonde hair, hazel-green eyes, and fair skin with light freckles across the bridge of my nose. I tan a little, but nothing compared to Faith.

It is always interesting to me how many people over the years have thought that Faith and Ella were sisters. They look nothing alike. Ella has a square jaw line and does not have strong cheek definition and has a cute button nose compared to Faith's long, narrow nose, but most people only see the blond hair and blue eyes.

Normally I share my day with Faith, but my heart just isn't in it tonight with everything that happened today. I don't want to admit to my perfect sister, whom I look up to, just how messed up my life is right now. She couldn't understand. Besides, I need to get over this self-pity; look at where Faith is right now. And I certainly don't need or want a lecture from Mom about the locker thing. In Mom's eyes, it will be my fault. I might as well have taken the marker and wrote 'Bitch' myself.

Mom actually cried last fall when Sam and his friend Drake decided to toilet paper the trees in our front yard on Halloween. They got several of my friends' houses too, not just mine. But the next morning, before my alarm on the cell went off, Mom came charging through my door, sobbing. "What did you do?" It was more of a shout than a question.

"What?" I mumbled still half asleep and trying to figure out what was going on. I fought off the covers and sat up. "What time is it? My alarm didn't go off yet."

"You need to get up and clean that mess up before you leave for school."

"Mom, I don't know what you're talking ab—"

"Oh?" Sniff. "The front yard?" Somewhere between a shout and utter disappointment. "You managed to get our front yard toilet papered." And now she was pissed. "Get up and get dressed."

She turned on her heels and stormed out of my room, slamming the door behind her.

I can only imagine what she would say about today's proceedings.

I settle into the chair between Faith and the window, kick my boots off and cross my legs so my feet don't touch the floor. My English assignment comes first since Mr. Jones called me out today. I open my folder for my assignment and am perplexed (Lyla's favorite word since she learned the definition last year during an assignment) by the envelope in the pocket. Then I remember Mr. Jones handing it to me at the end of class today. I stashed it away and completely spaced it but now my interest is piqued.

I remove a folded piece of paper, white with light blue and silver snowflakes fluttering around the edges and a deeper blue writing fills the center that reads:

CONGRATULATIONS

*You have been selected by your peers to represent the sophomore class as a member of the **Winter Formal Queen's Court!***

This is an honor bestowed to only one representative for each grade. The crowning of the Winter Queen will take place prior to the East Brook vs. Clairmont Varsity Basketball Game Friday, January 20th.

The Winter Formal Dance will be held Saturday, January 21st at 7:00. Attire for both events is formal for you and your escort, a fellow student at East Brook High School. You may use the locker rooms in the alternative gym to change at halftime of the varsity game for the remainder of the evening.

Please report to the Media Center at 7:45 tomorrow morning for pictures and complete the enclosed questionnaire to Mrs. Conner, The Student Council Sponsor.

This will be a night to remember!

And below it is the form asking for information: parents' names, escort's name, clubs and activities I am in, and honors I have received.

I close my eyes and let the grin spreads across my face. Deep down I felt I would get this honor, but last fall MyaNika Shilling was nominated to represent our class for homecoming, so I've been having doubts. This is the first nomination since Sam and I broke up. I had hoped I could earn this honor without Sam by my side and here it is. My status wasn't ruined by Sam breaking up with me. I let out a deep breath.

46

Lyla is going to explode! I reach for my phone and click on Lyla's number to share the news. I swear last year she was more excited than I was when they announced the Winter Queen Court over the intercom.

We had gym seventh period along with Sara. The last five minutes of the class, while we were in the locker room changing, the principal came on the intercom. My heart started racing, butterflies fluttered in my stomach, and I could barely hear a word he was saying over the sound of blood rushing through my ears even though the entire locker room of freshman girls was dead silent.

I tried to act as normal as possible in case my name wasn't called so I continued digging through my locker, not once looking up. My hands were shaking as I fumbled with my silver hoop earrings and the heart necklace Sam had gotten me for Christmas a month earlier. Then I heard Mr. Clifton's deep burly voice say, "And the freshman representative is Fiona DeW—" Squeals and shrieks engulfed the locker room cutting Mr. Clifton off. Most of the shrieks were from Lyla and Sara.

"Oh. This is so great." I finally looked up to see Lyla's face beaming at me, you would have thought Mr. Clifton had announced her name. "You can get that purple dress you were drooling over at the mall last weekend."

All I could do in that moment was smile. I didn't want to be too extra about it.

"I wanna go with!" shouted Sara, bouncing up and down.

"Maybe Faith and Ella will drive us," Lyla continued, still beaming.

My eyes wide. "Did Faith make it?" I was so wrapped up in my triumph that I hadn't listen for Faith's name.

"Uh, um…" Sara stammered and looked to Lyla.

"Did anyone hear Faith's name announced?" Lyla shouted so the entire locker room could hear.

"I think so," someone answered.

"Couldn't hear for you girls screaming," someone else called who didn't seem to be as excited as us.

"We have to find her." I grabbed my stuff and the three of us scurried out of the locker room as the bell rang, going against the grain of traffic that was trying to leave the building.

The buzzing from one of the monitors in Faith's room snaps me back to reality. I look down at Lyla's picture on my screen, followed by the word dialing. My thumb hovering above the end call and when I see it goes to voice mail, I click end.

I let out a sigh as I look to Faith and realize I have no one to share this with. Faith can't respond, Ella is missing, and Lyla isn't taking my calls. If I hadn't pissed her off today, she would be right here with me, and I wouldn't have to tell her anything. She would have read the letter over my shoulder. But I'm obviously the last person Lyla wants to talk to right now and telling her in a voicemail after what happened earlier, I don't want her to think I'm flexing. Telling Mom and Dad is futile and telling Faith is bittersweet. If she were awake, she would be the one crowning this year's Queen, a tradition always performed by the previous year's Winter Queen.

"Hey Mom, Dad?" I fold the letter and return it to my folder. "Do you mind if I go home? I need to get up early in the morning and I still have some reading to do for English."

"You usually study here." Mom turns to me, and I can't tell if she is concerned or annoyed at my question.

"Yeah, just a long day at school and I had a hard time concentrating last night on my homework. I just really want to focus and get to bed early."

"Well, you usually stay with your sister." Mom lets out a sigh, "But if you feel like you need to go home, I guess you should do what you need to." Mom doesn't take her eyes of Faith.

"Sharon why don't to take a break and ride home with Fiona. I will stay with Faith a little longer." Before Mom can argue he adds, "I don't need to be up as early as you in the morning. You need to get a good

49

night's sleep too. You are no good to either of our girls if you don't take care of yourself."

"I guess you are right," Mom sighs letting Dad know she is not happy about this. "I just hate leaving her here."

"I know." Dad bends over to kiss her head. "I'll stay till visiting hours are over, then make my way home."

"Call if anything changes." And for the first time in a month, Mom walks out of the hospital at a normal time.

This time with Mom on our way home is the most time we've spent together, outside of the hospital since the accident. Neither of them has said it, but I know they blame me for Faith's condition. And they are right, it is my fault. I was the one driving the night of the accident, and too fast according to the accident report. Of course, I have no memory of it to know why I was driving so fast. Or why I was driving Faith's car.

Mom and I were close when I was little, but after the Terrace Grove Campground end of the year bash, everything changed. She's disappointed in me and looks at me differently now. But when the four of us, Faith, Ella, Lyla, and me are together, Mom seems to forget about all that.

The four of us are always laughing when we are together no matter what we are doing. Like the time we were going on vacation.

Lyla made a comment about something silly, and Faith and Ella started giving her a hard time. We were all laughing so hard that when we got out at a restaurant to eat, Dad made us go to the bathroom to get ourselves together, including Mom. That did not help one bit and we stayed in the bathroom laughing for an hour. Dad finally gave up and ordered us all food to go.

All that changed this past month and I really miss those moments.

"Hey, Mom?" I glance over at her in the passenger's seat.

"Hum?" No "honey," no smile. Not even a "yes?" Just a grunted hum. She doesn't even look over at me. Her focus remains out the front window and her hands are knotted in her lap.

"Um, I was thinking. Maybe we can do something this weekend." I look her way again. Her mouth is a straight line, and her face is hard. "I don't have a game tomorrow night."

When I don't get a response after what feels like several minutes, I let out the breath I've been holding.

"I-I wasn't thinking anything big," I continue, my voice a little softer. "Maybe dinner on our way into the hospital together?"

"Umm." Mom nods her head slightly and purses her lips.

I look to the road for several moments, my hands tight on the steering wheel, ten and two just like I was taught, hoping to make her happy. When I glance to the passenger's seat, she is still looking straight ahead staring out the window, showing no emotion at all.

I turn my focus back to the road.

My stomach churns and I regret saying anything at all. I try to push my emotions away, but the silence is killing me. I take the next exit toward home and realize my knuckles are white from my death grip I have on the steering wheel. My jaw is clenched so I take a deep breath and exhale, releasing my muscles. I hadn't realized I was grinding my teeth until now.

"Or maybe we could go shopping after we see Faith? I don't, like, need anything. Just something to get our minds off things." I shrug keeping my eye on the road waiting and hoping for a response. But I get no response from her. So much time passes, I'm not even sure what to do.

"You know, Mom, I'm still here." I let out a breath and continue. "I know you hate me right now and I don't know how to make things right and I'm so sorry for what I did to Faith, but please don't turn your back on me. I might not be lying in that hospital bed, but I am hurt and in pain too." My voice catches on my last words, and I feel the all too familiar stinging behind my eyes, they are about to betray me.

We drive in silence the rest of the way home. I pull in the driveway and shut the engine off and jump at Mom's voice.

"I don't hate you, Fiona." Mom is still looking straight forward like she is trying to open the garage door with her mind.

I sit back and wait for her to continue, but she doesn't.

Mom releases her hands and slides them, palm down under her thighs and looks away out the passenger's window for what seems like an eternity.

I let out a sigh and reach for my bag in the back seat and turn back to open the door.

Mom's voice is sharp in the quiet darkness stopping me from moving.

"I don't know how to be there for you right now. I don't feel I can trust you. And I'm hurt. I am angry. More than angry. I'm pissed. Both of my girls were almost taken from me." She pauses to get her voice under control. "And Faith isn't out of the woods yet..." Her voice trailing off with a sob.

"Mom—"

"You shouldn't have been driving that night. You are not an experienced driver, and you shouldn't have been driving that damn car Faith wanted so bad. It is too powerful."

I didn't bother to point out that Faith was an inexperienced driver when she got the car for her birthday.

She turns to me with tears streaming down her face, brow furrowed and pain in her eyes.

"Why were you driving? Please tell me that?" she begs bringing her hands together like she is praying. After a few moments of silence. "Why won't you help us? Help us understand what happened. Help us put the pieces together to help find Ella?" Mom sits motionless, staring at me. The pain on her face crushes my heart. She throws her hands in the air and tosses her head back on the head rest.

I swallow hard. I have nothing to say that will help my mom understand.

"I can't remember," I mumble looking down at my hands, my fingers resting over the bottom of the steering wheel. Tears flowing freely in the darkness of my vehicle.

"Just what exactly where you girls doing that caused you to not remember, Fiona?"

I close my eyes and squint hard trying to block out my mother's words. My jaw clinches and fist tight in my lap. I take in a gulp of air between silent sobs to calm myself down and exhale as quietly as possible.

"I swear, Mom, the whole night is a blur. I-I remember talking to you," I mumble, and I wipe away the tears with the back of my hand, "then, Dad coming into the kitchen and us leaving the house. That it, I promise I don't know what happened."

The night is silent again, I turn my head away from Mom and swallow down my tears, so she doesn't hear them. I feel my face crumble with the pain, but I can't let it go. Not when Mom is trying so hard to be stoic.

The cold night air rushes in when my mom swings open the passenger door. The hardened snow crunching under her boots as she slams the door and rushes past my Jeep fumbling in her purse for the keys to the front door. I watch through tear-stricken eyes as my mom disappears in the house without me.

Chapter 3

"Say cheese," Mrs. Conner says, and the flash blinds me before I can respond. "Let's get a couple more, Fiona, I'm not getting that usual spark in your smile."

"Tilt your head a little more to the left." Directs the photographer and I hear the *click, click, click* of the shutter.

I take in a deep breath and exhale, trying to relax and give a genuine smile, which never comes naturally to me.

I think back to Sam and Lyla making fun of my school picture this year and feel a giggle bubble up.

"What are you doing here?" Sam spat. Lyla busted out laughing while looking over Sam's shoulder at my class picture.

"I don't know. I was trying to smile—"

"You look constipated," Lyla said, which got an agreeing nod from Sam and more laughter.

My cheeks flushed; I couldn't argue that. I did look constipated. And scared. Constipated and scared. And now I will look constipated and scared for infinity in the East Brook yearbook. Excellent.

"There, I think we got a few good ones." Mrs. Conner nods while looking over the photographer's shoulder at the digital shots.

"Oh. That one. I like that one best." Mrs. Conner looks up from the camera with a smile and says, "Do you have your info sheet completed for me?"

"Ah, no, actually I don't." The heat rises in my cheeks, and I am suddenly aware of eyes on me. I notice out of the corner of my eye that the person dropping off a library book at the desk has become interested in my conversation with Ms. Conner. Leigha Overbay. A senior, and Sam's new girlfriend for the last two days.

"Ah, I have all but the escort." Last year that was a no brainer; I didn't even have to ask Sam. *He came up to me after the big announcement and asked, "What color tie do I need to get?"*

Lyla answered, "Purple. Don't worry, we will get you a swatch of material so you can match it." And that was it.

Mrs. Conner takes the paper from my hand and dismisses my concern with a wave of her hand.

"Well, that's okay, just let me know who the lucky young man is as soon as possible." Mrs. Conner turns back to the photographer and motions Kaylor, the freshman candidate, to take a seat in front of the camera.

I thoughtlessly take a piece of hair around my finger and thumb and begin twirling it as I turn to leave for class.

The ten-minute warning bell sounds for first period. I'm usually, just, now walking into the building, which is why none of my friends want to ride to school with me. It's an odd feeling to be here this early.

I grab my notebook for first period and my art supplies for second period at my locker and make my way down the hall. When I walk into first period, Mrs. Shipley does a double take when she realizes I'm the first student to arrive, then glances at the clock in the front of the room. *I bet she never thought this day would happen.*

"¡Buenos dias, Fiona. Ha llegado a la hora!"

I recognize the first part to be, "Good morning, Fiona," but have to process the second part, and honestly, I don't really care. So, I just respond, "Si," and take my seat. A minute before the bell rings, Lyla strolls through the door with a few of our friends. I try not to act concerned about the giggling, but I hope she takes the seat next to me.

I keep my eyes focused on my iPad as Lyla walks by my row and the open seat next to me and sits two rows back. I do my best to act like I didn't notice as I find my Spanish homework and upload it in the Canvas assignment.

Lyla doesn't even look my way and I realize Mrs. Conner and the other candidates are the only ones who know I made court. Well, besides Leigha. But she hardly counts.

I should have tried harder to talk to Lyla last night. I should have drove to her house on the way home from the hospital and cleared everything up right then. But Mom would have expected me to explain why I had to stop at Lyla's. But I was relieved that she didn't question why Lyla wasn't with me.

"Good morning, East Brook. Please stand for the Pledge of Allegiance." The class stands and begins saying the pledge along with Mr. Clifton. Once the moment of silence is complete, students take their seats, and I can't help wondering if Mr. Clifton is going to announce the Winter Court nominees.

"Congratulations to the Lady Eagles for their victory over Redmond. The final score of the varsity game was 45-39 with Jaylah Lawson scoring 22 points, 7 rebounds. MyaNika Shilling had 11 points and 4 rebounds. Way to make us Eagle Proud."

I feel a little ping in my chest as I wait for Mr. Clifton to continue.

"The Student Council will be sponsoring the Winter Formal Saturday January 21st in the school cafeteria at 7:00. Dress is formal and tickets will be on sale during lunch next week leading up to the dance. Check the posters around school for more information. The Winter Queen crowning will take place on Friday January 20th before the varsity basketball game. And your Winter Queen Court Nominees are—"

My heart is in my throat, my palms are sweaty, and I have butterflies in my stomach. It's like I don't know I am already on court and waiting to learn my fate like every other student at East Brooke. *What if he doesn't call my name?*

"Kaylor Smith representing the freshman class." I look back down to my iPad pretending to check my inbox and hold my breath. "Fiona DeWitt representing the sophomore class," Mr. Clifton continues. I slowly let out my breath, but there are no cheers this year.

"Shanna Findley representing the junior class and Takiesha Williams representing the senior class. Congratulations ladies." Mr. Clifton goes one about tonight's swimming and diving meet, but I don't hear much after that.

This class is mostly sophomores and a few juniors, so I'm not surprised that there isn't as much excitement about the announcement as last year, but Lyla and my friends not saying anything hurts. I do receive a few "Congratulations," including Mrs. Shipley.

I don't turn around to see Lyla's response. I know under different circumstances she would be ecstatic. But since I didn't tell her about court before the announcement was made, I have no doubt Lyla will take this as a slap in the face. Big yikes. But I'm not sure how I could have told her last night after what happened yesterday. Or without sounding self-absorbed. I just should have begged her to call me back. *Damn it! I should have gone to her house.*

Just then, I realize I didn't reach out to Officer Quincy last night to check on Ella's missing person's case. I need to call today so I make a note on my calendar to remind me after school.

The class continues as if nothing happened, and I guess nothing did happen for most of the students. We conjugate verbs and read from the text orally to practice our Spanish accents, which we suck at. Mrs. Shipley is assigning our homework when she is interrupted by the intercom.

"Mrs. Shipley, sorry to interrupt," calls the front office secretary.

"Si?"

"Will you have Fiona DeWitt come down to the main office and have her bring her things, thank you."

"Si!"

Before Mrs. Shipley can say anything, I'm gathering my things.

"Do you have the assignment written down Fiona?" Mrs. Shipley ask, thankfully in English so I know what she is saying.

"Si," I respond purely out of habit and try to disappear without drawing any more attention to myself.

"Good morning, Fiona." Mrs. Smiley has the perfect name for her personality and job as the face of East Brook. She is the first person you see when you enter the front office. But today she looks a bit sheepish, or is that pity that I see on her face? Before I can respond, she glanced to her left. I follow her gaze and notice the two police officers standing there. Turns out I don't need to check in with Officer Quincy after all.

"Sorry to pull you out of class Miss DeWitt, we just need a few minutes of your time." My eyes drop to the ground as I give a nod of understanding. Not sure what's worse, getting called to the principal's office or finding cops waiting on you when you get there.

I recognize both officers. The older officer with thinning gray hair and a pudgy middle is Officer Buchanan. The tall younger officer that looks like he might have been a college running back is Officer Quincy.

I follow them into the conference room Mrs. Smiley directs us to. Officer's Quincy and Buchanan are assigned to Ella's missing persons case, and this is not my first meeting with either of them, but this is the first time they came to see me at school.

In the conference room, Officer Quincy, the nicer one of the two, instructs me to take a seat. Officers Quincy sit across the table from me, and Buchanan takes the seat at the head of the table and next to me. Buchanan, with his short, thick stature seems to grimace a little fitting into his seat and reaches up scratching his balding head. Quincy, on the other hand has a head full of dark hair and dark eyes that matches his skin and stands at least a foot taller than Buchanan. And, yes, he fits in his chair nicely. I can't help smiling that Officer Quincy is just Lyla's type. Tall, dark, and handsome, although she goes for basketball players.

Mrs. Smiley shuts the door behind her as she leaves the room. I take a deep breath, close my eyes, and try to get control of my racing heart.

"Miss DeWitt," Officer Quincy begins. "I know this is difficult for you, but we found some new information that we hope you can piece together for us."

My palms are sweaty, so I wipe them on my jeans and keep my gaze on my iPad in front of me. I'm already biting my bottom lip.

"I really don't remember anything. I'm sorry—"

"We understand that Fiona," Officer Buchanan reassures me, his voice gruff compared to Quincy's. But even with his reassurance, I can't shake the feeling that he doesn't believe me. "We are hoping that maybe this information may trigger a memory." He releases his clasped hands, opening his palms to me.

"Anything if it can help find Ella." I look up, first at Quincy, then Buchanan for the first time. Buchanan's beady eyes on mine make me feel about five years old.

"Good. We know you want to help." Buchanan nods and places his big, gnarly hands on the table, fingers laced together. "The night of the accident, do you recall if Ella was in Faith's car?"

I open my mouth to answer, but I feel my lip quiver and no words come out. I drop my eyes to my lap and realize my thumb is bleeding from a hangnail I've been picking at and lift it to my mouth to stop the bleeding.

"Take a deep breath, close your eyes and go back to that night," Quincy instructs. I follow his orders and allow that day to come flooding back to me like it does every night in my dreams. I'm usually safe from this nightmare while at school, but not today. The nightmares have caught up to me.

"Now, you told us earlier that you remember leaving your house with Faith, and Faith was driving." Quincy's voice light and calm. I take another deep breath to relax and nod.

"Yes, we were still laughing at my parents," I explain.

"Where were you going?" Quincy continues.

I lean back in my chair, take a deep breath and exhale hoping to relax some and remember more.

"To the mall. We always get Mom and Dad each one gift that we pick out together. You know, so they have something from both of us of equal value." I smile. "We started that when Faith got her license and her first job at the boutique in town. She decided to get each of them a nice gift that Christmas and I was worried my parents would like her gift better since I was in seventh grade and didn't have as much money as she did."

"Okay. So, you leave the mall and where do you go?" Quincy asks. Buchanan must be letting Quincy take the lead on this, only stepping in if needed.

"I'm not sure." I feel on the cusp of something...important but it's just out of my grip. "I think Faith received a text as we were pulling out of the mall. I remember her handing me the phone, telling me to read it since she was driving."

"Do you know who it was from?" Buchanan's voice surprises me. I rub my thumb over the stinging hangnail and try to block out the pain, focusing on the memory.

"I can't remember," I admit shaking my head, eyes still closed.

"Can you see the text?" The hasty tone of Quincy's voice gives me a start. He even sounds closer like he is leaning over the table toward me.

"No. I-I can see the face of the phone, but the screen is blurry." I picture the screen and the light coming from the screen but can't make anything out.

"Who do you think the text would have been from?" Buchanan jumps in.

My eyes spring open at the sudden change in voice to find Buchanan leaning forward wide eyed, forearms and hands flat on the table.

"Well, I know we were supposed to get in touch with Ella after shopping so maybe—"

"You think it was Ella?" Buchanan turns to Quincy.

"Maybe…" I shrug, "I assumed we went to see her since we had the accident by SWU." I look to the picture of the current school superintendent on the wall behind Buchanan. I bet he is disappointed that this is the conversation taking place in his school's conference room.

"Let's start there. Take a deep breath and close your eyes again. Go back to that moment, where did you go shopping?" Quincy's voice smooth and calm now. I close my eyes and hear the squeak of the leather chair as Quincy leans back.

I clear my throat before starting. "The plan was to go to the new outdoor mall, Kingston Town Center. But I don't know if we did or not." I lean forward and place my elbows on the table, resting my forehead on my fingers and rub my fingers across my forehead like you do when you are stumped on a hard Algebra question hoping to rub the correct answer out of your brain.

"Let's say you did. Picture yourself in the passenger's seat as you were that night. Does anything stand out to you while Faith is driving?" Buchanan voice gravely but calm.

"Ah, no." I sigh, dropping my shoulders. "Wait, we are on the interstate." I sit up in my chair, my eyes fly open.

"Which one?" Quincy interrupts. "Can you see anything that might tell you where you are?"

"Ah, not sure." I close my eyes again and search for that memory. "Wait, there. I see a road sign for Cincinnati—"

"Does it say anything else?" Quincy asks.

"Yes, but I can't make out...numbers. It's one of those green signs that says how many miles to go until you get to Cincy." I sit up straight and exhale. Relieved I finally remember something helpful.

"Great job, Fiona." Buchanan reaches across the table to pat my head like you would a dog. "Can you make out the numbers?"

"Um..." I squeeze my eyes closed harder hoping it helps me remember more. "No, the sign goes by too fast. Sorry." I slump back in my seat and turn to the look at the picture on the wall to my left. If only I could dive into that blue ocean staring back at me. Just float away.

"Okay, I know when we spoke previously, you said the three of you were to meet up but you're not sure where you were going?" Buchanan looks at me questioningly.

"Yes. I remember. When I asked Faith, she said Ella wanted it to be a surprise."

"What time was this?" Buchanan questions, and pulls out a pen, clicking the end so the ball point pops out. Then he opens the little notebook and looks down at his notes.

"I'm pretty sure this was on our way to the mall. I remember Faith telling me Ella has a surprise for us and that we were meeting her later." I squirm in my seat, making the leather squeak under me.

"Any chance you can remember what time the text came in? The one we were just referring to?" Quincy asks as he stands and paces the room.

"I think I glanced at my phone as we were leaving a store. It was the last store we went to. I remember because we had parked there and planned to hit that store last. I'm positive it was after 9:30."

My eyes blink open at the new memory, both officers hanging on my last word, waiting, wanting more.

"I-I didn't realize we stayed at the mall that late," I added when they don't say anything.

"Can you remember if you were at KTC?" Quincy asks and leans over placing his hands on the back of the chair across from me.

"Yes, I recognize the parking lot in front of Nordstrom's," I add, but I don't see anything else after that.

"Great. That's great Fiona," Quincy reassures me and stands up crossing his arms.

"I feel like I am just not much help at all," I add, looking down at my lap, I play with a loose thread on my ripped jeans.

"Trust us, you are." Quincy nods, pulls out the chair and takes a seat.

I let out a sigh of relief and look back up to Quincy.

"Alright," Quincy jumps back in, "Let's try again. Close your eyes. Can you remember if Ella was ever in Faith's car that night?"

I close my eyes and take a few seconds to focus back on that road sign, but nothing. "I just don't know for sure, but it's possible. Maybe we picked her up on the way to the party?"

I open my eyes to see Quincy and Buchanan quickly glance at each other.

"What?" I look between the two of them, my eyebrows raise, and I sit up a little taller in my seat.

"You just said 'Maybe we picked her up on the way to the party,' like you knew you were going to a party either with Ella or to meet her there," Quincy informs.

"I did?" I lean forward wanting to know what else I missed.

Buchanan chimes in. "Let's look at this line of thinking. Your accident was by SWU campus, so it makes since that you were there to see Ella. If you were going to a party with Ella, where would that be?"

"Well, now that I think about it, Ella hadn't been home much over Christmas Break. I asked Faith a few days before we went shopping where Ella was, and she said she was staying with friends off campus. I thought it was odd that she wouldn't want to come home and see her friends and family over break, especially since she hadn't been home in months. But Faith didn't seem to think anything of it. She said 'Ella likes it there. Besides, it's only thirty minutes from Brookston.'"

"Ella lives in the dorms at SWU, right? But she said she was staying with friends?" Buchanan flips back a few pages in his notebook and looks up over his readers.

"Yes. But I think the dorms close over break," I add, tilting my head to the side. Quincy nods in agreement.

Buchanan opens a file he had in front of him, takes out a picture and slides it over to me.

"We found Ella's car parked off campus. According to Ella's parents, you are right, she didn't come home for break. Mr. Grunwell said Ella was planning to come home Christmas Eve and stay for the remainder of the break. They assumed she was staying with Faith or her other high school friends."

I study the picture of the black five-year-old Kia Sportage that looks brand new except for the damaged driver's side mirror which Ella never got fixed. "It's definitely Ella's car," I sigh.

"This is where we found Ella's car and her parents were shocked to learn she had been at SWU this entire time. Does anything look familiar?" Quincy asks, drumming his thumb on the table.

"I remember Mom E—that's what we call Ella's mom—telling us that she called Ella's roommate and the dorms when they couldn't find her."

I take the second picture in Buchanan's file, really scrutinizing every inch of the picture. The houses on the street look familiar, all are similar and something you would see in the old parts of town. "Nothing stands out to me. They look familiar but nothing specific about them."

The squeak of Buchanan's chair causes me to look up. Quincy is looking down and Buchanan's brow is furrowed.

"So how does this have anything to do with Ella being in Faith's car? I mean, if her car was there and we actually did go to a party there, wouldn't that mean we met Ella there?"

"Honestly, we were hoping you could help us with that, but that was my thought exactly." Quincy sighs, drops his hand to his lap and places his elbows on the chair arms.

"But we don't know if this is where the party was. The police canvased the area when her car was found. Most of the houses are college rentals. When the police spoke to the tenants, many were already home for break. No one could verify if there was a party on this street that night."

"So, you don't know why Ella's car was there." I drop the picture on the table and fall back in my chair. "I'm no help."

"Actually, you are Fiona." It's Buchanan this time and he sounds more like a dad trying to reassure a child. "Your memories are coming back and telling us we are on the right track. You're filling in the blanks as to how and why you were at SWU that night." Buchanan shakes his head and shrugs. "We were just hoping for more. That's all."

"Me too." I shrug and look away to let my hair cover my leaking eyes, just as Quincy slides a box of Kleenex my way.

Quincy's voice is soft, "We reached out to the detectives assigned to your accident case and asked them to canvas the accident site when the Grunwells reported Ella missing. We are looking into a connection between the accident and Ella's disappearance. They recovered a cell from the accident site under a shrub about twenty feet from where Faith was found."

"So, you do think there's a connection between our accident and Ella being missing?" I ask, my head spinning, trying to take in this news.

"It can't just be a coincidence that two girls from Brookston, Indiana are in a car accident right off campus on the 23rd of December, and a SWU student goes missing within a day or two later who is also from Brookston, Indiana. Not to mention you three have a very close relationship." Buchanan tilts his head and crosses his arms over his chest to make his point.

And he is right. It is an awfully big coincidence but, hearing the cops say it is hard to take.

"Anyway, the detectives found the phone and we believe it was in Faith's possession as she was thrown from the car," Quincy finishes.

"I'm sure she had her phone with her—"

"Well, that's the thing," Quincy adds as he clasps his hands together, fingers intertwined and glances at Buchanan before he begins. Buchanan nods and Quincy continues. "The phone was severely damaged from the wreck. We assumed it was Faith's cell since Faith

73

was in the passenger's seat, but we still had our IT department take a look at it to see if they could get anything off of it; in case there was any information that could help."

"Any luck?" I straighten up in my seat and lean forward biting my lip again, hands in fists.

"They were able to recover the cell number and it turns out that it's Ella's phone, not Faith's." Buchanan pauses to let that sink in.

My eyes narrow on Buchanan. "Why would Faith have Ella's phone?" I say to myself more than asking them.

"We don't know, but we are still hoping to get more off the phone. IT is currently trying to retrieve texts and pictures. We'll have you look through them once we do." And with that, Quincy and Buchanan thanked me for my time and instructed me to return to class.

I sit in my chair replaying the conversation and the information I just learned.

Faith had Ella's phone on her. Why?

I throw my head in my hands and squeeze my eyes shut. I feel a headache coming on and I need to talk this out with Lyla. I take my phone out and text: "we need to talk about Ella. lunch? PLEASE!"

By the time I answer the officer's questions, second period is well underway. I open the door to enter class, all eyes turn toward me.

"Sorry." I hand my teacher the pass and make my way to my assigned seat and get a few congrats on the way. Luckily, my seat is in the far row of art tables so the eyes watching me must turn back to the white board as I pass. I take my seat and bring my iPad to life trying to catch up on the project we are working on.

The rest of the morning follows in similar fashion. Nothing memorable happens but that's good. Several more "congrats" and "are you excited?" come my way, which makes me feel better about making court and the butterflies stir with each comment. Of course, there was talk about escorts, dresses and who they think will win. I even get a few, "I'm voting for you" and "I hope you win." I take a deep breath feeling myself relax a little and hope this is an indication that things at school might be getting back to normal. I need as much normal as I can get as everything outside of school is a hot mess.

***

I look over my lunch options as I stand in the lunch line and realize Lyla didn't text me back. I certainly thought she would respond when I brought up Ella. My stomach churns as I look at the half-baked pizza that is always served cold. It's all just too much. Faith fighting for her life, Ella missing, Lyla mad at me and me needing to remember. Or maybe it's just the idea of this crappy lunch.

My heart warms at the memory of Faith and me complaining to Mom and Dad about the school lunches last year.

"What?" The look of disbelief all over Dad's face was hysterical. "School lunches rock!"

"Ugh. There are so many things wrong with that statement." Faith rolled her eyes, and I started giggling and almost spit out my Sprite.

"First, you're too old to say 'rocks,'" Faith continued, Mom started giggling too but she tried to play it off with a wave of her hand.

Dad looked over to Mom with the same look of disbelief. "I don't know what you're laughing about. You are just as old as I am."

"I am not!" Mom shrieked and dropped her knife and fork to the table with a thud of her hands. "You are seven months older than me. And I agree, you should not be using the word 'rocks.'"

"Unbelievable. Who would have thought my girls would turn on me? But seriously, how can the school lunches be bad? We loved the square pizzas they served. I always bought two slices," Dad added proudly.

"You wouldn't be buying two slices of the crap we're served." Faith tilted her head as she focuses on cutting the steak Dad grilled for dinner.

"I swear they just take them out of the freezer the night before to thaw and they don't even bake them." I paused long enough to swallow my bite of mac and cheese. "And there is hardly any cheese or toppings on them."

"That doesn't sound good at all." Mom shook her head and forked her salad.

The cashier rings up the PB&J, apple, and bottled water as I punch in my lunch code to pay. I turn to walk to the table where I usually sit and feel that all too familiar wave of nausea roll through. A big group of us usually sits together which includes Lyla, Sara, Jessica, and several others. Normally there is no question, everyone knows to leave an open seat next to Lyla for me to have or vice versa, but now, I'm not sure what to expect.

Time seems to move in slow motion as I walk across the cafeteria, my legs heavy, my stomach in knots. I strain my neck to see over the crowded tables, hoping to see an open seat. My heart leaps to my throat when I see Sara sitting on one side of Lyla and Neveah, a JV cheerleader on the other. Across from her is Jessica and several others mixed in.

Clearly, I am not sitting by Lyla. I quickly glance around trying to find a seat at the long lunch table that could easily seat twenty students.

I approach the table and let out a sigh when I see a spot open about four seats down from Lyla and next to Avery and Tarin.

I put a smile on my face like I planned to sit with Avery today.

"You two don't mind, do you?" I ask in a low voice hoping no one else hears. I set my food down and throw my leg over the long bench seat before anyone answers.

"Saved it just for you." Avery pats the seat next to her and skootches over like this is an everyday thing.

"Thanks." I sit down and let out a quick breath to calm my nerves. I turn to my water bottle for a drink before unwrapping the plastic wrap from my sandwich.

"Nuh-uh," I hear Sara bark just as another voice half whispers. "She did not."

I can't help myself; I glance in their direction to see what the fuss is about. My friends are all huddled together, Jessica leaning over the table, ass in the air and elbows on the table holding her up. My friends are hanging on Jessica's every word and take turns glancing my way. Except for Lyla, who is focused on her food and taking a drink of chocolate milk.

Avery and Tarin are quiet but keep eating, not acknowledging the commotion.

"I wonder what that's about?" I ask softly and just then the group I usually sit with picks up their trash and walks passed us to the common area, following Lyla's lead. Tarin watches them leave and once out of sight, she leans over the table and in a hushed voice says, "Jessica told some students in second period that you didn't care that Faith is in a coma."

"What?" I shout louder than I intend. I look around and see a few eyes in my direction. I lean into the table to get closer to Tarin and Avery. "I didn't say that!"

"She also said that you were jealous of Faith and planned the whole thing." Tarin takes another bite of her bread stick, then puts it down and lifts her eyes to me mine. My mouth hangs open and I try finding my words. Finally, they come.

"Why would she say that?" I demand, keeping my eyes on Tarin, only turning when I hear Avery's voice.

"Apparently, she told Colin the same thing, at least that is what he told me last period." Avery tilts her head as she looks to me with eyebrows raised, revealing faint lines in her forehead. I pick my mouth up off the table, blink a few times, and realize my throat has gone dry. I feel like someone has reached out and wrapped a giant hand around my throat squeezing it tight.

"She must have heard us talking after school last night about the accident. But I have no idea where she come up with all the other crap." Avery puts her plastic fork down and keeps her eyes on mine.

"I-I..." My mouth opening and closing like a fish on land gasping for air. I swallow the lump in my throat and try to make since of it all.

"What the hell? I never said anything like that." I wait for someone to tell me it's all a dream. No one speaks. "I mean some things I did say but they were totally taken out of context. That fucking bitch!" I feel the heat rise in my cheeks and the burning at the back of my eyes. I need to get out of here.

I jump up so fast from the table, my knee bangs the underside of the table as I straddle the bench to get out. I turn from the table, leaving my lunch sit and walk as fast as I can to the bathroom, not caring that half the students left in the cafeteria are watching my melt down.

I take a hard left around the corner into the bathroom and screech to a halt when I find myself face-to-face with Jessica.

"How could you?" I demand.

"I heard you say you didn't care." Jessica looks over her shoulder to see me moving toward her. Her eyebrows shoot up and she shifts her weight to the foot farthest from me, then turns back, reaching for paper towel and dries her hands.

"No, I didn't!" I throw my hands in the air, eyes wide, and take a step toward Jessica. My heart racing and fist clenched.

"Yes, you did!" Jessica screams as she takes a step back and places her hands on her hips.

"I did not say that I didn't care, Jessica. Faith is my sister." I swallow down tears, my voice catching in my throat.

"Yes, right in front of your Jeep last night." Her volume raises and her face grows flushed. Her sandy blonde hair swings with each movement.

"I love my sister. Why would I ever say that?" I throw my hands up and look up to the ceiling shaking my head, my voice matching hers.

"I heard you and I also heard what you said to Avery." Jessica leans forward pointing her finger at me.

"Jessica, you know that is not what I meant." We are about a foot apart and I could reach out and strangle her. "You are taking it out of context."

"I. HEARD. YOU!" Jessica yells just inches from my face, almost spitting on me.

My eyes narrow, my teeth clench as my mouth goes hard and I feel a fire in my stomach. My blood is boiling. I draw my arm back, my right hand clenched in a fist, and I step toward her with my opposite foot as my entire body moves toward Jessica, my right arm trailing my shoulder, fist high just like my dad taught me. Just for a second, I see fear on Jessica's face, but as quick as the fire in my gut flashed, I am paralyzed. My fist stops an inch from Jessica's nose. Jessica looks like a deer frozen in head lights, face pale and eyes wide.

"No," Tarin dives in between us. Avery is right behind her and wrapping her arm around my shoulder, pulling me back just as the bell rings to end lunch. Tarin is on the other side of me, pulling on my arm to lower my fist. Jessica hunches her shoulders and scurries out.

"What happened?" Avery asks eyes wide and looks around. I'm sure the confrontation only lasted about thirty seconds but, in that moment, it seemed like forever.

"I...walked in...and...saw Jessica...and just lost it," I spit out in between sobs. I hate crying at school, and I am pissed at my body for betraying me. "I just...I ran into her...I had to know...why she said it." My shoulders heaving up and down with each gasp.

We are now the only ones in the bathroom, and I am leaning against the wall with Tarin and Avery on each side trying to comfort me. I lean over, my elbows on my knees and hands covering my face to hide the tears. My slick bottomed boots begin sliding out from under me. I don't fight it and slide to the ground, knees bent, my forehead on my knees and arms around my legs trying to make myself as small as possible.

"I swear I didn't say that." My voice raw, my words bubble out in sobs.

"I know you wouldn't say anything like that," Tarin assures me. "She is just jealous of you."

"I agree with Tarin." Avery continues, "I heard Jace likes you."

"What? We are just good friends. And what does that have to do with anything?" I raise my head from my knees and turn to Avery. My vision blurry and face red from ugly crying.

"Last fall in English, I heard her talking about Jace. She has a major crush on him," Avery whispers and then mouths the word "major" with a nod.

"Right, and remember how pissed Jessica was when she found out that Jace went with you to hang up missing flyers for Ella last weekend?" Tarin asks. "You might not have noticed. It was during lunch when you told Lyla how many flyers you and Jace got up. Jessica was sitting down a bit from you. I watch as her face turn red, mouth grew hard, and her eyes narrowed with every word you said. I knew then she wasn't a true friend to you."

"So, she goes around making shit up, telling people that I planned my sister's accident?" I sit up and hold my palm in the air. I drop my hand and lay my forehead back on my knees.

Tarin and Avery stay with me the rest of the hour and my sobs finally stop. I get up off the floor, my legs and back stiff and my knee pops. I look in the mirror to take in the damage, my eyes are puffy and red, no way can I go to fifth period looking like this.

"Why don't you go to the nurse and tell her you're sick," Avery suggests. "That way you can hide out until you are ready to go back to class."

The three of us walk to our lockers and I have to admit, Avery's plan is better than mine. I don't have a plan.

Both give me a hug for encouragement, and they head to their next class. I look at myself one more time in the distorted magnetic mirror I have hanging in my locker. I take a deep breath, glance around to make sure the locker bay is empty and stand there for a few more seconds debating my options.

"Fuck it." I grab my white puffer coat with faux fur around the hood and slide it on. I throw my notebook, folders, the novel we are reading in English, and iPad in my bag and slam my locker shut as I turn my back on my day.

My heart is racing as I make my way through the quiet halls on high alert. When I get to the exit by the student parking lot undetected, I let out a deep breath I didn't realize I was holding. I make my way through the blue double doors and am met with falling snow that wasn't supposed to start until around 2:00 this afternoon.

I dig for my keys and try yanking my hood up at the same time which proves to be useless.

Once in my Jeep, I shake the snow out of my hair and lean my head back on the seat, closing my eyes. I love my Jeep and how Dad was a little surprised by my choice of vehicle. Three weeks before Faith's sixteenth birthday, she was given the choice of Mom's two-year-old, Dodge Durango or choosing a vehicle within reason.

"I want a new, Garnet Red, V8 Camaro with a drop." I couldn't help but giggle at Faith's confidence. I was certain, even as a seventh grader, that a Camaro was not within reason.

"That's my girl." Dad gave Faith a light punch on the arm before Mom could be Mom and ask the most embarrassing question ever.

"What's a drop?"

"Ugh...it's a convertible, Mom." Faith rolled her eyes.

"Absolutely not." Mom's disapproval put an end to further discussion which resulted in Faith storming off to her room and slamming her door. Honestly, I was shocked that she even had the guts to ask for a car like that. I knew she wanted one, but did she really think she was going to get it?

Faith must have realized it too because she came out of her room about ten minutes later and apologized for her childish behavior. She even took it one step further by saying, "I also understand that my behavior is not the way to prove that I am responsible enough for a car."

The morning of Faith's birthday, my sleep was interrupted by a high-pitched squeal. I climbed out of bed and made my way to the horrid sound coming from the kitchen and notice a small, opened box thrown on the table atop ripped wrapping paper and bow. Faith was still squealing and hugging Mom and Dad as she bounced up and down in the kitchen with her new keys in hand.

"Well, let's go check it out." Dad might have been more excited than Faith if that was possible.

"Okay." Faith took off toward the door in her boxers and tank top, even though it was only March. I ran back to my room to grab my phone and shouted over my shoulder. "We need pictures, no, a video."

By the time I got back, everyone was outside and there was more squealing. I reached the door and started filming Faith as she unlocked the driver's door and crawled inside. She didn't get a brand-new Camaro with a drop top, but she did get a used red Camaro with a V6. She was giddy with excitement.

Dad crawled in the passenger's seat and started going over a few things about the car, but before they got too far Mom steps in. "Okay, guys. We need to lay down a few ground rules before your dad has you starting the engine and pulling out of the driveway."

"Right..." Dad reluctantly agreed with a huff. "Ground rules. Okay, let's go back inside. We can eat breakfast while we go over everything."

Mom had already made Faith's favorite breakfast casserole, so we fill our plates and sit at the table. Dad made it a point to make sure I paid attention to all of this since I will be riding with her and would be getting my license in a few years.

Mom and Dad take turns running through the rules. "We must know where you are at all times. No one is to be in the car but Fiona, and of course Lyla and Ella once their parents give permission. And finally, you must maintain a 3.5 to get the Good Student Discount."

I laughed. "Like she will ever have lower than a 3.9," I added with an eye roll and stuffed my mouth with another bite of delicious birthday casserole.

"Well, we just want to be clear. As long as your GPA is a 3.5 or higher, we will pay your insurance," Mom added. "However, if it drops below 3.5, you pay."

"You are also responsible for buying your gas. You will need to budget that out of your paycheck," Dad jumped in while he dug out another serving of breakfast.

"Okay—"

"Oh. And that car is not to leave the driveway in snow or ice. It is not made for it," Dad interrupted Faith before she could continue.

"Of course, Dad." Faith did a really good job of fighting off the eye roll because I know Faith wanted to say, "Well, duh…" but she was playing it smart. "Maybe Mrs. Keelin will give me a raise. I have been working at the boutique since last summer."

"It never hurts to ask." Dad nodded his head. And with that, Faith sprinted to her room to throw on a pair of jeans, sweatshirt, and boots so her and Dad could play in the new car.

I started to help Mom with the dishes when she looked at me with a halfhearted look of exasperation and said, "Well, you might as well go too." And that was all I needed to hear. I ran to my room and threw on the first thing I could find and was out the door.

When it was my turn to choose a car for my sixteenth birthday, I'm pretty sure they knew I wasn't going to choose Mom's now five-year-old Durango. But the surprise on Dad's face when I told them I wanted his two-year-old Jeep Wrangler Unlimited was priceless.

"Really?" Dad tilted his head and smiled.

"Yes. Didn't you ever wonder why I was pushing you to get the blue one over the red? I've had this planned for years," I admitted and threw in a huge smile.

"Is that why you pushed me to get the Fuel wheels?" Dad asks and I couldn't hide my smirk. "I should have known there was a reason you pushed for the addons." Dad shook his head, but you could see pride on his face. "And here I was just proud I had a daughter that knew what any of it was," he added with a wink.

Mom laughed and looked from Dad back to me. "I'm not sure your dad is prepared to part with it."

"I guess the other option is to buy me a new one." I turned to Mom, tilted my head, and shrugged my shoulders hoping to look adorable. "Then I can pick everything out I want on it. We'll need another lift kit, Throttles, and 35s."

"Um ...no. Faith didn't get exactly what she wanted." Dad gave me a stern look, then let out a sign. "Let me think this over. Maybe we can work something out." Dad leaned back in his chair, put his thumb and index finger to his chin, and pretended he was rubbing his nonexistent beard.

"Thank you, Daddy." I jumped into his lap for a hug like I did when I was five years old.

Of course, I got the Jeep on my birthday, and I am pretty sure his display of disappointment was purely for Mom so she wouldn't be to upset when he showed up in his new Cadillac Escalade. The whole reason he chose the Jeep was because Mom insisted that we didn't need a big SUV since Faith and I were getting older. And the Durango is big enough for all of us when we travel.

The buzz of my phone jolts me back to reality. I glance at the screen to see the notifications popping up. The latest Instagram post, a picture of Ella from last year with the caption: @fionarenee first your sister, now Ella?

The warmth in my heart fades as reality takes hold. Even though I've only had my license since the beginning of November, it seems like forever ago and it's definitely a different world now. I take a deep breath and exhale and toss my phone on the passenger's seat without reading anymore posts.

"What the hell happened that night, Fiona?" I rub my hands over my face and through my wet hair.

I push in the clutch, my truck rolls backward a few inches before I press the break and I turn over the ignition. *I have to get out of here.*

Chapter 4

The snow is coming down harder now as I pull out of the school parking lot, but the roads aren't bad enough to need 4-wheel drive. I have no idea where to go except to see Faith.

My stomach churns at the thought of sitting next to my perfect sister. *How could she even begin to understand what I'm going though at school?* Besides, Mom usually stops in to see Faith between meetings during the day and I don't need a run in since it's 12:15 on a Friday.

At the highway intersection, I automatically turn in the direction that takes me back toward Brookston. The roads are starting to turn light gray with the snow. The dark clouds lingering overhead indicate it's not stopping anytime soon.

I look around at the snow-covered trees and white rolling hills that are only found in the southern part of the state. I resist the temptation to pull off the road to make snow angels.

Without a second thought, I blow by the road I turn off to go home and I let out a deep breath and sink into my seat. My stomach calms and my grip on the steering wheel lightens. My Jeep seems to know where to go. Where I need to be.

Ten minutes later, I turn off the main road and pull down the shifter to put my Jeep into 4-wheel drive. The entrance to Brooks Summit Slopes is no longer black, but a beautiful, untouched white and has a few steep inclines before getting to the lodge. The parking lot is sparse since it's a school day, but by 4:00 pm, you won't be able to find a spot, especially with the snow forecast for tonight and tomorrow.

Lyla, Sara, me, and a few others from our crew planned earlier in the week to head to Brooks after school to hit the fresh snow since we don't have a game tonight. I'm sure Neveah and her fam will be here but only to hang in the lodge and flirt with the guys. You won't see them on the slopes.

After parking in a primo spot, I hop out of my Jeep and walk to the back, pleased I put my gear in the back before I left the house this morning. I reach in for my Burton snow pants and slide them on over my leggins. I change into my boots and coat in the parking lot, pull my gray beanie on my head letting my hair flow freely. I grab my gloves and board and I'm on my way.

I stop long enough to scan my season pass at the ticket office; a process quicker than usual since no one is here yet. I look up expecting to recognize the face behind the glass. Brooks hires a lot of high school kids in our area, and I usually know most of them. But today there is an older gentleman working the booth that I don't recognize. He does a

92

double take when he sees me, probably wondering why I'm not in school.

At the base of the hill, I strap my lead foot into the binding and skate to the ski lift. This might be the only time I haven't waited in line at Brooks.

The ride is peaceful, and I take in the beauty of the snow-covered trees. At the top of the hill, I step off the ski lift and quickly move out of the way, so I don't get ran over by the chair and I giggle at the memory.

"OMG. Lyla, look at that dime!" I pointed to the shaggy blonde in an orange coat.

"Where?" Lyla's head snapped in the direction I was pointing. "Oh, the one on the K2? He is gorge! We need to take that line," Lyla said as she hopped off the lift. "Fiona."

"What?" I was still looking at the hottie. "Oh, crap." I hopped off the lift but not fast enough to get out of the way.

"Ugh!" Pain shot through the back of my upper thigh and butt as the lift chair rammed into me and threw me to the ground.

"Face plant," I heard from behind me followed by laughter.

"And she wasn't evening skiing yet," another voice added. I didn't bother to look back. I didn't want them to see my face.

I struggled to get off the ground and out of the way, so I didn't get trampled. Suddenly, two hands grabbed my shoulders and started pulling me, then I heard her laughter. Lyla didn't want me trampled but she was enjoying my humiliation.

"At least there wasn't a yard sale," she added, a reference made to a snowboarder who bites it on the slope and loses all their gear. "Jace would have loved that!"

"Shut up," I hissed. I got to my feet and grabbed my board and hurried away from the ski lift hoping no one saw me, but I couldn't outrun Lyla's laughter.

With a smile on my face from the fresh memory, I skate over to the line I plan to take. I strap my other foot into the binding and adjust my straps. I stand up and look out over the valley at the base of Brooks Summit and to the adjacent hill, which is Brookston. The rolling hills glisten with snow-covered grounds, trees shadowed with white powder as large snowflakes float in the bluish gray sky. The snowfall slows and for just a moment, the dark sky opens letting a ray of sunshine through the clouds illuminating Brookston with its glittering treetops.

It's a view an artist dreams of and it takes my breath away, like someone punched me in the gut. My legs buckle beneath me, and I sit back on the cold ground taking in the moment, barely noticing the tears streaming down my cheeks. Everything I know and love about Brookston is forever changed.

Unaware of how long I've been sitting here or that my ass is freezing, I start to feel a little lighter; like the tears washed away some of the overwhelming emotions I had buried inside.

With a deep breath in and an exhale, I wipe away the dampness from my cheeks and stand up. The snow is falling heavier now so I pull my goggles over my eyes and butter the tail of my board, so my lead leg is in front. I rock forward just enough to get over the lip of the hill, just like Jace taught me, and I carve.

Even though it's been a while, my body knows what to do and autopilot takes over leaning into the movement as my weight shifts from the backside to the frontside of the board. The stiffness in my knees and back left over from the accident begin to loosen and subside with each motion. I feel more alive at this moment than I have in weeks.

The rush of the ride, the chill of the air on my skin and the wind blowing through my hair takes me far away from the bullshit of the day. I am free in this moment. No worry, no guilt, no sadness, no anger- a calmness takes over my heart. I am at peace on this hill. Exactly what I need.

I lean into the frontside of the board at the bottom of the run and turn toward the ski lift, gliding as far as I can before taking my back leg out of the binding. I dig my heel in the snow, and skate toward the lift.

"Fiona, wait!" I stop in my tracks and look over my shoulder to see who is calling me. Jace is carrying his board under his arm and jogging in my direction.

"I heard you skipped out and figured this is where you'd be," Jace says with that crooked grin. My heart skips a beat and a smile spreads across my face. Yeah, I'm crushin' on him.

"Who told you I skipped?" I look around like a kid worried they are getting caught while sneaking a cookie before dinner.

"I, ahh…" Jace stammers a little trying to decide how to say it. "Well, I heard about what happened at lunch."

"Of course, you did," I say flatly and look down at the ground. I'm sure everyone knows by now.

"You know I don't believe any of it, Fiona, but you know how Jessica and those girls love spillin' tea. So, when I didn't see you before fifth period, I asked Avery. She said she thought the nurse, but the nurse said she hadn't seen you. So, I figured you might have skipped out."

"And you took that to be your cue to skip?" I cross my arms over my chest and cock my head to the side.

"I couldn't let you get all the sweet cherry pow pow." Jace gives me a wink and a light punch on the arm.

I drop my head back, bringing my hands to my head to keep my beanie on and let out a laugh at Jace's use of slang for fresh snow.

"At least there's no roadkill out here yet." I giggle and look up to the hill above us.

"I knew I could get a laugh out of you," Jace says proudly, and straps his lead leg into the binding. "Ready?"

"Yep." I turn and lead us to the ski lift. A smile on my face; Jace skipped to hang with me. I laugh out loud when I realize how pissed Jessica will be when she hears about it.

I follow Jace down the hill avoiding the jumps to be safe. At the bottom of the hill, Jace turns to me and holds out his fist to bump.

"Nice run." He bends over to unbuckle his back foot, as do I.

"Little rusty but I am working out the kinks. Let's see if you can keep up with me this time," I tease, my cheeks burn not only from the wind but from smiling. Even at my best, Jace would blow me away on the slopes. He's one of the best snowboarders at Brooks.

We make our way back to the lift to take a different run. There is a small line forming now; people must be leaving work early to hit the slopes. I have no idea how long we've been out here, but I'm starting to feel tired, and my knees are aching.

This time I lead. I choose the line and feel ready to try a small jump. As soon as I hit the lip of the jump, I know I'm in trouble. My body weight is off balance and I try to correct myself as I land but it's useless. My board slips out from under me as my butt hits the snow, and I continue to tumble head over heels while rolling down the hill. I'm completely disoriented when I finally come to a stop and begin looking around trying to get my bearings. Jace can't be far behind, and he might not be able to avoid me.

"You okay?" I hear and finally find him to my left. "I could tell you weren't solid on the jump, so I went around it."

"Yeah," I stammer, trying to get up. "Just gonna be a little sore tomorrow."

Jace lets out a weak laugh. "I bet. That was a hard hit. Need help?" But Jace is already helping me up before I can say no.

"Thanks, I think this is it for me. Besides, I don't want to be here when the rest of the squad gets here."

Jace goes quiet, looks around then down at his gloved hands. I can tell he isn't sure what to say.

"Jace, I completely understand if you're staying. I don't blame you. Don't worry about me."

"I'm not," he says with a smile and reaches out pushing my shoulder. "I was just thinking about what we are going to eat at the lodge."

I let out a laugh. "I am a little hungry," I admit and my stomach growls on cue.

"Last one there buys." And Jace takes off.

"Hey." I follow right behind him.

I order a soft pretzel and Jace orders nachos. We take a seat in a booth by the window so we can watch the slopes and of course make fun of a few wipe outs.

"So, how are you doing, Fiona?" Jace asks between bites.

I look to my pretzel, avoiding his eyes and find I've been breaking it into little pieces.

"I'm fine." I shrug and dip a piece into the cheese.

"Um, by the looks of your plate, I would disagree." Jace nods toward my destroyed snack. "C'mon Fiona, you don't have to pretend with me. Spill it."

"I…" I sigh. "I just don't know what I did to deserve this. I mean, even if Jessica doesn't like me, why would everyone else take her side? I'm just pissed. Seriously, to think I don't care about my sister?" I lean back against the hard back of the wood booth, rub my fingers together to get the salt off and look out the window at the skiers and snowboarders.

"Everyone knows you love your sister, Fiona. And you know Jessica is just salty." Jace reaches across the table, taking my hand in his and squeezes. My heart jumps and I snap my head back to look at my hand in Jace's. He releases my hand as soon as I look back.

"Why is she so salty? She's always acted like my friend. I mean we don't hang a lot, but she is friends with Sara, so Jessica has been around more lately," I say more to myself than Jace. I go back to tearing my pretzel into small pieces.

"I think she is jealous of you," Jace sighs. "I'm not trying to be mean, but she is pretty basic."

"What does that have to do with me?" I drop my pretzel on the plate and my hands to my lap as I look out the big picture window and watch a skier glide effortlessly side to side down the slope.

"Well, she's basic and you...you're, you know..." My head snaps to Jace as he shrugs. My brow furrows, and the corners of my mouth turn down waiting on him to finish. "Not." I watch as Jace keeps his eyes on his food. He scoops up some cheese and chili onto a nacho chip and pops it in his mouth.

"I'm not really sure what to do with this information," I admit and continue watching as Jace. We sit in silence for a few moments as he chews his food and takes a drink of his Pepsi. Jace keeps his eyes turned down at the table.

"I'm not sure there is anything for you to do about it. It is Jessica's problem she is salty and jealous. Not yours." Jace finally look up and points at me.

"But it *is* my problem. She is making it my problem by starting all this shit." I swallow hard and try to relax my hands I have clenched into fist.

"Actually, it's not. It's all about how you let her problem affect you." Jace takes another sip of Pepsi and goes back for another chip. "Hey, look at it this way," Jace says between bites, "At least you know who your true friends are and who they aren't." Jace licks cheese off his thumb and fore finger, then wipes his hands on a napkin. "Well, except for Lyla," Jace mumbles though another bite.

"Yeah, I really fucked that up, Jace. I didn't mean to hurt her. I just didn't think about what I said first." I lick my thumb and press down on a piece of salt on my plate and bring it to my tongue.

"You and Lyla will be fine. You just need to talk. Hear her out." Jace nods, slurping the last of the Pepsi in the bottom of his cup.

"Maybe, but right now, she won't even acknowledge me." I take another piece of pretzel, dip it in the cheese and bring it to my mouth when I notice Jace has stopped eating and is watching me. Suddenly self-conscious, I feel the heat in my cheeks as I chew my food.

"Are you sure you don't want to stay? You're gonna miss one hell of a night. Half of East Brook with be here." Jace tilts his head with eyebrows raised. Those blue eyes staring into mine.

"Ah, I'm good. Thanks for hanging with me today." I feel the smile spread across my face, a little disappointed I need to leave. I hate not being included but I just don't think I want to be here tonight.

"My pleasure." Jace picks up the plate with my shredded pretzel and throws it in the trash. He walks me to the exit of the lodge, and I lean in to give him a hug and thank him again.

"That's what I'm here for." He pulls back from the hug first.

With a laugh, I wave bye. He doesn't say anything but waves back as his smile starts to fade. I turn to walk to the back of my Jeep and place my board in the back. I remove my snow pants and boots then slide on my furry boots. When I open the driver's door, I quickly look over my shoulder and see Jace is still standing there, like he is on guard protecting me. I give him a quick smile, climb in, and drive away.

I'm drawn to each electric pole I pass and see Ella's face staring back at me. The missing posters are faded and flimsy from the January weather.

Guilt runs through me as I should have went looking for Ella today. *But where? Do I just start walking around SWU campus calling out her name like you do when your dog gets loose?* I make a mental note to make new posters and get them up this weekend.

There's at least four inches of snow on the ground and road crews are out plowing and salting. But they can't keep up with the pace of the snowfall so most of the side roads haven't been touched. The highway isn't too bad, but I keep it in four-wheel drive to be safe.

I pull in the driveway and my heart skips a beat when I see the tire tracks in the snow that leads to Mom's side of the garage. Usually, Dad is not home at this time and if Mom is able to get out early on a Friday evening, she goes straight to the hospital. She was gone when I woke up this morning and I was hoping to avoid her tonight after last night's fiasco.

"Shit. Shit, shit." The butterflies return to my stomach, my palms are sweaty, and I'm biting my lower lip. Somethings wrong or she would be at the hospital.

I yank off my beanie in case she is looking through the window waiting on me.

"Shit, Faith!" My heart is in my throat at the thought that something has happened to her.

I shut off my Jeep. I throw my gloves and beanie in the back and jump out of the Jeep, leaving my bag in the back. As I rush to the door, I pull my hair back into a messy bun hoping to hide the wet pieces.

The front door swings open before I can even get my key in the lock. The door slams against the foyer wall and I jump expecting the glass pane to shatter. I would be grounded for two weeks if I had slammed the door that hard.

"Is it Faith?" I ask, panic in my voice, and stop in my tracks when Mom steps onto the porch.

"What the hell is this?" Mom shoves her cell phone in my face.

"I-I don't kno—"

"I can't believe you." She cuts me off as I try to grab the phone in her hand.

"Mom, you're moving too much. I can't read the screen." I try to sound calm hoping that might help defuse the situation, but my brain scrambles to understand.

"With everything else we have going on and I have to get this text from Sam's mom. What the hell do you think you're doing?" And for the first time I look at her face. Her mouth in a straight line, jaw clenched, eyes are red rimmed and watery, you can see all the creases on her scrunched up forehead.

"Mom, I swear. I don't know what you are talking about." I take the phone out of her hand. She shuts the door and walks away crying, leaving me standing on the front stoop reading the text that has her so upset.

"Hi Sharon, I hate to bother you, but I just saw this on Sam's phone and thought you should know. This is a screen shot of the Instagram post a friend texted to him. He swears he doesn't know who posted it. A teacher friend of mine told me Netflix and chill means having sex."

I scroll down the screen and see a post from da'man69, who I have never seen on Instagram before but says he's from Brookston, IN and has an inappropriate cartoon picture for his profile pic. Below the username is a picture of a half-naked girl straddling a guy with his jeans around his ankles on a couch in a dungy room. The girl has long blonde curly hair with strawberry blonde roots that hangs to cover her face. If I didn't know better, I would think it was me.

Below the picture, the caption reads: Netflix and chillin' W @fionarenee 2day. #53X #gettinsom

And apparently that is what the person sharing this post was going for. My eyes go wide, and my mouths hits the ground as nausea rises in my stomach. I stand there frozen, staring at the picture. I can see at the bottom of the screenshot the message Arron Brewer wrote on the text to Sam: "dam langford, your ex is a thot"

105

I feel the blood drain from my face. I turn and in one long step, dive to the side of the front porch, throwing myself over the railing and empty the content of my stomach. Twice.

Hanging on to the rot iron railing, my legs give out and I crumble to the ground right on the front porch as sobs rake through my body. I bury my face in my coat and scream as loud as I can, the echo rings back to me from the woods across the street. Snow is falling on top of me, and I stop screaming when I run out of air. I do everything I can to not take another breath in. Please, just let this be done, even if that means I just took my last breath right here on this porch.

My body doesn't listen to my pleas and takes over breathing. My lungs suck in as much air as possible, even though I wish they wouldn't. My knuckles white with the death grip I have on the cold black railing. No one is running to help me.

My head rests against the railing, tears freezing to my cheeks, as I reach for my phone in my back pocket. Then remember I tossed it on the front seat at Brooks. I stay still for a few more moments hoping I vanish into thin air, but that doesn't happen, so I pull myself off the frozen concrete and stagger to my Jeep. I reach across the driver's seat without getting in to grab my phone. My screen comes to life when I hit the power button, I have at least twenty notifications from Instagram plus several text messages.

Most comments are in response to a picture of Jessica and me arguing in the bathroom at school that I didn't realize someone took; and speculation about why I skipped out. Spencer Halcomb commented: "thehalk04 bet @fionarenne got roasted"

I look at the next comment from Sara, I know she is referring to me: "sadiehawkins get what u deserve"

Unable to read anymore, I scroll down and there's the post from daman69 with a look-a-like me having sex which now has 47 likes and endless comments ranging from support to ridicule.

"Mom." I slam my door and race up the front steps and into the house. "Mom? Where are you?"

She doesn't answer but I can hear the whimpers from the kitchen. I have no idea what to say to make this better.

"Mom?" I ask shyly, trying not to upset her more than she already is. "Can we talk?"

Mom is sitting at the kitchen table, elbows on the table and her face in the palms of her hands. I notice tear drops landing on the wood surface.

"I just don't understand," she mumbles through covered hands. "Everything is such a mess...with Faith and Ella." She lifts her head up to me as I turn from the sink wiping my mouth after rinsing it out. I notice her drawn forehead and red, pained face. "The doctor said we should let you go back to your life, that normalcy will help you get your memory back and recover. But this?" She waves her hands frantically in the air and points to her phone. "This is what you do? After what happened at the Terrace Grove party? How could you?" She drops her head in her arms on the table and sobs.

Nausea rolls again and I turn back to the sink. Luckily, I have nothing left but dry heaves. I tilt my head to drink straight from the faucet, something I would be scolded for under normal circumstances, and spit out the water. Leaning over the sink, forearms resting on the edge for support, I stare at the drain at the bottom.

"Mom," I sniff, wiping my mouth, and turn from the sink to look at her. "I know this looks really bad—"

"*Looks*?" Mom cuts me off and raises her head to look at me over her arms. Her eyes buggy.

"Mom. I swear I was not having sex with anyone today. Or anytime..." My words trail off as I see the knowing look on my mom's face.

"I don't know what to believe. Do you know how bad this makes you look? Me look?"

My eyes go wide, and I jump back like I've been slapped. I take a deep breath and close my eyes trying to stay calm.

"I know, Mom, and I am really sorry you had to see that. I don't know who daman69 is or who is in that picture, but it is not me."

"Did you skip school today?" Her face hard, eyes staring at me.

"Well, I-I can explain." But she just continues to stare. "So, at school, Jessica Brindle started a rumor that I'm jealous of Faith, and that I purposely had the accident to hurt Faith. But Mom, you know how much I love Faith and Ella. I would never do anything to hurt either one of them."

"I know you wouldn't do anything to purposely hurt Faith or Ella. But you obviously ran your mouth about something to piss Jessica off."

"What?" My eyes huge, unable to believe what she just said. "I didn't do anything." I swallow fighting back tears. "Or say anything for that matter."

"You need to learn to keep your mouth shut. You can't trust everyone you go to school with," she scolds.

"I know that!" I scream. "I didn't do anything!" I toss my hands out to my side and let them drop as I step back from the table.

"You did skip school." Mom's voice sharp.

"Yeah, after Jessica attacked me in the bathroom about the rumor *she* started."

"That's not the point. If you had stayed in school like you should have been, this 69 person would have no reason to post anything about you. But because you skipped, that leaves an opening for more rumors. This whole thing could have been avoided."

The heat in my face is back along with the burning in the back of my eyes.

"Unbelievable." I turn on my heels and storm off toward my room.

"You're grounded for one-week, young lady!" Mom shouts after me.

"Ugh..." I stomp my way down the hall and slam my door shut.

A second later, Mom opens my door and whips out her hand. "Your phone."

Without looking at her, I toss it on the dresser, and I throw myself across my bed with boots hanging over the edge and bury my face in my pillow. I can't hold back the tears anymore and I let out an imaginary scream in my pillow.

I feel the weight of my four-legged fur ball, Merida, jump up on my bed. Merida is a beautiful white and brown ragdoll kitty with blue eyes. We rescued her from the shelter when I was twelve; she was my birthday present.

I roll over on my side, kick my boots off, and I cuddle up with Mer at my chest. She curls up next to me purring and snuggles in with her unconditional love.

I think back to when we got her to distract me from this hell. *Her name was Madeline, and it wasn't quite right. After a few days I realized how brave this tiny little girl was with her curious nature and felt Merida was a better name.*

Laying here stroking her soft fur, I need to draw from Merida's courage, strength, and bravery. Something I just don't seem to have right now.

Chapter 5

All is dark but the glowing light next to me. My heart is about to jump out of my chest. Something isn't right.

I squint my eyes to adjust to the dark and try taking advantage of the glow to search for what I'm missing. I don't know what that is, but...gone. It's gone. Like a missing limb. It's always been there with me, but now it's severed.

I feel a pull to my right and whip my head around, but I find nothing. The glowing light disappears with a flash, fear prickles down my spine. This fear is not for me, but for something or someone else.

Suddenly, a dim light appears ahead of me. It draws me in like a moth to a flame, disoriented and confused, I have no choice but to run toward the light. I see something red in the distance.

My heart is pounding, lungs are heaving, and I hear my footsteps beating against the pavement. I watch the red object grow closer. It's a car. Faith's car.

"Here's the key." I hear as the pointy metal lands in my hands. I'm now behind the wheel and driving. I'm not sure where I'm going but I must turn right at the stop sign.

I'm distracted by the return of glowing light. I look to the passenger's seat and I'm not alone. Unable to make out the person sitting next to me as long hair is blocking her face, I focus on the glowing light coming from the phone in her hands.

"C'mon, C'mon." Her words are panicked, preventing me from recognizing the voice.

I glance back to the road, then the passenger. The long hair hiding her face is glowing blonde.

"Faith!" I shoot up in bed. Heart pounding and covered in sweat, I'm frantically looking around my room. But it's gone. The light is gone. She's gone.

Dad bursts through the door as I'm searching for my phone before remembering Mom has it.

"Are you okay?" I look at Dad's face, this isn't the first bad dream he has come to save me from. But you would think at six-teen, the nightmares wouldn't be happening anymore.

"I think so," I try to catch my breath and try to bring my heartrate to a level below that of a hummingbird. "It was so real but none of it made any sense." I look to my dad and shrug my shoulders.

"Another nightmare?" I look to my mom standing in my door frame. For the first time I notice my mom's puffy red eyes.

"Ah, yeah," I sigh and look down at my shaking hands and stuff them under my blankets. I take a few more deep breaths to calm myself.

"You okay?" Mom asks, not stepping into my room.

I nod and swallow, and when I look back up, my mom has her back turned to me and is walking away to her room.

My dad stands at the end of the bed and gently scratches Merida's chin; her purr brings me comfort.

"Do you wanna talk about it?" Dad asks softly and moves to sit on the edge of my bed.

"No, I think I was looking for someone, but I never saw who, or couldn't figure out who it was. It was all fuzzy and distorted, jumping around a lot. But I had a strong sense that I needed to find...something. Or someone."

"Maybe you were looking for Ella." Dad reaches out and smooths the ridges in my comforter from me jumping up.

"Yeah, maybe so." I let out a deep breath.

"How about I make us some hot chocolate? You know I make the best." I look up to see a tiny smile on my dad's face, one eyebrow raises.

"You came in to sit with me. Why couldn't she?" I ask softly as I pull my knees up to my chest, wrapping my arms around my shins, and tuck my chin down so my forehead rests on my knees.

"She's going through a lot right now, Fi. She had a hard life growing up, you know. She just wants the best for you. Both of you girls." Dad reaches out and wraps his hand around my foot and gives it a little squeeze like he always does when we have a talk.

"It doesn't feel like it." I raise my eyes up over my forearms to peer at my dad, trying to hide the tears.

"Give her some time, Fiona. She loves you. She just needs...time," Dad sighs and gives me a hug.

I look up from my dad's embrace and see my mom standing at the door again. When Dad sees Mom, he turns to me and says, "Okay, get some sleep."

Dad stands and turns, then disappears down the hall.

"I'm really sorry, Mom. I didn't mean for any of this to happen." I lay my forehead on my knees and hear my mom walk to my bed, sitting in almost the exact same spot Dad just left.

"But it did and here we are." Mom wipes her nose with a tissue and looks to the picture I have on my dresser of Faith and me, then the one of the four of us and a recent picture of Lyla, Sara, and me in our cheer uniforms at Homecoming.

"And you're right, I shouldn't have skipped today. I was just so angry. I had to get out of there." I shake my head and lower it back to my knees.

"There are always consequences for our choices. Some good, some bad but always a consequence. That's why we're in this mess now with Faith and Ella."

I blink several times trying to understand her accusation. Luckily, my face is hidden behind my legs because I don't think I could hide the shock of her words.

"Is there anything else going on that you need to tell me?" Mom places one hand over the other on her lap.

I'm just about to say no, then I remember. "Oh, I'm up for Winter Queen this year." As I say it, I realize the irony in this situation. My classmates nominated me Tuesday, several days before the locker graffiti and the Jessica thing.

"Really? Wow." Mom's eyes go wide. "I can't believe anyone voted for you with everything that's happened."

This time my face isn't hidden, and I am positive she left red marks across my cheek from the back of her hand as she slapped me.

"Try to get some sleep." Mom stands up, walks to the door, and turns the light out as she leaves.

I sit in the dark, feeling the sting. It's just Merida and me, again.

I lay back on my bed, head resting on my pillow, and I stare at the stream of moonlight peeping in through the crack in my curtains. Mom's words ringing through my ears.

I can't believe anyone voted for you…

You obviously did something to piss her off…

But here we are.

The record in my head is stuck on repeat mode.

I can't believe anyone voted for you…

I shouldn't do it, but I can't help myself. I reach for my school bag and grab my iPad. As soon as I turn it on, I am once again face to face with all the notifications from the day. I ignore them and tap on the Instagram app and my eyes are drawn to the message icon.

"Ugh." I roll my eyes at the messages. Merida presses the top of her head to the palm of my hand, something she does when she wants to be petted.

My curiosity gets the best of me, and I click on the messages. I have eight dm's, one each from Tarin and Avery, two from girls on the cheer squad and four from Lyla.

My heart skips a beat when I see Lyla's name and I click her message first. I scroll to the first post for the day, wanting to read my messages in chronological order. The first message she sent was at 3:30 pm today and read: "Getting worried. I've text you several times this

117

afternoon with no answer. Then I called after seventh like 100 times, but I just get your voicemail. Call back."

I start to write back: "Hey. Sorry, I turned my phone off, then Mom took it away when I got home." But I notice Lyla's next message before I hit send.

This message came through at 4:15 pm today: "Getting pissed. @brooks but ur not here. Hoped we could talk..."

The third message came in at 6:23 pm: "WTH Fi? ignoring me now? Some friend."

My hand freezes on Merida's back, my eyes widen. I blink and reread the message. Then I see the fourth message received at 9:12 pm: "You know what, you are so selfish. I'm not even sure you consider me a friend anymore. All I have done lately is stand up for you when people talk about how stuck up and bitchy you have become. And this is what I get as a thanks? You turn your back on me?"

My hands ball into fist and my jaw clenches.

"What the hell?" My eyes narrow on the screen. I scroll back to the first message and reread them all again. "She knows me as well as Faith does. How can she even say that I don't consider her a friend? I'm not playing this game. If she or anyone else wants to believe Jessica and what everyone else is sayin', well fine. I don't need them." I nod to Merida.

I delete my original message to Lyla and simply write: "I'm done!"
Send.

I turn my iPad off so it doesn't buzz all night and toss it on the floor.

***

"Mer, move." I push Merida off me and wince at the soreness in my body and try to find my iPad all in one motion. My alarm must die. I reach my arm over the side of the bed and feel the leather cover. "Found it," I mumble into my pillow.

"Shit!" I jump up fighting my way out of the covers when I see 8:00 staring back at me. "I'm late."

"Ugh…" My foot catches in the sheet and I barely get my arm up to catch myself on the dresser and I fumble my way to the bathroom. Merida steps aside but keeps a close eye on me. I can hear Mom in the kitchen.

"Fiona. I have an appointment then I'm heading to the hospital. Eat something before you leave."

"Mom, I'm late. I don't have time to eat."

Mom's footsteps get louder as she walks down the hall, stopping at the bathroom door. She leans on the door jam and crosses her arms over her chest.

"What do you mean you're late? You need breakfast before you go to the gym."

"The gym?" I turn to my mom while bent over the sink, toothbrush in my mouth. "It's Saturday?"

Mom lets out a small laugh at the puzzled look on my face. A sound I haven't heard since before the accident.

"Yes." Mom nods and turns away. "Eat something."

I look in the mirror, puffy eyes, pale skin, and toothpaste running down my hand, I let out a sigh of relief.

I rinse the foam away from my mouth, grab a towel from the rack and follow my mom to the kitchen.

Mom grabs her coat, purse, and keys before turning to walk out.

"You will be at the hospital today, right?" Mom asks but, it's not a question.

"Yeah, after practice."

"Do you really think you are ready for this?" Mom asks watching me as I get a bowl from the cabinet. "I'm just worried it's too soon."

"I'll be okay Mom," I mumble and get the Apple Jacks from the pantry and milk from the fridge.

Mom stops when she sees the milk.

"Do you remember the time we were eating breakfast and you and Faith got on one of your laughing kicks? We thought it was over but then you said something right as Faith was taking a drink—"

I throw my head back and laugh. "She laughed so hard; milk came out of her nose." I start giggling at the memory and I feel like someone is stabbing me in the ribs. I look up at mom. "What made you think of that?"

"Oh, I don't know. Just miss my girls. You two sure made things interesting," Mom sighs and turns to leave.

"Make things interesting Mom. She is still here," I add as I pour in the milk and return it to the refrigerator, then take a seat at the table.

"Not like she was." Mom turns back to me but her smile fades. I lower my first bite of cereal back to the bowel.

"I have faith, Mom." Right then, Merida jumps up on Faith's chair and sits down, putting her front paws on the edge of the table like she belongs. "So does Mer."

"I'm not sure Mer does." Mom raises her eyebrows and turns to Mer sitting pretty in Faith's seat.

"It's a love hate relationship with those two. Remember the day I picked her out at the shelter?" I croak. "Mer wrapped her paws around my neck, put the top of her head under my chin and started purring. But when Faith tried to take her from me to hold, she started hissing and went crazy."

Mom lets out a "Huh." Close enough to a giggle so I continue.

"Faith turned to Dad and said, 'Dad, you can't let her get that cat. It's cra-cra.'"

I dip my finger in the milk and reach to Faith's seat and let Mer lick it off.

"Fiona," Mom says with disgust.

"I know, don't feed her table food."

"Not only that, but while she's in the chair at the table. It is a very bad habit," Mom says. "Besides, she should not have milk."

I continue eating and watch Mer watching me, hoping for more milk. Maybe once Mom is gone.

"I'm leaving," Mom announces. "Don't overdo it on you first day back. Especially after skiing last night. That's the last thing we need." Mom slides her Burberry purse over her shoulder.

"I was snowboarding Mom." I shove another spoon fool of cereal in my mouth.

"Not the point. Just take it easy," She calls over her shoulder. "Oh, here." Mom takes my phone out of her purse. "You're not off the hook, but you really should have this in case something happens, and you need to call. With the weather and all."

"Got it." And with that Mom is out the door.

In my room I dig my favorite purple leo out of the draw and another pair of black leggins. Once changed, I check my bag to make sure I have athletic tape, headbands and my knee and ankle brace. Then I throw in a pair of black spandex shorts, clean clothes, socks, underwear, bra and two towels so I can shower at the gym. Oh, and flip flops for the shower. *Eww!* I grimace at the thought.

In the kitchen, I grab two bottles of water and pull my furry boots on as a text message dings. I jump across the kitchen to grab my phone hoping it's Lyla. It's from Mom. "We got about five inches of snow last night so take your time and use four-wheel drive."

I text back: "k"

I slide my coat on and walk out the door.

I make the ten minute drive to All Stars Gymnastic Center and the parking lot is packed.

I find a parking spot and head to the door. A beginner gymnastics class is already working on beam and a few high school girls are on the floor stretching. I turn and walk to the area where we put our bags when I notice a group of girls huddled together whispering. I recognize them all, including my friend Sara who has sided with Jessica, but Lyla isn't here. I wonder if Lyla thought I would still pick her up this morning.

123

The thought slips away when I hear a *shh* and turn to see Sara's group looking my way. When they see me turn to them, they all look away like they've been caught stealing something but go right back to giggling and whispering.

"Did you see the Insta post?" I hear Sara ask.

"No! What happened?" another girl from Washington Heights askes.

My stomach rolls and the blood drains from my face.

"Here, I took a screen shot of it," Sara says passing her phone around.

"Holy Shit! That *is* her," another girl says. The whispering continues and I turn away, breathing hard, my mind racing.

Another girl who attends Washington Heights get ups from the from the group and walks toward me. She comes to my side and wraps her arm around my shoulder leaning in and whispers to me.

"Hey Fiona, I just want you to know, I didn't know about any of this. I just saw them all talking and walked up right before you came in. I am not taking anyone's side and I didn't look at the picture."

"Thanks," is all I can say and try to smile. I know she sees the tears in my eyes.

"Whatever the picture is," the girl continues, "I don't believe it was you. It is so easy to photoshop shit now."

The group starts laughing louder and I try hard to resist looking, but I cave and take a peek. I swallow down the lump in my throat and notice another girl on the JV squad at school smiling at the conversation, but her face clearly indicates that she is only trying to save face with Sara's group.

I take a deep breath, put a smile on my face, push down the tears and walk over to a few girls who are stretching and join them.

"Hi girls. What's up?" I really don't know what else to say.

"Hey Fiona, sorry to hear about what's going on. I can't believe they actually think you would say something like that," a friend of mine who cheers for Lincoln High ensures.

"Yeah, it's ridiculous," a cheerleader on the freshman squad at East Brooke adds. "Everyone knows how close you and Faith are. And Ella."

I wince when I hear Ella's name. I need to put up new fliers.

"And who is the daman69 anyway?" another girl from Lincoln asks. "Why would anyone believe that is you?"

My stomach flips at the thought of the Instagram picture.

"What are you going to do about it?" another girl asks, and I realize all their eyes are on me.

"I-I don't know. I want it taken down, but I don't know who posted it," I admit, my stomach queasy.

"What did your parents say? You did tell them, right?" another girl asks, and I lean into a stretch for my achy back.

"Ah, well, my mom knows. She is not happy about it." I don't want to say too much. I don't want to talk about it at all.

"I bet she isn't," my friend from Lincoln adds. "What did the cops say?"

"The cops?" Bile rises up my esophagus. "I-I don't think I want the cops involved—"

"What? You parents didn't call the cops?" another girl says louder than I prefer, and I find the groups eyes on me.

"Shh…" I say before I can stop myself.

"Fiona, that picture is serious, and the cops can track the person who created the account. You also need to report the post to Instagram and print off a picture of it to give to the cops," one of the girls say.

"I bet it's a fake account someone created," my friend from Lincoln chimes in. "A few kids from my school created a fake Tumblr account just to throw shade at another student they didn't like. The cops were able to track it."

"Excuse me." My head is spinning, and my stomach is in knots. I get up and run to the locker room and open the first stall I find. My forehead breaks out into a sweat and my stomach muscles tighten and heave. There goes my breakfast.

126

I wipe the tears on my checks away with the back of my hand and grab tissue for my runny nose. I take a few deep breaths to calm myself down, raise my arms up resting my hands on my head and close my eyes. I continue breathing in and out until my heartrate returns to normal.

I take the emotions and shove them back into the pit in my stomach and turn to open the stall. I lean over the sink running cold water over my face and rinse out my mouth. I wish I had put a toothbrush and tooth paste in my bag. I lean into the mirror resting my hands on the edge of the sink and look at the scar on my face that I usually keep hidden by my hair when I hear giggling coming my way. Sara and another friend of ours round the corner as I try to pull a few strands of hair down to cover my scar. Sara and my friend stop in their tracks, eyes go wide, they turn to each other, and bust out laughing. They continue past me leaning into each other whispering.

I watch them in the mirror head into the last two stalls still giggling. I take one last look in the mirror. I walk out of the locker room, throwing the paper towel away at the door and take in a long deep cleansing breath in the hallway before I exit.

When I get back to the floor, I take my place and listen as the girls' chat about the latest news.

The next two hours are filled with skills, lead up work and tumbling. My brain wants to do a normal workout, but my body doesn't agree so I take is slow and work up to a backhand spring on the crash pad. I'm going to feel this later.

When the doctors felt I was out of the woods following the accident, they explained what happened to my body. I was lucky they said. I didn't have any major ligament damage, but the accident did leave me with a sprained knee and ankle along with other cuts and bruises that would heal over time. They also called in a plastic surgeon for the cuts on my face from hitting the driver's side window when the car flipped. The scars shouldn't be too bad they said. But their biggest concern was the contusion on my brain from said window. Or so I was told; but with medication, they were able to keep the bleeding under control and I didn't need surgery.

Thank God they did not shave my head! But the scar from my temple to my cheek bone is very noticeable.

I'm aware of the stares and gossip from Sara's group throughout the session as I have my hair pulled back so they can see the scars. I realize this is the first time anyone but Lyla, Sara and my parents and Ella's parents have seen my scars. I try to ignore them and focus on my work, and I take some extra time to stretch as everyone heads to the locker room. I hang back on purpose to avoid my former squad. Besides, this would be a good time to get my physical therapy exercises in.

I prefer to shower at home after practice but it's out of the way to go home, then drive to the hospital. I grab what I need from my bag and place the rest of my stuff in a locker. I look around to make sure I'm alone and quickly slip out of my leo, wrap myself in a towel and run to the shower hanging my towel on the hook as I step in.

One last rinse of my hair, I turn the water off and wipe the water from my eyes. I reach for my towel hanging outside the shower when I feel the cold concrete. I continue feeling around and find the curvy shape of the metal hook but no towel.

"Shit," I whisper.

I peek out from the shower curtain to see if it is on the floor. I see cool gray tile, but no towel. I look to my locker, it's still closed, then around the locker room. No towel.

My heart races and my breathing is heavy as I realize someone stole my towel.

My vision becomes distorted, and I feel like I might pass out. I lean my face against the cool concrete to combat the heat in my cheeks and calm my stomach.

My mind races as I fight between disbelief and survival. *This can't be happening.*

I listen for any indication of guilt outside the shower stall but all I hear is silence and the drip of a leaky faucet. I close my eyes and stay where I am, frozen in fear.

I take a deep breath and exhale, push myself off the wall and peek out the shower curtain. No one there.

I pull the shower curtain back with a shaky hand, cross my arms over my chest and sprint to my locker as quickly as I can in wet flip flops; my feet squeaking and slipping all the way. I reach my hand out for the lever on my locker before I even get there so the door swings open as I approach. I grab the second towel I brought with my other hand almost simultaneously. The towel drapes open, and I catch the edge with my other hand when I hear "click, click, click," followed by giggling.

"Hey!" I look up in the direction of the giggles coming from the hallway that leads to the exit and catch a glimpse of a red hoodie, hood up, with the All Stars Logo on the back as the culprit runs out the door of the locker room.

I wrap the towel around myself and shuffle to the hallway to see who it is, but the locker room door swings shut, and the culprit is gone.

"Fucking bitch." I start to chase but stop in my tracks realizing I'm dripping wet and am only wearing a towel.

I grit my teeth; my body still trembling and try to catch my breath. I sink to the floor right in the hallway.

Why is this happening to me? What did I do to deserve this? First the fake Instagram post and photoshopped picture, now this?

I press the heel of my hands hard into my eyes hoping to push away the sting of tears when I realize anyone could walk in on my pity party at any moment. I force myself off the floor, I wrap my arms around my body, hunch my shoulders and walk to my locker.

I decide right there that I will not change or shower in the locker room here or at school in the future. Just like I promised myself my freshman year that I would never where a skirt to school again after a junior boy pulled up my skirt in the hallway. Or joggers after a senior boy pulled my pants down after school when I was in the seventh grade. Just one more thing to add to the never do again list.

To protect myself, I take my bag the bathroom stall and lock myself in and change as fast as possible. Which isn't easy as I didn't take time to completely dry myself off.

I glance around the gym as I leave the locker room to see if anyone looks guilty but the girls from my training session are gone. I see my coach by the vault, she waves unaware of the incident. I wave back robotically, not really feeling present in the moment. I'm still on high alert.

At the door I pull my hood up since my hair is still wet, put on my gloves and make my way to the Jeep. I throw my bag in the back and climb in, push the clutch in and turn the engine over. I shift in to reverse and start to back out when I notice something on my windshield and hood.

I shift into neutral, pull up the emergency brake and climb back out. Draped across my hood is the midnight blue bath towel, the one stolen from me. I snatch up the towel and take another look around to see if anyone is watching. My fists clenches around the towel; my blood is boiling.

I lift the wiper and I remove the piece of paper that has been folded twice. I unfold the paper once and recognize the picture on the inside immediately. I unfold the paper again and see Ella's picture staring back at me on the missing flyer. The handwriting across the bottom is sloppy, rushed like someone was trying to avoid getting caught. But the message is clear.

Watch your back.

Chapter 6

"There she is," my dad says when I enter the room. The smell of the deli order I picked helps cover the stench of medicine and sickness.

"Are you excited to see me or the food?" I ask over the beeping of Faith's machines.

"Food." But he places his hand on my shoulder and squeezes, then takes the food and sets it on the table.

"Mom even remembered to ask for plates and napkins when she ordered," I add trying to get a laugh out of her. Usually, we are never prepared when we get takeout. In the summer we like to meet for lunch in the local park and never have utensils. Finally, Mom got smart and left a roll of paper towel and paper plates in her car.

"She's a thinker that one. That's why we call her mom." Dad always refers to Mom as a thinker, which is why she makes all the big decisions in our house. I don't believe that is completely true, but Mom is on top of things. Except paper plates and utensils.

"Uh-hum. I know what you're up to," Mom says flatly.

Dad puts on his best bewildered expression and says, "What? Me?"

"You're just trying to score points with me." Mom quickly unwraps one end of her sandwich takes a bite of her sub like she hasn't eaten in days. "So, I'll get you that new putter you want for your birthday." Mom finishes with a mouth full of food. Something Faith and I have been scolded for doing.

"I would never." Dad raises his eyebrows and looks at Mom as he places a hand over his heart feigning shock. I give a little smile, but I'm just too disheartened to laugh.

"You okay? Did something happen at practice?" Dad's parenting radar is going off and I hear the rip of his chip bag opening.

"I'm ok, just tired. Practice went well, maybe a little sore, so I probably need to get ice."

"Eat first." Mom hands me a plate with half an Italian sub, and my stomach churns again. I take the sandwich, trying to act normal but this time Mom notices. "Are you getting sick? You look piqued."

"I hope not. Just stress, I think. I have a big project due this week plus the game tonight."

"I was worried practice, and a game tonight would be too much," Mom adds in a motherly tone. "And no way should you have been at Brooks yesterday."

I watch Dad start to open his mouth knowing he is about to ask what Mom is talking about. Then he looks to me and must see the discomfort on my face as I squirm in the chair next to Faith. Dad takes another bite of his sandwich and looks down at his plate.

I bite my lip as I look to Faith knowing she would understand how I feel right now. Mom is very good at making me feel...less than. Faith see's it clearly.

I take Faith's hand just to let her know I'm here. "Hi Fay. Love you."

I stall a few more seconds before taking a bite. Surprisingly the sub tastes good and seems to calm my stomach a little.

"Maybe I just needed some food," I say to let Mom know that I am not sick and go for another bite.

I finish the first half of my sandwich and go for the second. Once my hands are free and my mouth is no longer full of food, I take Faith's hand and start telling her about practice, purposely leaving out the part about the locker room.

I skip over snowboarding yesterday to avoid an argument with Mom. Plus, Dad doesn't need to mediate.

"Officer's Buchanan and Quincy came to talk to me at school yesterday about Ella—" That's when I feel it. I freeze.

"What is it?" Mom sits up in her chair dropping her sandwich onto her plate. Her and Dad are staring at me intently.

"I think I just felt her fingers move." And they are out of their chairs before I can continue. Mom tries setting her plate on the bed table, but she misses, and the sandwich rolls of the plate and onto the floor. Dad keeps his sandwich in his hand and is standing at the end of the bed. His hand wrapped around Faith's foot, just like he did with my foot last night during our talk.

"Faith?" Mom is at her side holding her other hand.

"Let's not get ahead of ourselves." Dad interjects knowing how easily Mom jumps to conclusions. He walks around the corner of the bed and rubs Mom's back with his free hand.

"Yeah, what if I just imagined it? Or maybe it was just a reflex or something," I say hoping that I didn't jump the gun. But deep in my gut, I know what I felt.

"Faith honey. It's Mom, can you hear me?"

All three of us staring, non-blinking at Faith, afraid we might miss her next movement. After several seconds, Faith doesn't make any other movement and I watch silently as tears fill my mom's eyes. Dad wraps his arms around her stroking her shoulder trying to calm her down.

"I just don't know how much longer I can take this." Mom sobs and lays her forehead on Faith's arm.

"We have to stay strong." Dad gives Mom a kiss on the back of her head. "She needs to feel positive energy surrounding her."

"So, Faith, I have some good news." I look to Mom and Dad to see if I should continue. I felt her hand move when I was talking about the

136

events of my day. Maybe somehow me talking about things makes her want to join in. So, I keep going, "I was notified Thursday that I made Winter Queen Court. How great is that? But I really need you to help me get ready. You know, just like last year." I keep my eyes on Faith hoping for a response while still holding her hand.

"I know I won't win, but it will still be fun to get ready together. I want to see you crown the winner."

"Oh. It would be so great to see you both in the ceremony." A smile spreads across Mom's face. "No matter what the outcome of the vote is."

"Yeah." I glance at Mom. "Faith, I was even thinking I could wear your blue dress you wore to junior prom."

"Ah, you both always look so good in royal blue." Mom gushes and pulls a chair up from behind and takes a seat. "It's perfect for your skin tone."

"Well, it looks better with Faith's blue eyes." I tilt me head toward Faith as I look at Mom.

"That's not true. You girls both have beautiful eyes." Mom tilts her chin up as she looks at my eyes. "Your eyes are just like your father's." She drops her chin with a nod.

"I'm surprised you don't want your own dress Fiona," Dad says.

"After last year's approval process?" I give my dad the best stink eye I can pull off. "No thank you." I finally get a giggle from Mom.

"It wasn't that bad." Dad shakes his head and scrunches up his face. Then he places a hand on his hip and takes another bite of his sandwich.

"Let's see...The first dress I had to take back for being too short. The second dress was a two piece—"

"That's an absolute *no*." He mumbles through a mouth full of food and stops chewing long enough to give me a stern look and points his finger at me.

"And the third dress went back because it had areas of nude bodice between the beaded areas. Even though it was *not* see through."

"Doesn't matter." He swallows. "You're not wearing it." Dad shakes his head back and forth.

"I get it. So, this year to save us all the hassle and headache, I decided to go with a dress you already approved."

Dad frowns and drops his sandwich from his mouth. "That kinda takes the fun out of being a dad."

I tilt my head back and let out a true belly laugh, and it feels good. Except for the soreness in my abs from gymnastics and the pain in my back from snowboarding. But the laughing feels good.

"Just to make me feel like I am doing my job, let's go over this dress again." Dad walks back to his chair and shoves the last bite of his sandwich in his mouth as he sits back enjoying this way too much. Mom leans over and picks up what's left of her sandwich on the floor and piles it on the paper plate.

"Ugh." I roll my eyes. And even Mom is shaking her head, I see a smile cross her lips.

"It is floor length, royal blue chiffon with a mermaid bottom," I begin.

"I don't know what any of that means." He looks at me quizzically.

"It means that it is a fitted dress that flares out above the knee." I stand and run my hands down my legs and flare my hands out at my knees hoping this will help him get a visual.

"Okay, go on." He nods in approval. I hear Mom choke back a giggle.

"The bodice of the dress—"

"You mean that part that is supposed to cover your body?" He leans in closer to me, elbows on his knees.

"Ugh. Yes Dad." I throw my body back into my chair, my head rolling back over the seat to show my exasperation, another one of Lyla's favorite words, about the whole process. I lift my head and look to Mom for help.

139

"You're on your own for this one." She holds up her hands and looks away. Mom still has a big grin on her face.

"I so need Faith to have my back on this. The bodice is lace, *but* you can't see through it," I add when I see my dad getting ready to argue. "It does have see-through lace on the sleeves, which are long and an open back. But I swear it is in good taste."

Even though I am playing along to Dad's game, part of me knows this is a delicate subject, last year after I brought home the third dress that got returned, Dad gave me the list of unacceptable dresses.

"A short dress must be no more than two inches above your knees, no two-piece dresses, no cut outs, no low V neck fronts, no thigh high slit in the front and no nude cut out areas." Of course, I ended the conversation with a very dramatic "FINE!"

"Well, I will take a look at it when we get home before I say yes or no."

"Dad!"

"Oh Robert. Now you're just being ridiculous. Faith wore it two years ago," Mom scolds, only calling him Robert when he is in trouble.

"Thanks Mom. I just thought it would be nice to wear Faith's dress. Especially if she can't..." I can't bring myself to say it. "And it is a beautiful dress." I keep my eyes on Faith.

"Well, I think it is smart." Mom nods. "Plus, blue is a good color for Winter Formal, and it has sleeves, which is good since it's January."

Dad smiles and reaches over for my hand. "You will look beautiful honey."

"Thanks Dad."

I turn my focus back to Faith and gasp. "Her eyes are open."

"Oh my God! Her eyes are open," Mom repeats. "Faith. Can you hear me?" But Faith doesn't respond. She looks to be staring at something across the room.

"Faith if you can hear me, squeeze my hand." I watch her face intently; Mom and Dad are silent. A second or two passes before I say, "I need you. I need your help finding Ella."

I look up to find them both staring at me, waiting for a response.

"She did it again. She squeezed my hand," I exclaim. And Mom erupts in squeals, Dad is hugging Faith the best he can since she is still lying in the bed. I continue watching Faith's face.

"Thank you. Thank you. Thank you. I am so glad you're back," I gush.

"I'm going to go find a nurse or doctor." Dad is out the door.

"Faith honey, we love you. We've been worried sick," Mom says through tears, but these tears are for a different reason.

141

I close my eyes and let my head fall back so I am looking to the ceiling, tears spilling from the corner of my eyes as gravity runs them to my ears. I don't even know how I have any tears left.

I sit back up and lean toward Faith, her hand still in mine and bring it to my forehead and I say a pray.

"I am so sorry. I don't know what happened, but I had no intention of ever hurting you. I hope you can forgive me. Please get better soon. I miss you and Ella." Once again, I feel a small squeeze of my hand. Her way of telling me we will be okay.

Dr. Patel enters the room with my dad in tow. I step back from the bed; Mom is still at her side where Dad joins her. Faith is staring across the room. Nurse La'Tonya enters the room.

"Hey gurl. I didn't see you sneak in," she says to me as she moves toward Faith and begins doing her thing.

"I came in about an hour ago." I watch La'Tonya check Faith's vitals and the monitors as the doctor is talking to Faith and looking in her eyes with a small flashlight.

"You must have come in while I was on my lunch break," La'Tonya adds as I step back in the corner trying to stay out of everyone's way. I have no clue what they are doing but they seem to know and that's all that matters. Mom tells the doctor about Faith squeezing my hand, so he asks her to do the same. He doesn't indicate if she responds or not. La'Tonya looks at me and smiles and I feel myself let out the air I've been holding in.

Once the doctor finishes his exam, he turns to my parents and says, "This is a good sign, but she has major trauma, so she isn't out of the woods yet. There is a lot of healing that needs to take place but at least she is conscious and with intermittent response."

"Why isn't she looking at us?" Mom asks, looking from Faith to the doctor.

"Well, no two people come out of a coma the same," the doctor shakes his head. "So, we really don't know what to expect exactly. Many times, the patient has a hard time focusing and it is common for the patient to stare off into space. In some cases, the patient is conscious but can't respond to requests such as squeezing your hand, so the fact that Faith is squeezing your hand is a good sign. But healing does take time and we will continue looking for improvement in her responses, visually, physically, and eventually verbally."

"Remember, Fiona was in a medically induced coma, and we brought her out when the bleeding in her brain was under control," La'Tonia chimes in. "This is a different situation so you can't expect Faith to be able to communicate the same way Fiona did." La'Tonya adds as she walks to me, wrapping her arm around my shoulder and pulling me in for a hug.

"That is true." Dr. Patel nods. "Different circumstances."

"Is there anything else we can do doc?" my dad asks looking between the doctor and La'Tonya.

"Continue doing what you're doing, talk to her, share stories; tell her about your day. She can hear you; she just can't respond yet." The doctor taps on the computer screen adding a few things on Faith's chart before continuing.

"Contact Dr. Milroy and inform him of the changes," the doctor instructs and La'Tonya nods.

"Stay strong Fiona. Faith needs you," she whispers squeezing my shoulder. I nod and La'Tonya walks out of the room.

Dr. Patel looks back at my parents. "I will discuss everything with the neurologist, but I am sure he will come in for an evaluation. I wouldn't be surprised if he comes in this afternoon. Do you have any questions for me?"

Mom and Dad look at each other. "I don't think so," Dad responds cautiously like we all should have tons of questions we are ready to ask. But we all know the one question we have, he cannot answer.

"Well, I am sure you will. Don't hesitate to ask. Sometimes it helps to write them down as you think of them." Dr. Patel puts his stylus back in his pocket. Turns and smiles at my parents.

"Thank you," my parents say in unison.

144

"I'll be back to check on you soon Faith." He pats Faith's hand and turns to walk out of the room.

We all sit keeping a watchful eye over Faith, wanting to see any further sign or response. Finally, after several minutes I ask Mom if I can call Mom E, Ella's mom, to tell her the news and that I won't be there today.

"I think it would be good for you to go see them," Mom says. "They need to see you and it will be better to hear the news in person. Just remember, they are still grieving so even though it is good news, it may be hard for them to hear."

I give Faith one last kiss on the forehead and squeeze her hand but no response. I walk around to my parents and give them a hug from behind.

"Be careful Fiona." Dad's favorite saying.

"Send our best to Denise and Dave."

"Sure Mom. Let me know if anything changes."

I know I am not supposed to use my phone, but I can't help it. I have to call Lyla. Guilt rips through me, Lyla should be here for this. But then I think about her text last night and my guilt turns to anger.

Ella and Sara would be the other two I would call to share the news, but both are out for obvious reasons.

I sit in Jeep a few more minutes trying to think who I should call. I finally give up and pull out of the parking garage.

As I merge onto the interstate, my cell rings. I check it expecting it to be Mom or Dad with more news, but when I see the screen, I smile at the name.

"Hey Jace, what's up?"

"You sound happy." I can sense he is smiling on the other end. "Good news I hope."

"Actually yes, really good news. Faith opened her eyes today and even squeezed my hand twice!"

"Wow. That's great. So, she is out of the coma?" Jace asks, the line quiet for a few seconds as I think how to answer.

"Technically yes. It's kinda weird. She still has a lot of healing to do and may take time before she is fully responsive."

"Did she say anything about the night of the accident?" Jace interrupts.

"Ah...no, she isn't talking yet. She is just staring at a spot across the room, but the doc says that's normal, many patients just coming out of a coma can't focus."

"Hum, I guess I just thought that when someone wakes up from a coma, they can talk. I mean you were talking the day you came out of yours when I came to see you."

"Apparently it can happen like that, but you just never know. And I guess it was different with mine somehow since it was medically induced. I don't really know how to explain it."

"I'm just glad she is doing better," Jace adds.

"Me too."

"Does your ass hurt?" Jace asks and I can hear a little giggle on the other end of the phone.

"What?" I let out a laugh at this strange question.

"You know, your spill you took at Brooks yesterday?"

"Ah, yeah. I forgot about that with all the excitement. A bit sore but I will survive." I nod on the other end of the phone. "But yeah, I'm pretty sure my ass is bruised though. And my pride."

Jace let's out a large laugh at my ass and pride hurting.

"Hey so what are you doing after the game tonight? Shaunce's parents are out of town so he's having a party." Jace is quiet waiting for my response, and usually I am all about a party. Well, I was all about a good party. And Braxton Shaunce has bussin parties.

"I don't know," I say. I am sure he knows about the Insta picture, but I don't want to tell him about being grounded. Or what happened in the locker room today.

"When was the last time you went to a party?" Jace interrupts trying to get me on board.

"Um, I don't know. The night of the accident I think." The last party I went to a few weeks ago, I only stayed for a few minutes so that doesn't count.

"Ah, well, that is definitely too long for *the* Fiona DeWitt. You need to be there," Jace exclaims.

"I'll think about it," I finally say and feel a bubble of nerves in my stomach.

"Great. See you there." Jace hangs up before I can correct him.

Ella's parents' house is about five miles from my house and out in the country where we are in a subdivision. The house looks dark when I pull up but there are tire tracks in the snow on the driveway that stop before the garage, so it wasn't Ella's parents leaving and returning.

I look at the clock as I park, 2:58 pm. Several hours past the normal time I stop by. Maybe they decided I wasn't coming. I hop out of my Jeep and march through the snow on the unplowed driveway and follow another pair of footprints to the door that look like UGGs. I ring the bell and wait several minutes when the door finally opens. Ella's dad, or Dad E as we call him, answers the door looking tired and disheveled.

"Fiona." He looks a little surprised and even confused. "I must have fallen asleep on the couch. Haven't been sleeping well lately. Come in, come in."

"Hi Dave." It sounds wrong as soon as I say it, leaving a bitter expression on my face. We always call him Dad. When Faith, Ella, Lyla, and I are talking amongst ourselves and need to referrer to one of our three sets of parents, we add our initial to the end of Mom and Dad, so we know who we are talking about. Mom L and Dad L belong to Lyla, Mom E and Dad E belong to Ella and Mom F and Dad F belong to Faith and me. A solution Lyla came up with after the second time we all ended up at different houses because we had the wrong parents in mind.

"Dave? Who the hell is that?" he asks. Eyes narrowing in on me with a chuckle.

I give a little "I'm sorry" giggle. "Okay Dad." I hang my head like I've been scolded.

"That's more like it. Now give your dad a hug. I could really use another one." He takes me in his arms and hugs me like I would expect him to if I were Ella. After a few moments, "It's really great to see you, Fiona. Denise and I are so glad you still come by. It helps us keep Ella and Faith in our hearts."

We don't say a word as we walk to the kitchen. I sit at the island, and he walks around to the fridge and takes out milk. I watch quietly as he pours two glasses, slides one to me, then gets the plate of chocolate chip cookies.

149

"I made these this morning when I couldn't sleep."

"My favorite." I reach out for one without asking or being instructed. Ella's parents always told us to make ourselves at home and we do.

"I remember. I thought you might like a snack after practice today." I recognize the question without being asked. He moves around the island and sits on the bar stool next to me.

I swallow my bite.

"I should have called but I got grounded from my phone. I promised Mom I would only use it to call her on my way to the hospital."

"I understand, I was just surprised to see Lyla show up this morning without you." I freeze mid chew at Dad E's words before recovering. He watches me a few moments, then continues, "Anything you want to talk about? You know, with your adoptive parents?" Dad E nudges my arm with his elbow. "Sometimes we adoptive parents can be a little more subjective than biological parents. Biological parents mean well and all..."

A smile crosses my face. I've always felt that I can talk to Ella's parents. When I first started hanging out here, I was shocked just how much Ella and Faith shared with them. Not at all like at my house. Ella's parents know who's dating who, what the latest gossip is and any drama taking place because Ella and Faith share it all with them. I never tell my parents anything, well until yesterday.

I consider telling Dad E about everything but then decide against it. They have enough to worry about right now. My drama won't help them so what's the point?

"Thanks. I'm good. Just skipped out early to hit the slopes at Brooks yesterday." I shrug as I break the cookie into two pieces.

"Ahh, fresh snow. Don't blame you, but I bet your mom didn't like that too much."

"*Noooo* she did not." And got a hearty laugh out of Dad E.

"Well, I'm glad you made it by. Mom has a migraine, so she has been sleeping all day. I know she will be sad she missed you."

"I can always stop by tomorrow if she is feeling better." I haven't done any homework yet and I know I will go see Faith, but I hate the thought of Ella's mom being so distraught. Last week when I stopped by, she cried the whole time I was here. It was devastating and I wanted so bad to tell her everything. But I don't know everything or anything to help her.

"I know she would appreciate that, but you need to take care of yourself and be with your family too."

We are both quiet for a few moments and I reach for another cookie. Man, he makes a good cookie. Dad E breaks the silence first.

151

"So how are your parents holding up? We didn't make it to the hospital this week."

He doesn't say it, but I suspect the longer Ella is gone, the harder it is for them to come see Faith.

"They understand. You have a lot you are dealing with too. Shoot," I scold myself when I remember.

"What's wrong?" Dad E drops his cookie in his glass and fishes it out with his finger and thumb.

"Ah, I saw a flyer for Ella yesterday and it had taken a beating from the weather. I planned to make more and get them out this weekend."

"Fiona, you have done plenty to help Ella and we love you for it." Dad E hesitates and I think he is going to say something else, but he takes another bite of his cookie, them mumbles, "Any word on Faith?"

"Actually, things are a little better." I shrug. "Mom even giggled a little today when Dad and I were playing around." Dad E gave an all-knowing grunt before I continued. "Then today, we got a little good news."

"Really. Is Faith doing better?" His eyes bright as he looks at me.

"She came out of the coma, but she is not completely responsive yet," I add quickly before he gets too excited. He listens intently to every word I say as I recount the experience.

"That is such a relief. Oh man that is great news. This will bring Mom some hope. And lord knows we *all* need it."

"I was worried about telling you guys," I admit, biting at my lip and soak my cookie in the milk.

"What? Why?" Dad E's bright eyes fade away.

"Well, because," I let out a sigh, "I worry that you blame me for what happened and because we haven't found Ella yet—"

"Fiona. You can't honestly think we would wish ill of Faith and your family...or blame you." Dad E interrupts.

"No, I know that. It's just...I just..." Not sure what to say it, I take a deep breath. "I know how much you are hurting not knowing what happened to Ella. I feel so guilty about everything, I worry our good news will hurt you more." I pick at the cookie on my plate afraid to look up. "You know how much I miss Ella, right?" Without moving my head, I look up to Dad E.

"Oh, honey! I know, we know how much you love Ella. And we know you miss her and would do anything to fix it." Dad E reaches out wrapping an arm around my shoulder and pulls me in for a hug. "Of course, we wish this wouldn't have happened. To Ella, to Faith and to you. This certainly hasn't been an easy time for any of us. But I don't know how you can think Ella is your fault?" Dad E waits patiently as I get my thoughts together, then releases my shoulder.

153

"The detectives on Ella's case came to talk to me Thursday," I explain and share with Dad E that they found Ella's phone.

"So why did Faith have Ella's phone?" Dad E interrupts, dropping his fist to the counter. But to my relief, doesn't freak out.

"No idea and they are still trying to get info off the phone." I keep my eyes on the cookie. "They said it was in pretty bad shape but IT is working on it. I'm sure they are waiting to get more information before talking to you." I continue and explain about the Cincinnati mileage sign and the photo of Ella's car in front of the house.

"Yeah, office Quincy spoke to use about Ella's car on Thursday. Or was what Wednesday?" He scrunches up he face as he is thinking about the days. "Hell, I don't know. All my days are running together. What else came up?"

"I made a comment about going to a party that night, so they are wondering if we met up with Ella for a SWU party or something. That would make sense why Faith and I were by SWU when we wrecked. Maybe Ella was in Faith's car at some point and dropped her phone. I just can't remember..."

"But you think it is your fault Ella is missing?" I look up to find Dad E looking at me quizzically.

"I don't know. I just know I need to remember what happened so I can know for sure if we were with Ella. And if we were, I might be able

154

to give the detectives something to help find Ella." I sigh and dunk my cookie again.

"Fiona, you are being too hard on yourself. We know you would help if you could. And even if you were with Ella that night, it's not your fault."

"I hope not, but I have to accept my responsibility in all of it. And I feel like I am failing everyone."

We sit in silence for a few seconds, Dad E turns his head to look out the window. Then he takes a deep breath and exhales.

"I catch myself asking, 'Why? Why did this happen?' but then I remember my grandfather's words. 'Things happen for a reason, good or bad, we just don't always know God's plan until way down the road.' I've racked my brain for hours trying to figure out why this happened and what it is that we are supposed to learn from it..." He trails off.

"Any answers?" I ask lightly and put the last of my cookie on the plate. I just can't seem to finish it.

"No. But in my heart, I know Ella will come back to us, and Faith too." Dad E nods. "Maybe our lesson is to trust God."

"Maybe. It sure would be easier if he just came out and told us."

Dad E's shoulders shake with laughter, but I see him wipe a tear away with the back of his hand. Then to lighten the mood, he switches topic. "So, what's the plan tonight?"

"After the game? I don't know." I look down to my hands and press my finger on a crumb and bring my finger to my lips.

"Now, there has to be something going on. No parties?" Dad E sits back in his chair.

"There's a junior party. But I just don't feel like I should be at a party right now," I add with a shrug and go for another crumb.

"And what?" He lets out a little giggle. "You think you should be sitting at home punishing yourself?" Dad E leans forward in his chair, elbows on the island, hands clasped together.

"I don't know." Which is a lie. I do know. I'm afraid I won't be wanted. But also, yeah, I do feel like I should be punishing myself.

"You know, Ella and Faith would not want you sitting at home, wasting your nights away worrying about them." He looks at me waiting for a response. "Besides, I'm sure Lyla would miss you if you're not there."

"Yeah, you sound like my friend Avery. She said the same thing the other day. About the Faith and Ella part." Not wanting to talk about Lyla, I leave her out.

"This Avery sounds like a smart girl. Maybe you should call her and ask her to go with you."

"Maybe." I nod as I consider it.

"Well, as much as I love your company, it sounds like you need to make a phone call and get ready for the game and a party." Dad E stand up and takes the empty classes of milk to the sink.

"Are you kicking me out?" I ask in an accusing tone and hear Dad E giggle. "I mean, I am sure there were plenty of times over the years that you and Mom wanted to get rid of us. Like the time you kept telling us to quiet down and we just kept laughing all night."

Dad E throws his head back with laughter. "That was every time you four were together! Why do you think we bought you guys a tent? We figured at least during the summer you could be as loud as you wanted in the backyard." He leans against the counter and places his hands on his hips. "And we could catch up on much needed sleep."

A smile spreads across my face and I giggle at the memories of us camping out and thinking it was the greatest thing ever.

"So, you're gonna go to the party, right?" Dad E gives me the stink eye.

I stand up, get a paper towel, wet it, and wipe down the island throwing the paper towel and crumbs in the garbage.

"Well, I guess I have too, right?" I raise my palms in the air like I am daring the universe to tell me otherwise.

"That's my girl."

Dad E walks me to the door and gives me another big hug as we say our goodbyes. I wave one last time as I back into the turnaround in the driveway and follow the tracks previously made by Lyla's Mom. AKA Mom L.

Shaking Lyla out of my thoughts, I think about Dad E's words, and I decide to call Avery.

"Fiona. It's about time you called me back. I've called, text and even DM'd you."

"I know, sorry. I got grounded for skipping yesterday, so Mom took my phone last night."

"What? How did she find out?" Avery asks, but before I could answer, she adds, "And how are you calling me?"

"Well, she caved this morning about the phone because the roads are bad." And it hits me that I can't go to the party tonight after all.

"But Braxton is having a party!" Avery shrieks and I can picture the horrified look on her face.

"Actually, that is why I'm calling to see if you are going to the game first. But I just remembered I'm grounded, so not sure I can, unless..." And the wheels start turning.

"Unless what?" Avery asks, her patients is running thin on the other end.

"We got good news from the doctor today so maybe Mom will let it slide." I feel a little hope in this line of thinking.

"You definitely have to ask her. We're talking a Shaunce part here! And call me back as soon as you do." Avery hangs up before I can say anything else.

I run scenarios through my mind, trying to decide the best plan of attack when I pull in the driveway. The sky is growing dark which makes it look later then it really is. But there are two sets of tire tracks leading into the garage, so I know Mom and Dad are both home. Butterflies swarm in my belly as I work up the nerve to ask about the party. Normally there is no discussion or reversals when it comes to groundings, but I might as well try. Besides, Avery and Dad E are right. I do deserve to have a little fun.

The smell of chili hits me when I walk in the door. I hear Dre from *Blackish* on TV sharing a history lesson and when I enter Mom and Dad both have a glass of wine even though it is only 5:00.

"Is everything ok?" I ask concerned. I really expected them to still be at the hospital.

"Yes, the neurologist came in and wanted to do a few tests, so we decided to come home. He said he would call if anything changes," Dad explains and takes a sip of his Merlot.

"Oh, good. I was worried." I let out a huff.

"How are Denise and Dave?" Mom asks looking up from the TV. "I didn't see them this week, I need to call."

"Ella's mom wasn't feeling well so she was sleeping. Dad E made cookies which were so good." I put my hand on my stomach. "I told him about Faith, and he was really happy. He said if Mom E is feeling better tomorrow, they will plan to see Faith."

"Good, I am glad Dave is getting Denise out of the house. I've been worried about her." And Mom turns back to the TV show.

"The chili is ready in the crock pot, figured you might want to eat before the game," Dad adds. "Your mother made it, not me."

"That's a relief." I get a giggle from Mom, and I walk into the kitchen.

"Ha Ha," Dad adds sarcastically.

I eat a quick bowl of chili, feed and water Merida and start to get ready for the game. Merida sits on the counter at the edge of the sink while I fix my hair, minus the stupid bow they want us to wear. I take time to put on foundation and eyeliner; usually I just wear a tinted foundation, powder, and mascara. I figure on game nights and special occasions I can fix myself up a bit, but the result is not as good as when Faith does my makeup.

I hate leaving Merida, I hadn't planned to be gone so much today. I spend a few minutes playing with her, waving her favorite feather cat toy before I put on my uniform. I've learned with anything I

I have to wait till the last minute to get dressed or I will have Merida hair all over it.

I put on a pair of leggins under my skirt to keep my legs warm, pack my cheer bag and a change of clothes for after the game. And as always, I pack extra stuff for the game. I hate not being prepared. I give Merida one last pet and a treat, put my coat on and head to the door.

"Okay, I gotta get going." I call as I round the kitchen and realize I didn't ask them about the party. I notice Merida jumps up on the couch and stretches as she moves towards Dad's lap.

"Fiona, be home by 1:30," Mom calls when I stop at the door and turn to her. My eyebrows go up and I try to contain my excitement in case she forgot I was grounded.

"Love you guys. See you after the game." I wave bye.

"Be careful, Fi," Dad's voice rings behind me.

"I will." I don't turn back in case they suddenly remember and change their minds.

Chapter 7

"Let's Go Eagles. Let's Go!" *Clap Clap.*

The JV Squad is cheering as I enter the cafeteria where the athletic boosters take tickets.

The varsity squad is not required to cheer at the JV game, but we do come to the game to support the JV team and the cheerleaders. With fifteen minutes to tip off, several varsity girls are already here.

I wrap my coat tight around me and wonder why we aren't wearing our long sleeve body suit under our sleeveless uniform. As I approach the gym, the cheers get louder, and I see the JV squad does have their long sleeve body suits on. I look at the varsity girls sitting in the bleachers, and it becomes clear.

"Umm...Takiesha?" I call our captain before I get to the group on the bleachers. Shelby looks my way, then turn to Lyla and whispers as she points to me. Lyla throws her head back upon seeing me and lets out an overly loud laugh. Knowing Lyla, she is making her point that she is on their side.

"Hey Fiona," our captain calls. "I was surprised to see Lyla come in without you."

"Well, we had a little falling out last night." I keep my voice low, surprised that she doesn't already know.

"Really?" Takiesha's eyebrows furrow and mouth in a frown. She quickly recovers and continues, "Well, you two will work it out. Did you get the text from Shelby about wearing your body suit tonight? I can't believe I forgot to tell you all at practice." Takiesha shakes her head in disbelief.

"Umm, no." And there it is. Shelby is the person Lyla has been riding home with.

"Seriously? She didn't text you?" Hands on her hips.

"Nope." I shake my head once and feel my face flush.

"I had to work this morning, so I called her on my way in and asked her to text everyone. She told me she would. That pisses me off. I'm sorry, Fiona. We'll just have everyone change out of them."

My heart drops. I don't want attention drawn to it.

"Uh, maybe there is an extra in the cheer closet," I suggest and cross my fingers.

"OMG. You're awesome. Let's go see." Takiesha waves me to follow her. "But it's still wrong that she did that."

"Please don't say anything to her or anyone else. I don't want to make a big deal out of it." I turn and walk toward the storage room.

163

A few minutes later I walk out of the locker room with the right uniform on but two sizes too big so the arms flap. I pin them between my arms and sides so you can't tell and flash a brilliant smile for good measure. Out of the corner of my eye, I enjoy watching Shelby's smile turn to a sneer as I round the corner and enter the gym.

Before she notices me watching her, I look past Shelby like she doesn't exist and take a seat next to Takiesha.

"Oh, I forgot!" With my back turned to Shelby and Lyla, but loud enough for them to hear. "Congrats on Winter Court. I didn't get a chance to tell you yesterday."

"You too." She smiles back.

"I know you are going to win," I add to put the focus back on Takiesha.

"Ah, thank you. But I think everyone has an even chance. We have really great girls on court this year."

I force a smile and nod.

"Hey how's Faith?" Takiesha asks and I'm relieved for the subject change.

"Actually, we got some good news today. She is out of the coma but not completely responsive yet, but it's a good sign." I smile, cross my arms over my chest and rub my palms over my upper arms for warmth.

164

"That's awesome. I hope she can make it back for Winter Court," Takiesha adds.

"Me too." I know that is highly unlikely, but I keep it positive. I glance over my shoulder and notice Lyla's pouting lower lip which is a sign she is fighting tears. Even though I'm mad at her, I instantly feel guilty. She shouldn't have found out about Faith like that. I try to remember the last time she visited Faith; *Wednesday, I think. Has she gone to see her without me?*

I wonder if I should say something to Lyla, but before I can, she grabs Shelby's arm and pulls her up from the bleachers and the two scurry out the gym doors.

"Hey! Wait for me!" Sara jumps up and follows on their heels.

"Have you chosen a dress yet, Takiesha?" Daveona, a junior asks which draws me back to the conversation about Court.

"My mom and I went shopping today and I found one I like, but I haven't decided yet." Takiesha tilts her head like she is thinking back to the dress.

"Oh, what color is it?" a freshman asks.

"I have a picture." Takiesha presses the thumbprint to open her phone and scrolls through the pictures. "It's gray with beads all over. I love the dress, but I am not sure of the color."

Everyone ohs and ahs when they see the dress.

"That color is perfect with your skin tone and black hair," I assure her, and everyone agrees.

"What are you going to wear, Fiona?" Daveona asks.

"I was just talking it over with my parents today. I think I am going to wear Faith's junior Prom dress. The royal blue one."

"Oh my gosh. I remember that dress." Another senior exclaims. "It's beautiful. When I saw your sister walk in that year, I couldn't stop staring. Of course, I was only a sophomore who got invited by a junior. I felt completely out of place being there, but Faith totally looked the part in that dress. All she was missing was a tiara."

"Which she of course won that night on junior Prom Court." Takiesha giggles.

"Ah, maybe I shouldn't wear that dress. I don't think I can live up to that." My eyes go wide, and I add a grimace to prove my point. Again, I am reminded that I can never live up to Faith's legacy.

A few of the other girls' giggle. They probably agree with me but are too nice to say it. At least to my face.

"It will be perfect, Fiona." Takiesha throws her arm around my shoulder and gives a squeeze.

"Thanks. I have big shoes to fill." I can't help but giggle. "Literally, Faith's feet are bigger than mine. I'm gonna need to find shoes to wear."

After the game I follow Avery back to her house to change for the party. She lives on the other side of our school district called Decatur, which is also where Shaunce's parents have their farm. Usually, his parties are in the heated pole barn next to the house and since we have to park in a field, I offer to drive.

Tarin is sitting on the bed in Avery's room when I come out of the bathroom.

"You ready?" Avery asks.

"Yep."

"I seriously cannot believe your mom let you go. I didn't think she would," Avery clarifies as she climbs in my Jeep.

"Me either." I throw my hands in the air. "I didn't even have to ask. But my curfew is 1:30."

"That's okay," Avery reassures me. "If we want to stay, I am sure we can get another ride home."

"So, how did your date go Thursday night Avery?" I ask as I swing my coat on.

"Ah, well it was just the two of us and it was okay, but I don't think it's going to work out." Avery crinkles her nose and shakes her head.

"You know that already?" I giggle and look over out of the corner of my eye. Avery starts laughing.

167

"Um yeah, no chemistry." She drags out the *no* to emphasis her point.

"Ah…that bad huh?" I ask and hear Tarin laugh.

The Jeep is silent except for Erica Banks singing Buss It.

"So," Tarin stalls before continuing. "We were just talking…we think you should ask Jace to be your escort for Winter Court."

"Funny you should say that." I giggle. "I was thinking the same thing, but I didn't know if he would want to." I look in the mirror to Tarin in the back.

"Why wouldn't he?" Avery looks at me quizzically.

I shrug and take the next turn while keeping my eyes on the road. "I don't know, were not dating so he isn't obligated to—"

Avery interrupts with her throaty laugh.

"Um, I think any guy would love to be your escort for the evening." Tarin leans forward between the front seats.

"I don't know. I'm just not sure Jace is a suit and tie kinda guy. He's a jeans and cowboy boots kinda guy."

"Don't forget that sexy cowboy hat," Avery sing-songs.

"Ummm-mmmm, bet he clean up good," Tarin quips and we all laugh so hard Avery snorts.

"I have to admit," Avery adds with a shake of her head. "There is something sexy about a cowboy hat." Which brings out more giggles.

"What is it with you and cowboy hats?" I laugh and take the next turn.

"Cowboy hat, sexy smile and some abs, woo wee!" Avery puts the back of her hand to her forehead and gets more giggles out of us. Then turns in her seat to me.

"Promise you will talk with him about it." Avery has full on puppy dog eyes.

"I promise, I will at least ask him." I glance back at her. "And, yes, I will let you know."

Avery nods in response as Tarin shifts the conversation.

"Alright ladies. Who's the brave one to walk in first?" I look in the mirror and Tarin leans back in her seat.

"That's Fiona's job," Avery says quickly and throws her thumb toward me.

"What? Why me?" I glance at Avery.

"Because you're you and that's what you do," Avery explains, just that simple.

"I don't think so tonight." My stomach turns and my palms grow sweaty just as they always do right before I arrive at parties, athletic events or anywhere there is a crowd.

"You can't break your behavior pattern," Avery scolds. "You always enter like you own the place everywhere you go."

169

I've never really thought about it before, but I guess I do. And suddenly the conversation reminds me why I shouldn't have come to this party.

"I think I'll pass the torch to Avery." I don't want to admit how insecure I feel right now. Avery's squeal makes me jump and turn to her.

"I don't know if I can." Her voice higher than normal and her hands balled into first that she has brought to her chin.

"Sure, you can. You just have to decide that it's no big deal and, in your words, 'you own the room.'"

"I'm not as brave as you." Avery leans over and nudges my shoulder with her elbow.

"Bullshit. You are one of the bravest people I know." For the last few years, people have said Avery and Tarin are bitches but neither of them shows any sign that it bothers them. They do their thing and don't seem to care what others say. I envy that.

"Okay, okay, I will go first. But if I freak out, you have to push me through the door. And you guys better be right behind me." Avery turns and looks at each of us.

"Got it. Push you through the door." I nod and round the last curve.

Tarin giggles behind me.

I pass the Shaunce's Farmhouse and turn into the next driveway, which leads to the pole barn. Cars are everywhere, parked on both sides of the drive and in the field past the barn.

I drive into the open field and park next to a car I don't recognize. I know we won't get stuck but luckily for the cars parked out here, the ground is frozen and snow-covered, or they might.

We climb out and Tarin proudly smiles and says, "Look what I got..." dangling a bottle of Fireball in front of us.

"Awesome." Avery grabs the bottle first. "Everyone has to take a drink before we go in."

"Pass," I say and shake my head. "I'm driving," I add when Avery and Tarin turn to me in disbelief. That is one thing I never had to deal with when Lyla, Sara and I went to parties. Lyla didn't have her license yet, but Sara and I took turns being the DD and babysitter for the night, so we would all be safe.

"One drink at the beginning of the night is not going to hurt you," Tarin scolds. "Besides, it will help calm your nerves."

"I was hoping you couldn't tell." I snap my head toward Tarin.

"We couldn't tell until you decided that I needed to enter first. That gave it away," Avery admits. "Anytime you change your behavior people notice, especially you."

"Fine." I grab the Fireball and take a big swig, "Gha…" I grunt at the fire in my throat and hand the bottle off to Avery. "Let's go."

"There she is," Avery sings as they scurry behind me to keep up. I'm not running but I fear that if I slow down, I will change my mind before we get there.

As the barn gets closer, I can hear the thumping of the music grow louder along with shouts and laughter. My heart is racing, and my palms are clammy, but I stay the course.

I reach out for the doorknob and jump back with a yelp as the door suddenly swings open in my direction. My eyes bug out and the person exiting the barn literally laughs out loud, but only once. Then I realize it's Sam with his new girlfriend, Leigha.

"I can't believe you came," Sam says with a laugh. "What a bunch of losers." He pushes passed us and wraps his arm around Leigha's shoulder and leans in to whisper in her ear. Both giggling as they walk around the corner of the barn.

"What an ass," Avery snarls.

Even though he has been an ass to me the last few days, no one else seems to notice. Everyone else acts like he is the greatest guy in the world.

"I bet they are sneaking off to have sex," Tarin mumbles.

"Tarin," Avery scolds. "But yeah, they are totally having sex."

"Forget him." I walk through the door and into the florescent lights of the barn.

I keep my chin up as I walk past a few groups of kids to the left standing around talking and a group on the right playing beer pong. I find the keg and make my way there trying to ignore the stares when I walk past the group including Lyla and Shelby playing Bloody Hell.

"What the hell is she doing here?" a classmate I befriended in third grade when she moved here from Oregon, purposely says loud enough for me to hear.

I stop in my tracks, and Avery stumbles a bit trying not to run into me. I turn back, lean in and whisper something to her while wrapping my arm around her shoulder, Avery leans toward me on cue, and I whisper, "Just pretend I said something funny."

Avery tosses her head back letting out a giant laugh as her braids swing loosely except for the pieces around her face set in edge control. I take her arm in mine, a gesture so comforting to me, and we make our way to the keg. I know I am not supposed to drink, but I need to do something that looks natural. I grab a cup and pump the tap a few times and begin pouring a drink. I hand it to Tarin as Avery slips another cup under the stream without missing a beat.

Once we all have our cups, I turn to look for Jace and spot a group of guys playing euchre, but he's not there.

Then I hear. "Woohoo!" which is clearly coming from Jace. I turn in his direction and laugh when I see the corn hole game set up inside. Why not, the barn's big enough since they moved all the equipment out.

"Oh! My! Gawd!"

I spin in the direction of the commotion. Of course, it is the group playing Bloody Hell and they are passing around a cell phone, Lyla right in the middle of it again with that obviously loud laugh.

My heart aches at the realization I'm being ostracized by my former squad. But when I glance back to Lyla, I see her smile fade as she looks at the phone and passes it back to Sara.

"You came." Jace's voice snaps me back as he raises his cup in the air to celebrate. I take a look at him from cowboy boots to cowboy hat and my heart skips a beat and I fight off a giggle thinking that Avery will approve.

"Yep." I hold out my arms in grand gesture. "You didn't think I would miss it did you?"

"I was hoping not. Hey Avery." He tips his hat to Tarin. "Tarin." I can't help but smile at what is such a Jace gesture.

"Aren't you the perfect gentleman." Avery bats her eyelashes in typical flirty Avery style.

"Ah…" Jace fumbles to cover his flushed cheeks. "Glad you got this one here. She's been spending too much time away from friends."

"Technically, she got us here. But totally agree," Avery says.

I watch the game, we chat and Jace joins us when he isn't throwing, along with the other guys playing.

To everyone's surprise, the guys haven't lost their touch even though it's been too cold out to play. The score is only 7-6 because they keep cancelling each other's tosses out.

I watch as Jace focuses on his opponent's board, his corn-filled bag hits the center of the board at the rim of the hole and falls right in giving his team a three-point lead. Cheers go up but not for long as his opponent also throws his bag directly at the center of the board making a clean hit for three points, again canceling each other out. This continues for the next three tosses and the score remains 7-6.

"For crying out loud." I roll my eyes at Jace. "This game is going to take forever." I glance over my shoulder to see what else is going on and notice Sara huddled in another group showing them something on her cell phone. The group is laughing and carrying on about whatever they are looking at.

"Did you see her uniform tonight?" someone asks.

"Yeah, she looked like shit. What, did she have to borrow Bertha's leo?" The group giggles.

"At least she had something on," another classmate chimes in and the group breaks out in squeals.

My stomach roles and I shiver as I think about the Instagram picture.

I make myself turn back to the game and do my best to ignore the laughing at the other end of the barn. I force a smile and laugh at some joke. But I have no idea what was said.

I chug my drink and realize Avery isn't next to me. I look around and notice she's talking to a junior, BriAna by the keg. Avery has a look of dismay as she listens, so I start to make my way over and brace myself for the talk about the Insta pic. Avery's eyes get big, and her mouth drops to the floor. Avery does not hide her emotions at all. BriAna gets quiet and drops her eyes to her glass when she notices me coming. My stomach drops when I see pity in Avery's expression. I take a breath and put a fake smile on my face.

"What?" I ask impatiently, looking from Avery to BriAna.

"Apparently..." Avery pauses trying to decide the best way to tell me. "Well...um, Sara, I guess has a picture of you..." And she trails off letting it sink in hoping that she doesn't have to say anymore, but I'm not following.

"The Insta picture? That's not me." I shake my head thinking about the picture Sam's mom sent to my mom.

"No. Another one." Avery waits, giving me time to think before continuing. "I guess she took a picture of you changing in the locker room today," Avery whispers. "Or somebody did, but she has it."

My eyes bulge and mouth hits the floor. I hadn't thought about that picture since I left Dave and Denice's.

I pick my mouth up and blink a few times digesting the information.

"You mean that's what they're passing around?" I ask through gritted teeth, my skin burning red. "Did you see it, BriAna?" I turn to her, her eyes focused on her cup like she is hoping it will swallow her up.

"I did," BriAna says sheepishly and looks up at me like she is afraid of me. "But I swear I didn't know what it was. It doesn't show much anyway. They are making a big deal out of nothing Fiona." She reaches out and places her hand on my arm. "You can't even see your face so it could be anybody. The locker door is in the way. And the towel is covering you, kinda. All you see is side boob and leg."

I'm frozen in place and bile rises at the thought of the picture being passed around. I am half naked and being passed around like a joint.

"At least they didn't get you when you were completely naked," Avery tries to comfort me. "Do you want to leave?"

I turn my head as little as possible and look toward Sara, Jessica, and their fam out of the corner of my eye.

"No. They are just being bitches and I am not giving them the satisfaction. They want to humiliate me and if I leave, they win." I lift my head up and set my jaw.

I should stand up for myself, but that's what they want. A confrontation to embarrass me and make me look bad. They would all team up on me. And what if it turns to a fight? I hate confrontation and the vultures at this party would be drooling for a fight.

"*Gurrlll*, you gonna kick her ass, right?" BriAna leans toward me.

I shake my head no and take another drink. But damn I'd love to punch Sara.

"Good for you." Avery grabs my cup to refill it. "Besides, if I had a body like yours, I wouldn't mind showing it at all." She hands me the cup back. "But I totally think you should kick her ass."

The corn hole game finally comes to an end with Jace's team losing. The next opponents step up to take on the winners, so Jace and his partner disperse into the crowd, and we follow as the giggles and comments about the picture continue.

"Nice legs, DeWitt. I'd like to have them wrapped around me some time," Jackson Simmons, a junior, says when I approach the group. I know he is just giving me a hard time but of course everyone else giggles.

"Ah, thanks. And I know. I see you staring at them every time I cheer," I retort in my most disinterested voice possible, which gets out right laughter and jabs from his friends. Simmons, which is what everyone calls him, is not bad looking, but he is kind of a creeper. No amount of alcohol would make that happen.

"Face it, Simmons, you don't stand a chance with DeWitt," Jace corrects.

"It's a shame that towel was in the way," a junior adds.

Before I could tell him to kiss my ass, a friend of Sam's, who must be hammered, slurs, "Watch it. Langford will kick your ass."

"Really? Why would Langford give a shit?" A senior asks. "He's screwing Leigha."

I feel a fist ripping through my chest and everyone goes quiet after that.

A few guys glance up from the table and peak at me, trying to be inconspicuous, but I notice.

"Okay, let's play poker. Who's in?" And just like that, the conversation is redirected, and I mouth the words "Thank you" to my classmate Deontae Sprigs who brought up the game. He gives me a nod and continues. "25 cent opening bid. Dealers choice. Let's go Kings and Littles."

I take a seat at the card table next to Jace, toss the $10 I have to the banker for the buy-in and ante up.

"I need a refresher course, what's kings and littles?" I whisper to Jace.

"Kings and the smallest card in your hand are wild. So, if you have two kings and your lowest card is a five, you have three wild cards," Jace explains.

"Ah, got it." I look at my cards and move them around in my hands.

All around I hear cheers, laughter, kids getting drunk and the smell of skunk seeping through the back door of the barn. I purposely keep my cup close, pretending to drink but it's still full.

I hold my own for a while in the game, with Jace's guidance, but realize it's getting late, and I need to go.

Dealer calls three card guts and since I only have a dollar left, I decided to go for it. The game is called guts after all and let's face it, I need some guts right now.

"Everybody in?" the dealer asks and looks around the table.

One by one the players hold their cards over the table waiting for the count.

"Alright, on three. One…two…three…"

I hold my three cards and look around the table to see who else held theirs. Only two people dropped them so the rest of us are still in.

I'm sitting two seats to the left of the dealer and the first player raises a quarter.

"I'll call and raise you 50 cents." And I toss the rest of my chips in the center of the table and hear "Oohs" all around. The table goes quiet as players look over their cards and decide to call or fold. I glance around the table again and notice only two others call it.

"You know DeWitt. Think she's got something?" I hear the player next to Jace ask.

"Shit if I know." Jace throws his chips in which gives us four players still in.

"Show em'," the dealer announces.

I flip my cards over and look around the table. I'm showing a pair of nines, Jack high which beats the other two players. But when I turn to Jace, he has a big grin on his face.

"Sorry, DeWitt." He is showing a pair of Jacks, which beats my hand.

"Son-of-a-bitch." I throw my cards on the table. "I'm out."

I scoot my chair back to get up from the table when I hear. "Thanks for the money, DeWitt." Jace has a smug look on his face.

"Ass." I punch him in the arm to make my point and turn away from the roaring laughter at the table.

As I walk toward the keg, I notice Simmons and Tarin are talking, just the two of them. Then I notice how close Tarin is to Simmons.

Oh, Tarin. Not Simmons. But it is clear, Tarin's crushin'.

I find Avery talking to a few guys on the other side of the barn, so I change my direction.

"Hey, did you notice what's going on over there?" I nod my head in the direction of the keg.

"Yep," Avery sighs. "The heart knows no boundaries," Avery offers and chugs her drink.

"I think it should know that one." I shake my head and the rest of the group giggles. "I hate to break up the party, but I need to get going if I am going to make curfew. You guys staying?"

"I would stay, but I think Tarin wants to go." Avery gives me a disgusted look.

"Really? Tarin?" I look at Avery for clarification.

"I think she is planning to bring Simmons' back my house."

"Are you ok with that?" I look to her for an answer.

"My parents aren't home, so I don't give a shit." Avery shrugs.

"Let's go then." I turn to call for Tarin and start walking toward the door with Avery, Tarin, and Simmons in tow. I shiver at the realization that I have to pass Sara, Jessica and several other classmates huddled close to the door on our way out. We zig zag through the crowd and as

182

we get closer to the group, Sara looks over her shoulder and directly at me.

"Thank Gawd, she's leaving." Sara turns away from me and her group busts out laughing.

I ignore Sara and keep walking, but my stomach is churning, and the sting is back at the back of my eyes.

"I can't believe they let her in anyway. Why would they want a murderer here?" another student says. I stop in my tracks, Avery running into the back of me. For just a moment, I see red, and my hands wrapping around Jessica's neck.

"Not worth it." Avery puts her hands on my waist and pushes me forward like she knows what I'm thinking.

I step out the door we came in and let out the breath I was holding trying to keep my composure in the barn.

Avery throws her arm around my shoulder, and I quickly wipe my eyes with the back of my hand. Thankfully it is dark out and Avery doesn't say anything.

Avery and I are huddled together as we walk through the field trying to stay warm.

Tarin and Simmons crawl in the back and Avery in the passenger's seat.

"Nice, I'm in the backseat of DeWitt's Jeep." And the creeper shows up. I look up to see Simmons' grinning face through my rear-view mirror.

"Don't get used to it, Simmons. You'll be exiting soon," I add in a disapproving tone which gets a chuckle out of Avery.

I don't like being mean to anyone but let's face it, some people deserve it.

"Gladly," Simmons murmurs and I glance in the rear-view mirror to see Simmons leaning into Tarin. He whispers something in her ear which gets a giggle out of her.

The trip to Avery's is less than ten minutes and Avery and I keep ourselves distracted from the goings on in the back seat by singing along as loud as we can to Rockstar, which reminds me of middle school. I reach to change the channel when Monsters comes on, but Avery pushes my hand away.

"I love this song." Avery joins Band of Horses in singing the lyrics.

I feel tears bubble from the open wound in my heart; thankfully it's dark. I don't share that this was Sam and my song. It's too private. Too painful.

We pull in the drive and Avery jumps out, but Tarin and Simmons don't notice. I quickly turn the radio down to save myself from the memories.

"Uh-um..." I look to the back seat trying to get their attention and hope no one notices my face.

"Sorry," Tarin mumbles and Simmons helps her out of the back seat.

"You guys have fun," I shout with an all-knowing tone of voice which gets more laughs and giggles.

"Text me when you get home, so I know you are okay. Proud of you!" Avery calls.

"Okay." I nod but don't look her way.

"Just don't text Tarin," Simmons shouts back.

"Wouldn't think of it," I yell over the giggles. I push the clutch in, shift into reverse and turn around in the wide part of the driveway. Avery leaves the outside light on until she sees me pull out onto the road. I give a beep as I drive away.

Once on the road, I let out a breath and think back over the night. *The wrong cheer outfit thanks to Shelby, Sara's comment and then her passing the picture around. Running in to Sam and Leigha probably on their way to have sex and now the song.*

And what did Landon mean by, "Langford will kick your ass"? Does he know something I don't?"

Suddenly my stomach rolls when I think of the picture, Sara's picture, and the Instagram picture. It's all too much.

Fifteen minutes later I am in my driveway to beat my curfew by ten minutes. As I climb out the driver's side, I notice the lights of the car following me into our addition roll past my house, but don't think much of it.

The house is dark, but the outside light is on at the front door. I try to be quiet in case Mom and Dad are sleeping. I know they need it.

I pick Merida up as soon as I see her hoping this prevents her from meowing. We tiptoe down the hall passed my parent's bedroom. The door is cracked but the room is dark, and I can hear the light snoring of my dad sleeping.

I pull the door the rest of the way closed without latching it, so they won't be disturbed and make my way to my room. I avoid turning on the overhead light, instead using the light from my phone to see. I shut my door quietly and change into my dad's old college t-shirt I love to wear and shorts for bed.

I don't even bother brushing my teeth or washing my face. Faith's voice rings through my ears. "Fiona. It is so bad for your skin to sleep in your makeup." But right now, I don't care.

Merida and I climb under the covers and settle in. I swear she sleeps just like me, lying on her back, covers up to her chin and sometimes she has her paws on top of the covers which is so stinkin' adorable I can't stand it. Tonight, she curls up at my side, in between my ribcage and my arm and rests her head on my shoulder.

I reach my hand around her belly to stroke her soft coat. Merida purrs and reaches her nose up to my chin, so I turn my head and give her a kiss and a smile spreads across my face. I take in a deep relaxing breath and exhale.

"Sweet dreams, pretty girl." As I start to drift off to sleep, I hear a text beep through on my phone.

Through blurry eyes, I struggle to see the screen and don't recognize the number but the text reads: "First your sister, then Ella. Who's next?"

Chapter 8

I scrunch my face and twitch my nose hoping to stop the tickle. The room is filled with cats, much like the Humane Society's cat room and I am frantically searching for Mer. Several cats are following me trying to get my attention. I should stop to play with them but where is Merida? Again, there's the tickle on my nose which makes me squirm and I see the red feathers of Mer's favorite toy. The tickle continues to grow becoming more than I can bear. And the feathers. All these feathers. Mer has to be behind all this, if I could just get the feathers out of the way.

"Shit!" I screech as I smack my hand to my face trying to get those damn feathers. And I realize Merida is the culprit. Specifically, her ginormous tail.

Merida is lying on my pillow, something she knows she is not to do, and is wrapped around my head like a pair of earmuffs with her tail under my chin. But her tail is so long and full it curls back around at the end and lands right at my nose.

"Mer," I grumble and reach my arms over my head to pick her up.

"Ouch," I wince at the stinging in my back. "Uh, I think I might have over done it this weekend."

Mer stands up, stretches, then sits beside me cleaning her paw. I try sitting up, my abs scream horrible things at me. I release my muscles and fall back in bed staring at the ceiling.

"Well shit. I haven't been this sore since...I guess since I was in the hospital from the accident. At least I had pain meds for that." I turn to Merida like she might respond. But she sits there watching me like a concerned parent and when I reach for my phone to check the time, she goes back to her task of cleaning her paws.

My heart skips a beat when I remember the text I received last night. I read the text one more time, realizing it wasn't a dream and my headache reminds me that the text was the final straw that caused me to cry myself to sleep.

I drop my head back to the pillow. I shouldn't have gone to that party.

I bring my phone back to my face to see the time and I try sitting up but decide it will be less painful if I just roll over and fall out of bed.

"Nope, I was wrong." As my knees and hands hit the floor.

I hobble my way into the Jack and Jill bathroom that connects Faith and my rooms, Merida close behind and turn the water on as hot as I can stand it. A few minutes later, my muscles begin to loosen; I could stay here all day. Or until the hot water runs out.

I can hear Faith now: "You put ice on sore muscles, not heat." But the hot water feels so good.

Merida is sitting on the bathtub ledge watching the water swirl down the drain. I thought cats hated water, but this is our daily routine when I shower. Sometimes she even paws at the water trying to catch it.

Finally, I force myself to step out of the shower and I twist my hair up into a towel and throw on a State t-shirt I got when I visited Faith at college in October and a black pair of Nike Pro Shorts.

The growling in my stomach guides me to the kitchen. Blessed cold pizza.

I lift a corner piece out of the box and take a bite while reaching in the cabinet for a plate. I grab a Coke from the fridge and sit down at the table and reach in the box for another slice when I see mom's note:

At the hospital. Get your homework done.

Mom

10:15 am

Even with cell phones and text, Mom still leaves a handwritten note. It's something she did growing up with her family and has always done with us. If she gets up early and goes for a walk in the hills behind our house, she stills leave a note letting us know where she went and the time she left.

One more slice of pizza, of course sharing a pepperoni with Mer, I turn my focus on my day. I haven't done any schoolwork all weekend and I want to go see Faith. I putt the pizza box back in the fridge and the empty can in the recycle bin, I rinse off my plate in the sink and place it in the dishwasher, then I make my way to the bathroom to brush my teeth.

I look at my reflection in the mirror, my hair is a mess. I brush it out before pulling it back into a bun when the chimes of the doorbell make me jump. Merida hops down and runs toward the door. I'm sure she assumes the visitor is here for her.

I peek out my bedroom window and my heart jumps to my throat.

"Sam?" My body instantly tenses, and I freeze for a second before running to the door, swinging it open.

"What were you thinking?" His voice loud but not a shout and he pushes his way passed me into the foyer, letting the glass door shut behind him. "Simmons?" He turns to me, and a shiver rolls down my spine from the ice in Sam's glare.

"What?" I ask trying to figure out what he is implying.

"Oh, don't act like you're innocent." Sam's face flushed, hands on his hips.

"I have no idea what you are talking about." I shake my head and throw out my palms as I step back.

"Really. Everyone else knows. It's all over Instagram." Sam stands up tall, at least five inches taller than me and crosses his arms.

"What are you talking about?" I cross my arms over my chest and feel my eyes narrow on his.

"You hooked up with Simmons last night." He leans in about a foot from my face.

"The hell I did!" I bob my head and step away from his anger.

"You know he's spilling tea, Fiona." His voice chokes up on my name.

"About what?" I place my hands on my hips and shift my weight to one foot. But Sam just raises his eyebrows to make a point and nods in my direction.

"Eww. Um, curve even if he tried," I growl. "Come on, you know me better than that. I would never hook up with him. He's so sus."

"He left the party with you. Several people saw him get in your Jeep." Sam stares at me unblinking.

"Umm, yeah. Did *they* not mention that he and Tarin were all over each other and he climbed in the back seat with her? Or that he got out of my Jeep with Tarin at Avery's house and stayed there last night?" I wait for his answer, but he gives me nothing.

"You haven't texted me or called me back since Wednesday. And you expect me to answer to you?" I shove my index finger in his chest.

"I don't owe you anything. Get the hell out." I stand by the open front door, one hand on the doorknob and waving my other hand in a gesture for him to leave.

Before I can react, he crosses the foyer pushing me against the wall, hands on my hips trapping me there with his mouth crashing down on mine. It isn't a tender kiss but a strong, forceful, angry kiss. Like he is trying to take back what's his.

I've been so thirsty for this moment since last Saturday and now it's here. I've begged for him to want me again and here he is, but deep down I know this isn't real. He only wants to prove to himself that I still love him. That he can have me back in a heartbeat if he wants, but I can't find the strength to resist.

When he feels me give in to the moment, he picks me up, closes the front door and carries me across the room. Sam lowers me to the couch resting my head on the pillow, and he hovers over me as my leg drops off the edge of the couch, my foot hitting the floor.

His hand finds my leg and he runs his fingers along my skin, his hand catches behind my knee pulling my leg toward him, his fingers still grazing the skin of my thigh and over my hip. His lips leave mine trembling as he places kisses along my jaw and now my throat. His hand feels like ice on my flushed skin as he finds his way under my t-shirt and up my side.

My head falls back, eyes close and I release a low murmur. I'm barely aware I have my leg wrapped around his waist and my fingers are twisted in his hair.

Suddenly, I realize that Sam is on top of me, we aren't dating, and he has a girlfriend.

"Stop!"

"What? Why?" But he continues to caress my body.

"This isn't right." I grab his moving hand with mine before it goes any further.

He lifts himself enough to look into my eyes and sees the glistening of tears I'm fighting. With a sigh he drops his hand from my shirt and his forehead to my chest. He turns his head, so his cheek is resting below my collar bone and forehead at the nap of my neck. He has to be able to hear the fast, loud thumping of my heart.

Neither of us move or say a word. We just lay here like this, not wanting the moment to end.

"I shouldn't have come." He sits up and holds his hand out to me, pulling me up. I look over at him sitting next to me. Sam is bent forward with his elbows on his knees, his head bent down looking at his clasped hands.

I start to ask Sam why he came here today, but I'm afraid of the answer.

"I really thought you loved me," he whispers. I turn to see his eyes looking through me. That look takes my breath away.

"I do." Almost breathless. But the sadness in his eyes is clear he doesn't believe me.

"I just don't understand, everyone thinks we've already had sex at Lyla's party last fall. Why are you stopping this?"

I think back to that night at Lyla's party in her parents' RV, I remember feeling out of the loop of what was going on. *Did Lyla and Sara plan to get Sam and me alone? Was Sam in on it?*

Several classmates saw Lyla and Sara lead me and Sam into the RV and before I knew it, Lyla and Sara left us making out on the couch. So later when we went back to the party, everyone knew where we were and speculated on what we did.

"That's not the point. I'm just not ready for all that comes with it. It's bad enough knowing everyone thinks we already did and what they are saying. It would be so much worse if it were true. At least I know what happened. Besides, it's not about everyone else. It's about us."

"That's exactly my point, Fi." Sam throws his hands in the air and lets them drop. I know I should tell him about Terrace Grove, but I can't bring myself to say the words, so I swallow them down deep and bury them again.

Sam looks away from me and back down at his hands. Without saying a word, he stands up and walks to the door. I follow him, not sure what else to do. He opens the front door, turns to me, both hands in his front pockets. The sun is shining through the glass door highlighting his blue-gray eyes which remind me of an angry ocean against the stormy sky.

I hunch my shoulders, cross my arms over my chest suddenly self-conscious and look toward the floor where I notice my nail polish matches Sam's eyes.

The longing in my gut almost makes me cave. Even if I did change my mind about sleeping with Sam, and I really want to, it can't be under these circumstances. He must prove he loves me, and I need to be able to be honest with him.

Sam clears his throat which draws my attention back to his lips and up to his pleading eyes. I'm afraid to speak. I just might beg him to stay. I want him to stay. I want him to want to stay.

Suddenly, he turns to leave, maybe deciding he gave me enough time to change my mind.

He opens the glass door and walks away without saying goodbye.

As quickly as I can, I shut and lock the door not waiting for him to get into his car. The pain rips through my chest and my legs give out as I sink to the floor unable to hold back my sobs. I wrap my arms around my body as I lay on the foyer floor in a fetal position, gut wrenching sobs rack through my body.

***

Based on the light now coming through the windows, it is well into Sunday afternoon. I don't know how long I've been lying on the tile floor, but my hands and feet are blue. I use the bottom of my t-shirt to wipe the remaining tears from my face and notice the throbbing is back in my head.

I push against the wall to help pull myself to my feet and realize just how much my body aches. I look around, everything is familiar, but nothing seems real. It feels fuzzy and distorted. Like deja vu.

Once in my room, I dig out a pair of sweats and sweatshirt from my closet and fuzzy socks from my drawer and slide under my comforter.

My emotions raw. I feel hallow.

***

"Fiona." I barely notice my mom sitting next to me on my bed. "I expected you to come to the hospital—are you okay?" she asks when she see my eyes.

197

"Just not feeling well I guess."

"You probably overdid it this weekend. Are you running a fever?"

"I don't think so." But Mom feels my forehead with the back of her hand.

"Think you can eat anything?"

My stomach turns at the thought of food. I shake my head and pull the covers over my mouth.

"Let me get you some water." She leans down to give me a kiss.

"Mom? How is Faith?" I ask and hear her sigh.

"No change today. The doctor reviewed her test with us but nothing new." Mom turns to leave my room when I hear Dad ask, "What's wrong?"

"Says she's not feeling well." They continue to whisper but I can't make out what is being said.

I zone back out into my nonexistent state of oblivion only slightly aware that Merida is with me.

I sit up to drink the water Mom brings in and slip back under the covers silently begging sleep to end this pain.

***

The sound of my alarm doesn't wake me, but it does slowly draw me back to the present. I'm not sure how long this transition took, but my body just takes over knowing what it needs to do to get ready for school, like it's on autopilot.

Mom pokes her head into the bathroom while I am washing my face.

"How are you feeling this morning?" I look up just in time to catch her worried face in the mirror before she forces a smile.

"I'm fine," I mumble through my hands as I rinse my face and pat it with a towel trying to hide my appearance. All the while my mind is flashing to Sam and our encounter yesterday. My heart jumps at the thought of his hands on me. Him kissing my neck. A knife slashing through my heart as I relive him turning his back to me and walking away.

No tears. Please no tears.

"You don't sound fine. Maybe we should stay home and call the doctor," she says, her head leaning on the door.

"No. Ah, I mean, I have so much going on today. I can't miss school," I answer keeping my face low to avoid her scrutiny.

I just want to sink into a hole and die yet I can't bring myself to miss school. I can't bring myself to stay away from Sam. He is like a drug in my veins, and I can't rip them out. Maybe he will be waiting for me at school to tell me everything is okay.

"Is there something going on I need to know about?" Mom sounds more accusing than concerned.

"What? No. Why?" I turn to her.

"This all just has to be a lot to deal with and Lyla hasn't been around much which isn't normal. I'm sure she misses you—"

"Huh. Not quite," I interrupt. "She seems to have fallen on the side of Jessica and her friends."

"Oh, I don't believe that. There has to be more to it—"

"Trust me. There's not." I push my way past her and into my room. "I've got to go. I can't be late."

She follows me but stops at the door, hands on her hips. I pull on a pair of jeans, trying to avoid eye contact but out of the corner of my eye I see her throw her hands in the air in defeat and disappear down the hall.

After checking Merida's food and water bowl, I grab my coat and bag and head to the door. I can hear Mom in the kitchen, so I try to avoid that area, but Mom gets me before I get out the front door.

"You're not eating?"

"I'll grab something on my way." But she knows I won't.

"This conversation isn't over young lady," Mom calls as I walk out.

All the way to school, all I can think about is Sam and yesterday and what it all means. *Why did he come to my house? Just because there were rumors that Simmons left with me? Or was that an excuse? He had to know that Simmons left with Tarin. Right?*

I walk into school and pass through the senior locker bay to get to mine. There are two hallways I can take to get me there, one is closer than the other, but as of late, I take the longer one to avoid Leigha's locker.

I breathe a sigh of relief as I turn the corner without seeing Leigh, or Sam, but stop dead in my tracks as my heart hits the floor. There they are. Sam and Leigha. His arm around her shoulders, standing very close and leaning into each other. Leigha is saying something and giggling but Sam is straight faced and glaring at me.

He breaks the stare and looks back at Leigha with a flat smile at what she just said. I bite my lip and beg my legs to move as I scurry past them keeping my head facing forward.

My ears ringing, hands clenched in fists and that all too familiar sting in the back of my eyes.

"Fiona." I turn to see Mrs. Conner motioning me over. I take a deep breath and exhale trying to calm my nerves. I'm not looking forward to this conversation. I know what it's about.

"Hi Mrs. Conner." I try to keep walking, but she steps in front of me.

"Good morning. Have you decided who your escort will be?" She opens her notebook and clicks her pen, then glances up and waits.

"Oh, no. Sorry, I know who I am going to ask, but I just haven't done it yet."

"Well, I need to know by tomorrow morning. Okay?" Mrs. Conner blinks waiting for my response with that sweet smile on her face. I clear my throat so I can respond.

"Of course." I turn and walk away and quickly dab at the corners of my eyes.

The day goes by painfully slow. Every time the bell rings to end class, my mouth gets dry and my stomach queasy wondering, hoping I find Sam waiting for me. Each time the next bell rings to begin class, my heart sinks because I didn't, yet I feel relief that at least it's over for now.

I talk to Jace today during lunch and before sixth period, but it seems forced. I found myself looking over my shoulder, worried Sam would see us. The guilt made it impossible to ask the question.

Or is it hope causing me to avoid asking the question? Hope that Sam will come to his senses and make things right?

But when I see Sam get into Leigha's car after school, I know it's over. I need to move on.

"Jace!" I shout when I see him walk out of the building.

His face lights up like a Christmas tree when he sees me and jogs my way.

"Hey. What's up?" he asks as he comes to a stop about a foot away.

"Nothing." I let out a breath and realize I have butterflies. "Actually, there is something..." I look to the ground and bite my lower lip.

"Spit it out, DeWitt." Jace giggles. "I've never known you to be shy about anything although you've seemed a bit preoccupied today." Jace raises his eyebrows as he watches me.

A laugh escapes me, and it feels good which reminds me why I value Jace as a friend, even when Sam was determined that we couldn't just be friends. Sam was insistent that Jace wanted more. No way was I losing Jace's friendship.

"Well, umm, I know we're just friends and all, but I consider you to be a great friend..."

"Yeah?" I hear humor in his voice. "I like where this is going." He grins. "Seriously, I consider you to be a great friend too," he says with a little sarcasm. "What's this about, Fiona?" Jace reaches up and rubs his hand on the back of his head.

I sigh and roll my eyes knowing Jace is doing everything in his power to make this as difficult as possible. And loving every second of it.

"Will you be my escort for Winter Court?" I spit it out in a one swift breath. And suddenly I'm holding my breath again. It never crossed my mind that he might actually say no.

"Of course." I didn't think it was possible, but his face lights up even more, like the star on top of the Christmas tree. "So, like, what do I have to wear?"

"Well, it's formal but you don't need a tux. A suit will do." I nod.

"I wonder if I can still wear the suit I wore to eighth grade graduation?" Jace brings his hand to his face and rubs his chin as he considers this. Something a mad scientist might do when they are coming up with a new plan.

I try my best to suppress a laugh in attempt to display my repulsion at the idea of him wearing a suit that looks like an NFL Player wore to the ESPY's. Besides, he has grown like a foot since then.

"Um, for your sake, I hope it's too small. For my sake, hell no." My eyes huge to make my point.

"Ugh..." Jace covers his heart with his hand and drops his head back feigning insult. "Well just what am I supposed to wear?"

"My dress is royal blue, so I think a black suit and tie would be good."

"Sounds boring." He scowls and crosses his arms over his chest. "But if that's what you want, boring it is."

He can't seriously be waiting for me to give him the okay on a crazy suit. "Yes. That's what I want. Boring." I let out a giggle.

"Fine." Jace rolls his eyes.

"Thanks for doing this Jace. It means a lot to me." I give him a light punch on the arm.

Jace turns serious, drops his arms, and shoves his hands in the front pockets of his jeans. "Of course, Fiona. You didn't actually think I would say no, did you?" He cocks his head to the side and my heart goes to my throat.

"Uh-um." I clear my throat. "It did cross my mind, but not until the question was out there. I didn't know if this was your sort of thing."

Jace takes a step back showing surprise and confusion on his face. "It's not about my sort of thing. You're my friend and you asked me to be there for you. That's what friends do."

The truth in those words sting a bit.

Feeling lighter as I leave school, even hopeful, I head to the hospital. If I can get Jace in a suit that doesn't have some strange pattern, maybe anything can happen.

I'm relieved to find Faith's room empty. I need to talk to her about everything that happened yesterday with Sam.

Faith is still non-responsive but that doesn't stop me from pouring my heart out about everything and how much I miss Sam. It's funny how it seems easier knowing she isn't able to respond.

"I just can't believe he would do this to me. Do you think he still loves me or is he messing with me?"

I look at Faith with her bandaged head and blank stare. The bruising on her face from the latest surgery is turning a greenish yellow.

"How dare he treat me like this. Who the hell does he think he is anyway? I don't deserve this," I say trying to convince myself more than telling Faith.

"Faith, I know you can't respond to me yet, but I need you back. I need you. Just telling you about this whole mess makes me feel better. Stronger."

I watch Faith's face for a few moments hoping for a change, but nothing.

"Oh, I don't think I told you Saturday. I spoke to the cops working Ella's—"

I freeze when I feel Faith squeeze my hand. It must be from me mentioning Ella's name.

"You miss Ella too." Another squeeze and a smile spreads across my face. "Well, the cops said they found an iPhone at the accident sight about twenty feet from where they found you. It's basically unusable but they have their IT people trying to retrieve anything from it that might help. Turns out it is Ella's phone." Again, another squeeze. "They said they would let me know if they find anything else out."

"There's my girls." I turn to see Mom walk in the room.

"Mom. Faith squeezed my hand again." I look to Mom and back to Faith.

"That's great news." She gives me a pat on my shoulder, leans into kiss Faith on her forehead and takes the seat on the other side of Faith. "You seem to be feeling better."

"Yeah, a little I guess. I think I'm just tired." I tell Mom about Faith's responses to my story and about asking Jace to be my escort.

"Oh, that'll be so great to share the night with a friend like Jace. You two used to be such good friends before..."

"Sam?" I ask. "It's ok, Mom. Yeah, I agree." But the pinch in my heart indicates differently.

"I just don't understand." Mom shakes her head. "You and Jace talked almost every night in elementary. And then Sam came along and that ended."

"Jace and I were still friends, just..."

"Sam was jealous," Mom says sternly with a nod. "He didn't like you being friends with Jace."

I stare at my mom wondering how she knew this, but she doesn't take her eyes off Faith. I always thought she liked Sam. Maybe I was wrong.

I stay another hour before heading home. On the drive home I'm lost in thought and memories of Sam and me. I try to bring back the strength I felt in the hospital, but it's gone. I need Faith's support.

I pull into my driveway and barely notice the car parked in our turnaround. I'm startled when the interior light comes on as the driver's door swings open.

"Sam?" I blink and my heart leaps to my throat.

I pull up to the garage and he is waiting next to my door. Before I can make a move, my door swings open, and he is blocking my exit.

"We need to talk," Sam announces and my annoyance flares at his command.

"I don't think there is anything to talk about." I turn and grab my school bag giving me a few seconds to gather my thoughts and hopefully my strength, then push my way past him. I start to walk toward the door, leaving him there, but he grabs my arm and swings me around to face him. Before I can respond, he moves in for a kiss.

My eyes go wide as I fall back slightly, his finger under my chin bringing it up to his lips, he wraps his arms around me pulling me in. I sink into the kiss, close my eyes and am right back where I thought I didn't want to be anymore, but what the hell do I know.

A sudden flash of the fury I felt in the hospital rips through me as I remember he went home with Leigha after school. I place my palm on his chest and push him away.

"What do you think you are doing?" I take a step back and pull the strap from my bag back on my shoulder.

"Kissing you." Sam looks confused and I see the faintest smirk. If I weren't still mad at him, I might laugh.

"You have some nerve." I turn on my heels and scurry up the front steps of my house.

"I broke up with Leigha," he calls after me and I stop in my tracks and wince when I realize it was long enough for Sam to notice.

"You're too late," I snap over my shoulder. I start moving again without looking back, but I can hear him following me.

"Fiona." I turn at my name and curse myself for not having more self-control.

"What?" I try to give him my best I don't give a fuck expression.

"I'm sorry. I don't know what I was thinking." Sam lowers his head, hands in the pockets of his coat.

I toss my head back letting out a laugh. "I do!"

"Look, I know I treated you wrong. I've been really stupid. I got wrapped up in...in..."

"Sex? And Leigha?" I finish what he doesn't want to say.

"Ah, look, I'm sorry. I don't know what I was thinking." Sam rounds his shoulders into himself and shivers.

"You were thinking you wanted to get laid." I glare at him.

Sam starts to say something but stops and looks away.

"What do you want from me, Sam?" I sigh and throw my arms out wide. I'm tired of this game and, just plane tired right now. But when he turns to look at me, the pain on his face softens my anger.

"I want you to forgive me. I want us to be a couple again. I want you to ask me to be your escort and tell me everything will be ok." Sam admits and runs his hands over his face and through his hair. "You're the only one who knows me. Knows about my family. The only one I can talk to."

I look up to Sam and see the little kid I remember him to be back in elementary school and that pulls at my heart strings. I know how hard it is for Sam to share his feelings. And I know that comes from his upbringing in a volatile home. Deep down, I believe him.

"I can't," I admit and look away breaking his stare.

"You can't? Or you won't?" Sam voice isn't accusing, just sad.

"Both." My answer surprises me as much as it does Sam. Sam pulls back but keeps his eyes on me waiting for me to explain.

"I already asked someone to be my escort—"

"Jace?" he interrupts through gritted teeth.

"Yes." My eyes meeting his with a sense of pride that I made the right choice and now he knows what it feels like to be in my shoes. I force myself to stay strong, but my cheeks flush under the weight of his glare.

Sam's face is red with fury, but he doesn't say a word. I know him well enough to know he won't beg, but he is hurt. Good.

"I need to check in with the detectives about Ella. Goodnight Sam." I turn my back on him and walk through the front door, leaving him standing on the porch.

Chapter 9

Officers Buchanan and Quincy both rise as I walk in the conference room in the main office.

"Good morning, Fiona." Office Quincy nods. "I apologize I didn't return your call last night."

"I understand. It was later than I realized when I called." I set my things on the table and pull out a chair. I take a seat on the edge of the maroon leather chair like the ones in Mom's office and place my elbows on the conference table.

"Sorry to pull you out of class again, Fiona," Office Buchanan chimes in.

"No worries, I'm guessing this has something to do with Ella's phone? Did you get anything else from it?"

"We did. Not much but possibly something." Quincy slides over a picture. "Does this mean anything to you?"

"It's just letters." I frown at the picture as I run my finger over the edge of the photo.

"Right, this is the last text on the phone we found," Buchanan explains as he points to the picture.

"'*bqr,*' does that mean anything to you Fiona?" Quincy leans in placing his hands on the table.

"No, I have no idea what it means. Who was the text to?" I focus on the letters hoping something registers. Flashes of the night come back. The Cincinnati mileage sign. The mall parking lot. Faith and me laughing in the car. But no letters.

"We don't know. IT hasn't been able to track the text yet. But it doesn't look like the text was sent," Buchanan answers. "Could it be some type of code? A restaurant, directions? Anything?"

"Code? Like, what kind of code?" My eyes snap up to meet Buchanan's over the picture.

"Not sure. Maybe how they call Over the Rhine, OTR?" Buchanan shrugs, then sighs as he leans back with a squeak of the leather.

"I wish I could help but it doesn't mean anything to me. Sorry." I look back at the picture, then drop it on the table.

"What about Faith's phone?" Quincy asks as Buchanan glances at Quincy then back to me.

"What do you mean?" I slide back in my chair and frown.

"Well, after our last talk, we went back over the accident file." Buchanan stops long enough to let this sink in. I shake off a shiver and wrap my arms around my body. "According to the report, you managed to have your phone on you when you were taken to the hospital. Ella's phone was found the day the Grunwells reported Ella missing, but we assumed it was Faith's until IT got into it last week. So, Faith was in the car with you, where is her phone?"

My mouth dry, my tongue feels too big for the space between my teeth. I wish I had a bottle of water but apparently schools do not offer this when students are interviewed by the cops.

"I…" I swallow trying to make my mouth work. "I don't know."

Quincy sits back in his chair and looks out the window while resting his chin on his index finger.

"I searched the car." Quincy looks back to me. "But I didn't find anything else. There's nothing left in the car. It's burnt to a crisp."

"When the Grunwells filled a missing report on Ella," Buchanan jumps in, "we didn't know the connection between the girls in the accident in front of SWU's campus and the missing person report because Ella's missing person's report wasn't filed with us until Christmas Day. But based on the timeline and that you three are all from Brookston, we decided it need to be considered that the two cases are connected. You confirmed that for us last week with your memory of driving to Cincy that night," Buchanan explains.

"Cincinnati PD were handling your accident case since it took place in their jurisdiction. When we made the connection of the three of you,

I requested the phone from evidence so our IT could start working on it," Quincy added.

I'm paralyzed in my seat. This new information is too much. My head is spinning, and I feel the throbbing of a headache coming on.

"What are you thinking Fiona?" Buchanan leans in. I blink a few times trying to get my thoughts together.

"I just think it is odd that Faith was with me in the car but where is her phone? It never crossed my mind that Faith's phone is missing. Maybe it just burned up in the fire but why did she have Ella's?" I lean to the side of my chair, elbow on the arm rest and rub my temple where I feel the throbbing.

"We've been discussing that too. It's possible they got their phones mixed up, but not likely," Buchanan says. "Not with phone cases and such. If it was in the car, it's gone. And the investigators on the scene didn't know to look for a third phone."

"Is it worth checking the car again?" I ask, desperate for answers. "Even if it is a melted lump, at least we know where it is."

"We searched it thoroughly last week. There was nothing left Fiona. I don't think it will do any good. Thanks for your time," Quincy offers and both officers stood up. As they are walking out of the conference room, Buchanan stops and turns to Quincy just outside the door.

"It might not be a bad idea to let her look through the car," Buchanan whispers. "It could jog her memory."

I make my way into seventh period and hear the whispers as I pass.

"She was called to the office again. The cops where there waiting on her," a girl in our class says.

"Nuh-uh," chimes in another student.

"No way," a third student snaps.

"Maybe she really did try to kill Faith," a fourth student adds and giggles and sh's follow.

"What about Ella? I bet she had something to do with her disappearance too," the first girl whispers.

"Maybe that's what the cops were questioning her about. I wouldn't put it past her," the fourth girl claims.

"You don't really believe all that?" a guy questions.

"Can you imagine Fiona in jail? Orange is not her color," the second girl clarifies.

"I think the only thing funnier than her going to jail would be if she is pregnant," the first girl adds and the group giggles.

I act like I don't hear them as I walk to my seat, but I feel their eyes still on me as nausea rises in my stomach.

I'm thankful for my seat in the back row. I place my books on the desk and slide down into the seat recounting the conversation I just had with the police.

"You okay, Fiona?" I turn to look at a student I have known since first grade, Jaleena Laughery.

"I'm fine. Thanks, Jaleena. How are you?" I try to act as normal as possible.

"It's not right what they are doing," she whispers back and glances in their direction. I follow her eyes to the group of students spilling tea.

Not sure how to respond, I give a weak smile and turn to Mr. Ellison who is going over the homework assignment. I try to focus on his words when I feel the vibration of my phone in my back pocket. I wait until Mr. Ellison's back is turned and pull my phone out concealing it with the massive history book on my desk.

I click on the text from Avery: "plans 2nite? we should hang"

I lift my eyes up to see what Ellison is doing and I quickly type back: "hospital after school come with not staying long"

Avery didn't really know Faith. Yeah, she knows who she is, everyone does, but Avery never met her through me, so I'm surprised when she says yes. I text back: "my locker after class"

"k" Avery text and I giggle at the kissing emoji Avery includes.

"Something you'd like to share Fiona?" Ellison barks. I fumble my phone almost dropping it and slide it under my book.

"No, Mr. Ellison. Sorry." I glance around at all the eyes on me and smirks on their faces, I feel the pink flare in my cheeks.

"I'm sure that is not your phone you have out, right Fiona?"

"Correct, Mr. Ellison. Not my phone," I squeak with a nod and clasp my hands together on top of my desk.

"If there is nothing further, may we move on?" Mr. Ellison turns to me, hands on his hips. This is not a real question.

"Of course," I say before I can stop mouth. Mr. Ellison blinks at my response, stares for a few seconds then shakes his head as the class erupts in laugher.

I slink down in my chair even further and find relief that Ellison has managed to draw the attention of the class to the historical event displayed on the whiteboard. I am clueless as to what it is since I didn't do my homework and just don't give a crap at this point. All I can focus on is the ticking clock on the wall, *tick, tick, tick*, with each second that passes. Only nine more minutes.

I sigh in relief when the bell rings and move from my desk to the hall.

I make my way to my locker after class and hear Avery's laughter ringing out through the locker bay before I see her. A smile spreads across my face.

"Do you care if we stop by my house? I want to change," Avery explains.

I look Avery up and down checking out her outfit for the first time today. Wide leg jeans, cropped gray sweatshirt and red high-top converse. I look down at my own almost identical outfit but with white Doc Marten's and a white turtleneck cropped sweater.

"Do I need to change?" The question in my voice is met with full on Avery laughter.

"Not at all. You are wearing a cashmere sweater with Docs."

"But it's practically the same as your outfit." I look down at my oversized sweater and hold out my arm to check the material.

"Hardly, Fiona." Avery rolls her eyes at my lack of understanding. "My outfit is too casual."

"Huh, I guess I don't see the difference." I fiddle with the edge of my sweater taking a better look and get another giggle from Avery.

I follow Avery in her mom's old Camry to her house. We're in and out in ten minutes and heading to the hospital.

lWe are both quiet as we walk through the halls to Faith's room. I expected Avery to be chatty but maybe she is being respectful of me. Or maybe she is just not sure what to expect.

"Wow, is that Faith? It doesn't look like her at all," Avery admits. Her bluntness brings me out of my own thoughts. She's right, the body lying in the hospital bed still doesn't resemble Faith. But hearing someone else say it is hard to take.

"I'm sorry, Fiona, I shouldn't have said that," Avery sighs and takes my arm in hers to comfort me.

"No, you're right. It's doesn't look like Faith," I agree with a shake of my head. "I guess I keep trying to convince myself it does. There is still so much trauma." I shrug as I look at my sister staring at the wall across from her.

I sit next to Faith, I start sharing my stories of the day, a little self-conscious of Avery hearing everything too. Things I wouldn't normally share with anyone but Faith. Avery sits quietly for most of it but chimes in on que when there is something funny to add. I know Faith will love Avery once she gets the chance to know her.

"Hey girl." I turn to see nurse La'Tonya walk in and right up to me for a hug. "Who is your friend?" La'Tonya asks turning to Avery.

"This is Avery, she is keeping me company this evening." I smile and turn back to Faith.

"Hi," Avery responds with a quick wave.

"Girl, I love your hair." La'Tonya waves her hand.

"Thanks." Avery shrugs and adds, "This is what happens when your mom is black, and your dad is white." I smile at Avery's unapologetic response.

"Isn't her hair snatched?" I ask. "I mean, I have naturally curly hair too, but do you think my hair would ever look that amazing? *No.* And I certainly can't pull off the braids she had in last week."

"Well, both you girls have great hair. When I don't have a weave in, mine is a hot mess," La'Tonya adds as she continues to check Faith's chart.

"Anyone with naturally curly hair knows you just never know what you're gonna get each day," Avery adds with a laugh.

"Never truer words. Okay, you girls can stay in the room, but I need to check Faith's back. She's getting a couple of bed sores we need to watch." La'Tonya pulls on latex gloves as she walks to the other side of Faith's bed.

"Do you need any help?" I offer like I always do but know La'Tonya isn't going to take me up on it. And I am glad. I'm not sure I have the stomach for it.

"No girl, I got it." Latonya waves her hand at me.

"Do you mind if I watch?" Avery asks. My eyebrows raise as I look to her. "I want to go into nursing."

"Really?" Both La'Tonya and I ask at the same time. It suddenly hits me that we are only two and a half years away from making this decision and I have no idea what I want to do. But now that it is brought up, I can totally see Avery as a nurse.

"Just stand right over here, Avery," La'Tonya instructs.

La'Tonya explains to Avery what she is doing. Avery nods and listens intently. La'Tonya answers Avery's questions with patients and you can see the pride she takes in her work.

La'Tonya looks at me. "Fiona, you okay?"

"Yeah, I just hate that she is in pain. I almost think I can feel it. Or it reminds me of my pain from the accident." I keep my eyes on Faith's.

"Keep up your faith. She needs it now. Plus, we are keeping her pain meds regular, so she isn't feeling anything," La'Tonya reassures. "Okay, all done. I am going to keep her on her side for a bit. I'll be back in later to move her again." She rips off her gloves and reaches in her pocket, removing a small notebook and pen. She scribbles something on the page before ripping it out of the notebook and hands it to Avery.

"Here." La'Tonya flutters her eyelashes and flashes a bright smile. "If you have any questions about nursing schools."

I raise my eyebrows at the exchange taking place. I swear Avery's cheeks flush when she looks back up to La'Tonya.

"Thanks, La'Tonya," I sing-song and wave before turning to scrutinize Avery.

"You girls be safe going home now," La'Tonya calls from the door.

I lean into Avery and nudge her arm with my elbow hoping to get a response out of her.

"She is hot!" Avery fans herself off and slides down in her chair.

"So...ya gonna call her? I think there might be chemistry there." I wink which gets a giggle out of Avery.

"Do you think I'm crazy?" Avery meets my eyes and raises her eyebrows.

"What, for being interested in La'Tonya? Ab-so-lutely not! She *is* hot!" I pretend whisper.

"How old do you think she is?" Avery leans over to me and raises her eyebrows.

"Well, I remember her telling me that she did a college program her junior and senior year of high school with Ivy Tech, so she only had to do two years in college to get her BSN. She graduated last spring, so

223

maybe twenty, twenty-one?" I shrug and watch as Avery bounces in her chair, which is interrupted by the beep of Avery's phone.

"It's Tarin. Apparently, Simmons is having a few people over to watch the SWU game tonight. She wants us to come by."

"Really? Who all is going to be there?" I ask, not sure I should really be there.

"She says Jace and a few of his friends are there. Tarin invited a couple other girls. We don't have to stay long, let's just stop in and say hi."

"What time does the game start?" I ask thinking it is a legit question.

Avery turns to me with a look like I have three heads. "Who cares?"

"True." But secretly, I enjoy watching the SWU games, especially with the season they are having. It's something my dad and I do together. I've even tossed around attending SWU when I graduate.

We stay with Faith a while longer then decide to head out around 6:30. To my surprise, Avery is quiet when we first get into my Jeep.

"How do you do it?" she finally asks.

"What do you mean?" I glance to Avery. She is looking down at her hands in her lap and picking at the growth on her manicured nails.

"I mean, keep going to see her every night. Doesn't it break your heart?" Avery looks over with sadness in her eyes.

224

"Yes." I turn back to the road, my eye bulge. "Every time. And knowing I'm the reason she is there rips my heart out. But the idea of her lying in that bed and me not being there with her kills me."

"I guess so." Avery turns to look out the window. "It was an accident by the way. You can't blame yourself. You know Faith wouldn't want that. She wouldn't blame you."

I shiver and reach for the knob to turn up the heat.

"How did you learn about Ella anyway?" Avery's voice soft, she looks down at her hands in her lap. "If you don't want to—"

"No, it's okay. Well, while I was still in the hospital from the accident, Ella's mom came to see Faith and me a few days after Christmas. We call her Mom E btw. I was awake by then and Mom E asked when I talked with Ella last."

I think back to that conversation.

"I'm not sure. I think at least a week or so before...Faith had been texting with her, but I just assumed she hadn't texted me because she was busy with finals. And I didn't want to bug her," I shrugged slightly and felt a pinch in my back.

"Has she text you or Faith since the accident?" Mom E leaned toward me in the hospital bed. "I thought for sure she would be here to see you both. She was supposed to come home Christmas Eve, but we haven't seen her."

225

"What? She didn't come home for Christmas?" I gasped and tried to sit up right. "Why not?"

"We don't know—"

"I didn't want to worry you with the news just yet Fiona," Mom interrupted Ella's mom. "I was worried she wasn't stable enough." Mom glanced to Denise in apology. "She has only been out of the coma for a few hours."

"I understand." Mom E took a breath and continued. "We called the campus police Christmas Eve, and they informed us that all the dorms were shut down. Ella had to be out of the dorm by the sixteenth."

"I-I don't have my phone." I looked around trying to find it. "Did you call the police?" I looked to Mom E who could only nod as she wiped away tears.

"How long have I been here?" I turned to Mom, and she was already digging in her purse.

"Oh, they gave it to me when they brought you into the ER. The nurse said you still had it in your hand when you came in. I forgot I had it." She handed the cell to me, and I hit the power button.

"What day is it?" I asked, trying to turn on my phone.

"It's Wednesday; you've been here since Friday night. The doctor kept you sedated until this morning." Mom reached in her bag for the charger, took the phone out of my hand and plugged it in.

"Here, I'm sure it's dead." She handed it back to me.

My energy level was dropping but I wanted to help so I pushed through and impatiently waited for the phone to come to life. I can't believe Ella isn't here with Faith.

"I have tons of texts, voicemails and DM's." I scrolled through the messages searching for Ella's name. "I don't see any messages from her. I'll texted Lyla and ask her." I focused on the screen, fighting off the fatigue that was creeping in.

"Ly, just got my phone back have u heard from ella?"

I closed my eyes and waited for Lyla to reply. My phone beeped within seconds. Lyla responded: "OMG! ur awake! mom is bringing me in later. no, called and text her but no response. hasn't she been to see you guys?"

My arms felt heavy and my brain foggy. It took me longer than it should have to text back: "no, Mom E is here haven't heard from her they r worried"

"what? like missing?" Lyla texted back.

I text: "idk, just learned she never came home for xmas. they called the cops"

227

I looked up from my phone and saw the anticipation in Mom E's expression. I shook my head no and I watched her shoulders drop followed by a sniffle in the tissues she was holding. My mom wrapped her arms around Denise and pulled her into a hug.

"Have you contacted her roommate?" Mom asked.

"Julia said she hasn't heard from her in weeks. I don't think she wanted to tell me but when I shared that Ella didn't come home for Christmas, Julia admitted that she hadn't seen Ella much the last month of school. Said she was always out and staying with friends."

"What did the police say?" I interrupted.

"They are doing everything they can." Mom E shrugged as her shoulders shook.

"I can't believe this. Faith and now Ella." I was fighting to keep my eyes open when my phone rang.

"Ly—"

"Oh my god. Ella is missing. Was she like kidnapped? She wouldn't run away. What do we do? I mean when was the last time anyone saw her..." Lyla was rambling so fast; I couldn't even concentrate to keep up. "How do we find her?"

The line was quiet, and I realized Lyla was waiting on a response.

"Um..." I rubbed my forehead trying to fight off the fatigue. "I don't know." I tried to be as quiet as possible, wishing I could get out

228

of bed, so Mom E didn't hear me. "Her parents filed a missing person's report. But no one knows who saw her last."

"Do you remember anything? I mean, the last thing I knew was you were going to text me when you and Fay were leaving to come get me. Did you two meet up with Ella? Faith said we were going to after we shopped." Lyla paused again.

"I-I just don't know. I don't remember anything after leaving our house." I laid my head back and closed my eyes again.

"Who else might have seen her last?" Lyla asked desperate for answers.

Feeling exhausted, I sighed, trying not to get annoyed. She was worried and wanting to help but I didn't have the answers.

"Mom E called her roommate. She said she hadn't seen her much the last month of school."

"What, like she disappeared a month ago?" Lyla's voice squeaked.

"No, apparently she wasn't staying in her dorm much." I took a deep breath. "Lyla, the nurse just came in, I will see you when you get here," I lied. I hit end call and closed my eyes trying to figure this out.

"I'm so sorry to bother you with this," Mom E added. "You need to rest, and you have enough on your plate with Faith. I'm going to go to the police station to see if they have any information. Get well Fiona." She gave me a kiss on the forehead and turned to leave.

"Mom E," I called. She turned around to look at me. "We will find Ella."

Denise wiped her cheeks and nodded, then turned and walked out of my room.

"Mom, I need to sleep. Go be with Faith."

Mom leaned down and kissed my forehead. "I'll be back soon."

I gave my mom a smile, laid my head back and closed my eyes hoping I would wake to find everything back to normal.

I don't say anything else, and Avery lets it go.

"So, what do you think I should do with my hair Friday night?" I already know what I am doing with my hair, but I need to change the subject.

Avery lets out a sigh. "I think you should wear it down and straighten it." She turns to me.

"Really?" I catch her smile from the corner of my eye. "Straight? I never wear my hair straight."

"That's why you should for Friday night. Then wear it up Saturday. What color is your dress again?"

"Royal blue. Oh, that reminds me. I need to drop it off at the cleaners tomorrow to get it pressed."

"Should we do that tonight?" Avery asks, turning away from her phone to look at me.

"No, they'll be closed by the time we get back to Brookston."

"Did you get an appointment for your hair?" Avery asks.

"Yep. Tomorrow right after school. Just getting highlights."

"I think you should do something funky." Avery wiggles in her seat.

"Um, no. Don't even start on your crazy ideas for my hair." I let out a laugh as I think about what Avery would have me do.

"Nothing over the top—a few royal blue streaks?" Avery's voice rises.

I turn down Simmons' long driveway, my eyes narrow on the gunmetal gray Mustang.

"Is that Jace getting into Kenton Downing's car?" I ask. Avery leans forward for a closer look but doesn't respond.

I pull my Jeep off to the side of the driveway. Kenton pulls up next to us as we start walking to the house.

"Where you guys going?" Avery leans in the passenger's window.

"Pizza run," Kenton replies with a nod.

"Hop in." Jace opens the passengers' door. "Just going to Brookston Pizzeria. Gone no longer than thirty minutes."

"Okay." I climb in the back of the car. I'd much rather hang out with Jace and even Kenton than Simmons, even though it is odd that Jace is hanging out with Kenton. Kenton is known to be a bit rough.

"Where's Riley?" I figure she is here if Kenton is.

Riley is on the outskirts of our friend group and known as the class bully, but I've never had a run in with her. Each month she chooses someone new to harass. Avery was on the receiving end of Riley's bullying our freshman year. Riley was relentless, and no one seemed to know why Avery was the chosen one.

"I don't give a shit where that bitch is," Kenton retorts and my eyes go wide.

"Wow. Did you two break up?" Avery asks sliding in the back seat.

"Nah, she's just pissed cause I didn't want to hang out with her tonight," Kenton calls as he turns out of the driveway.

Avery and I remain silent not wanting to say the wrong thing.

"I hear you got my boy Jace to agree to wearing a suit Friday night." Kenton eyes me in his rearview mirror. He's never been inappropriate with me, but I wouldn't want to be alone with him.

"I just hope I don't regret it," I joke and get a laugh from Jace.

"Don't worry, Fiona. I got a boring black suit and tie. You will be pleased."

"Ah...thank you. Pictures by any chance?" I lean forward to Jace.

"What? Pictures? Of the suit?" Jace looks over his shoulder to the back seat and I realize he is serious. "Why would I do that? You'll see it Friday night."

232

"Typical male." Avery laughs.

"So, what's up with you and Langford?" Kenton changes the subject.

"What? Sam? Nothing." I feel myself scowl. And I look to Jace and wish I could see his face.

"Heard he dumped Leigha. You can't tell me you weren't involved—"

"I'm not. I wasn't!" I bite my lip annoyed Kenton brought this up in front of Jace.

"Not buying it, Fiona. Saw Langford leaving your neighborhood last night."

I blink, my stomach flips and I feel my face getting hot.

"You didn't tell me he came to your house last night," Avery hisses and turns to me and I can barely see her face in the dark, but her eyes are wide.

"It wasn't a big deal." I roll my eyes. "He was there when I got home."

"And?" Kenton is not letting it go.

"Fine. He told me he broke up with Leigha and he wanted to be my escort, but I said no, Jace is my escort and I told him to leave." I hear Jace let out his breath.

233

"Well, Sam's loss. Jace's gain." Avery elbows me and I narrow my eyes at her.

"All right, I drove. One of you has to go get the pizzas," Kenton pulls in not quite between the white lines and puts the car in park.

"I have the money so it's me." Jace hopes out of the car. When the door slams shut, Kenton turns to me with a smirk.

"Jace is a good dude. Don't break his heart, DeWitt." Kenton finishes with a wink.

"Think Simmons ordered enough pizzas?" Jace says as he climbs back in the car.

"How many is that? Six? Seven?" Avery asks leaning forward looking at the boxed stacked on his lap.

"I thought Tarin said it is a small get together?" I turn to Avery.

"One pizza per dude sounds about right," Kenton adds. "You girls can share a pie."

My stomach growls and I realize I haven't had anything to eat yet. That might not be enough.

Once at Simmons' house, I crawl out of the Mustang and offer to help Jace with the pizzas. Headlights are coming up the driveway behind us, but I don't pay any attention to it. Kenton helps Avery out of the car, walks to the passenger's side and grabs the pizzas out of Jace's hands.

"Got em' dude. I'm starving." Kenton and Avery laugh as they walk ahead of us.

"How did you get hooked up with Kenton?" I lean into Jace to whisper.

"Well, Simmons handed me the money and told me to keep the change if I go get the pizzas. I was heading out when Kenton rolled up. Told him what I was doing, and he said, 'get in' so I did."

"Oh, well that's kind of a relief," I whisper, which gets a laugh out of Jace, and I feel his hand on the small of my back.

"He's not so bad but yeah, not my normal squad," Jace leans in and whispers. My heart skips a beat.

I hear footsteps running up the drive behind us, I glance over my shoulder just in time to see Sam charging Jace at full speed.

"Jace!" He glances over his shoulder as the full weight of Sam's body slams him to the ground.

"Keep your hands off my girlfriend," Sam yells. The screaming must be my own as Sam and Jace wrestle around of the frozen ground.

"I'm *not* your girlfriend!" I shout. "Sam! Get off him." And suddenly Jace is on top and landing a solid right cross to Sam's face.

"Stop it!" My shouts draw everyone out of the house.

Sam has the upper hand again and my blood is boiling.

Without thinking, I step into the rumble and reach down grabbing Sam's arm attached to the hand he has wrapped around Jace's neck and pull as hard as I can. Jace sees the opportunity and shoves Sam with everything he has throwing Sam backward. My head flies back with the crack of Sam's skull smashing into my forehead. The momentum throwing me backward to the frozen ground.

Avery and Tarin rush to my side, picking me up off the ground, and drag me away from danger. I get my feet under me and watch as Kenton and Simmons pull the two apart with Sam still working to get to Jace. Kenton releasing Jace, turns to helps Simmons drag Sam to the car he came in.

"Take him home, Brewer. You need to cool off, Langford." Simmons leans in the car as he throws Sam in the passenger's seat.

"You okay, Fiona?" Jace turns to me.

"Yeah." Avery and Tarin have me surrounded and are dragging me into the house. Tarin digs through the freezer and places a bag of frozen peas on my head before I'm even seated.

"That's one way to get a party started." Kenton holds up his bottle of beer.

"You can always count on DeWitt." Simmons holds up his hand waiting on me to give him a high-five. I roll my eyes and reluctantly give in.

"Funny," I scoff. "Where's Jace?" I look around the kitchen.

"He's in the bathroom checking out the damage," Simmons adds with a nod down the hallway.

"How bad is it?" I ask leaning back in my chair trying to peek around the corner.

"Not bad enough for you to need a new escort." I glance up to see Jace making his way to the kitchen with that smart-assed grin.

"I'm so sorry, Jace. What an ass." I look up at his bloody lip. "Your shirt is ruined."

"Totally worth it," Jace adds as he applies ice to his lip. "How's your forehead?"

"It's fine." But I wince as Avery puts the ice pack back on it. "I just hope it doesn't form a bump. I might have to get bangs tomorrow if it does."

"Bump or no bump, you will be beautiful." Jace holds my stare.

"And you will not get bangs," Avery clarifies.

"All right. Tip off in five minutes. Help yourself to the pizza and head to the living room." Simmons is directing traffic, and everyone falls in line grabbing pizza and drinks.

I move to the living room with the peas still on my forehead, I take a seat on the floor and try to focus on the game, but my head is throbbing. Every cheer when SWU scores and the swears when they screw up feels like a nail being pounded in my head.

"How long are you wanting to stay?" I lean over and whisper to Avery.

"I can find a ride home," she whispers back.

"Are you sure? I'll take you home. My head is just hurting." My arm holding the icepack is starting to hurt so I switch hands.

"I'm sure it is. No worries at all. Are you okay to drive?" Avery asks.

"Yeah, it's not that far." I push myself off the floor. "Thanks for having me over Simmons."

"Thanks for providing the pre-game entertainment, DeWitt." Despite the pain I laugh at Simmons remark.

"I'll walk you out." Jace jumps up and follows me to the door. "You sure you're okay to drive?"

"Promise." He opens the door to my Jeep, and I climb in. "Are you okay?" I ask for the first time.

"Never better. Text me when you get home. Okay?" Jace adds with that crooked smile that causes my heart to skip a beat.

"Sure. See you later, Jace." He shuts the door and I let out the clutch. Jace stands watching as I back out of the drive.

Chapter 10

"Are you going to the office in your robe today?" I stop when I see my mom sitting at the kitchen table. She is usually dressed and ready to walk out the door when I get up.

"Don't be silly. But wouldn't that be a sight?" Mom takes another sip of coffee and I let out a giggle, wincing at the throbbing in my head. Mom doesn't even look up from the paper we still have delivered every morning.

"What? I like the crinkle of the newspaper when I turn the pages." She shrugged one day when Faith pointed out that she can subscribe online. Faith rolled her eyes at my mom's hopelessness to catch up on technology.

"They would think I've lost it for sure." Mom's words bring me back.

"What?" I ask, my brow furrows, and I wince again.

"Oh, nothing." Mom waves her hand. "I was just thinking how everyone at my office would react if I showed up in my robe and slippers. Actually, I rescheduled my appointments today. We—" She looks up from her paper and her eyes go huge.

"Good God, Fiona!" She jumps up and rushes to me. "What did you do to your forehead?"

"I'm fine. Just a little bump." I try to pull away from her hoping to hide it.

"That's not a little bump." Mom puts her hands on my shoulders, so I have to face her. "And it's black and purple."

"I was accidentally headbutted last night. No big deal."

"Huh, I say it's a big deal. That's going to look great Friday night." Mom drags out her sarcasm.

I grimace when I touch the knot on my forehead.

"Let's get some ice on it." Mom turns to get a baggie of ice.

"I did last night."

"Well, it needs more." Mom doesn't turn to look at me as she digs through the freezer for ice.

"Great." I throw my hands up in the air. "Just what I need. Maybe Jill can help me style my hair at my appointment tonight, so I can cover it up."

"Let's hope."

"Geesh. Does it really look that bad?" I place my hand on my forehead and turn to run to the bathroom to check it out.

"Holly crap. I have a horn coming out of my forehead." My eyes big in my reflection as I turn my head side to side while inspecting the damage.

"It's not that bad." But Mom's face is not convincing as she stands holding the bag of ice and leans on the bathroom door jam.

"Well, I wouldn't say it's a horn," she adds when I turn to stare at her.

"Okay, so take this ice and go lay back down for an hour or so." Mom pushes me in the direction of my room.

"What? Why?" I look over my shoulder as she keeps pushing. "Mom! I have school." I stop and turn to her so she will stop pushing me.

"Nope. Not today. That's what I was telling you before I saw your horn," Mom says and continues when she sees me start to argue. "I took the day off and called Dr. Saunders yesterday. She is getting us in today at 9:30."

"But I'm not sick. I don't need to go to the doctor." I stomp my foot on the ground like a five-year-old having a tantrum. "I need to go to school."

"Fiona, stop acting like a baby. It doesn't hurt to have a checkup. All the stress and guilt you are carrying can't be good for you. Plus, you hardly eat anymore."

"That's not true. I had pizza last night." Suddenly, I realize that I didn't eat last night with the fight and all. Mom doesn't need to know that though.

"Still, we are going to the doctor today and then we need to get you a dress for the dance Saturday."

"Well," I huff. "I didn't think about a dress for Saturday night's dance," I admit and cross my arms over my chest with a pout, and Mom tries to stifle a giggle. "That does seem to make up for making me go to the doctor when I don't need to go. Plus, I can hide my horn for one more day," I sigh. "But I'm not happy about this."

"Okay then." Mom giggles. "It's a date. And we will ask Dr. Saunders if she can do anything about your horn." And she walks away. "Take advantage of the morning and sleep in."

"Not going to argue with that."

***

Dr. Sanders is in her early thirties but still looks too young to be a doctor. Mom decided a few years ago when Faith turned fourteen that it was a good idea for the two of us to have a female doctor that we were comfortable talking with.

I shift uncomfortably in my seat thinking about the time Faith brought me here a few days after the Terrace Grove party. I was thankful then that Mom had decided to have us change to Dr. Saunders, but it still makes me squirm. Sitting in the waiting room it reminds me of that night.

Lyla and I were so excited to be attending our first high school party and one so well known as the one at Terrace Grove Campground End of the Year Bash.

As the beer flowed, Lyla and I drank. Both giggling and buzzed from the beer and the hottie kept flirting with me. When the guy Lyla had been eyeing finally came to talk to her, he asked her to be his cornhole partner for the next game. She giggled and gladly said yes.

I stayed where I was, leaning against the table for support and watched Lyla make her way to the cornhole games.

"Hey beautiful." I jumped and stumbled a little as the hottie sat on the table next to me. "What's your name."

I told him and we chatted about school, summer, and sports. Then he leaned in and kissed me. I couldn't believe it. This hot older guy kissed me. I melted.

"Let's go for a walk." He took my hand and we walked through the woods to the riverbank. He sat down and patted the ground next to him.

243

I stumbled as I sat down spilling my drink. He leaned in for another kiss.

"How's that?" he whispered.

"Mmm..." was all I could say, my head spinning. I felt warm and fuzzy all over.

It was sweet and gentle, and my head spun again when he laid me back on the grass. I looked up at the stars as they made circles.

I felt his hand at the hem of my dress, tugging at it. He pushed it up as his hand moved from my hip toward my chest. I reached for his hand to stop him, but he pushed my hand away.

"I—"

"Shh, shh, shh," he whispered as I try to push myself up and move from under him.

My mouth was dry. I couldn't breathe from the weight of his body and my head was spinning out of control.

I tried to say no, but it came out mumble from under his mouth. My stomach rolled and I closed my eyes. He continued kissing my neck and I felt his hand under my bra.

I tried pushing him away, but I was weaker and drunk. I sucked in a breath of air and tried to scream, but he covered my mouth with his hand.

"No need to scream," he whispered. "We're friends, right?" His hand was on my thigh, and he tugged at my underwear.

I was pinned under him. I couldn't get away. I couldn't vocalize my scream. The stars were no longer happily spinning; the sky was a blur.

When he was done, he stood up and zipped up his pants. He reached out a hand to help me up. I didn't take it. I sat up on my own, head still spinning, my stomach rolled, and I looked away from him. "Whatever," he grumbled. "You might want to fix your hair before you go back." He turned to walk away, then turned back. "No one needs to know Fiona." Then he disappeared into the trees.

I waited as long as I could, hoping he was out of ear shot. I pushed myself up to my knees, leaned over and emptied the contents of my stomach.

I heard his voice, "no one needs to know" over and over, like it was branded into my memory as I cried myself to sleep that night.

Faith realized almost immediately that something wasn't right and insisted I tell her. Two days after the party, I finally gave in and sobbed as I told her what happened. I said that I thought I wanted to have sex with him, but it was a mistake. I didn't want her to be mad about what really happened. I wasn't sure at the time what had happened, but I didn't want anyone making a big deal out of it. She insisted she needed take me to the doctor to get tested, so we did.

A few days later, Mom got the call about the test results. That's when shit hit the fan as my grandma used to say and was the day I lost my mom's trust.

"Fiona." The nurse's voice snaps me back to the present, saving me from spiraling out of control. I let out a breath and turn to Mom.

"You coming with me?" I ask as I get up from my chair. Normally she doesn't come in the room with me anymore but since this was her idea, I figured she would.

"No, she knows my concerns. I want you to feel comfortable talking with her."

I give my mom a little thank you smile and follow the nurse through the door.

"Good morning Fiona. How are you?" the nurse asks.

"I'm good thanks." I ball my fist up as I lie through my teeth, then I see the nurses eyes go wide.

"What's going on with your forehead? I don't have that in the note from your mom's call yesterday." The nurse looks back through my chart.

"I got headbutted by a big butthead last night." I roll my eyes as I walk through the door.

"Yikes. Was this an accident?" She looks back over her shoulder as we walk down the hall.

"Yes. But the fight that I was trying to break up wasn't. This is what I get for getting involved."

"Well, at least you tried to help." She pats my shoulder.

"Not sure it was worth it," I continue and hear the nurse giggle.

"Okay, I need you to step on the scale." The nurse redirects me.

"Ugh." I roll my eyes again.

"I know, no one likes this part." The nurse gives the scale a few seconds to respond. "Are you trying to lose weight? Cause you don't need to if you are." She glances up at me from my chart.

"No, I'm not, just had a lot going on lately." I look away trying to mask my eyes.

"Well, you're down about six pounds from your last visit, and trust me, you didn't have that much to lose. Okay, let's go into room three." She points in the direction of the room, and I begin walking ahead of her.

In the room the nurse checks out my visible accident scar and asks me the gauntlet of questions before Dr. Saunders comes in. I answer them honestly as there is no reason to lie. They can read my chart and have seen me at my worst. But I always wonder what they are thinking.

"Dr. Saunders will be in in a minute." The nurse turns and leaves the room.

"Thanks."

The knock on the door comes less than a minute later when Dr. Saunders peeks her head through the door. "Hi Fiona, how are we doing today?" She asks with a bright smile. Then she sees the horn and walks right to it.

"Did this just happen?" she says as she takes a long look.

"It happened last night. Accident. Well, the fight wasn't but me being headbutted while trying to break it up was." I try to keep my voice calm, so I take a deep breath and let it out.

"I see." She sits down on her stool across from me. "So, I know why your mom scheduled this appointment, but why don't you tell me what's going on."

I look to the window trying to keep my composure. I feel the sting of my eyes threatening to betray me, so I take another deep breath and share my guilt over Faith and Ella and that I just learned that Ella's missing case is connected to the night I can't remember. I don't go into detail about Lyla, Sara, Jessica, or Sam, I just can't. Besides, what good would it do? When I finally have nothing left to say, I sheepishly turn back to Dr. Saunders who silently staring at me.

"Wow," Dr. Sanders' voice is soft. "That is a lot to take in. No wonder you're stressed." Dr. Saunders asks a few more questions but then she asks the big one.

"Fiona, I can figure from all we talked about how you are feeling so let me ask you this, what do you want?"

"What do you mean?" I look to her eyes and blink a few times.

"Well, if you could change things right now, what would you change? What do you want?" Dr. Saunders asks.

I clench my fists up so the arm cuffs of my PINK sweatshirt swallow up my hands. Now if they would just swallow the rest of me.

My eyes bulge. "To make this all go away and go back to the way it was before all...this..." My voices breaks as I wave my handless arms around and I gulp back a sob.

"So, you mean like for none of this to have happened?" She raises her eyebrows.

"Yes! Exactly." I wipe away the tears with the cuff of my sweatshirt.

"Okay, that helps me know where we need to start. Let me get your mom."

A minute later, my mom follows Dr. Saunders back to the exam room. She enters with a smile to my relief as I'm wiping away my tears.

"So, Mrs. DeWitt. Fiona and I had a great talk today and here's what I'm recommending going forward. I do think Fiona will benefit from therapy. Fiona is not in denial about anything that has happened,

249

but she is struggling to accept what has happened and how to handle it. In therapy she will get tools to help her work through her emotions and help her accept and move forward with what's happened."

Dr. Saunders turns to me.

"Fiona, as soon as you accept that things will never go back to the way they were, you'll be able to move forward. That does not mean that things won't be okay or get better with Faith and Ella. But the events that have taken place will always be there. In therapy you will learn how to move forward with your life. How does that sound?"

I wipe away tears and nod, not sure what else to do.

"I will have my nurse schedule your therapy sessions and get the paperwork through your insurance. Now, aside from the weight loss, your vitals are good. So, I want to see you back in three weeks, and I want you to track your meals. I'm not so much concerned with the food you eat at this time, I'm more concerned that you are eating three times per day. If you have a hamburger and fries for dinner, just write that down. Your goal is to eat something at each meal. Of course, the healthier the better. But *just eat!*"

"Got it," I sigh with a nod.

"All right, I will get you some meal tracking forms, but there are a few apps on your phone you can use if you prefer. Just look up meal tracker apps. Do you have any questions for me?" Dr. Saunders looks from me to Mom and back. We both shake out head no. "Okay, we are all set, we will call with your therapy information."

"Thank you, Dr. Saunders," Mom says and shakes her hand.

"Thanks," I add not as happy with the outcome. Not sure I know what a happy outcome would be.

"Oh," Dr. Saunders turns back to us before leaving the room. "Continue to ice that forehead for the next 24 – 48 hours. Twenty minutes on, twenty minutes off. NSAIDS for the pain."

"Okay," I say with a nod, and we make our way out of the office.

"That wasn't so bad now, was it?" Mom asks as she looks at me over the hood of her SUV.

"I don't need to go to therapy, Mom. Please don't make me do this. I'm fine," I beg with a little whine.

"Fiona Renee, this is for your own good. No one has to know either." Mom's words are clear. She isn't changing her mind, and this is yet again a secret from the rest of the world. Just like the Terrace Grove party.

"Fine. But we still get to go shopping, right?" I look at Mom across the car before I climb in the passenger's seat.

"Yes. We are shopping," Mom confirms with an exasperated sigh and a giggle.

In the passenger's seat I check my phone for any new updates. I have a text from Avery: "skippin w langford?"

What? I text back: "hell no! PISSED at him"

But I can't help wondering why she would think that. Then I hear my phone beep. Avery again: "thats the word on the street since ur both gone 2day"

I text back: "WTF? im with mom"

I immediately text Sam: "u skipped?"

Avery text back: "dont worry about it u know how everyone spills tea"

Ugh...I text: "bet jessica and sara are loving it"

Avery text: "just jealous bitches post a selfie w ur mom and location"

"k" I drop my phone to my lap annoyed about the latest tea. My phone beeps again, this time Sam: "yep come 2 my house"

Ugh! I punch the screen hard on my phone: "no"

Another beep and it's from Sam: "come on fi"

My anger flares when I think about last night: "wth happened last night?"

By this time, we pull into my favorite burger joint, my stomach growls and I remember that I haven't eaten anything since lunch yesterday. The hostess seats us in a booth by the windows and the server takes our drink order. I'm lost in thought about Sam skipping and the latest rumor about me. I'm sure Sam doesn't mind.

My thoughts are interrupted by the beep of my cell. This time it's Jace: "wtf fiona? skipping w langford"

Of course, Jace heard about it. My heart sinks and I close my eyes. Then I type: "no, swear, dr appt and now w mom for lunch and shopping"

Another beep comes in from Jace: "doesnt matter to me but u should know everyones spillin"

I take a breath and release it: "yeah avery just text me no idea he skipped till just now"

Our server brings our drinks and takes our orders and I check my phone again for a response from Jace, but there's nothing.

"Okay, this is our day so phones off. That includes mine too." Mom powers down her phone. "Besides, I'm sure all that texting is what started all your problems in the first place."

"What?" I drop my hands on the table, my phone still between my fingers and stare at my mom who is still looking at her phone.

"Well, I just mean that what you put out there on social media, text, and on the internet never goes away. And it is easy for your words to be taken out of context. That's probably how all this started with the

Jessica thing." Mom looks up at me unapologetically as she shoves her phone in her Michael Khors purse.

"Fine," I add through gritted teeth. I turn my cell off and put it in my pocket.

Lunch is delicious and I'm starving. I finish everything on my plate. Once Mom drops the *it's all your fault* attitude, lunch isn't so bad, and Mom starts talking about dresses. Maybe she feels some relief from taking me to the doctor. Whatever it is, it's nice for a change.

At the mall we hit up several stores but it's not until what must be the 10th store that I find a dress I like, and I think Dad will approve.

I step out of the dressing room in a burgundy V-neck sleeveless A-line dress with a short tulle skirt and sequined beaded bodice. The beading carries onto the straps of the dress and creates finger like projections of beading through the pleats on the waist and into the tulle skirt in the same rich burgundy color.

"Oh, Fiona. That dress is beautiful on you," Mom gushes.

"Thanks, Mom. I really like it. But is it too red for the winter formal?" I turn to look in the mirror.

"Oh, I don't think that matters. Besides, you are wearing the blue formal Friday night, right?"

"Yes. That reminds me, I need to take that to the cleaners in Brookston when we get home."

"You haven't done that already? You better hope they can get it done by Thursday evening. Nothing like waiting till the last-minute, Fiona."

I feel the heat rise in my cheeks and I bite my lip to keep my mouth shut.

"Okay, let's see the second one." But I am already turned away and walking to the dressing room.

I take one last look mirror at this beautiful dress. It's not my style but I am drawn to it.

The second dress is a two-toned sequined beaded dress that transitions from silver on the top to ice blue on the bottom and stops two inches above the knee. Below the waist of the dress, the silver and ice blue begin to blend together then separate with scatterings of the opposite color throughout the silver top and ice blue bottom. The illusion neckline is straight across with the sheer layer creating long sleeves scattered with silver stones and a few ice blue. It sparkles everywhere.

"Wow." Mom steps back and covers her mouth with her hand.

"Will you zip this up?" I turn around, move my hair out of her way and look up to the mirror when she is done.

"I just don't know, Fiona. I love them both. They are completely different." Mom is standing behind me, looking over my shoulder at my reflection in the mirror and for the first time, I see the resemblance between me and my mom. I was always so positive I looked like Dad, I never realized I have Mom's facial structure.

"I know. I don't know which one I want," I sigh.

"Maybe you should wear one Friday night and the other Saturday night," Mom says but I'm pretty sure she is joking.

"I kinda feel like I should wear a long dress Friday. Plus, by wearing Faith's dress, it's like she is with me in a way."

"Have you tried it on?" Mom's eyes lock on mine in the mirror.

"Ah, no. I didn't," I mumble.

"Faith is taller than you, it might not fit. It's probably too late to get it altered." Mom is standing behind me, I see tears in her reflection in the mirror despite her smile. I don't know what to say so I just nod.

"Oh, let's get a picture together." I grab my phone out of my coat and wait for it to power up. I turn to face the mirror; Mom wraps both arms around me and places her hands on my shoulders and tilts her head toward mine.

I open Instagram and upload the picture with the caption: "Mom and me day! #dressshopping #winterformal #can'tdecide"

And click, share. *There. That should take care of the rumors.*

"Okay Mom, which one?" I turn to her and wait.

"Oh, I don't know. They are both beautiful, but I think the burgundy dress really makes a statement on you. It looks great with your hair and skin. However, the silver and blue dress is amazing. The colors go with the winter formal theme, but you are wearing a blue dress on Friday. And even though the blue dress has sleeves, they are sheer so that doesn't do any good in this cold weather."

"You're not helping." I roll my eyes and throw my hands up.

"Okay, let me take a picture of you in this dress and then we will take a picture of the red one and you can send them to Lyla."

"I think I will send them to Avery."

"Still no luck with you and Lyla?" Mom looks up from her phone.

"I haven't even tried to talk to her. She is always with Sara or Shelby and now Jessica." I look to my feet and try to imagine what shoes I would look best.

"You must have really pissed her off."

I flinch at my mom's words, my eyes going wide. "Smile," Mom adds as she snaps the picture. The blood drains from my face and I blink several times trying to recover.

"Are you kidding me?" I slap my hands on my hips and shift my weight to my left hip.

"What? I was just taking a practice," Mom justifies while still playing with her camera.

"It's not about the picture, Mom," I snap at her.

"I don't know why you are taking this tone with me Fiona—"

"Oh really? You can't understand why I am angry at you?"

"Fiona! This is not the time or place, young lady. Now put the other dress on and drop the attitude." Mom spins me around, moves my hair out of the way and unzips my dress.

"Oh! I think it is. Almost every comment out of your mouth has been an attack on me—"

"It has not been an attack on you," Mom protests cutting me off.

"Really? 'Your texting is probably how all this started' or 'I'm sure you ran your mouth' or just now when talking about Lyla, you said, 'you must have really pissed her off.' Like it was all my fault. Have you ever considered that there are two sides to this story? Maybe it's not just what I did, Mom." I see the surprise register on her face. "Maybe I tried to talk to her, to apologize for what I mistakenly said. Maybe I never apologized for not calling her back the night of the accident when she was supposed to go with us. I know she is mad and hurt about it, but the truth is…the truth is I am relieved that she wasn't with us that night. I am so thankful that I didn't call her back and we didn't go pick her up to go shopping as we had planned. It's bad enough that…"

"I—you are right. I didn't know," Mom says softly shaking her head and crosses her arms over her chest.

"No, you didn't. You just assume the worst from me." My voice louder than I intend for it to be.

"I do not, Fiona." Mom brings her hand to chest. "But you have to admit, this all looks a bit one-sided—"

"Are you kidding me right now?" I grab my head in my hands like I'm trying to prevent it from exploding. "When are you going to accept that I am not Faith? I'm not your perfect little Fay!" I throw my arms out and stomp my foot.

"I know that! I don't want you to be Faith. What in the world every gave you that idea?"

"Seriously? Umm, every time you compare me to her. Grades, test scores, sports, cheerleading. 'Why aren't you class president like Faith is, Fiona?' or 'Faith already has her homework done. What's taking you so long, Fiona?' I am trying my best but honestly, I don't even know who I am anymore! Or who I ever was!"

I feel the tears pooling in my eyes and I fight back a sob with a breath. My mom's eyes wide with shock.

"I've spent my entire life walking in Faith's footsteps, trying to fill her shoes. To be loved like Faith, popular like Faith, as smart as Faith, to be respected by my teachers and coaches like Faith, but what about

259

me? When do I get to just be Fiona?" I smack my chest with my hand, and I feel the heat in my face.

"What do you mean, Fiona? You *are* Fiona." Mom frowns and her brow furrows.

"Yes, but am I this version of me only because I am Faith little sister? I've tried so hard to live up to her name and I keep failing—"

"I wouldn't call this failing Fiona; you are trying to find your way." Mom shakes her head. "I never realized this is how you felt, I thought you loved being—"

"I do! I do love being Faith's sister." A tear rolls down my cheek, my voice is small. "But I just, sometimes I want to be Fiona. Just Fiona. Not 'Fiona, the next Faith,' cause I'm not. I can't live up to that. I need to find my way, which means making mistakes and screwing up. But I need to be able to do that without being constantly compared to Faith."

I keep my eyes on the ground, afraid to look at my mom. But after a long moment of silence, I hear my mom's voice, weak and sad. I look up through my eyelashes while keeping my head down.

"Okay, well, I get that, and I have somethings to work on. I didn't mean to…I just want the best for you. For you both." My mom brings her hand to her face and runs her fingers over her forehead, then wraps her arms around her shoulders like she is trying to protect herself against the cold.

"Mom, I know you didn't, and I know you love me. I don't believe you did it on purpose or meant to hurt me. But it does hurt, I just want you to love and accept me for me. Mistakes, weakness, and all. Do you realize that every adult in my school that knows Faith compares me to her? And I know I don't live up to their expectations. I know they don't mean to either, but I just feel like a disappointment. Especially lately."

"Oh, honey. You *are not* a disappointment. And I do love you and you're right." Mom nods her head. "Maybe I should talk to Dr. Saunders about both of us going to therapy. Maybe we can work on this together." Mom turns to me, and I raise my eyes to meet hers.

"Really? You would do that for me?" My heart warms at my mom's offer.

"Of course, I would. And I probably should have been seeing a therapist this whole time too. I am sure there are some tools that could help me handle all this better. But I really think you should ask Lyla to spend some time with you, so you can work things out." Mom watches me a few seconds before continuing. "I miss her, and I know you do too. We are missing Ella. Faith isn't Faith right now, it's hard to not having Lyla around too, isn't it?"

I nod, feeling the tears flooding the dam and breaking free as I fall into Mom's embrace.

I'm not sure how much time passes or how many people wonder what's wrong with the crazy chick, but Mom stands there holding me. The tears finally slow, and the sobs quiet but Mom is still holding me. I lift my head to wipe my face. Mom brushes my hair away and hands me a tissue, then gives me a kiss on my forehead.

"I'm sorry, Fiona. I've just been so lost in my own grief that I never considered that there was more to it. I didn't know Lyla was supposed to go with you that night. But I guess I shouldn't be surprised. You four are inseparable." Mom shakes her head and I catch her wince as she realizes her words. "But that is why you need to talk to Lyla. Away from school. Away from other students. On neutral ground so to speak." Mom lifts my chin up with her finger. "Promise me you will think about what I've said."

"Okay," I nod.

"Now, let's get your dress and get out of here. You need to get Faith's dress to the cleaners."

I change out of the dress and back into my joggers that match my PINK sweatshirt. I place the dress back on the rack and open the door to find Mom standing there with her camera pointed at me.

While driving back from the mall, Mom takes a few calls, so I figure it's safe to get my phone out. I find a text from Avery saying she wants to see pics of the dress, but I don't feel like telling her the story. Still no text from Jace, I'll deal with that when I get home, just can't face it now. But there are three texts from Sam: "where r u"

"need my fi"

"call me"

My heart skips a beat but then I think of Jace. He is such a great guy. Funny, caring and I can't deny that he does look damn good in a cowboy hat. Plus, I've already asked him to be my escort and I'm not doing that to him.

I drop the phone in my lap and look out the passenger's window, letting my mind race. I barely notice we are in the driveway until Mom shuts the engine off.

"Thanks for the dress and lunch, Mom." I climb out of the SUV and get the dress from the back seat.

"Well, I just hope you are happy with the dress," Mom adds mindlessly. Her mind is already on work.

"I am." I climb the steps to the front door. Mom is following me but then stops at the bottom of the steps.

"Ah, I need to get to the office. I have an offer on the Delmont Dr. property coming in. And you need to get that dress to the cleaners and

263

try to catch up on any homework you have from today. I'm sure your teachers can send you your assignments online."

"Got it," I call over my shoulder. I don't bother explaining that all my assignments are online.

Mom doesn't follow me in the house. She turns back to her SUV and opens the door.

"Oh, tell Sydney to run my card number for your hair, Fiona," Mom calls.

"You can Venmo it you know!" I shout to Mom, which gets me a look like yeah right. I giggle as I push my key in the lock and turn the tumbler.

"And ask her how you can cover your…horn." Mom slams her door and starts her engine.

I wince at the remembrance of my horn. I check the bathroom mirror after hanging up my dress. Yep, still there.

With a sigh, I turn to enter Faith's room and walk to her closet without looking around.

Sometimes I go in her room and lay on her bed, just to be close to her. To try and remember anything to help her and Ella. But right now, I need to get her dress to the cleaners. She keeps her formal dresses to the back left of her closet. There are so many formals; at least six. One for each year of prom, which for Faith was all four years, and then one for junior and senior winter court.

I peek in the bag I'm sure is the royal blue dress and take it off the rack. I drape it over my arm and walk back to my room.

Merida stretches out for a belly scratchin', then I check her water before I leave. I give her belly one last rub, place the garment bag over my arm and turn to walk out the door.

The Brookston Cleaners has been in business long before I was born and is owned by the Ressler family. Kellan Ressler is a year older than me, and his sister graduated with Faith.

I walk into the cleaners and am reminded that Jessica works here on nights and weekends when I see her employee picture on the wall along with a few other classmates.

At the desk I ring the bell since no one is out front.

"Fiona, Hi. I don't have extra help during the day," Karen Ressler apologizes as she comes to the front. "Shouldn't you be in school?"

"Yeah, had a doctor's appointment and I just got back. Needed to get this dress in ASAP."

"Is this for your mom again?" Karen asks as most of what I drop off is for Mom or Dad, not me.

"No, actually this is Faith's dress. I just need to get it pressed."

"How is she doing?" Karen looks up over her reading glasses.

"Ah, better. She is showing signs of improvement but not completely responsive if that makes any sense. Still a long way to go."

"I'm sure, but it sounds hopeful. So, what are you doing with the dress?" Karen pauses to wait for my response, holding the garment bag up by the hanger.

"I am wearing it Friday night for the Winter Court Crowning. I just thought it would be nice to have Faith with me, ya know?"

"Isn't that sweet. And congratulations." Karen types on the computer keyboard, then prints out a pick-up slip for me. "Okay, here is your ticket, I have it under your name, and I will make sure it is ready for you to pick up tomorrow night."

"Sounds great. Thank you." I turn to walk out the door.

Chapter 11

After leaving the dry cleaners, I can't help thinking about Sam's text.

Why did he skip today? Is he really hurt by Jace and me or is he just jealous that I wouldn't ask him to be my escort? Why would he care after what he did to me? Maybe he really is hurt that I chose Jace. Maybe he does still love me.

My mind jumps to the day our freshman year when Sara and Neveah confronted me about Sam.

"OMG Fiona. We think you and Sam would be perfect together," Sara said when she slid into the seat next to me.

"What? Sam? Like dating?" I laughed at the suggestion. I dipped another limp French fry into my ketchup.

"Yeah, think about it. The big shot football player and the cheerleader?" Neveah smiled at me and raised her eyebrows waiting for a response.

"Wait, who's 'we'?" I stopped eating and looked up to her and back to Sara.

"Well, we were waiting on our ride after the freshman cheer practice yesterday and several of the players came out of the locker room. You know, we were all just hanging and chatting, Sara started

teasing Sam about why he and Dominique broke up, Jada asked him who he likes. We couldn't get anything out of him, but Sara suggested that the homecoming couple should date."

"Seriously? Because we are on court together?" I questioned and took another bite of the spicy chicken sandwich. Sure, I thought Sam was cute, but so did everyone else. But I never thought of him as a boyfriend.

"Ah, you don't see it?" Neveah grabbed my arm from across the table. "Not because you are on court together but because you are perfect for each other."

"How? I really don't know Sam that well. I mean, sure we have gone to school together forever, but—"

"But what? You're both are super talented and smart, and he is hot. You're basically already each other's date for the homecoming dance. And you aren't dating anyone right? What more is there?" Neveah said then started bouncing in her seat. Sara was squeaking and clapping her hands next to her. I looked from Sara back to Neveah wondering if they know something I didn't but couldn't help but smile at their enthusiasm.

By the end of the homecoming dance, Sam and I were a couple. It was that simple.

We talked every night, walked to and from classes together. We just seemed to fit. I became the person he turned to when things got rough at home. And for me, he was the only person besides Lyla that knew my insecurities and inferiority complex when it came to Faith. We talked for hours about everything and hung out when we could.

Sam was the first person I confided in when I got a C+ on the English exam that I had studied my ass off for. He was so sweet about it.

"Fiona, it's only one test and you know you are smart."

"No, I'm not. Not like Faith."

"Who cares about Faith? I know you love her and all, but you shouldn't be comparing yourself to her. She is her own person just as you are. And frankly, I love you more so…"

"That's sweet. Just wish my parents could see that," I sighed.

"Parents suck. I'm proud of you. That test was really hard. You have nothing to feel bad about. Just think how bad you would have done if you hadn't studied at all."

I couldn't help but laugh. "Sometimes I wonder why I bother studying at all. I might even do better."

"That's not the answer," Sam scolded. "Then you wouldn't get into college. I see big things in your future, Fiona DeWitt. Big things."

"Like what?" My heart soared that he thought of my future.

269

"I don't know yet, but you aren't someone who settles for less, so I know they are going to be big," Sam added with a nod.

I giggled at his confidence.

"VIP. Very Important Person. Don't know why I'm important but I am." I shrugged and laughed out loud.

Sam laughed. "I like that. We're a couple of VIP's. Together we are unstoppable," Sam added.

Without even realizing it, I miss my turn to go home and find myself pulling into Sam's driveway. Feels just like old times. I jump out of my Jeep and look up to see Sam standing at the door in a pair of basketball shorts, no shirt, and a big smile on his face.

"I knew you'd come." His smug grin annoying me a little. I roll my eyes.

"Wow. A bit cocky, aren't we?" I stop at the door. Place my hands on my hips and shift my weight to one hip.

"Not at all. I just know you, Fi." His lips turn to a devilish grin. "How was your doctor's appointment? Are you sick?"

"No, Mom just felt I needed to get a check-up. With everything going one, she is worried." I shake my head and shrug.

"How's Faith?"

"Better."

"That's good." But when Sam smiles, the cut on his lip from the fight last night breaks open and starts bleeding. "Shit."

He rushes to the sink in the kitchen to rinse off the blood. I get a washcloth from the bathroom and a few ice cubes from the freezer.

"Sit down on the couch." I wave my hand to the living room. "Jace got your lip good."

"Lucky shot," Sam quips.

I take a seat on the couch next to Sam facing him and wrap the ice in the washcloth. Sam winces as I place the ice on his lip.

"What the hell happened last night? Jace and I are just friends." I ease up on the pressure on Sam's lip.

"Not if he has anything to say about it." Sam's eyes meet mine. "Fiona, trust me. He doesn't want to be just friends."

"And that's for me to decide. Not you." I hold his stare.

Sam blinks and pushes the ice away.

"Look, I don't know what is going on with Jace and me, right now we are just friends, and I am not sure that I am ready for anything more. But if I am, it's none of your business."

Storm clouds roll though those blue-green eyes. Sam raises his hand to my forehead gently sweeping my hair out of my eyes and off my face.

"Holy shit, Fiona. Your forehead." Sam sits up and puts his hands on the sides of my face and tilts my head to get a better look.

I pull my head out of his hands and shake my hair back over my horn.

"What happened to your forehead?" Sam leans back again, dropping his hands to the couch as his forehead creases.

"You don't remember?" I watch him closely.

"What? Is that from last night?" Sam's face grows pale and eyes wide.

"Um yeah, you headbutted me, ass." I look away from Sam to the ice in the washcloth for a few seconds.

"I didn't know what I hit. It was you? I thought maybe it was Simmons. And you know he has a hard head, so I wasn't worried."

"Nope, I'm the lucky one." I raise my hand with the washcloth filled with ice and the ice rattles.

"I'm sorry. I didn't mean to hurt you. Does it hurt?" Sam rubs his thumb over my horn as lightly as possible and I close my eyes to avoid wincing at his touch.

"Does your lip hurt?" My attitude slips out.

"Stupid question." Sam sits up, brushes the hair from my forehead and places a very gentle kiss on my horn. I brace myself for pain, but the kiss is so light, I barely feel it.

He continues the kisses along my forehead and down my cheek until his lips meet mine. He pulls away with a wince.

"Did I hurt your lip?" I bite my lip and raise my eyebrows. I can't hide my smirk.

"Totally worth it." He places a finger under my chin pulling me in for another kiss.

His hands run down my arms to my waist, picking me up and places me on his lap. He wraps his arms around me and deepens the kiss.

Absent mindedly, I place my hand on his shoulders for balance. As I fall deeper into the kiss, my free hand wrapping around his neck, and I grab a handful of hair. Our bodies press together, and I'm lost in our kiss. Suddenly Sam pulls away.

"What's wrong?" I frown searching Sam's face. "Your lip?" I look at his swollen bottom lip.

"Nothing." He looks in my eyes. "I know you aren't ready, and I don't want to pressure you."

I let out a breath with a shiver, Sam lowers his forehead gently to mine and we sit silently in this embrace. I should tell him about Terrace Grove. That might help him understand. But he will want to know who it was and that I cannot tell him.

"I-I...I should go. I have a hair appointment at 4:00. Let's hope she can hide my horn," I grumble. Sam lets out a low laugh.

"You got a horn." Sam laughs harder.

"Stop it!" I laugh and punch his shoulder. "It's not funny."

Sam's laugh fades but his smile stays intact.

I get up from the couch, Sam follows me to the door taking my hand and turns me around for one more kiss. I almost tell him I want to stay.

"Bye Sam." I put my hand up to stop his advance.

"Fi." He kisses my hand before releasing it.

Lightheaded, I turn and walk out the door and climb into my Jeep. Sam is still watching me from the glass door. I pull to the end of his driveway and stop as a black car with tinted windows rolls by. I pull out behind the car and follow it back into Brookston and watch the car turn off in the direction of my house.

I continue to Studio B and find a spot in the parking lot and lean my head back on the headrest. I sit there for a few minutes since I'm early. When I climb out of my Jeep, I see the same black car out of the corner of my eye drive past.

***

"Hi Fiona, you're early," Sydney greets me at the counter.

"Yeah, I need to look though some styles. Take your time."

"Okay, I am a little ahead of schedule. I'll grab you when I'm ready.

I take out my phone I haven't checked in a while, I see a few text from friends, Takiesha asking if I am okay. Avery giving me the latest updates about the day I am missing. And text from Jace: "sorry i overreacted. u and sam r none of my biz just think he is an ass and u deserve better"

I start texting back but what do I say? 'You're right Jace. None of your business'? Or, 'you're not overreacting, just made out with him'? How about, 'he really is a good guy but yeah, can be an ass'?

Ugh. Everything is so messed up.

My stomach rolls trying to figure out what to say, so I just don't respond.

"All right, Fiona, ready for ya." I glance up from my phone to see Sydney smiling at me. "Congratulations by the way. I saw in the paper that you're on Winter Court."

We talk about my hair options, how to cover my horn and what Sydney recommends for color. Sydney pulls up a picture on her iPad. It has a deeper red for the low lights and icy blond for the high lights. I decided to go with it before I chicken out. When she is finished, I look in the mirror amazed at my hair. It's definitely not what I would normally do but I love it.

"Hi Fi-Fi." Dad takes a second look and askes, "What happened to your hair?"

"You don't like it?" I stop in my tracks, take a piece of hair in my hand and looking down at it.

"I didn't say that. But it's different." Dad smiles and turns back to his paperwork.

"Well, at least it covers your forehead." Mom nods and looks back to Faith.

"Right. I wasn't into the red, but Sydney showed me a picture and assured me it would not be orange."

"So, you like it?" Dad looks up from the report his is studying.

"I do. I really do. I mean it's different, so I have to get used to it, but—"

"Then that's all that matters." Mom nods and looks to Dad.

"So, any news on Faith?" I walk to the bed and take a seat next to Faith and across from Mom. "Hi Fay. I've missed you."

"No, the doctor said everything still looks the same. It's just a waiting game. But her cuts and bruises are healing, and swelling is going down a little each day." Mom nods and brushes a curl away from Faith's face.

"That's good," I admit but Avery's comment about Faith not looking like Faith flutters through my mind. She's right, Faith still doesn't look like my sister.

"Did you get the dress to the cleaners?" Mom asks, leaning back in her chair, letting Faith's hand rest on the bed.

"Yes, I did. It will be ready tomorrow night."

"Are you sure you don't want to wear your new dress tomorrow night?" Mom asks.

"Wait a minute." Dad lowers the paper in his hand and sits up in his chair leaning to one side. "I did not approve a new dress. I only approved Faith's dress."

"D-A-D... Not again." I roll my eyes and throw myself back in the chair. But both Mom and Dad are giggling now.

"That's enough, Robert," Mom scolds while giggling. "He is giving you a hard time Fi. I already showed him the dress and promised that the dress is not too short," Mom explains, and I release a sigh of relief. "So, what shoes are you going to wear?"

"Well, when I got the dress from Faith's closet, I picked up her nude stilettos and then a strappy silver pair with a thicker heel. Something she must have bought at school; I've never seen them."

"Oh, yeah. She called asking me if she could get a new dress and shoes for a formal she went to. I bet those are them."

"I didn't know she went to a formal." I frown at my sister lying in the hospital bed. This is something she should have shared with me.

"I don't think it was a big deal. A friend of hers asked her to go. Just friends." Mom shrugs. "You know Faith, she is picky about dating."

"I liked that she never dated much in school," Dad chimes in looking over the top of his papers at me. "But I did miss giving boys the what for."

"Not that Faith couldn't have had her pick," Mom adds. "There were always boys hanging around, asking her out. She just didn't like any of them I guess."

I think back to when Myles Kemper asked her out last year. After a few dates, she finally told him that he was a nice guy, but she just didn't want a boyfriend. I thought he was gorge and couldn't believe she didn't what to date him. He was a star athlete and star student when he graduated East Brooke two years before and is premed at Indiana. What else can you ask for?

I push away the wonder about Myles Kemper and focus on Winter Court.

"Anyway, I like the shoe but haven't tried them on. They will probably be too big, but I can always stuff tissues in the stilettoes I guess."

"What about those sheer stilettos with the crystals on them you wore last summer for your cousin Gwen's wedding?" Mom asks.

"Oh, yeah. I forgot about those. They will be perfect with Faith's dress." I turn to Faith. "Hear that Faith? I don't have to wear your stinky shoes after all."

"You look tired, Fi." Dad tilts his head as he shuffles his papers back into his briefcase.

"Yeah. It's been a long day. And I'm getting a little nervous about Friday." I fight off a yawn.

"That's to be expected. Go on home, Fi. Get some sleep," Dad protests. "We will be home in a little bit." Dad leans over and takes Mom's hand in his giving it a squeeze. I look to Mom who nods in agreement.

"All right. I will take you up on that." I yawn again as I stand up and stretch a little before I move.

"Be careful going home, Fi," Mom adds as I turn to Faith.

"Okay." I take Faith's hand and give it a squeeze. "Come back soon, Faith."

I leave Faith's room and turn to walk to the elevator noticing the corridor is empty. A shiver runs down my spine. I'm not alone.

I turn to look over my shoulder and see the door swing shut to the stairwell at the end of the hall. I shiver again and scurry to the elevator repeatedly pressing the down arrow while glancing over my shoulder and back down the hall. No one there.

"Come on, come on, come on."

I exit the hospital, cell in hand, and search the parking lot for any sign of life. The lot is mostly empty and eerily quiet. Once in my Jeep, I lock the doors, close my eyes and let out my breath.

"Fiona, you are being ridiculous. Do you actually think someone is following you?" I scold myself. "Get it together."

Just then, I hear the roar of the engine behind me, and I look in the rear-view mirror to see a black car role past me in the parking lot.

My blood runs cold, and my hands freeze on the steering wheel. I can't see anything behind that dark tint, but that is definitely the same car I saw today in Brookston.

I watch as the car pulls out of the parking garage. I quickly reach for my phone and fumble it, dropping it on the floor.

"Shit!" I search the floor below me and feel the edge of the phone and barely get my fingers on it. There, I got it but as I open my camera,

I'm too late. The car peels off and speeds out of the parking lot. It's gone.

Suddenly I am back in Faith's car, and we are driving on a crowded side street, I assume close to SWU which is lined with parked cars.

"Keep your eyes open for a spot, Fiona," Faith said to me. "I don't want to park too far away."

I watched out the window as we slowly passed parked cars. A shiny black car parked under the light grabbed my attention. A new model Charger with black wheels and tinted windows.

I shake my head at the memory. I need to find out if the car I saw today is the same one parked at the SWU party we went to.

Chapter 12

"Ahh…" I step out the front door, throw my head back and find peace in the light falling snow landing on my skin.

I ask my phone for a weather update.

"One to two inches of snow this morning. Possibility of snow showers through the day Friday with a big front moving in late Saturday evening into Sunday bringing a potential of three to five inches."

At the end of the driveway, I stop and look toward the cul-de-sac hoping to see the black car, but it's not there. I let out a sigh to calm my nerves, until I remember that I have to face Jace today.

The snow begins to cover the roads, so I shift into 4-wheel drive. *Just breathe, Fiona. Take in the beauty of the drive.* The untouched snow-covered yards. Driveways and roads not plowed. The kids waiting for the bus making snow angels while Mom yells out the door telling them to get out of the snow.

A smile creeps on my face at the memory of Faith, and me making snow angles in the front yard while we waited for the bus.

"You girls stay out of the snow," Dad called as we walked out the door.

"Wait till he shuts the door," Faith whispered and glanced over her shoulder to see that he was gone.

"All clear." Faith tossed her backpack aside, jumped as far as she could out to a fresh patch of snow and fell backward giggling. I followed her lead.

"Dad is going to be mad," I laughed.

"You only live once Fi." The beep of the bus startled us, and we both jumped up screaming.

"I told you girls to stay out of the snow," Dad yelled from the front door. I looked over my shoulder and saw my dad trying to act mad, but he couldn't hold back his smile.

"Bye Dad. Love you!" We blew him a kiss and he shook his head and closed the door. Faith and I scurried to the bus, giggling the entire way.

"Fiona!"

I turn as I step out of my Jeep and see Jace walking to me. I guess it's going to be sooner rather than later.

"Hey, I texted you last night. Did you get it?" Jace asks stopping by my Jeep.

"I did." I nod my head and reach across my Jeep for my cheer bag and my school bag.

"Look, I'm not going to lie, I didn't like that you and Sam skipped—"

"But we didn't," I interrupt as I turn to Jace.

"I know, but you know how it is when you hear shit. So anyway, sorry I acted all crazy." Jace looks to the ground and then back to me.

"It's no big deal. When you texted me, I didn't even know he skipped. I was just shocked at the whole thing."

"I get it. At first, I was angry and not sure if I should believe you, but I do. If you say you didn't skip with Sam yesterday. I believe you."

"I, um—"

"What the hell, Fiona? You skipped school with Langford?" Jace's friend Isaac trots up to us interrupting me.

"I. Did. Not. Skip. With. Sam. Ugh!" I roll my eyes, turn toward the building and start walking, but I can hear the giggling behind me.

"Not cool dude," Jace says, but I hear humor in his voice.

"Sorry man. Sorry Fiona," Isaac yells. "Just giving you a hard time." Isaac laughs.

"Whatever!" I yell not even turning back but I smile at Jace's giggle.

"Catch ya later, Fiona," Jace calls. I give him a wave over my head without turning around and call over my shoulders, "Bye Felicia!"

And they bust out laughing at the old insult.

I walk through the senior locker bay and take out my phone pretending to look something up to avoid Leigha.

"Slut!" My head snaps up without thinking and I look in the direction of the voice and find myself on the receiving end of the evil eye from Leigha and her friends. I look back to my phone and try to ignore the heat in my cheeks.

"She thinks she is so special because she's Faith's sister," one of them says.

"I can't believe he broke up with you to go back out with her," another voice adds.

"It's only because she is on court and Sam wants to be her escort," Leigha justifies. "He told me she was a second choice anyway when they started dating. He wanted to get back together with Dominique."

Robotically I make my way down the hall as giggles erupt behind me.

"Hey DeWitt." My head snaps up to find Simmons holding up his hand for a high-five. "Heard you skipped with Langford yesterday—"

"I did not!" I interrupt. "Ugh! I was with my mom."

"Well, you better check your Instagram and get your story straight." Simmons winks and turns to walk away.

I walk to the closest bathroom and start scrolling Instagram. I lock myself in the stall and look back to my phone. Sure enough, just posted three minutes ago, a picture of my Jeep in Sam's driveway with a post that reads: Gyoung23 @fionarenee skippin with @slangford

My phone beeps and I see a text from Avery. It's a screen shot of the picture.

I text: "just saw it, in the bathroom by our locker bay"

Avery texts back: "omw"

I step out of the stall thankful no one is in the restroom but me. Avery bounds in. "I thought you didn't skip with Sam." Avery puts her things on the sink and turns to me.

"I didn't. I went over to talk to him after I got home from shopping," I admit and feel my shoulders droop knowing this will get back to Jace. "I was pissed about the fight and wanted to know what his problem was."

"Ah, Fiona, I think we all know what Sam's problem is. He's jealous," Avery says, then raises her eyebrows and smirks. "So, did you two hook up?"

"It wasn't like that. I was putting ice on his lip, you know, from the fight the other night and he…he kissed me. Nothing else happened, I swear."

"Well, it's not me you have to worry about. I just want you to be happy." Avery turns to the mirror and looks at her hair. "But what about Jace?" She pulls lip gloss out of her Gucci crossbody purse.

"I started to tell him this morning, but we were interrupted." I throw my hands in the air and stomp my foot. "Stupid Isaac!"

"So, what are you going to do?" Avery drops her lip gloss back into her purse and looks at her lips one more time, wiping away excess gloss under her lower lip. Then turns to me.

"I don't know. I—" I cut off when I see Riley walk into the bathroom.

"You are such a thot!" Riley shouts when she sees me. "What the hell gives you the right to get in my boyfriend's car?"

"What?" I shake my head at her trying to figure out what she is talking about. "Oh, you mean Tuesday when we went to get the pizzas?"

"You know what I mean. You got in the car with Kenton." Riley stops and throws her hands on her hips.

"Yeah, in the backseat with Avery." I hiss. "Jace and Kenton were in the front. Jace asked us to go with them. It's not like I want Kenton or anything," I scoff with an eyeroll and look back to the mirror.

Riley is about three inches taller than me and when I turn back from the mirror, she is in my face and looking down at me.

"I should kick your ass right now." Riley throws her arms out to her sides and lets them drop with a smack on her thighs.

Avery jumps in between us. "All right. Let's go." She grabs my arm and pulls me out of the bathroom.

"Bitch!" Riley yells and follows us out of the bathroom.

I look over my shoulder expecting to see her following us but am relieved to see she isn't.

"WTF? I didn't do anything. I was in the back seat," I cry still looking over my shoulder.

"She is just using that as a reason to turn on you." Avery still has her arm in mine and pulling me to her locker. "You know how that bitch is."

"Kenton? Eww," I say making a face. Avery stops in the middle of taking a notebook from the top shelf of her locker and looks right at me.

"Ignore it, Fiona. She isn't worth it." Avery stares into my eyes to prove her point.

The bell rings to let us know we have five minutes to get to class.

"Ignore it. Okay? See ya at lunch," Avery calls as I rush off to my locker.

"K." I throw my bag, coat and hat in my locker and grab my iPad, slamming my locker shut and rush off to class.

During first period, I decide I need to talk to Sam, but don't get a chance to till after 3rd period.

"Sam," I call when I see him round the corner by his locker.

"Hi." Sam looks up. His eyes go wide but face grows into a smile.

"Who did you tell?" I question and cock my head to one side letting him know this isn't a social visit.

"Tell what? I didn't tell anyone we skipped together. They assumed because we were both gone yesterday."

"I know that. I mean about me coming over later. Did you tell everyone we made out?" I shout a little too loud and Sam glances around seeing who all is looking for tea.

"I didn't say anything to anyone. Apparently, Gabe Young left school early and passed my house before you left." Sam moves in and places his hands on my hips. "I swear," he says. And for a second, I think he is going to kiss me, right here in the locker bay. I recover quickly and step back.

"Whatever." I roll my eyes. I want so badly to be pissed at Sam, but I have no one to blame but myself. I turn and walk away.

"Come on, Fi. Don't be pissed," Sam calls after me, but Sam being Sam, doesn't chase me down.

I put my materials away in fourth period since the clock indicates we have about two minutes before the bell rings. And because lunch is next, I quickly grab my things and make my way to the door hoping to be the first out, so I can beat the long lunch line.

I swing the heavy wood door open, pleased I am the first there and find myself face to face with Neveah and her cousin Kinsey Marsh glaring at me.

Kinsey graduated with Faith and at one point she, Ella, and Faith were friends. I don't know what happened to dissolve the friendship, but she has clearly taken Jessica's rumors to heart. Kinsey was never an athlete but started lifting weights her senior year and has become quite the badass. A badass who has come back to her alma mater to torment me.

Quickly, I turn to another student at the door beside me and start talking as the butterflies swarm my stomach. The bell finally rings, and I make my way out the door and down the hall, using every ounce of self-control to refrain from looking back. But I give in and casually glance over my shoulder as I turn toward the food line. My stomach flips as Kinsey's glare feels like two lasers on my back as she continues to follow me down the hall.

Once inside the cafe, I release a sigh as a bead of sweat rolls down my back. I'm suddenly not hungry but I grab a PB&J and an apple. At the register, I punch in my account number and glance around the cafeteria for Kinsey.

My heart leaps to my throat when I spot her, but she is at the other end of the cafeteria from where I sit and talking with a few seniors before turning to walk back to the front office. *Calm down, Fiona. Maybe she wasn't even here for you.*

But that's a lie and I know it. She is stalking me.

"You okay?" Avery stops eating as I sit down.

"Yeah. Fine. Why?" I look to Avery but still take another look around the room for Kinsey.

"You look like you just saw a ghost." Avery waits for my response before taking another bite of food.

"No, no ghost. Just nervous I guess." I fight to open my chocolate milk and notice my hands shaking, so I shove them under the table to hide them and turn to face Avery.

"You shouldn't be nervous. Excited yes. Nervous no." Avery shakes her head and smiles as she swings her arm around my shoulder. "Oh, I meant to tell you this morning. I love your hair. But priorities you know." Avery says running her fingers through it.

"It's not too much?" I hold the apple below my chin waiting on her response.

"Not at all. It's perfect. It's the first thing I noticed when I saw you. But had to hear the tea first."

I giggle at Avery's honesty.

The bell rings signaling the end of lunch. I open my locker and feel a presence coming toward me.

"Really Fiona? You lied to me." I look up to see a red face Jace with his brow furrowed.

"No, I didn't—"

"Well, the picture is pretty evident that you were at Sam's—"

"But I didn't lie. I didn't skip with Sam yesterday." I swallow the lump in my throat.

"So, you didn't go to his house yesterday?"

"No," I mumble and let out a sigh. "I did." I look down at my iPad in my arms and pick the torn edge of the cover.

"When were you going to tell me?" Jace's cheeks are red.

"I-I tried this morning, but we were interrupted."

"So, what actually happened yesterday?" Jace asks and leans toward me, extending his arm and placing his hand over my head and on the locker next to mine.

"I don't know. I just felt that I needed to talk to him. About what happened Tuesday night, about...I don't know." I know I am rambling but can't seem to stop. "About why he is doing this to me now. When he was the one to break up with me. And I was pissed that he attacked you."

"So, the rumors about you two making out aren't true. Nothing happened."

I bite my lip and look down at my shoes. I feel Jace tense and walk away.

"Jace," I cry, but he keeps walking. "Jesus Fiona. What the hell is wrong with you?" I scold myself.

I zone out through most of fifth period, replaying the scenario over and over again in my head trying to figure out what I should have done differently, I just can't believe I did this to Jace. *He doesn't deserve this. I don't deserve him.*

I try catching Jace after fifth at his locker, but he isn't there. I send him a text: "Hi, we need to talk"

He texts back: "I don't think there is anything to say"

I write: "I'm sorry. I never meant to hurt you."

I stand there staring at my phone, waiting for a response and the tardy bell rings. I'm late to class and nothing. I walk down the hall, phone in hand, I finally hear a beep and my heart races: "u did"

My heart sinks. I have to fix this. I text back: "I know and am sorry What can I do?

Another beep: "idk"

A sick feeling runs though me as a new thought hits me. I text back: "are you still going to be my escort?"

I stand there staring at my phone for what seems like an eternity, I finally get a response: "don't know"

Ugh. Before I realize it, I am texting Avery: "Jace says he doesn't know if he wants to be my escort now"

Avery responds back: "y? is this about the picture?"

I respond: "no, came clean about kissing S yesterday. J feels I lied to him"

Avery types back: "do you still want J to be your escort?"

I think about everything that has happened with Jace and with Sam. Then text: "idk, so confused"

A few seconds pass before I get a text back: "u need to decide what u want before you talk to him"

The rest of the afternoon drags on. I try catching Jace after sixth, but I see him walking down the hall in the opposite direction. Again, I try finding him after seventh, but he doesn't come back to his locker, so I head to cheer practice.

Takiesha sent a text to me about attending practice tonight but not needing to change since we are not cheering tomorrow night and the squad will be working the cheers without us. I go to our practice location and take a seat to observe cheer practice. Takiesha starts the practice with announcements, time, and uniform to wear tomorrow night and the plan for what cheers need to change since the two of us won't be cheering.

Practice wraps up and I make my way down the corridor to the athletic exit where I park. Someone is following me but I'm checking my phone hoping to find a text from Jace and not paying attention to who is in the hall with me.

I remind myself I need to send Quincy a text about the black car following me as soon as I get home. I wish I had gotten a picture.

At my Jeep, I dig my keys out, unlock my door, open it, and toss my bag across the seat.

"Fucking slut!" someone calls, and I instantly recognize the voice as footsteps approach me.

My eyes narrow and my teeth clench. I turn to see Riley walking toward me.

"Fuck you, bitch!" I put my foot on the sidestep and slide into my seat but before getting my door closed, Riley's arm reaches into my Jeep, and I feel the sting of her hand across my face.

My whole body trembles and I see red. In one quick motion, I grab the door handle with both hands, and I let out a scream in my head. Every muscle in my body goes ridged as I jump out of my Jeep, swinging the door as hard as I can at Riley who barely jumps out of the way in time; her eyes wide and jaw drops. Before she can respond, I'm on her. My left hand wrapped around her neck and pulling her toward the ground while I swing with my right.

"Hey! Stop it!" I barely hear the voice for the sound of blood whooshing though my ears. But the voice and footsteps on the blacktop continue running toward us.

"Let go!" the voice shouts.

Pain rips through my scalp as Riley pulls my hair, but I keep swinging. Then I feel the pressure across the front of my chest as I am being pushed away and realize someone is trying to break us apart. I tighten my grip and swing again.

"Ouch! You bit me!" I hear the voice say and finally realize it's Sam.

Someone else shows up, Riley's grip on my hair loosens and Riley is dragged way.

"Kenton, get her out of here. You okay?" Sam asks pulling me back toward my Jeep.

"I think so." I gasp for air and take a few breaths trying to get my bearings. "I don't know what happened. I just had enough." The whooshing sound loud in my ears, I feel the burning of my skin. I wipe my hair out of my face and feel my heart racing.

"It looked like you had had enough. I was really trying to save Riley from you," Sam says.

Surprisingly, I hear myself laugh but my hands are shaking, and my breathing ragged.

"And she bit me." Sam's voice going a little high. "What the hell is that?"

"I helped Kenton get Riley in his car," Brewer says as he jogs up to us. "You okay, Fiona?"

"I think so. Thanks," I mumble.

"What about me? I was just in a girl fight," Sam argues. "Girls are mean. She bit me."

Brewer's shocked expression turns to laughter at Sam's words.

"It's not funny. I think she broke the skin." Sam pulls up his sleeve to check.

"Langford got his ass kicked by a girl." Brewer laughs, and I hear myself snort.

"You guys are assholes," Sam snaps, and we laugh harder. I throw my head back in laughter and fall back on my Jeep for support.

"If you girls are okay after your fight," Brewer says, "I'm gonna take off." He turns to leave, and I can still hear him laughing.

"Fuck you," Sam calls back and I only laugh harder. The Jeep is the only thing holding me up.

"Are you gonna keep laughing or are you gonna thank me?" Sam puts his hands on his hips and tries to hide a smile. I'm still bent over giggling. I finally catch my breath and stand.

"Thank you for the laugh, Sam." And I lose it again. I lean forward to put my hands on my knees to hold myself up. "Ah..." I start taking deep breaths to calm myself down.

"You're just lucky wrestling got out when it did." Sam starts laughing with me.

"Whew." I stand up and take a breath. "But seriously, thank you. I didn't even realize she was behind me."

"What was that about anyway?"

"Oh, you know Riley. Avery and I rode with Kenton and Jace to get the pizzas for Simmons Tuesday night. That's all the fuel she needs to be a bitch. She'll pick on someone else next month."

"Yeah, but you're the first to stand up to her," Sam says proudly and pats me on the shoulder.

"Seriously, I don't know what happened. She called me a slut and I said, 'Fuck you bitch.'"

"That will do it." Sam laughs. "You okay to drive?"

"Yeah, I'm fine." I nod and take a deep breath.

"All right, so the important stuff. What color tie should I wear?" Sam asks as he steps close to me and starts to put his arm around me.

"For what?" I put my hand up and press on his chest to stop him.

"Well, I don't know what color dress you are wearing, so what color tie do I need?" He steps back and puts his hands in the pockets of his Letterman's jacket.

"Sam, I don't know what you are talking about." I shake my head and frown.

"For court tomorrow night. You know, I need to match what you're wearing, so we don't clash."

I blink a few times and realize what he is saying.

"Sam. Jace is my escort." I step back to give myself space from Sam.

"What?"

"I already told you. I asked Jace to be my escort and he said yes."

"But yesterday. What about yesterday?" Sam asks, those stormy eyes are back. "That meant nothing to you?"

"I don't know. I mean, it didn't mean nothing, but I don't know what that was. I got caught up in the moment I guess." I shrug and look away feeling embarrassed about our make out session.

"Wait a minute. You came to my house, made out with me, you still want Jace to be your escort and you just 'got caught up in the moment?'" Sam throws his hands out, turns away from me and runs a hand through his hair.

"Don't blame this on me. You broke up with me. You broke my heart. And for what? To have sex with Leigha. Now you're trying to turn it on me because I'm moving on?"

Sam spins around to face me again.

"Fi, we never—Wait." Sam's eyes grow hard. "So, you *are* moving on. With Jace?" Sam crosses his arms over his chest.

"Yes! No. I don't know. Maybe." I look down and kick the tire of my Jeep.

"You are a thot." Sam turns to walk away.

"Hey, fuck you," I yell and cross my arms over my chest.

"You're not ready," Sam calls as he climbs in his car.

I look around the empty parking lot, then back as Sam pulls away leaving me standing alone in the cold.

Chapter 13

Merida meows and rubs up against me when I walk through the door.

"Hey pretty girl." Merida's in my arms before I finish my greeting. She takes her place on my shoulder, which becomes her perch as we make our way to my room.

My cell rings.

"Hey, Mom," I say when I hear my mom's voice on the other end.

"Just checking on you, I thought you were coming to see Fay?"

"I was, but it was a hectic day today and I have so much I need to get done for tomorrow night." I shake Merida off my shoulder so I can remove my coat. Merida digs her claws in trying to keep her place.

"Well, we understand. Just miss seeing you. Do you have money for food?" I hear Mom rummaging through a file or something. She must have brought work to the hospital with her again.

"Don't worry, I'll find something." Merida lands on the bed along with my coat and bag.

"Just remember what Dr. Saunders said, 'you need to eat three meals a day.'" Mom's voice is stern.

"I know, I know. I promise." I roll my eyes at my overprotective mother, but it's been so long since she has been concerned about me, I find comfort in her smothering.

"Okay, call if you need us. Wait." I hear Mom ask Dad, "What? Oh, Dad says he'll pick something up on the way home if you haven't eaten anything yet."

"Oh, thanks. I'll let you know. Be safe." I click the end button and reach over to pet Merida. I feel guilty about her flop.

I kick off my boots, change into joggers and barely get my t-shirt on when Merida returns to my shoulder.

We make our way to the kitchen hoping to find something to eat. I lean my head in for a Merida snuggle and she returns the love so she must not be to upset about her flop. I don't feel very hungry after what happened in the parking lot, but I promised Mom and I want to stay on her good side, so I pop a plate of broccoli and chicken casserole the neighbors brough over yesterday in the microwave.

The smell of cheesy casserole catches my senses and my stomach growls letting me know I need food. I plow through my first helping and go for a second saving a few pieces of chicken for Merida.

After putting my plate in the dishwasher, I walk back to my room, stopping at the bathroom to check my face in case Riley got me. Nothing there.

"Ouch." Pain shots through my right temple when I pull my hair up in a messy bun. That must be from Riley pulling my hair. At least it's not visible to my classmates; unlike the scar from the accident. I take another look at my face in the mirror hoping the scar has faded. Then I look to the horn on my forehead. Still there.

"Ok Merida, I have to get some homework done tonight. Oh, but first…"

I scroll through my phone for Officer Quincy's number, look at the time, after 7:00, so I decide to text him instead: "Sorry to bother you but I was wondering if there was a black Charger with black wheels and tinted windows around the house where you found Ella's car at SWU?"

I set my phone aside knowing I probably won't get a quick answer. Merida hops down onto my desk and helps me get my iPad and notebook out of my bag. I sit down at my desk and turn my iPad on to find that it only has three percent battery.

I dig for my charger in my bag. "Crap, Mer. It's in my locker. Let's see if Faith has one in her desk."

I walk through the bathroom to Faith's room, flip on the light and sit down at her desk. It feels so weird to be in her room knowing she hasn't been here in over a month.

I focus on why I'm here and look around her room for a charger. I see pictures of all of us on the corkboard above her computer and a framed picture of all four of us at a concert. Faith and Ella surprised Lyla and me with Lizzo tickets last summer. It was our last big bash before Faith and Ella left for college.

Of course, there are several pictures with other friends I recognize from her class. Pictures at Homecoming, football and basketball games, parties, and spring break trips. I smile at the picture of Faith and Ella getting their tattoos after high school graduation. Ella got an arrow on her right wrist while Faith had "faith over fear" tattooed on the inside of her left foot. Ella is all smiles. Faith looks like she was about to pass out.

I put the picture back in its place and look through Faith's desk drawers, but no iPad charger so I guess I will have to use Faith's computer.

"What's her password again?" More asking myself but I look at Merida like she might be able to tell me. "Oh. It's the last four digits of her cell number, 8262."

The computer flashes to life and I move the cursor to click out of the programs she has open when I see the messages from Ella.

I glance through the DMs and wonder why they are still up. These messages are from October. Then I see a message form Faith to Ella: "When can I meet your new guy?"

I didn't know Ella had a guy. I read on and find Ella's response: "Not this weekend. He will be out of town."

Faith wrote back: "You just texted yesterday saying he is having a party and I should come."

Ella wrote: "Yeah, sorry. Got my weekends mixed up. Party is next weekend. You'll be back at school, right?"

I can feel Faith's disappointment. I know she misses Ella. I'm not surprised when I read Faith's next message: "Oh well, we can still get together when I'm home on break."

Ella responded: "I don't know. My break isn't when yours is, and I've got a lot to do at school with midterms coming up. Maybe."

I lean back in the desk chair and remember back to the day Faith left for college.

"Faith, promise me no matter what, we will find a way to see each other when you are home for breaks." Ella sniffled through teary eyes.

"What? Of course. You're my biffle." Faith and Ella busted out laughing.

Mom leaned into me. "What's a biffle?" I rolled my eyes at her ignorance.

"B.F.F.L.," I replied. Mom was still looking at me. "OMG, best friends for life."

I look back to the DM stream and Faith's next message: "What the hell Ella? You didn't want to see me two weeks ago when I was home for my grandma's birthday either. Something isn't right. What aren't you telling me? We tell each other everything."

Ella responded: "Just a lot going on. It's not you, I...I just need time to work things out with X."

Faith asked: "Who is X Ella? Your boyfriend? I don't understand why you can't even tell me his name."

Ella wrote back: "He's just a very private person. He wants to keep our relationship between us."

I start running scenarios through my mind about why Ella doesn't want Faith to know about her guy. Or why Ella hasn't said anything to me about him. I wonder if Lyla knows him, but I can't find that out right now.

Suddenly I hear Faith's scolding me for my conspiracy theories.

"There you go again, Fiona, overreacting. 'You're only sixteen, what the hell do you know.'" Were Faith's exact words to me when I suggested to Faith that she had a crush on her psych professor last fall.

But something doesn't feel right about this.

I scroll through the messages hoping to find something that will help find Ella or lead me to this X person. Maybe he knows something.

I find Faith's next message: "Ella, I love you like a sister and don't want to see you hurt. Something doesn't sound right about this guy. The picture you sent, the one he got mad about you sending, why did you crop him out of it?"

Not reading Ella's response, I scroll through the stream of messages to find the picture Faith is referring to. And there it is, sent two days before this conversation. The picture is clearly Ella with someone sitting behind her. His arm around her waist and the other around her shoulders, but everything from the top of Ella head up is cropped out. I see what looks to be Greek letter on his sweatshirt, but part of the symbol is covered by Ella's body. It's definitely Ella, but she doesn't look good. Her makeup and hair are done, but she looks thin and pale, and a bit dazed. And it looks like the guy might be propping her up or something.

I see why Faith is concerned.

I scroll back to the last part of the conversation, Ella responded: "I told you. He is a very private person. He doesn't like to be in pictures, so I cut him out."

Faith asked: "Ella, are you okay? Is he hurting you?"

Ella sounded annoyed when she responded: "Why would you think that? He was just really pissed when he found out I sent you that picture but absolutely not."

That's where the conversation ends. My mind races trying to figure all this out. *Ella may have a boyfriend and she won't or doesn't want Faith to meet him. Or the boyfriend doesn't want to meet Faith. Do Ella's parents know about him?*

I think back to the night when Ella showed up at our house with a busted lip and crying.

She wouldn't tell Lyla and me what happened, but we could hear her through the bathroom door telling Faith, "It's over. Hunter is such an ass." We listened as she told Faith about the fight she had with Hunter because he supposedly cheated on her with one of their friends. When she told him she was breaking up with him, he backhanded her causing the busted lip.

A few days later, she and Faith came home from a party and Ella was buzzed. She went into this big, long lecture about never letting a guy put his hands on you.

I hear the beep of my phone which snaps me out of my thoughts. I grab my phone off Faith's desk and my heart skips, a text from Jace: "in your driveway"

I race to the door and find Jace standing there waiting on me. Jace steps in when I open the door.

"Jace, I'm—"

"Stop Fiona." Jace holds up his hand. "Look, I'm not your boyfriend and you aren't my girlfriend, so you owe me nothing."

"Actually, I do." I look up to meet his eyes.

"No, you don't." He stops me. "But I'm not going to lie, it hurt that you lied to me. I thought we had something. I thought you were over Sam, and we had a chance."

My excitement rises until I realize Jace used the word had. Past tense as in, not now.

"Now I don't know what to think," Jace continues. "Maybe you should have Sam be your escort."

"No. I don't want him to be my escort—"

"Fiona, I don't think you know what you want," Jace interrupts and leans against the door jam, putting his hands in his coat pockets.

"I know I want you to be my escort. I know I told Sam so tonight when he *assumed* he was going to be my escort. And I told him no Monday night when he wanted me to ask him. And when he showed up on my doorstep last Sunday saying he loved me and wanted me back, I could have asked him then, before I asked you, but I didn't. I chose you Jace."

Jace lets out a fake laugh. "Funny way of showing it," he mumbles and looks down at the ground.

"I didn't know you had feelings for me." My voice catches and I swallow hard. "I thought we were friends." I feel myself frown.

"Oh, c'mon. Like you didn't know." Jace stands, throws his chin up as he crosses his arms.

I blink and open my mouth to respond, then close it. Speechless. I'm speechless. Then I see the pain in Jace's eyes and my heart flips.

"I never meant for any of this to happen. I never meant to hurt you, Jace. And if you say you don't want to be my escort, I understand. But I don't want Sam or anyone else to be my escort." I look in his eyes hoping he sees me, hears me. And I realize this *is* what I really want.

We are so close I can feel his breath on my lips, and I know we are going to kiss. My heart skips a beat and I have a warm fuzzy feeling in my toes.

"I gotta go." Jace steps back and turns, pushing the glass door open.

I stand there wide eyed, mouth agape watching him leave. I try calling for him, but nothing comes out. Then finally, "Will you please still be my escort?" My voice weak and crackling.

"I'm not sure. I need to think about it." Jace slides into the driver's seat and leaves.

I'm left standing on my front porch, the cold dark night closing in, my heart sinking, red flaring in my cheeks. It's bad enough I was dumped by Sam but now Jace and he wasn't even my boyfriend.

The roar of the car ignition coming to life that is parked down the street snaps me back. The car speeds past my house and even though it's dark, I know it's the car I saw yesterday. *Who lives down there?*

I watch the taillights disappear into the night.

Chapter 14

"She's here," Sara whispers to Jessica when they see me and turn to run ahead of me.

I look down at my phone as I enter the hallway leading to my locker and look up just in time to see Riley in my path. I try to maneuver around her, but I feel Riley's shoulder crash into mine, throwing me backward and off balance. I fight to get my footing, but my boots are wet from the snow and my feet slip out from under me. I crash to the floor, landing on my ass. My phone flies out of my hand and lands hard on the concrete with a smack.

I reach over to grab my phone before it gets trampled when I hear Riley and her friends giggling.

"OMG Riley! Did you see that knot on her forehead? You must have done that last night," Jessica croaks, and I look up to all three of them laughing at me; Sara is pointing.

"Did you slam her head into her Jeep?" Sara asks.

"I hope you put a dent in her precious Jeep," Neveah retorts.

"How awesome would it be if her phone just broke," Riley adds as the three turn to each other laughing.

"You kicked her extra ass, Riley!" Sara squeals and my heart is in my throat as I struggle to get off the floor and notice other students stop to watch and laugh.

Riley looks back at me and flips me off. I turn away and am faced with the crowd of eyes gathering to watch the show. I grind my teeth, reach for my forehead to make sure my horn isn't showing and push my way through the crowd.

I rush to my locker and hear Nicole, the girl whose locker has been by mine since seventh grade. "What the hell happened with Riley?" she asks. "Sorry, not trying to be nosey but you know, everyone is spillin tea."

"Yeah, I've heard. Idk, I just lost it. She called me a slut and that was it. Shit." I screw up my combination and start over as the warning bell rings.

"Well, I will never admit this, but if you ask me, she deserves it. I'm on team Fiona," Nicole adds which should make me feel better, but it doesn't.

"Ah, thanks but there shouldn't be a team anything." I shove my coat and bag in the locker and reach for my books.

"This is high school, there is always a team," Nicole says with a nod. "Oh, and good luck tonight. I voted for you."

"That's sweet. We both know I won't win but thank you for trying."
I wave as she turns to leave.

I rush off to first period, trying to count my tardies. *Yesterday fifth period, I'm positive I have one from last week, and now this morning. At least three, that's an after-school detention right there. Ugh!*

I walk into class, hoping to go unnoticed and slide into my seat. I think I made it.

"This morning we will be going over- Ah! La reina candidata! The potential Queen has decided to grace us with her presence," Mrs. Shipley quips and I am greeted with giggles from the class. Lyla laughs the loudest, but when I glance in her direction, she is leaning in as Shelby whispers something in her ear.

"Sorry, I'm late. Got held up at my locker."

"Yeah, cause everyone wants to see if she got her ass kicked or not," a classmate retorts and laughter erupts.

"Enough." Mrs. Shipley holds up her hand and shuts it down. "Just glad you are here Fiona. Buena suerte esta noche."

"Gracias." My cheeks glow. I sink into my seat and my stomach churns.

"Are you nervous?" I turn to see the student next to me leaning in my direction.

"What?" I whisper back.

"You're fidgeting with your ring. I haven't noticed you doing that before. I suspect you are nervous for tonight."

"A little." If she only knew the half of it. I might not have an escort, half of the sophomore class hates me and would love to see me destroyed tonight, both Jace and Sam are pissed at me and no need to remind anyone that I'm responsible somehow for Faith and Ella.

Last year at this time, I was nervous but because I was excited and full of anticipation about being on Winter Court. Plus, I had the support of the freshman class, Sam to help me stay calm and Lyla and Sara never left my side. From the time I arrived at school for the ceremony, the pictures that followed in the cafeteria and when I went to the locker room to change. They were there for moral support, helping me enjoy every moment of the night.

The bell finally rings dismissing us from class. I need to find Jace and beg him to be my escort even if he never wants to speak to me again after.

I round the corner to Jace's locker bay, it hits me how dire this situation is. My hands start shaking and my mouth goes dry. This is not a time for pride to get in the way. But please don't let my voice tremble.

I quickly slide my hand in my pocket and clear my thoughts before reaching Jace's locker.

"Fiona. I was just coming to find you," Jace says before I have a chance to talk.

"Jace. I'm sorry—"

"Stop. We've already been over that. I thought a lot about this last night. We're friends, always have been and we still are. You don't owe me anything." Jace pauses to let that sink in. "Sure, I hoped it would turn into something more. I'm not going to lie, it hurts that you might not want that but no matter what, we are friends. We aren't dating so I have no right to be mad about anything."

"Jace, I—"

"Let me finish please." He leans in, placing a hand on my shoulder. "So, if you still want me, I would be honored to be your escort tonight."

A smile spreads across my face and I let out my breath. I throw my arms around Jace's neck to pull him in for a hug.

"Yes!" I let out a sigh. "I do." I feel a weight has lifted off my shoulders.

"Good. Cause you know, I like bought this hideously boring plain black suit and tie and stuff." He releases me sooner than I wanted.

I let out a laugh. "You probably could have gotten away with a crazy suit if you would have played your cards right." I giggle and Jace takes my arm in his as we walk out of the locker bay.

"Son of a bitch. Why didn't I think of that?" Both of us laughing, I notice Sam's ice-cold glare as we pass.

"So, where are we going?" Jace asks.

"Are you walking me to class?" I look up to meet Jace's eyes.

"If you are okay with it. Let's just call it practice or tonight." Jace straightens up trying to make himself taller and makes me laugh even harder.

I know full well that we are causing a scene, but I just don't care. Let them gawk and whisper. I am enjoying this moment with Jace. I feel strong and protected on his arm. And disappointed when we stop at my class not wanting this moment to end.

I haven't felt like this since, since...I don't know when. Last fall? Like I belong again.

Was it losing Sam that made me feel like I don't belong? Or did that happen after the accident?

But right now, I'm good. Excited even, and I think that might be because of Jace.

"See you later, Fiona," Jace says turning away.

"Hey, Jace. Don't forget rehearsal during fourth."

"Wouldn't think of it." He gives me that lazy smile and my heart skips a beat.

Reminiscing over my moment with Jace, my smile slips away when I overhear more whispers.

"Can you believe it? They haven't talked all week," a classmate whispers.

"Yeah, I hear Lyla is done with Fiona. I never thought they would split up," another girl chimes in.

"Well, apparently it was something Fiona said to Lyla about the guy Lyla likes," the first girl continues. "But I wouldn't think that would matter now since Lyla is dating Ethan Williams."

"The junior basketball player? He's hot," the second responds.

"Right? I guess Shelby suggested it to him. He asked Lyla on Wednesday to go to the dance and they went out last night," the first girl continues.

I tune out the conversation, I can't listen anymore. I feel like a knife is being stabbed in my heart. I should know this. I always know what is going on with whom. Especially my best friend. I think back to Mom's suggestion to ask Lyla to talk.

I turn at the bay before mine and look to Lyla's locker; she is talking to Sara and Jessica. I try to turn away before any of them see me. But it's too late. Sara sees me, points in my direction and whispers something to Jessica which gets both girls giggling.

I ignore the looks and gossip as I walk into third period when my cell buzzes in my hand. A voice mail form Officer Quincy. I pull up the text version of the message to read: "Fiona, got your message last night. I am going back through the tapes from the night of the party but the cameras at the church on the corner don't cover the entire street. I am also going to the impound lot to look over Faith's car again. I'll call if I find anything."

I walk into class and take my seat, thinking about the black car I keep seeing.

"Sorry for the interruption, will you send Fiona DeWitt to the office please?" Mrs. Smiley's voice rings over the intercom.

I look up to the clock, it's only halfway through third period. Too soon for Winter Court Rehearsal. I turn back to my teacher who nods his head. As I gather my things and stand, I notice all the eyes on me.

I exit the classroom with excitement in my heart and walk into the office with a smile on my face.

"Hi Fiona." Mrs. Smiley looks up from her computer. "Mr. Clifton needs to see you. Have a seat." She waves her hand to the waiting area.

"Oh, okay." I shrug and turn to move toward the chairs. My smile fades.

"What are you doing here?" I ask my mom, taking the seat next to her.

"I hoped you knew. Mr. Clifton called about an hour ago and said he needed to see me." Mom shifts in her chair and turns her head to look at me. Her blue eyes cool and mouth straight.

I tighten my grip on my things and try to stay calm, but the pit in my stomach is back. My heart jumps when I see Mrs. Conner come in the other door and cross to Mr. Clifton's office.

Mrs. Smiley answers the intercom on her phone, which is loud enough for us to hear Mr. Clifton call us in.

My mom stands tall, squares her shoulders and strides through the office before me. I follow, shoulders hunched over, arms wrapped around my iPad tight to my chest and I keep my eyes on her heals as I follower her into his office.

"Good morning Mrs. DeWitt." Mr. Clifton stands to shake my mom's hand like they have a business transaction. But I am positive they went to school together as his family is also from Brookston. "Fiona." Mr. Clifton nods in my direction as he takes a seat. "Please sit."

He gives us a moment to settle in and before he can say anything, my mom starts.

"Why are we here Mr. Clifton?" She leans back in her chair, crosses her legs, and intertwines her fingers together in her lap. She looks cool and confident in her black slim fit dress pants, charcoal gray ribbed

320

turtleneck and black suede healed booties that I have no idea how she walks in in this weather.

I drop my things in to my lap and sink down in my chair, glancing up to Mrs. Conner standing behind Mr. Clifton. Her face is pink, and she keeps her eyes on the ground.

"Well, Mrs. DeWitt. You know we love Fiona, and Faith…" He trails off and takes a sip from his coffee mug with the Eagles logo before continuing. "And I wish the circumstances were different as I know how challenging things are right now." He keeps his eyes on my mom.

I tilt my head slightly, hiding my face behind my hair, and see my mom give a knowing nod. I look back to my hands tight on the edges of the iPad as the bile rises in my stomach.

"We were made aware of a…" Mrs. Conner pauses and looks to me, "situation last night that took place on school grounds."

I close my eyes and sink further in my chair, fighting the gag reflex I feel in the back of my mouth.

"Fiona?" My mom's voice surprisingly calm, which draws my eyes up to hers behind my blonde curtain.

I look back down at my lap unable to find my words. I'm afraid it won't just be my voice coming out. I jump in my seat at the touch of my mom's hand as she reaches over and takes my hand in hers, giving it a squeeze.

"We received a report this morning that Fiona was in a fight after school with another classmate." Mr. Clifton pauses to let that sink in and I feel his eyes on me, but I keep my head down and bite my lip.

"Did a *teacher* see this fight?" My mom's voice catches my attention and I turn to look at her.

"Ah, no—"

"Then how do you know it was Fiona?" Mom interrupts, sits up straight in her chair, and tightens her grip on mine. "Who reported this…fight?"

"That's not important, Mrs. DeWitt," Mr. Clifton clarifies. But Mom cuts Mr. Clifton off before he can continue.

"Then it's a student's word against Fiona's," Mom adds with a nod expecting to wrap this whole thing up like she does when she gets an accepted offer on a property.

"Actually, we pulled the video footage from last night." Mr. Clifton swings his monitor around so we all can see it. My stomach heaves and I close my eyes willing my stomach to calm down, but I scan the room for a trash can just in case.

My eyes go wide as I watch the whole thing play out right in front of me. Riley calling after me, me turning to her, then starting to get into my Jeep, her slapping me and me going after her. Mr. Clifton lets it play until Sam and Brewer break us apart. Then he shuts it off.

I look to my mom, my lower lip quivering and see my mom still sitting tall, shoulders back and head high.

"That girl attacked my daughter. Fiona was only defending herself."

"Now, Mrs. DeWitt—"

"Don't you 'Mrs. DeWitt' me *Bob*. We go back a long way and I remember a time you got in a few fights. This was clearly an attack on my daughter." My mom lets go of my hand and leans forward in her chair.

"Sharon, you are correct, but my hands are tied. This was on school property. And with the pictures that are circulating, we feel—"

"The what?" my mom interrupts. "Oh, you mean the photoshopped picture on Instagram that Fiona had nothing to do with. We still don't know the person who posted it. But the police are looking into it." My mom sits back in her chair. My eyes pop learning that she went to the police about the picture.

"If that was the only picture, but it's not." Mr. Clifton looks to me as does my mom. I swallow and feel the sting of tears, but I know I have to tell.

"I-I didn't want to worry you and Dad about it, so I didn't tell you," I whisper. "You have enough to deal with right now."

"Fiona Renee, what happened?" I hear the anger in my mom's voice. I pause for a few seconds and fight back sobs and wipe the tears from my eyes. I let out a breath and wipe my tears again.

I tell her about the missing towel from the hanger in the locker room at the gym, and the picture, and finding my towel on the top of my Jeep with a note under windshield wiper. Then about the party that night where Sara was passing around her phone with the picture on it.

"Sara? Your friend Sara? Did she take the picture?" Mom's face growing red, fury in her eyes.

"I don't know. I didn't see the person taking the picture." I look down to my lap, my hands in fists. I swallow down a scream.

"Who is this Sara?" Mrs. Conner asks.

"Sara Hawkins," I admit. My mom looks directly into Mr. Clifton's eyes.

"Ah, shit, Sharon. Jim Hawkins's daughter?" Mr. Clifton lowers his head and rubs his hand across his forehead before looking back up.

"Ugh...the school board president's daughter?" Mrs. Conner gasps, looking back and forth between us. I nod while wiping my tears away.

"All right, I will look into it, but you need to let the police know about this too." Mr. Clifton makes a note on his desk calendar.

"This puts us in a really tough position, Fiona." Mrs. Conner shakes her head. I look up meeting her eyes and see pity on her face.

"Yes, it does. I agree that the fight wasn't instigated by you Fiona, but you did fight on school property which is an automatic three-day suspension." Mr. Clifton raises his hand to stop me as I jump to the edge of my seat. "Which won't start until Monday. The other student was sent home today and will be out all next week."

I slide back in my chair trying to make sense of it all.

"Now, with everything that has happened, Mrs. Conner and I feel that it would be better to have another student represent the sophomore class tonight."

My mouth drops to the floor, my eye become blurry and blood swooshes through my ears. I only hear bits and pieces of the conversation after that. Something about "already notified the next in line" and "you are still welcome to come to the festivities tonight and tomorrow night" but the rest is hit or miss.

My body is numb as all the blood drains from my face. I think tears are still leaking from my eyes. I barely acknowledge that my mom is out of her chair and in Mr. Clifton's face screaming things like "you can't do this to her" and "you know everything she has been through?" and "those pictures where not her fault."

I sit frozen in my chair not sure what to do. I continue listening to my mom advocate for me. Something I never thought she would do under the circumstances. As I sit here thinking over everything that has happened and how I just keep trying to ignore it all and shove my emotions back down. I realize it should be me advocating for me. Not my mom.

"No!" I raise my head and look directly at Mr. Clifton. My mom looks to me with a surprised expression. "You can't do this to me! I already have a target on my back, and you are making it worse." My voice growing louder. "Please! Please don't—

"Fiona, shh, shh, shh." Mom turns to me and puts her hands on my shoulders. "Calm down, Fiona."

"No! I will not calm down!" I jump up from my seat, pushing Mom off me and she stumbles back. My books and iPad scattering across the carpeted floor and under Mr. Clifton's desk as I look at my mom. "Everything has been taken from me! My sister. Ella. My memory. Lyla. My reputation and now…" I hold out my palms and wave them around the office. "The one and only thing I have to get excited about? And you." I lean on Mr. Clifton's desk and point my finger at him. "You are taking it away from me because of what Riley and Sara did to me."

"I'm sorry, Fiona…" Mr. Clifton stands and starts to walk around his desk.

"How could you?" My lower lip juts out and my eyes narrow stopping him in his tracks. The tears pick back up as I turn to Mom and fall into to her arms.

"Shh, shh, shh...c'mon." Mom takes my hand and wraps her arm around my shoulder guiding me out of the office, leaving my belongings of the floor. "I'm taking my daughter home."

Chapter 15

My mom opens the passenger side door, pushes me in, and slams the door. I have no idea who was in the hallway as we exited the building, and I don't care.

I hear Mom's door shut and feel her arm over my shoulders as she pulls me into a hug.

"It's…not…fair," I cry on Mom's shoulder. My sobs are so loud I wouldn't be surprised if students in the building can still hear me.

"You're right, Fiona. It's not fair. But you did fight on school property," Mom says quietly as she still rubs her hand on my back.

"SHE ATTACKED ME!" I scream and pull away.

"I understand that. But the facts are clear. You could have gotten in your Jeep and pulled away and ignored her," Mom says softly, and she still has her hand on my shoulder trying to comfort me.

My mind goes blank, and suddenly I have tunnel vision as I stare at my mom. I suck in a huge breath and let out a hair curling scream and start banging my balled-up fist on the dash so hard my thumbs smack the window on the rebound. I see red everywhere. I extend my fingers out ridged like I'm growing talons and I rest them on the dash as I suck in more air and scream again. This time when I suck in another breath,

I rear back and slam myself forward with everything I have. My forehead smashing into the dash. I draw back again and slam myself forward into the dash hoping to make the pain end. I rear back to go again, blood dripping from my brow when I feel Mom's arms wrap around me and the weight of her slim body crawling on top of me to hold me in down.

"STOP! Fiona, stop!" I barely register the panic in her scream as I'm fighting to get out from under her. "Please...stop!" she begs through terrified sobs.

My body goes limp, the sobs and screaming stop and I fall back into the leather seat with Mom on top of me. Her arms are wrapped around me in the tightest embrace I've ever felt but I don't feel anything else. And I don't care. I'm empty.

"Please, please. Fiona. Please don't hurt yourself. I love you," Mom cries.

I don't know how much time passes, but I guess she realizes I am no longer a threat to myself, and she shifts her weight off me and is on the console between the seats but hasn't let me go.

She drops her forehead on my shoulder, arms wrapped around me and she cries.

***

329

I must have fallen asleep or maybe passed out because when I wake up, I am still wearing the clothes I had on today; except my boots are off. Merida is by my side all snuggled up to me. My eyes feel swollen, and my head hurts. I lay my head back on the pillow and let the tears flow and dig my fingers into Merida's fur.

I take a deep breath and let it out trying to calm myself.

I look around for my phone and see it on the night table by my bed. Mom must have taken it out of my pocket.

It's 4:45 and school has been out for over an hour. The runner up is scrambling to find a dress and get ready. And here I am, siting on my bed, lost. I should be getting ready but there is no reason.

I look at my notifications knowing I am not going to read most of them, but I need to call Jace.

I blink and sit up in my bed. I wipe my tears with the back of my sweatshirt cuff to make sure I am reading the screen right.

A text from Lyla: "Fi, I just heard about Faith's dress and what Sara and Jessica did to it. None of this is right and they shouldn't get away with it."

My heart is pounding. Lyla texted me. I start to text back but read the text again. Then I notice the garment bag on the back of my door. Mom must have thought to pick it up.

I throw the covers off, Merida tumbling to the floor with a thud, and I crawl across my bed to reach for the zipper. Before I can unzip the bag, Mom walks into my room.

"You're up." She smiles and take me in her arms. "I'm not going to ask how you are, I can imagine." She releases me and steps back.

"What are you doing?" she asks leaning against my dresser watching me.

"Lyla just texted me telling me Sara and Jessica did something to Faith's dress." I hear Mom gasp.

I take out the hanger from the bag, hold the dress up and drape it over my arm. I look over the dress as tears stream down my face. Mom covers her mouth with her hands and shakes her head.

"I can't believe they are doing this. How did Lyla know?" Mom sits down at the edge of my bed, and I hang the dress back up but not in the bag and sit down next to Mom.

I pull up the text and hand the phone to Mom without taking my eyes off the dress. Faith's dress. They did this to Faith's dress just to get at me.

"She's right," Mom whispers so soft I barely hear her. She drops the phone in her lap and stares down the hall with the same blank look Faith has in the hospital bed. Then she blinks and her mouth turns to a frown. She looks back at my phone and starts typing something.

"What?" I look to Mom who takes a deep breath and sighs and hands the phone back to me.

"Lyla's right. They can't get away with this. I bet they are behind both of those pictures." Mom stands up and walks toward the door.

"Where are you going?" I ask. I thought she would stay with me.

"I have a few calls to make." Mom turns and walks to my door, but then stops and turns back. "Are you going to be okay? I will stay if you want me too. But I trust you, Fi. If you tell me that you are okay and you're not going to hurt—"

"I promise," I interrupt with a sigh and shake my head. "I was just so lost and angry, and I just felt it all seemed so...hopeless. I still am, but I'm not going to hurt myself."

"Please know that it is not hopeless. *You* are not hopeless Fiona. This is a rough patch." Mom takes a deep breath, turns to Faith's dress and says, "A really unfair rough patch," as she exhales.

"I'm okay, Mom." I try to smile and wipe away a tear. "I mean I'm not, not yet, but I'm going to be."

Mom watches me for a few moments, "Okay." She nods and gives me a smile, "Okay then. We're going to be okay." She takes my hand and gives it a squeeze with one last look at the destroyed dress.

"Oh, I called Jace and Avery for you. I knew they would be worried," Mom adds.

"Thanks Mom." I wasn't looking forward to those calls anyway. I am sure they have messaged me, but I can't bear to check.

"Fiona," Mom calls and I look up to see her leaning on the door frame. "I think you should go to the game."

My eyes go wide.

"What? Are you kidding me? Why?" My brow furrows. "Seriously? I don't think I can handle it. It all just hurts so bad." I shake my head. The idea of missing it is so painful, but the idea of going and watching the ceremony I was to be part of? I can't!

"I'm sure it does. But you have nothing to feel bad about. Or embarrassed about. Don't let someone else tell you how you should feel. Only you can do that." Mom lets that hang there for a few seconds. "Besides, I am pretty sure Jace and Avery would be happy to see you."

"How would I even get there? My Jeep is—"

"In the driveway," Mom interrupts. "Your dad and I went back to get it once I got you home."

"Hey Mom?" I wait till she turns back around. "Thanks for, um, everything today. But I'm not sure I can go to the game."

"Fi-Fi, your welcome. But I wish you would think about it."

"Um, what do you think will happen if I do?" I ask. Mom waits a few moments before answering.

"I honestly don't know. But I do think going to the game will help you take some control back." Mom shrugs her shoulders. "Just my thoughts."

Chapter 16

Merida is back on my lap as I sit at the end of the bed staring at Faith's dress. I think back to the nigh of Faith's junior prom. *She was stunning. Lyla and I were with Faith and Ella through each step of the pre-prom process. We couldn't wait till it was our turn.*

As I sit and look at the ruined dress, my emotions run wild. But Lyla is right. Sara and Jessica should not get away with this. And so is my mom; sitting here isn't going to help anything. The ceremony will happen no matter what. And all the girls on court deserve to be supported, even the candidate replacing me. I'm sure it's MyaNika Schilling.

I scroll through my phone and send a text to Avery: "hey, think i should come to the game?"

I bite my lip as I wait on Avery's reply. Then, before I change my mind, I find the picture on Instagram and send it along with the picture Sara took of me in the locker room to Officer Quincy with a text explaining what happened.

The text from Avery is clear: "YES YES YES!"

I smile as my stomach flip flops and I let out a sigh. I text back: "ill text u when I get there, need makeup help"

Avery responds with a heart and hugs emoji. Then I send Jace a quick text telling him I am coming to the game, and I will see him there.

I feel like I am having an out of body experience as I walk to the bathroom Faith and I share, plug in the curing iron, and bend over to rinse off my face. I'm here but I'm not. I'm just going through the motions. Autopilot has kicked in, otherwise I would still be sitting on the bed frozen.

I throw on a light layer of foundation, look at the bruise forming around the gash on my forehead from my break down earlier and decide to send Avery another text: "bring concealer, gonna need lots"

I brush out my hair and use the curling iron to make big, loose waves. I grab the makeup bag in the bottom drawer and finish getting ready.

Out of habit, I check Mer's water bowl and top off her food bowl, then head out the door before I chicken out.

I jump when my phone rings, my heart racing as I drive through Brookston. I don't think to look who it is. I just press the phone button on my Uconnect.

"Hello?" I say when the phone connects.

"Fiona, Officer Quincy. So sorry I haven't got back with you, but I need to talk to you about your text." I hear concern and impatience in his voice.

"I apologize for bugging you tonight, but I felt I needed to tell the police. They are doing more stuff too, but the picture is the worst," I add as I come to the four-way light.

"I need to know about all that too but let's focus on the picture." I can hear Quincy shuffling some papers around.

I nod, then add, "Okay" since he can't see me. "What do you need?" I swallow to calm my nerves.

"Who took the picture?" Quincy waits silently for my answer.

I explain that I am pretty sure it was Sara Hawkins and that she was the one passing it around. I tell again about the towel, who all was at the gym that day and the note left on my Jeep. I then explain about the Instagram picture and the name it was posted under and finally the dress and how Jessica and Sara bragged to a friend about damaging it.

"Any idea where these girls are now?" Quincy waits for my answer.

"I guess at their homes but will soon be at the game. Tonight's the Winter Court Crowning and I was supposed to wear the dress they damaged so I am sure they are planning to be there," I say while keeping my focus on the road through an S turn.

"Okay, I will look into this Fiona. I also want to let you know that I went back through the car today and as you know, there isn't much left of the car after the fire. I didn't find her phone. The fire might have turned it to ash."

"Oh, well thank you for checking." I try to switch gears to keep up with him.

"Don't give up, Fiona. We found a security camera a block away from where we found Ella's car. We've been looking for any footage that might show Ella. If you think this black car might help in some way, I will go back through the tapes. Maybe we can pull some footage from that night," Quincy explains. "I know this is a lot right now, but what is the concern about the black car?"

I explain about the car following me and Wednesday night at the hospital. Officer Quincy takes all the information down and says he will look into it. He tells me to be careful and vigilant. And to make sure my parents or a friend know where I am going at all times. He thanks me for my time and the line goes dead.

I pull into a parking spot at the school about twenty minutes before the varsity game is to start and send Avery a text: "two rows back from the main entrance, just left of the door"

Avery responds: "omw"

About thirty seconds later, Avery comes bounding out of the doors. I flash my lights at her, and she walks to the passenger's side of the Jeep. Avery stops in her tracks when she opens the door.

"Oh!" she exclaims, eyes wide. I assume she is talking about my forehead, but maybe she means the dress.

"Not talking about it. Get in," I demand.

Avery giggles and climbs in, and I hand her the makeup bag with all of Faith's goodies. She immediately leans over to my seat and takes me into her arms.

"I am so sorry. This is so much bullshit." She keeps hugging me and I pat her arm after wiping away a tear. Avery pulls back so I can get my eyes under control, and she hands me a tissue from the glove box.

"Thanks, but I can't talk about it." I swallow and look at the school's entrance.

"I am so proud of you, Fi. For standing up for yourself and for coming here. I can't imagine how hard this must be. But they won't suspect this," Avery assures with an all-knowing nod.

"I realized earlier that it doesn't matter if I am here or not, they would still try to hurt me somehow. I just can't let them win."

"Good for you!" Avery smiles. "How did you know it was Sara and Jessica?"

"They bragged about it and Lyla overheard them. She texted and told me." I wait for Avery to say something. When she doesn't, I add, "She said that they shouldn't get away with it."

I turn to Avery who is watching me carefully. I take in a deep breath and exhale. "After talking to Mom, I realized she is right."

"Did you two talk?" Avery asks quietly.

"Lyla?" I shake my head no, and don't add anything else.

"Are you done crying?" Avery asks and I turn to her with a surprised look on my face.

"Well, if you're not done crying, there is no point of doing your makeup. But we are running out of time, so get it together," Avery adds bluntly.

I through my head back and bark out a laugh, and Avery laughs with me.

"I think we are going to need more light." I turn on the overhead lights, then reach for my phone to get my flashlight. "Don't overdo it. Just a little please." I close my eyes and let Avery work.

Avery shines her light into the makeup bag and finds powder, eyeshadow, eye liner and mascara and sets them on her lap. She tells me how to hold the flashlight and what to do with my face. Look to the left, then right. Close your eyes, now look up. Then she tells me to smack my lips together and done.

340

I don't even bother looking in the mirror. I don't care. It's not about how I look. This is about Faith's dress and the hell Sara and Jessica are causing me.

Just then, my phone beeps. It Jace. His text reads: "down to the last five minutes of the jv game"

I text back: "omw"

I lay my head back on the head rest and close my eyes. I take in a deep breath and exhale. My stomach is in knots and my heart is in my throat.

"You got this, girl." Avery reaches over and takes my hand. "C'mon!"

As the door swings open to the school, I hear the 4th quarter buzzer ring and cheers go up. The band plays as the JV teams leave the floor and the cheerleaders jump up to do a cheer. I've done this a hundred times and can see it playing out even though I am not in the gym yet.

At the ticket table, everyone stops to stare, but I keep walking right past them. I don't give anyone the chance to turn me away. Avery flashes her ticket stub at the table and jogs up to my side.

The corridor to the gym is quiet as the fans are in the gym waiting on the Winter Court festivities, but I notice the stares and whispers from those lingering in the corridor. My head feels light and fuzzy, and luckily Avery's arm is intertwined in mine and pulling me along, or I might turn around and run.

I look to Avery out of the corner of my eye as she nods and smiles at me. I give a faint nod back, hold my head up high and take a deep breath in and exhale.

The band stops playing as I continue to the gym. The fans grow quiet, and the announcer's voice booms through the speaker.

"Welcome to the 17th Annual Winter Queen Crowing." Mr. Sheffield stalls giving the cheerleaders, band, and fans a chance to settle into their seats.

When I reached the gym entrance, Jace is standing at the edge of the crowd in his black suit and tie. I look down and giggle at the cowboy boots as I walk into the gym to meet him.

"Where's your hat?" I ask, still giggling.

"I thought that might be a bit much," he admits with that crooked smirk. Damn that smile can make a girl stupid.

"I'm going in, you two," Avery says and gives my arm a squeeze.

"You look amazing." Jace blinks. "I need to thank Sara and Jessica for ripping your dress." Jace raises his eyebrows a few times. "It's slashed in all the right places." He winks and I feel my cheeks glow red. And that's all it takes. Everything else, everyone else falls away. It's just Jace and me.

"Here," Jace fumbles with the plastic container which slips out of his hands. Luckily, I catch it causing us both to giggle.

"And representing the freshman class, Shanna—"

The crowd jumps to their feet, cheering, drowning out the announcer. My eyes drop to the ground, and I swallow the lump in my throat. My strength wavers as I realize I would have been called next if I hadn't attached Riley. If I hadn't defended myself.

Jace takes my hand in his to adjust the slap bracelet around my wrist but doesn't pull his hand away once the corsage is in place. It's perfect. Five white teacup roses nestled in baby's breath, sheer white ribbon and Ruscus leaves.

"It's beautiful, Jace." I look up to meet his eyes and my heart warms. A smile spreads across my face in spite of the tears threatening to spill at the corner of my eye.

"Not compared to you," Jace whispers with a straight face and brushes away the tear at the corner of my eye.

My stomach flips and I glance away to the floor feeling my cheeks flush.

I lift my eyes from the ground toward the gym and see Sam's eyes on me. Staring me down. Brewer leans over and says something to Sam, Sam just grunts, throws his head back with a nod and continues staring.

I turn back to Jace, take his hand, and pull him away.

"Let's go." I lead Jace to the end of the basketball court where the Winter Court starts their procession, and I have no idea what I am doing. I didn't actually think I would make it this far.

"This year's Winter Queen is..." The crowd is silent, but I notice the whispers in the stands. I look out of the corner of my eye and zero in on Sara and Jessica huddled together laughing.

"Takiesha Benning." The crowd goes crazy. Jace and I release arms to clap for Takiesha. We stand to the side and watch the crown being placed on her head and roses in her arms. Camera flashes are going off as the yearbook staff captures the moment.

I jump at the tap on my shoulder and turn to find Mr. Clifton standing next to me.

"Fiona, I am glad you came but your dress isn't appropriate—"

I cut him off with a stare. I turn to Mr. Clifton, square my shoulders, and raise my chin to him.

"I know, this is what Jessica Brindle and Sara Hawkins did to it. It was appropriate I assure you when I took Faith's junior prom dress to the cleaners Jessica works at. I've already notified the police." I hold my stare on him until he huffs, then turns and walks away.

The Winter Court starts to make their way off the gym floor. When Takiesha sees me standing there, she let out a squeal and comes running over to wrap me in a hug.

"Congratulations Takiesha, I knew you would win." I continue our hug and she pats me on the back.

"I can't believe they did that to you." She pulls away from the hug. "I am *so* sorry they did this. The girls here at school and Mr. Clifton and Mrs. Conner," Takiesha glances in Mrs. Conner's direction and I see her face turn pink.

"No biggie. Just wanted to support all of you." I turned to give the other girls a hug when they realize what I am wearing.

"What the hell happened to Faith's dress?" Takiesha steps back to take it all in.

"Ah, well. My mom picked it up from the cleaners this afternoon and apparently this is what Jessica and Sara did to it?" I hold my arms out and look down at the shreds of blue barely covering my body.

"Fiona, you need to tell someone about all this stuff," Shanna jumps in.

"I did, I called to police earlier and told them everything. About the pictures and the dress." I wring my hands together wondering if I did the right thing. I shiver as Jace puts his arm around my shoulder, suddenly feeling very exposed.

345

Jace must have notice my shiver because he takes off his suit jacket and wraps it around my shoulders. He is a lot taller than me, and the jacket almost comes to me knees. I feel relief that the rips in the dress are covered and I mouth "thank you" to Jace.

A commotion behind us interrupts our conversation and we all turn to see what's up. I stand slightly behind Jace and take his arm in mine when I notice the uniformed officers at the gym entrance and the detective talking to Mr. Clifton. Officer Quincy. Standing next to him is a female officer I've never seen before. I blink a few times to make sure I'm not seeing things.

Mr. Clifton points to the crowd then leads the detectives to the far end of the cheering section. Mr. Clifton and the officers stop in front of Sara sitting in the front row with the cheerleaders and Jessica right behind her.

The band stops playing, and the crowd goes silent, you can hear a pin drop. I look to Lyla who is standing frozen, eyes wide, and staring at Sara.

"Ladies, I need to speak with you," I hear officer Quincy say. My head snaps back to Sara and Jessica. I almost feel sorry for them.

"What's this about?" Sara asks and looks to Mr. Clifton innocently.

"I think it would be better if we talk about this in my office ladies." Mr. Clifton nods toward the front of the building.

"I didn't do anything," Jessica shouts. "I'm not going anywhere." She crosses her arms over her chest.

I look from Jessica back to Sara who has gone pale, and I notice Sara's father walking across the gym floor. As a board member, he is at most the games, and he does not look happy.

Officer Quincy leans over and whispers something to the girls and Jessica's behavior changes. Sara looks like she might cry, and Jessica's face goes so pale her skin is almost transparent. The girls stand and follow Mr. Clifton toward the exit.

I watch as Mr. Hawkins scurries to catch up to Quincy.

"What's this about? This is my daughter." Mr. Hawkins holds out his hand toward Sara as he tries to keep pace with Quincy's stride.

"We have been made aware of a situation involving your daughter and need to have her and Jessica answer some questions." Quincy didn't bother to look at Mr. Hawkins. He just kept walking, Sara next to him and Jessica next to the female detective.

The group heads out of the gym and for a second, everyone stands around looking at each other. I look to Lyla who is straight-faced and watching Sara leave the gym, ignoring Shelby who is whispering in her ear. My heart hurts for Lyla as I know she feels guilty that she might be the reason they are in trouble. But Lyla did not do this.

I walk toward Lyla and stop about a foot from her. She slowly turns away from the exit and looks right at me.

"It wasn't you. You didn't get them into trouble. This is about the picture Sara took." I let that sink in, but Lyla doesn't reply. "Anyway, I'm sorry. I'm sorry I haven't talked to you about anything the last month or so. Sorry, for what I said and for not talking to you after Brooks." I stumble on my words and clear my throat. "But thank you."

I turn and walk back to Jace. The band starts playing and the Varsity teams make their way back to the floor for warm-ups.

For the first time, I take another look down at Faith's dress. There are rips everywhere. Several on the bodice, even one showing my hot pink bra. The bottom of the dress has slits running high on my thighs and hips of course showing my underwear. Mr. Clifton is right; the dress is not appropriate. But I made my point, and Sara and Jessica are in trouble.

"Ladies," I say softly as I turn back to the court, "I'm so sorry if I ruined your night." I raise my eyebrows as I realize for the first time, they might think I was trying to steal their time. "I promise that wasn't my intent."

"Of course not!" Takiesha chimes in. I look to the other girls who are shaking their heads and agreeing.

348

"This was supposed to be your night too." I look to see MyaNika Schilling, the candidate taking my place and see sympathy on her face. All I can do is nod. After a few seconds of awkward silence, I clear my throat and rub my hands over the shredded material.

"Ah. Okay, I need to get out of this monstrosity." I laugh and turn to Jace. "Walk me out?"

"You're leaving?" Jace takes a step back. "I think you should stay and watch the game with me."

"Ah, Jace. I would like that. But it's been a rough day. I think I can still make visiting hours. I need to see Faith." I lean in and give Jace a hug. He pulls back and turns to walk me out, placing his hand on the small of my back. Electricity shoots through me at the touch of his hand.

Chapter 17

I skip gymnastics today and spend a few hours Saturday morning helping Avery and Tarin decorate for the dance. Specifically, the desert and candy table. As I'm walking out the door, my phone beeps. A text from Jace and I feel my cheeks tighten and a tingly sensation runs through my body.

"Want to ride to the dance together?"

I start to type yes, then I erase it and text back: "i would love to, but i'm going to see faith before the dance. i think it will be easier if i drive. meet me there?"

I climb in my Jeep as my phone beeps again. Jace responds: "of course"

My smile fades when I look up and see the note under my wiper. I freeze and stare at the note. I look around to see who is in the parking lot. No one in any direction but me.

I open my door and reach around the windshield for the note. I sit back down in my seat and swallow the lump in my throat and once again look around wondering if anyone is watching, then I open the note.

Written in scribble I don't recognize; I can barely make out the words.

"This isn't over bitch!"

I look around again, half expecting to see the black Charger, but the lot is silent.

The beep of the phone brings me back. I check my phone, another text from Jace: "are you planning to wear the corsage tonight?"

I text back: "yep"

I wait on Jace's response. "i was going to get you another one, but mom said you probably kept it"

I giggle and write back: "of course, i did. thanks for what you did last night. couldn't have done it without u and avery"

Jace responds: "of course just wish you would have stayed" followed by a smiley emoji.

I drop my head back and let out a laugh and text back: "driving. see you 2night"

In the hospital parking lot, I glance at my clock which reads 1:26. I think about how much time I need to get ready and when I need to leave the hospital.

Mom and Dad are at Faith's side, and both look up and smile when I walk in. I look to Faith to see if there is any improvement. I notice the swelling on her face is subsiding. She still doesn't look like Faith. The reconstructive surgery must have changed her facial structure.

Dad comes over and gives me a kiss on the head.

"How is she?" I ask. "I should have come to see her sooner."

"You've had a lot going on, Fi. Give yourself a break." I look up to my dad. "She knows you love her." He rubs my shoulder.

"She blinked last night." Mom beamed.

"And you didn't tell me?" I look at Mom, my eyes wide.

"Well, I planned to," Mom fumbles.

"She's telling you now, Fi." Dad is standing behind Mom with his hands on her shoulders showing a front of solitude.

"What happened? She didn't do that when I came in last night." I look at Mom and move to the seat on the other side of Faith, the leather squeaks when I sit.

"You came in last night?" Dad asks and looks up at me.

"Yeah, after I left the game. I didn't stay too long. Honestly, I was exhausted and missed Faith." I pull up a seat next to the bed. "So, what happened?"

"I-I was telling Faith stories about you, her, Ella and Lyla and..." Mom shrugs. "And she just blinked. Only once, but still."

"That's good, right?" My eyes dart from Mom to Dad.

"Doc says it is," Mom sighs and tilts her head.

"Let's give Fiona and Faith some time, Sharon. You need to eat," my dad says, urging my mom to the door.

"Honey, do you need anything?" Mom asks me and my stomach growls.

"Yeah, I haven't had any lunch," I admit and watch them stand up.

"What do you want?" I look to Mom standing in the door holding my dad's hand.

"Um, burger and fries please."

"Got it," Dad responds.

Once they are out of the room, I take Faith's hand and begin telling her about the last forty-eight hours since I couldn't bring myself to do it last night. I begin with the fight. Jace not being my escort, then forgiving me and being my escort. The fight with Riley and then getting suspended and kicked off court. Lyla refusing to talk to me, then her telling me about Sara and Jessica. Suddenly, I remember the messages on Faith's computer.

"I didn't know Ella had a boyfriend..." I feel Faith squeeze my hand. "I was on your computer doing homework and saw your messages. Why didn't you tell me? And why was she so secretive about him?"

I think back to the picture of Ella and some guy with his face cut out of his picture.

"I need to ask Mom and Dad E about him." Faith squeezes my hand again. I reach up and brush her hair off her face, just like I did when she got influenza her freshman year.

I knew the piece of hair that hung in her eye would bother her, but she was too sick to care. But I did. She wouldn't want it there, tickling her eyelid.

"I've been going to see them on Sundays. I think it is really hard for them to come see you. I know it is, but they still do. Oh, that reminds me. I got a call from Officer Quincy. He searched your car again for your phone, but no luck. Didn't even find anything that might have once been your phone." I sigh and look away from Faith.

I look to the bed at the blonde curly hair and blue eyes and squint trying to find Faith in there.

"Oh, another thing. Quincy said he is rewatching the video tapes that were pointed in the direction where Ella's—Aw, I know, Faith," I say when she squeezes my hand. "You miss her too." But as I watch her face, I have a sinking feeling in the pit of my stomach. I shiver at the sudden chill rolling down my spine and try to remember what I was saying.

After a few seconds, I realize I haven't filled Faith in on the black car or how I think it is stalking me or Wednesday night when I left the hospital. I shared my conversation about Quincy and the tapes and how I hope there is some connection that might help find Ella.

Faith blinks. My mouth drops open and I can't take my eyes off her, hoping she will blink again. I clear my throat and open my mouth.

"So, can you blink again for me?" I watch intently, leaning in toward Faith. The chair squeaking under me.

"You okay?" I let out a squeal at the sound of my dad's voice and turn to look at him coming in the room.

"Ah. Yeah. She blinked. I asked her if she would blink again—"

"And you couldn't take your eyes off of her afraid you might miss it." Dad smiles as he walks to me, wraps his arm around my shoulder and pulls me in for a quick side hug.

"Exactly." I sigh and fall back in my seat.

"Here. Eat," Mom says. "I put salt and ketchup in the bag."

"Thanks," I mumble as I rummage through the bag, pull out the burger and take a big bite.

I must have scarfed down my food in a matter of seconds because when I wad up the bag, while still chewing the last bite of my food, I look up to find Mom and Dad watching me wide eyed and mid bite.

"When was the last time you ate?" Dad asks as he chews.

"Um…" Thinking back over the last twenty-four hours. "Yesterday morning."

"Fiona," Mom scolds and I wince, my eyes meeting her frown. "You know what Dr. Saunders said. You need to eat three times a day. Plus, snacks."

"I know, I know." I throw my hands in the air in surrender. "I've been doing better and tracking everything. But I wasn't one bit hungry after what happened in Mr. Clifton's office."

"Well, promise me you will get back on track," Mom grumbles.

"Promise." I reach over Faith to Dad's plate of fries and steal a few.

"Hey!" He wraps his arms around his food to protect it from me. "Go buy your own."

"Already ate'em" I mumble through a mouth full of food.

"Okay, so tell me what happened last night at the game," Mom adds then takes another bite.

I take a deep breath and exhale, leaning back in my chair again and told them everything.

"So, the police came to the school and took Jessica and Sara?" Dad's eyes are wide.

"Well, Mr. Clifton took them to his office so they could talk. Mr. Hawkins went too." I shrug my shoulders. "I don't think they were arrested. But I've been avoiding social media lately, so."

"Shew. I bet Jim wasn't happy." Dad looks to Mom with a knowing nod.

"I don't think he was." I shake my head and think about how he basically had to run to keep up with Quincy.

"Well, I am glad they are looking into it," Mom says as she is replacing the lid on her half-eaten salad. "It's horrible what they did to you, Fiona. And they acted like friends."

The room is quite for a few moments, I'm not sure what to say.

"I'm proud of you for standing up for yourself. But you still need to be careful. And watch out, don't trust everyone." Mom stands, picks up Dad's empty food wrapper and walks to the trash.

"Yeah, I get that. I'm just sorry I put you both through this." I bite my lip and look down at the piece of hair I am twirling between my fingers.

"Okay, if you're going to be ready in time, you should get going." Mom points at the clock.

"We plan to be home before you leave. The dance doesn't start till 7:00, right?" Dad asks.

"Yes. Mom I could use your help with my makeup, can you be back by 5:30?"

"Of course, but it won't take that long to do your makeup," Mom corrects me.

"If I did it, it would," I admit and stand up to walk behind my parents and give them a hug from behind.

"Love you." Then I turn to Faith and kiss her forehead. "Love you too Faith." My stomach quivers.

At the door, I turn back to look at Faith on more time, then turn to my parents. I blow them a kiss and walk out of the room.

I realize the corridor is eerily quiet which is odd as it is 3:00 on a Saturday. I stop halfway between Faith's room and the elevator and look back over my shoulder toward the stair well. A black hooded figure disappears as the door swings shut.

A shiver runs down my spine and before I think about what I am doing, I take off running down the corridor hoping to catch the hooded person.

My footsteps light on the linoleum floor in my furry boots, my arms pumping, I reach the metal door and slide past in my worn-down boots with no tread stopping only when I grab the door handle. I swing the heavy door open and listen for steps.

I hear fast paced heavy steps echo through the stairwell and onto the concrete landing below. I follow. My heart pounding hard against my ribs. I hear the heavy metal door below me on the ground floor swing open and smack the concrete wall behind it.

My knees ache with each step, my muscles pumping, lungs burning. I get to the first floor and the adrenaline helps me swing the door open.

I step out into hospital lobby gasping for air. My head feels light. I raise my arms over my head to get rid of the cramp in my side.

I spin around searching in every direction, but no one's here. I bend over and rest my hands on my knees trying to catch my breath as I watch out the floor to ceiling windows along the front of the hospital for a black Charger.

I stand up and take the phone out of my back pocket and open my camera. This time I'll be ready for it. Sweat is beading on my forehead and running down my temples. I'm suddenly burning up in this hospital; my vision a little blurry. I need air.

I make my way to the exit, keeping my eyes open for the car. The cold bite of January feels good on my face as I step through the spinning doors.

I pay close attention to the parking lot, looking all around and keep my phone handy. But no car. At least no black Charger.

"Damn it!" I exhale.

In my Jeep, I take a few minutes with the window rolled down to let the cool air wash over my face and replay the situation in my mind but keep my eye on my rearview mirror just in case.

After several minutes I accept that the black car isn't coming out to play so I pull up my playlist downloaded on my Uconnect hard drive and scroll through the list. I smile when I see the song my dad used to torture us with when we were little. Over time it has taken a special place in Faith, Ella, Lyla, and my hearts and feels like just what I need. So, I crank up the volume to Beastie Boy's Paul Revere and before I know it, I'm driving down I-74 belting out the chorus:

"He told a little story that sounded well-rehearsed,

Four days on the run and that he's dying of thirst

The brew was in my hand, and he was on my tip..."

The digital clock on my dash shows 3:31 and I left out a sigh as I continue to sing. But the butterflies pick back up the closer I get to home, although I'm not sure why. The worst already happened yesterday.

I pull into the driveway and my phone beeps. Then beeps a second and third time.

"Shit. Now what?" I mutter to my phone and pull up the latest text. Relieved to see it is from Jace: "hi fi mom still went to the game last night and snapped some pictures"

I scroll through the pictures, and a smile spreads across my face seeing how handsome Jace is. I barely recognize who is standing next to him. I blink a few times and finally recognize the dress. Faith's beautiful and now ruined dress. I make the picture bigger.

I blink at the picture and zoom the picture out. I look more like Faith than I ever have. Avery did an amazing job on my makeup. *Wow, if only the dress wasn't ruined. Gawd. Is the dress really that bad?*

I jump out of the Jeep and run straight to the garment bag hanging on my closet door, zip open the bag and take out Faith's dress to look it over when I notice a picture flip out of the bottom of the garment bag.

I look down at the floor and see a face staring back at me. I recognize the face. I recognize the picture.

I drape the dress over my arm and reach down for the photo I saw on Faith's computer. A printed version only showing Ella. This photo has been cropped and the background photoshopped. One corner has a black edge. It looks to be burnt.

I think back to a night last Thanksgiving when I got a text from Faith. *"hey fi, leave the spare key under the mat when you leave. Ella is stopping by to get a few things from my room. I don't think I will get off work in time."*

I typed: "k, need me to get anything out?"

Faith responded: "no Ella knows where everything is. she needs a dress for a xmas party at the end of the semester, so she is looking through my stuff."

I toss the picture on my desk and turn back to the dress, place it in the bag and take it to Faith's closet. Then I go into the bathroom to

361

shower and do all the things girls need to do to look their best. I dry and straighten my hair when I hear the garage door go up.

I look at my phone, yep 5:30. I unplug my straightener and walk back in my room when the picture on my desk grabs my attention. The photo landed face down and I notice writing on the back in black sharpie. I pick the picture up, expecting to see the location the photo was taken or something to that effect, but struggle to make out the scribbled writing.

"12/3/22 53:22 LT 5105"

I stare at the scribble trying to make sense of it.

"Fi?" Startled, I turn to see my mom standing at my door.

"Oh. Hi, Mom." I drop the picture on my desk and turn to her.

"I picked up pizza on the way home. I figured I wouldn't have time to cook and do your makeup."

Mom watches me as I realize I hadn't even given dinner a thought.

"You nervous, Fi?" Mom asks and I am thankful she didn't point out that I hadn't thought about dinner.

"Yeah, a little." I nod. "But I think I'm more excited."

"Eat first, then makeup. C'mon." Mom motions me to the kitchen where I find Dad already seated and I take my seat at the table. Merida takes Faith's seat and I give her a knowing smirk.

"Merida," Mom scolds. "Faith will not approve of this." She wags her finger.

"She's a member of this family too," I say and slide a piece of pizza on my plate.

"Yes, but she should not be seated at the table." Mom gives me the eye.

"Merida, come." Merida hops down and I sneak her a pepperoni as a reward.

"Mom says you're a bit nervous, Fi. Why? After last night, I would say tonight is a piece of cake." Dad takes a drink and picks up the pizza for another bite.

"I don't know. I'm excited but…I guess it's just all the other stuff going on—"

"That reminds me." Mom cuts me off before I could tell them about the stairwell. "We have our first appointment scheduled for next Wednesday with the counselor. I was able to get an appointment at 4:00 so you don't have to miss school."

"I don't think I have practice Wednesday either." I look to the old school calendar still on the fridge. I've given up on trying to get her to sink her iPhone calendar with mine. Then I wince realizing that I am suspended through Wednesday. Thankfully, neither say anything about it and Mom continues.

"So how about we ride together, go to counseling, then grab dinner and go see Faith?" Mom looks back from the sink as she rinses off her plate and places it in the dishwasher.

"Sounds like a plan." I hop up and grab my plate as I eat my last bite of pizza. "Now, let's go do my makeup." I lead Mom to the bathroom with Merida on my heels.

"I found this on Pinterest, how about we do your hair like this?" Mom hands me her phone. "The colors are similar to yours and it really shows of the red and blonde which would look great with your dress."

I look at the picture and trying to imagine my hair like that.

"Can you do that?" I ask Mom, still looking at her phone.

"It's simple really, it's a variation of a braid called a fishtail. I used to do them for you girls when you were little," Mom says running her fingers through my hair.

"Really? I don't remember that." I look up from the phone to see Mom's face.

"Well, when your sister came home in tears because she was made fun of at school for wearing a fishtail, I stopped." Mom grabs my shoulders and turns me to face the mirror as she runs a brush through my hair.

"Faith was picked on in school?" I find her eyes in the mirror.

"Unfortunately, yes." Mom looks up to meet my eyes without stopping the work she is doing on my hair. "She came home several times in elementary crying because someone said something mean to her. Made fun of her clothes, her hair, anything really." Mom looks back to my hair as she continues. "Not unlike you, but Faith was picked on by a girl a few years older than her."

"You knew?" I watch her in the mirror, as she puts the brush down, and takes my hair into her hands.

"Of course. But you were always so strong. Determined to find your own way. You never said anything to anyone about it, but a mother knows," Mom sighs. "I noticed the comments and glances from the other girls. The school carnival, cheerleading for 6th grade basketball," Mom shrugs, "open houses."

"Why didn't you say anything?" I look to my own refection in the mirror and notice my watery eyes.

"You seemed to be handling it okay. I would have stepped in if needed but when you were upset, you would go out in the back yard and do your gymnastics. It was your coping mechanism. That's why I always made sure you stayed in gymnastics. Even when you took up cheer," Mom said as a matter of fact.

"I didn't realize, you were watching out for me in your own way," I mumble and look down at my hands.

365

"I was. Faith didn't handle it as well as you." Mom works effortlessly on my hair.

"I never knew." I sniff and reach for a tissue.

"Well, you were younger than her and probably just don't remember." I feel her tug on my hair a few times as I think over Mom's words. "See. All done, we just need to loosen it up and pull some strands out to give it a messy look."

I take out a mirror and turn around to check the back.

"How did you do that?" I look at my hair from every angle as I turn my head in different directions. Mom standing behind me.

"I'll show you some time, but now, let's do your make up. I was thinking since your dress is that deep red, you should wear red lipstick and we will keep the eyes natural."

"Red? Me? I don't—"

"Trust me. Everyone can wear red. It all about finding the right shade. And no, you shouldn't wear Faith's red. You can wear my shade."

Mom works on my face, and I follow her instructions. Look up. Look down. Close your eyes. Smack your lips together. All that silly stuff I used to watch Faith do each morning and Avery had me do last night.

"All done." Mom steps back with a smile.

366

I blink at myself in the mirror, surprised I look like me but also like the girl in the pictures with Jace.

"I guess I can wear red lipstick." I hear Mom giggle as she puts the lip stick back in her makeup bag.

"Finish getting ready, and I will be back in a few minutes." Mom turns, leaving me standing there in the bathroom staring in the mirror.

I slip into my new dress, the one with the beaded bodice and fluffy tulle skirt and sit down on my bed to slip into my new burgundy suede deep V-cut booties with a stiletto heels. A little gutsy for me to try and pull off without Faith or Lyla's help, but they just felt right. Especially since it is freezing out and the other pair I liked were strappy and open.

I walk to the living room and find Mom smiling with her hands clasped together. Dad lets out a whistle and rubs his hand across his forehead.

"Look out, boys. She's a heartbreaker." He shakes his head and laughter rolls through me.

"Dad. Stop it. Do I look ok?" I look to Mom first then Dad waiting for their response.

"Beautiful, honey," Dad says as he stands up, walks across the living room, and kisses my forehead.

"Not bad." Mom shrugs. "But I think something is missing."

I watch as she turns to the piano and then I look down at my dress. *Undies, bra, pantyhose, dress, shoes...that's it. That's everything.* Mom turns around with a small box and places it in my hand.

"These where your great, great grandmothers on my dad, your grandpa's side. I was going to give them to you at your graduation, but I think they are perfect for tonight."

I lift the box from mom's hand, it's a little heavier than I was expecting and open the lid. The sparkling garnet gems shine back at me. Earrings and a bangle bracelet.

"They are gorgeous." My eyes go wide at the pair of cluster drop earrings with a larger garnet in the center surrounded by two outer layers of smaller garnets, dangling from a smaller cluster of three garnets on gold shepherd hook wires. Below the earrings is a perfectly matched bracelet featuring five of the same garnet cluster with gold facets connecting each together and the center cluster has a larger garnet and an additional layer of small garnets.

"They are antique Bohemian Garnet pieces made in the late 1800's. They were a gift from your great, great grandmother's husband upon their marriage in 1910 and were originally his mother's." My mom shares as she takes each piece out of the box.

"I-I don't know what to say." I watch my mom put the earrings on me. "I'm afraid to wear them."

"Don't be silly. They are meant to be worn." Mom smiles as she takes my hand, which feels cooler than hers.

"Just don't lose them." Dad laughs.

"That's what I was thinking." I toss my head back and laugh, almost losing my balance in my tall heals.

"Right." Mom nods. "They are meant to be worn; not lost."

I look in the mirror and reach up to touch one of my earrings to make sure I am not imagining this.

"What about Faith?" I turn to Mom. "Shouldn't she at least have either the earrings or bracelet?"

"It's a set, Fiona. They stay together, just like you and Faith." Mom sounds motherly and I swallow hard thinking about Faith. "Besides, Faith was given her heirloom pieces already."

"Really? Are they like mine?" I ask turning my head in the mirror letting the garnets catch the light from the ceiling fan.

"No, yours are older. Faith received a sapphire ring and earrings from the Art Deco period, which was the early 1900s. They came from Dad's side of the family, and he gave them to her to wear at her junior prom. You know, the earrings she wore with the blue dress from last night."

I feel a pinch in my heart when I think about the dress.

"Fi, you okay?" Dad asks when he notices me lost in my thoughts.

"Ah, yeah. Just taking this all in." I wring my hands together to keep from touching my earrings or my face.

"There, now you are ready." Mom steps out of the way, so I can see my appearance. "Is Jace picking you up?"

"He offered, but I wasn't sure if I was getting ready and going back to the hospital, so I told him I would meet him there."

"I was hoping to get a picture of you two." Mom frowns.

"I'm sure there will be lots of photos taken at the dance, Sharon." Dad puts his arm around Mom.

"Well, let me at least get a few of you." Mom takes out her phone and I know there is no point in arguing so I pose and smile, and even make a duck face.

"Stop it with that face." Mom stops snapping and lowers her camera. "What's up with all you girls doing that with your lips in pictures?" But Mom isn't wanting an answer, so I try to think of something happy. Jace comes to mind and my natural smile comes through.

"Okay, okay. That's enough. I'll make sure you get a picture of us." I hold my hands up in front of my face. "Are you going to go back to the hospital?"

Mom and Dad look at each other.

"We are meeting the Wilson's for a drink," Dad says. "But I think we will probably stop on our way home." Mom seems to relax at his words.

"So, I'm going to go now. Love you both." I grab my coat and gold beaded clutch and walk to the front door.

"Oh, your corsage." Mom runs to the kitchen. I hear the fridge door open, and she meets me halfway.

"Leave it in the box until you get to school to protect it," she advises.

"Thanks Mom." I give her a hug.

"Have fun," Dad calls and waves.

"Be safe," Mom adds, but I can barely hear them over my own thoughts of Jace.

Chapter 18

I take the key out of the ignition but can't seem to move. I can't take my eyes off the couples walking into the cafeteria, arm in arm and hurrying to get out of the cold. I hear the group of freshman girls squealing and giggling before I see them and remember how excited Lyla and I were last year as we entered the dance.

Faith and Ella had decided to go stag to the dance.

"It's our senior year! Screw the boys!" Ella shouted from the front seat of Faith's car. "Let's go with our fam."

Faith giggled and nodded in agreement.

"So, does that mean we can ride with you?" I asked.

"Aren't you going with Sam?" Faith looked over her shoulder at me in the back seat.

"You know Mom's rule," I grumbled.

"No dating as a freshman..." all four of us finished in the same sing-song voice.

"What about you, Lyla? Not going with anyone?" Ella asked and passed the bag of Takis back to us.

"No. I'm holding out for MJ to ask me." Lyla beamed with excitement and rocked side to side next to me.

"So, he's talked to you?" Faith's eyebrows raised in the review mirror as she met Lyla's eyes.

"Nope, but any day now." And we all busted out laughing.

"So, you'll take us, right?" I sat up in the back seat and leaned on Ella's head rest.

"Of course, we will chauffer you two losers around." Ella blew me and Lyla a kiss.

"But you're lucky we love you," Faith added and turned up the volume. Ella started shuffling through her play list.

Last year at this time I was on cloud nine. My bestie by my side, my boyfriend waiting on me to arrive and Faith and Ella were safe.

The beep on my phone jolts me out of my thoughts. I pull up the text from Jace: "inside let me know when ur here"

My hand falls to my lap as my head drops back against the head rest and I stare at the roof. It would be easy to make an excuse and get out of here. I close my eyes and picture Jace's sexy smirk. My stomach flutters but not from anxiety, from excitement.

I text Jace back: "omw"

And before I have a chance to change my mind, I hop out of the Jeep and scurry on my tip toes to the door and remember Mrs. Conner's words last week.

"Fiona, you're on court. You don't need a ticket." She looked *amazed that I would ask.* But technically, I am no longer on court. I fight off a shiver as I open the door.

I swallow hard as I approach the table, my eyes darting around for anyone who might recognize me to help verify that I am supposed to be here. Then I look around again hoping no one is around to witness my possible rejection if they require a ticket.

"That color is beautiful on you, Fiona." I let out the breath I am holding when I hear Mr. Jones' words and give a weak smile.

Mr. Jones leans in and in a hushed voice adds, "That was very courageous what you did last night." He gives little nod and I see a faint smile cross his face. "Have fun." He waves me on.

"Thank you." My voice shaky.

As I walk past the ticket table, I am transported to a winter wonderland with varying types and sizes of spruce trees adorned with snow on each side of the corridor, snowflakes and clear lights hanging from the ceiling. I walk thought a tunnel of arches made of leafless branches covered in twinkling lights that was not there when I left this morning, and white felt covering the ground to look like snow.

The arched tunnel opens to the cafeteria where Tarin, Avery and I decorated the dessert table and candy bar which is adjacent to the dance floor. The dance floor is draped with white sheer fabric from the center of the ceiling out to the edges of the dance floor where the fabric gathers and hangs. Snowflakes float on the blue and white aggregate floor from the light in the center of the ceiling. My breath catches.

"Fiona." I turn to Jace who is holding out a dozen long stem red roses, I barely notice the music playing. "These are for you."

"Oh, Jace. They're beautiful." I scoop up the roses in my arms and sniff the fragrance of an open rose. I look back to him. "You didn't have to."

"I know." Jace rolls his eyes and shrugs. "I wanted to." Jace smiles that sexy crooked smile I imagined earlier, his hair styled like last night, but a little looser, shaggier. More Jace-like and it looks just as sexy. I look down and giggle, the boots.

"Thank you, Jace." I breath in the scent of the roses again and smile.

"Beautiful," Jace breaths.

"I know, can you believe this place?" I look around the cafeteria. "It didn't look anything like this when I left at 1:00 today. You can't even tell it's the same cafeteria we eat in."

"No," Jace whispers and shakes his head. "I mean you, Fiona." My eyes meet Jace's, I blush under the weight of his stare. My heart is beating so hard it could break a rib.

"Thank you, so are you." I giggle and roll my eyes. "Handsome. You look handsome."

"Thanks." Jace straightens up a little and adjusts his tie. "Shall we?" He holds out his arm for me to take just like he did last night at the ceremony we weren't a part of. We walk past the dance floor to the section of tables at the back of the room and look around for a seat.

I place the roses on a table and Jace helps me out of my coat. I sit down in the chair and place my purse on the table next to the roses.

Jace takes the seat next to me and takes my hand in his.

"So, what part of this wonderland did you create?" Jace asks and looks around.

"Ah, we put together the dessert table and candy bar." I point in that direction.

"Oooo...two of my favorite things." I laugh at his enthusiasm. "Let's go check out your work." Jace tugs on my hand, and I follow.

"Avery." I let go of Jace's hand to give Avery a hug. "You look amazing."

"So do you. Great color on you and that lipstick..." Avery teases. "Fiya gurl."

"Ladies," Jace says as he licks icing off his finger. "I have to say, you did a great job on the dessert table."

"You know we didn't actually make the desserts, right?" Avery leans around me to watch Jace shove the last bite of cupcake in his mouth.

"You didn't? Then what did you do?" Jace looks around. Avery starts explaining our work.

"That's a little disappointing. But it's still tastes great." He reaches for a white chocolate covered strawberry.

"I need to use the restroom, Avery? Jace I'll be right back." Avery follows me.

"I don't really, just wanted to have a minute to ourselves," I whisper to Avery who is huddled up next to me.

"Jace looks hella good." Avery giggles dragging out the word good. "So, what's up?"

"Nothing. Honestly, I just want to check the earrings Mom gave me tonight."

"I was going to ask. They are really cool. They look antique." Avery leans in closer to see.

"They are, apparently they were my great, great grandmother's and Faith was given a sapphire set a few years ago."

"Wow." Avery is now looking at my bracelet.

"I agree, but I'm kinda worried about wearing them." I reach for my earrings to make sure they are still there.

"Are you worried about losing them or what?" Avery asks.

"After the dress, shouldn't I be? And everything else they did?" I whisper and look around to make sure no one is in earshot.

Avery drops back from me. "What do you think they might do tonight?"

"I'm not sure, but when I left after decorating today, there was a note on my wind shield that read, 'this isn't over.'"

"What isn't over?" Avery crosses her arms over her chest and leans forward and I shrug. "Any idea who put it there?"

"Nope." I sigh and rub my hands over my arms to fight off a chill.

"Huh, that's odd. I wonder what it means?" Avery keeps her eyes down and frowns.

"I don't know, but I can't shake this feeling…" I pause and look around.

"What is it?" Avery asks impatiently as I wait for the couple to walk past us.

"I don't know. Something isn't right, but I can't put my finger on it. I swear sometimes I am being followed." I roll my eyes and shake my head at how ridiculous I sound. But when I meet Avery's eyes, I don't see the carefree look I was expecting. Instead, I see a pale faced Avery with wide eyes waiting on me to explain.

"I'm overreacting." I wave my hand in the air to push the thought away. "I'm sure it's just stress." And shake my head. "C'mon. Let me look at my earrings again."

I wrap my arm through Avery's, and we scurry to the bathroom. We come to a halt as we round the corner and see Jessica and another classmate. My smile fades and my eyes dart back and forth between both girls, and I notice Jessica's chest and arms are covered in hives.

I look over at Avery who is giving me that "what is *she* doing here look." I shrug my shoulders with a slight shake of the head to let Avery know I don't know. I straighten up, square my shoulders, and raise my head and continue to the mirror to check my reflection then wash my hands, Avery right by my side.

"I'm glad Takiesha won, but I voted for Kaylor," Jessica says louder than necessary as she leans in to look in the mirror.

"Well, you know who *I didn't* vote for," the other girl adds while reapplying a too-pink lipstick.

"No one voted for her," Jessica quips and crosses her arms over her chest placing her hands to cover her shoulders. Not a good night to wear a sweat heart neckline.

"I feel bad for MyaNika," say the other girl. "I mean, not only should she have been the sophomore class candidate in the first place, but she had to use someone else's votes. Or lack thereof."

"Yeah," Jessica adds. "I wish we would have found out earlier that MyaNika was our candidate. I would have voted for her."

I clench my teeth and feel the heat rise in my cheeks. My heart is in my throat. I need to get out of here, but I will not turn and run.

"I've been looking for you two." I look up at the sound of Neveah's voice as she enters the restroom. "Oh." Neveah looks to Avery and me like she is just realizing we are here. "I mean these two," Neveah quips waving a finger to Jessica and the other girl. "Not you two. No one's looking for you two." Jessica and the other girl giggle but I watch Jessica in the mirror. Red face, jaw clinched. She is pissed.

"I'm not even sure how you're allowed to be here if Riley isn't," Jessica hisses.

I focus on the image of my lips in the mirror, then turn my head side to side like I did at home to look at the earrings and hope I look natural. Avery quietly watches but doesn't say a word.

"I don't even want to be in here with her after what she did," Neveah grumbles walking to the exit with Jessica and the other girl in tow.

I watch from the mirror and release my breath as the trio rounds the corner. I close my eyes and take a few more breaths to calm myself.

"Forget them, Fiona. They are not worth it. Besides, they are just pissed about the dress thing and the picture." Avery looks in the mirror over my shoulder.

"Why? Because I wore the dress anyway?" I drop my hands to the sink and turn to look at Avery.

"Tarin overheard someone talking. Your mom called the owner of the cleaners last night and told them what Jessica did to the dress. The owner's pulled Jessica into the office this morning and fired her," Avery whispers with a smile on her face. "Apparently the owners are looking into pressing charges since she damaged someone else's property that the cleaner is responsible for."

"No shit?" I can't hide my excitement and let out a giggle.

"Notice Sara isn't here either?" Avery raises her eyebrows.

"Um, no I haven't noticed." I scowl as I think to why Sara wasn't with Jessica.

"Apparently, Sara is in trouble too, but no one knows if it is the picture or what? Supposedly the female detective that was here last night is with the child pornography unit or something. Sara admitted that she took the picture." Avery lets that sink in as she applies gloss to her lips. Then continues after giving her lips a smack. "I'm surprised the police officer hasn't contacted you."

I look to my phone and notice I have a voice mail message from Officer Quincy.

"I have a message..." I hold up a finger to Avery as I click play. "It's from earlier today."

Avery waits quietly as I listen to Quincy's voice coming through the speaker.

"Hi Fiona. I want to let you know that Sara admitted to everything. The locker room picture and coming into the cleaner to help Jessica ruin the dress. Sara is in trouble for taking and distributing child pornography, which is what the picture she took of you is considered since you are only sixteen. But she swears she did not take the Instagram picture. We will continue to look into it. Anyway, I just wanted to let you know. Also, I am still looking into the black Charger. I'll be in touch." And the line goes dead.

I drop the phone from my ear and turn to Avery.

"What happened?" Avery places her hands on my shoulder and give a little shake. I blink a few times replaying Quincy's words over in my mind.

"I-I-I guess Sara is in big trouble," I studder and wait for Avery to respond but she just nods with wide eyes encouraging me to continue.

"She admitted to taking the locker room pic. Apparently, that is distribution of child pornography as I am a minor. And that is not good." I can't move. Avery stands there unblinking as she realizes the severity of the situation.

"So, what's going to happen to her?" Avery asks and finally blinks.

"No idea." I shake my head and shrug.

"Wow. That explains the rumor that Sara is grounded and not at the dance." Avery halfheartedly chuckles. "I was tickled pink when I first heard about it, but now—"

"You kinda feel for her?" I say and watch Avery in the mirror.

Avery shakes her head. "Nope. That was really shitty what she did to you. She totally deserves to be in trouble."

I let out the breath I was holding.

"Yes, but this is big. Like, big trouble." I shake my head.

"And all because she is jealous of you. She is in big trouble because of her actions," Avery adds trying to reassure me.

I blow out another breath of air letting myself relax a little. Finally.

"*And* they didn't get away with it." Avery nudges my elbow with hers and I meet her eyes in the mirror and feel a small smile cross my face.

"So, I'm thinking about getting a tattoo." Avery turns her back to the mirror and leans against the sink.

"Really? Where did that come from?" I reach for a paper towel to wipe my hands.

"Yeah, I really like where your sister has hers." Avery nods.

"Oh, I didn't know you knew about that." I look to my wrist and adjust my bracelet.

"Well, I didn't until I went with you to see her. I like the location of hers." Avery nods.

"What—"

"I need the Winter Queen's Court and their escorts to report to the ticket table at this time," Mrs. Conner announces over the microphone interrupting our conversation.

The announcement feels like a punch in the gut. I swallow hard but remind myself that this is not about me. The girls on court still deserve the celebration.

Avery never takes her eyes off me but doesn't say word. She just gives me a big hug. I exit the restroom and search for Jace and find him still at the desert table.

"Still eating?" I ask.

"Yep." Jace nods putting his arm around my shoulder and leans into whisper. "You okay?"

I take another breath and exhale. "Yeah." I nod. "Everything is going to be okay."

"I mean, about watching the court dance…" Jace clarifies.

I watch as Kaylor and her escort are announced but the sting is not as bad as I thought it would be. She looks so happy; I feel a genuine smile come to me.

"No, no I'm not okay, Jace." I shake my head and fight off the thoughts trying to creep in about what I did to deserve all of this. I must have been a real bitch along the way cause karma just kicked my ass all over the place.

"But this is the way it is." I lean in to Jace for support as we listen to each candidate being called to the dance floor. I can see the candidates making their way under the arches of lit branches and a smile grows on my face imaging how it would feel to walk under the arches on Jace's arm.

From this side of the cafeteria, it is difficult to see the court dancing for all the students gathered around the dance floor. I stand on my tip toes to see but I'm too short. I look to Jace who is watching me. He takes my hand and pulls me around to the other side of the dance floor by the DJ where the crowd isn't so thick.

"Excuse me, excuse me..." Jace leads me through the crowd and stops at the edge of dance floor. Takiesha gives me a wave and I smile at her. When I look to MyaNika, she gives me a big smile and nods. Jace tugs lightly on my hand turning me toward him as we fall into rhythm with Ed Sheeran's voice singing Perfect.

385

A shiver runs through me when Jace places a hand on my lower back, takes my hand in his free hand and spins me around. I giggle, not expecting the move and feel my pulse rise as Jace pulls me in. That smirk, he's pretty pleased with himself. Damn, it's sexy.

I rest my hand on his shoulder, my other hand still in his and his arm wraps around my waist. His face grows serious, and my heart skips a beat. *Yes. Kiss me. Please.*

I rise up on my toes, hoping he gets the hint, but Jace is already moving in. He pauses just centimeters from my face, never taking his eyes off mine and I feel his warm breath on my lips. My eyes close as Jace leans in, his lips meeting mine. Soft, sweet, and gentle. Perfect.

My eyes flutter open as he pulls away and I register the cheers from the crowd.

"Woohoo!" someone yells along with squeals and whoops.

"Nice move, Brantley!" I recognize Simmons' voice and feel my face flush. Dammit. I bet it matches my dress.

"I've wanted to do that for a while," Jace whispers in my ear and my heart flips head over heels.

"I've wanted you to," I admit and look down at his tie suddenly self-conscious.

"I wasn't sure," Jace says and lowers his lips to my forehead.

"Wow. You really went for it. This is quite the stage to for not being sure," I add and look up to Jace laughing.

"I figured you wouldn't slap me in front of all these people." He looks around. "It was my safest bet."

The song fades away to a faster song and the students fill in around us on the dance floor.

"Wanna find a quieter spot?" I ask taking Jace's hand.

"With you? Yes." That smirk is back on Jace's face and sends a spark through me.

I lead him off the dance floor and see Tarin approaching us. "Fiona, I love that dress."

"Thank you. You look beautiful," I say, and Tarin turns to Jace.

"And you. It's about damn time." Tarin pokes her pointer finger into Jace's chest. Jace smiles and his cheeks grow pink. "Okay, I'll leave you two love birds alone." Tarin is swallowed up by the crowd on the dance floor.

Jace pulls out a chair at our table for me to sit. "Would you like something to drink?" he asks.

"Yes, please." I watch Jace walk away.

"OMG!" I turn to see Avery sit down in the seat next to me. "Finally!"

"What?" I giggle trying to look innocent, but I know my cheeks are glowing.

"Oh c'mon, you know what I am talking about. The kiss on the dance floor." Avery is giddy with excitement. "So, was it as amazing as it looked?"

"Yes." We both squeal. "So, what were you saying about a tattoo?" I ask trying to take the focus off me.

"Just that I like the location of Faith's tattoo. I think that's where I want to get mine."

"What are you thinking about getting?" I ask placing my elbows on the table and lean in to hear Avery.

"Not sure, maybe my birth sign with something else incorporated. I've been looking at some ideas." Avery adjusts her necklace to make sure the clasp is in the back.

"Yeah, I wish I had something cool I could get. You know, I don't really have anything I can do with my name like Faith."

"What do you mean?" Avery tilts her head.

"Well, like Faith's is 'faith over fear' which is pretty cool since Faith is her name."

Avery's brow furrows and mouth frowns. "That's not what I saw." Avery shakes her head and leans back in her chair.

"Well, that's the tattoo she got after graduation." I turn sideways in my chair. "Her and Ella went together. Ella got an arrow on her wrist and Faith got her tattoo on the inside of her foot."

"No, I mean the one on the back of her neck." Avery turns and runs a finger over her neck to show me.

"Faith doesn't have a tattoo on the back of her neck." My voice grows soft, and I shake my head.

"Yeah," Avery nods. "When La'Tonya let me watch her with Faith, I saw the tattoo on her neck when she rolled Faith on her side. I really like that location, but the tattoo she chose is odd—"

My ears start ringing and Avery's words blend into to background noise.

I think back to the day Faith and Ella got their tattoos. I wanted to go with them, but I had to work that morning.

"Let me see," I squealed when Faith walked in the door.

"OMG Fiona, it hurt so bad!" Faith proudly showed off her new tattoo.

"I love it, when I turn eighteen, promise we will get a tattoo together. Something for sisters." I bounced on Faith's bed as she looked at her foot.

"Absolutely not. This is my one and only. I thought I was going to pass out from the pain." Faith exaggerated each word. *"But of course, I will go with you."*

When did Faith get another tattoo?

I think back to the day she borrowed my black fitted crop top and red and black flannel shirt; the day we went shopping for Christmas. The day of the accident.

I was sitting on my bed when Faith walked in from the bathroom to my closet wrapped in a towel from her shower. She also had her hair wrapped up in a second towel and off her neck. Her back was turned toward me while she looked through my closet and she was wearing the rose gold toggle clasp necklace I got her for her birthday earlier this year, but no tattoo.

"Fiona. Fiona, what's wrong?" Avery's voice breaks through the memory. "You look like you saw a ghost." Avery places a hand on my arm, but I can't move.

"It's not Faith," I mumble but remain frozen in my seat.

"What?" Avery lets out a little laugh, but when I don't move, she continues. "Who's not Faith?"

"It's not Faith. I gotta go." I jump up knocking my chair backward.

"Fiona, you're not making any sense." Avery jumps up when I do, grabbing my chair to keep if from falling over.

I grab my clutch and coat and turn to run when Avery grabs my arm. "Fiona."

My roses! I take them in my arm and look to Avery.

"Tell Jace I'm sorry. I'll call later," I call over my shoulder and hear my booties clicking against the aggregate floor.

"Fiona, wait. Let me get Tarin and we'll come with you." Avery's voice calls as she tries following me.

In a trance, I run toward the door, pushing my way through the students.

"Fiona." Sam stops in front of me. "I need to talk to you."

"Not now, Sam." I push past him.

"Fi! Wait!" Sam calls but I keep going, through the doors to the parking lot.

I pull out of the parking lot and flashes of that horrible night come back to me.

Faith and me laughing at our parents who weren't listening to us before we left to go shopping. Faith driving as I rode in the passenger's seat. Then me behind the wheel of Faith's car. The person seated in the passenger's seat, long, curly blonde hair looking down at her cell phone. Faith not looking like Faith. Faith squeezed my hand, but only when I said—

The beep of my phone interrupts my thoughts. I answer the call.

"What the hell, Fiona?" Jace demands.

"I'm so sorry Jace. I will make it up to you—"

"Where are you going?" he interrupts.

"The hospital."

"Now? It couldn't wait?"

"I'll explain later. Promise."

"I would have went with you—"

"Jace, I can't talk now. I'll call you later." And I hang up the call as I pull in the hospital parking lot.

My heals click on the floor with each step as I rush down the corridor into to the room, I stop and look at the body lying in the hospital bed. I quickly glance around the room to make sure Mom and Dad are gone. LaTonya is the only one here.

"Fiona. What are you doing here? Aren't you supposed to be at a formal or something?" LaTonya stops what she is doing when I don't respond. "What is it, Fiona?"

Unable to bring myself to say it, I just stare at the bed.

"What's wrong?" LaTonya turns to me, but I keep my focus on the bed.

"Faith." I swallow hard to remove the golf ball from my throat. "That's not Faith."

"Gurl, you been smokin somethin' funny tonight?" LaTonya laughs. "You ain't makin' a lick of sense."

"That's not Faith." I walk to the bed and look down at the body under the blankets. Blonde curly hair, blue eyes, but the bone structure doesn't match, especially as the swelling is subsiding from the last surgery. "Faith doesn't have a tattoo on the back of her neck. She has one on the inside of her left foot."

LaTonya watches me then after a few seconds, she walks to the head of the bed and gently lifts Faith's head off the pillow to look at her neck, her eyes go wide.

"Ella has an arrow on the bottom side of her right wrist." Holding my breath, I wait to see LaTonya confirm my biggest fear.

LaTonya lifts Ella's arm and moves the hospital bracelets out of the way.

"Oh. My. God. I gotta get the doctor!" LaTonya scurries out of the room.

I pull the sheet from Ella's left foot, just to prove to myself that this isn't Faith, there is no faith over fear tattoo. I gently return the sheet and take Ella's hand.

"Ella?" She squeezes my hand. "Can you blink if you're Ella?"

I watch her face intently, waiting for Ella to blink, finally she does.

The room starts to spin, the voice in the passenger's seat the night of the accident replays in my head. Ella's voice. Ella was the one in the car with me that night. In the passenger's seat. That's why the phone the police found was hers. Not Faith's.

I slowly release Ella's hand and let it fall to the bed. I back away from the bed as Ella turns her head to meet my eyes. I stumble over a chair behind me but manage to stay upright on shaky legs. I make it to the door, never taking my eyes off Ella.

Ella opens her mouth, but nothing comes out at first. Then in a horse, painful whisper, "Find...her..."

Chapter 19

The cold winter air smacks my face as I rush out of the hospital doors. I shiver realizing I never put my coat on. I wrap my arms around my chest to fight of the chill and run across the parking lot as fast as my stilettos allow me to move when I hear a voice over my shoulder.

"Faith," the whisper echoes through the air. I stop in my track as a chill runs down my spine, and I turn in the direction of the sound, but no one is there. Just the rustling branches of the leafless trees in the wind and a light snow starting to fall.

I stand in the middle of the parking lot and look around, watching, convinced I am not alone.

I turn back to my Jeep and run. I open the door and jump in as quick as possible, locking the doors behind me.

I scan the parking lot, still no one there. No black car.

"Get it together, Fiona. You're losing your mind." I reach for my coat in the passenger's seat and slide it on as I fight off the chill. I jam my key in the ignition, press in the clutch which feels clumsy in heals, turn over the engine and shift into reverse.

I pull out of the parking lot, not sure where to go or what I am supposed to do. I start driving in the same direction I came and pass

SWU's main campus. The light up a head turns yellow, then red and I pull up to the line and stop. As I wait for the green light, I look at the street sign. High Street.

An image comes to mind, and I flash back to the night of the accident.

"Fiona, you just said 'left,'" Faith shouted in argument, but I couldn't control my laughter.

"I know. But I meant right. You know I don't know my left from my right." I was laughing at my own mistake.

"Ugh! You are driving me crazy. Is it left or right?" Faith laughed even though she was trying to be mad.

"Right. It's right." I looked at my GPS again. *"Definitely take a right on High Street."*

"If you get us lost, so help me God—"

"It's right. I promise," I shouted, and Faith followed my instructions. *"See, we are passing the front of SWU's campus. I remember Ella saying we would."*

The horn behind me blares and I look up to see the light has turned green.

I turn on to High Street and am now going the same direction Faith and I did the night of the accident. I glance to my left and see stone lions guarding the SWU campus all lit up with snow swirling around them.

The next light turns green, and I buzz through.

"Take a right at the next light. It should be College Street," I heard myself say from the passenger's seat of Faith's car.

I stop at the red light at College and High Street, I look to my left and see the location of the accident after we left the party. I'm suddenly back in that night and behind the wheel of Faith's car, my heart racing, hands sweaty and fear in my heart.

"Hurry! Follow them!" Ella screamed from the passenger's seat, panic in her voice. "Don't stop. You have to make the light!"

I pressed down on the accelerator of Faith's car, the engine roared as I turned the steering wheel hard to the left, throwing Ella against the window. The tires squealed against the pavement as the car rounded the corner, I glanced to the light as it flashed to red.

"Fiona!" Ella shrieked which drew my eyes back to the to the road.

"Shit!" I tried to correct my mistake but I over corrected and the car started fishtailing. Ella's screams filled the air and I tried again to get the car under control. I jerked the wheel back to the left, but the car flew over the curb and my ears filled with the sound of scrapping and crunching metal as the back-passenger's side corner panel clipped the fire hydrant sending us flying through the air.

The accident report said we flipped twice before coming to a stop 120 yards from the light.

The light in front of me changes from red to green and brings me back to the present. My heart is still pounding from the memory.

I turn right onto College hoping something or someone tells me where to go next. But nothing looks familiar as I pass a church on my left and houses on the right.

The first road I come to on my left is Illinois. But that's not it and I keep driving.

My voice pops in my head and takes me back to that night.

"Turn left on Dennis." I told Faith while still looking at my phone. *I looked up to search for the next street sign. "There, Dennis Ave." I pointed.*

Faith followed my directions and turned onto Dennis.

"Ok, at the first road, take a left and go two blocks and turn right," I instructed, Faith followed.

"This road?" Faith slowed down at the sign.

"Ah, Lake? Yep." I nodded and looked back to my GPS. "Take a right on Lake St. The house should be on your left."

I see the sign for Lake and turn right, then slow down to look at the houses. They all look the same, build in the same era. Brown brick with front porches varying only slightly in style and two concrete paths just

398

wide enough for the tires of a car running from the side of the house to a single car detached garage behind the house.

The houses look familiar because I've seen them before in the photo Quincy and Buchanan showed me. Where they found Ella's car. What was the number on the house in the picture? #4..3..6? Yes. #436 and I start searching.

I roll to a stop in front of #436 and look around for anything I recognize but nothing stands out to me. It's the same house, but different from the night we were here. It was lively and loud, music pouring from the seams and packed with people. Cars lined the street and every light in the house was on.

But tonight, the street is quiet, the house is dark and there is no sign of life. The house looks empty.

I pull over to the curb, and stare at the house. *I need to see the inside.* I step out onto the sidewalk and look around hoping something is recognizable to me.

I walk up the steps to the porch, and flash back to Ella standing on the porch with a solo cup in her hand.

"Faith! Fiona!" Ella ran down the steps and threw her arms around us both, sloshing half the beer out of her cup.

On the porch, I look through the window of the dark house, the light from the streetlamp shines in. It's empty. I hope for a memory, but nothing comes to me, so I walk to the door and turn the doorknob, but it's locked.

I notice the walkway leading to the back of the house and follow it. At the back of the house, the garage door is open to the detached garage. The door is three-fourths of the way down, but I can tell there is a vehicle in the garage. It looks to be a bigger vehicle, a truck or something. The chrome bumper is sticking out and I feel a distant memory that I just can't pull. Like I am forgetting something.

I jump at the sound of a car alarm and turn back to the street but see nothing. A nervous laugh escapes me when there is no one there. I turn to the back of the house and see the back door. I swing the screen door open and look through the window at the dark and empty kitchen. I knock on the door and hear no response, so I turn the knob and the door swings open.

"Hello?" I ask and hold up the flashlight on my cell on so I can see. I find the light switch and flip it on, but the electric must be off.

I shine my flashlight around the kitchen, the gray tile floor and white painted cabinets take me back to that night.

"C'mon, let's get you a drink." Ella pulled Faith by the hand to the keg in the kitchen. Faith kept my hand tight in hers.

"I'm driving tonight. I can't drink." Faith shook her head no.

"Oh, one won't hurt you." Ella grabbed two more solo cups and handed us each one. We waited our turn for the keg and the guy working the pump told Ella to slide the cup under the stream.

"Here ya go." Ella giggled handing Faith a cup, then to me when a guy walked up and wrapped his arm around Ella waist.

"I need one too." He leaned in and grabbed her butt.

"Get it yourself." Ella pushed his hand away. The guy started laughing and turned to the guy at the keg who laughs and slurs, "Dude, what do ya think you're doing?"

"Is this your boyfriend?" Faith leaned toward Ella and asked.

"Ah, no...he isn't here yet. So, where did you go today?" Ella changed the subject quickly and we followed Ella through the doorway to another room.

I walk the same path we took that night, through the doorway from the kitchen to the empty and dark dining room, I can see the card game going on that night, but I can't remember what they played.

Then I turn to the right and through the doorway to the living room where the couch was. Ella, Faith, and I sat chatting and catching up and I remember being interrupted.

"Ella!" Ella looked in the direction of her name and her smile dimmed when she saw his expression.

401

"I'll be right back." She walked over to the guy who kept looking in our direction. I remember biting my lip as I watched him, and Ella quietly argue.

"I'm sorry." Ella said as the guy swung his arm toward us and glanced in our direction. "I said I'm sorry. Okay?" Ella pleaded. I couldn't hear what else was being said but when I turned back to Faith, she was talking to a cute guy. When he saw me look his way, he introduced himself.

"I'm Trev." He held out his hand for me to shake. "Short for Trevion."

"Fiona." I nodded and then looked back in Ella's direction, but they were both gone. I look around the room, I didn't see Ella, but Trev drew me into his and Faith's conversation.

"So, you're the little sister, huh..." Trevion nodded.

A few minutes later, Ella came back, but she seemed shook.

"You okay?" I asked and reached out to touch her arm. I had an uneasy feeling in my gut.

"Yeah, I'm good," she said, but she seemed distracted and a little sloppy.

"Are you hammered?" I asked and giggled.

"No. Maybe..." Ella shrugged with a smile.

"How many drinks have you had?"

"One, two…" she looked into her cup. "Three…I think." Ella slurred.

"You need to slow down."

"Ella, do you know Trev?" Faith interrupted.

Ella looked at him, blinked her eyes and squinted. Her face seemed to grow pale. I turned to Trev and noticed the look on Trev's face. He was smiling but his eyes were…threatening.

"No, I…I…" Ella shook her head and took another drink from her glass.

I looked to Faith and wonder if she noticed their exchange, but she's smiled at Trevion, and he quickly recovered his expression.

My memory of that event fades so I move in the direction of the back room, which looks to be a small family room or den. My eye is drawn to the side door to my left and another memory floods back to me.

"Fi. Come with. I need to go to the bathroom," Ella said as she stood up and stumbled a bit then grabbed my hand.

As girls do, we took turns in the bathroom and checked our faces while waiting. It couldn't have been more than ten minutes when we returned to the couch down stars. But Faith wasn't there, and neither was Trevion.

"Hum, I wonder where Faith went?" I looked around the room and in the front room, she wasn't there.

"She must be getting a drink." Ella turned to the kitchen, and I followed. Trevion was whispering to the hottie Ella had words with. Both Trev and Ella's hottie went quiet when they saw us.

"Hey." I turned to Trevion. "Where did Faith go?"

The guy Ella was arguing with turned away from us.

"She said she needed to use the restroom and got up to follow you two upstairs." Trevion shrugged. "I figured I would use this time to get a beer." He raised his cup.

I glanced to Ella's hottie who was staring out the back window of the house ignoring our conversation.

"Uh, we didn't see her." I turned to Ella who was looking around the room and toward the stairs.

"She has to be here somewhere," Ella said and stumbled again.

I turned and walked from the kitchen through the dining room, not aware that Ella wasn't following me. I searched the house and was on the front porch when I thought I heard her voice. I went back into the house and entered the living room, but no Faith.

The room behind the living room was dark except for a glowing light that drew me in. I looked around but all that was there was an empty bookcase and a desk. The glowing light was coming from the left side of the room which had a side door with a window that allowed the outside light to stream through. The door was open slightly and I reached for the door handle and pulled the door toward me when I heard muffled noises coming from outside.

I looked down at the crunch of metal under my boot and saw the keys lying on the floor.

"Oh!" I jumped and let out a squeal as someone put their hand on my shoulder. "There you are," I said when I turned to see Ella.

I bent over to pick up the keys and held them to the light of the door. My stomach flipped as the light shone on the college ID holder, the royal blue and white Vera Bradly keychain ID holder with a capital S on the front. A Christmas Present from Ella when Faith was accepted to State.

"Faith's keys." I turned to Ella holding them up. "She must have gone outside and dropped them on her way."

"He—!" I recognized the muffled voice as Faith's. I swung the door open and stepped onto the concrete slab and felt the drizzle of rain hit my face. Ella was right behind me. My eyes adjusted to the dark and the sound of a door sliding open drew my attention to the road.

The rain created a haze, and I could barely make out the two hooded figures wearing all black. The bigger on of the two had his

hand over Faith's mouth and dragging her toward the street. She was
squirming and kicking her legs trying to get loose from his grip.

The creak of the floorboard to my right snaps me back to the present.

"Oh, shit." I turn my flashlight on the dark figures standing between me and the doorway to the kitchen and I cover my heart with my hand. "You scared me," I breathed and let out a giggle as I recognize the hottie Ella was arguing with at the party.

"Ah, I was just hoping to remember something, anything really, from the night I was last here with Faith." I wave my hand as I turn around in the room.

"That's not a good idea," Ella's friend says, eyes empty and glaring at me.

"Oh, you're probably right. I know, I should have waited till tomorrow or brought someone with me. I just really want to remember something that will help find Faith—"

"We would rather you not," the other figure adds and moves toward me. My flashlight hits his face and I recognize Trevion.

"Faith was a mistake," Ella's hottie hisses, and he cocks his head to the side.

My heart skips a beat at his words and a shiver runs down my spine.

"Um, hey, I'm not here to cause any trouble." My eyes dart back and forth from the two glaring at me, and I take a step back. "Maybe I should go." I look to the doorway leading into the kitchen where I entered, but the two have it blocked. Franticly, I glance around the room and wish I weren't wearing stilettos. I quickly turn to the living room doorway and run hoping to make it to the front door.

I dig my heels in to stop as Trevion jumps in front of the door blocking my exit. My heart is thumping, my breath quickens, and I have a metallic taste in my mouth. I look around the room for my next move.

Both sets of eyes watching, waiting, anticipating what I might try. Ella's guy moves toward me, and I take a step back.

Then I remember the side door behind me. I spin around and dart for the door. I feel an arm wrap around my waist, and I swing my elbow back as hard as I can hoping to make contact.

"Ouch! Fuckin' bitch!" I reach for the doorknob and feel the cold metal in the palm of my out-stretched hand as I turn and try to pull away. My head juts backward as my hair is being ripped from my scalp and my body is hurling through the air. Pain shoots through my skull and my ears fill with the bone-chilling sound of my head cracking against the bookcase and I slump to the floor.

I try to focus and get my bearings, but my vision is blurry, and I can't make out what's in front of me. I reach my hand out patting the wood floor around me searching for my phone as I try to get to my hands and knees.

"In here!" Someone shouts. And suddenly the room is filled with grunts, but my vision is blurry, and I can't tell what happening.

I run my hand up the wall and find one of the shelfs to grab onto to help me up. As I try to get to my feet, I hear the clattering of heels heading toward me.

"Fiona!" I look up in the direction of the voice, and squint trying to make out who it is. "We're here." My head is pounding, and everything is blurry and spinning.

"Avery?" I mumble.

"Yeah, c'mon. Tarin and I need to get you out of here." Avery drapes one of my arms around her shoulder and Tarin has the other and I'm on my feet, but they are doing all the work. My head feels like it is split in two and I feel something wet running down the back of my neck.

"Oh, shit! He's got a gun! Back off, Simmons." The room goes silent and Avery and Tarin turn in the direction of the scuffle and freeze, pushing me behind them.

"Let's go." I recognize the voice as Ella's friend and hear the two scurry out the back door.

"You okay?" a second voice asks.

"Sam? Is that you?" I question and look around trying to see who's here, but I can't focus.

"Yeah. Simmons and Jace are here too," Sam replies.

"I got her. I got her." Jace's voice getting closer, and I'm lifted off my feet, cradled in his arms, my head resting on his shoulder.

"Let's go!" Simmons shouts. "We gotta get out of here!" I hear the shuffling of everyone's feet on the hard wood floors.

"We need to get her to the ER," Avery instructs, and my world goes dark.

Chapter 20

I knock lightly on the bedroom door, not wanting to wake Mom if she's finally fallen asleep. I turn the knob and quietly push the door open peeking my head in her room. The pile of blankets is barely moving but I can hear her sniffle and I know she hasn't slept since the hospital notified her that the girl she has been holding vigil over for the past six weeks is not Faith. And the missing persons file on Ella is close and a new file open on Faith DeWitt.

As quietly as I can, I crawl into bed and wrap my arms around her and the dam brakes. Mom's sniffles become full blown sobs and she takes my hand in hers. My head throbs with each sob but I don't let go.

After a few minutes, her sobs subside, and she brings my hand to her lips for a gentle kiss.

"How are you feeling, Fi?" Mom whispers while wiping her tears.

"I'm okay."

"Don't lie to me. How are you feeling?" she scolds.

"I'm tired. And my head is throbbing. I feel like the stitches are pulling my scalp." I let out a deep breath. "And they shaved my head!"

Mom lets out a half sob, half laugh. "It's only a one-by-one inch square, Fiona. And it's on the back of your head."

410

"I guess it's the match to my horn." And a sob escapes my lips and Mom chuckles again though the tears.

"At least you have a sense of humor. Don't ever lose that, Fi." Mom rubs my hand. "You need to take another pain pill."

"I did a few minutes ago." I close my eyes.

"Did Jace leave?" Mom sniffs.

"I finally got him to leave a few hours ago. He looked like hell."

"He was worried about you," Mom mumbles.

"Yeah, I know," I sigh.

Mom rolls over to face me.

"What were you thinking going to that house alone? You could have been—"

"I know, I know. But that didn't happen thanks to Jace and Avery...and Sam. Hell, I even have to thank Simmons." I feel my eyes roll.

"Don't cuss, young lady."

"I think that's the least of our worries," I retort and get another half laugh, half sob from Mom.

"You are very lucky they followed you. I know things aren't good between you and Sam, but you need to call and thank him." Mom raises her eyebrows to make her point. "And the others too."

"Yeah, I know." I let out a sigh and rest my head on Dad's pillow.

"So, what where you doing at that house? Why did you go?" Mom asks and I feel relief that she is not accusing me.

"I-I don't know really. My mind was spinning after I realized Ella was in the coma and Faith was missing. I didn't know what to do but I had to try to find her. Then, as I was driving away from the hospital, things from that night started coming back to me. The directions I was giving to Faith that night that got us to the party." I choke back a sob, tears rolling down my cheeks. "I found it. I found the house. It looked empty and I just wanted so badly to remember what happened that night. Why was I the one driving away from the party? What was Faith—who I now know was Ella—so panicked about in the passenger's seat? I could feel my own panic all over again and I needed to know why. So many questions." Choking back a sob and use the back of my hand to wipe my nose. "I hoped going into the house would help me remember." My sobs take over, adding pain to my already throbbing head.

"Ah, honey. It will come back." Mom wipes away my tears and rubs here hand over my hair.

"We don't have time to wait for my memory to come back. Faith is missing. We need my memory now. I feel like I am still missing pieces—"

"Shhhh…Okay, okay. I understand your urgency, but right now, you need to rest. You took a really hard-hit last night. We are lucky it wasn't worse." Mom kisses my forehead. "Is your dad home yet?"

"No, he texted me and said he was putting up fliers around campus."

"I should have gone with him. I just couldn't bear to go today," Mom confesses.

"Everyone grieves differently. That was really heavy news you both got last night," I admit, only able to imagine how hard it must be to hear as parents.

"You too, ya know. You are the one who figured it out. How did you know?" Mom asks.

"Well, I just didn't see Faith in the person lying in that bed. But it wasn't until Avery went with me to the hospital last week. She wants to go into nursing so when LaTonya was checking Faith's, I mean Ella's back, Avery asked to watch. Then at the dance last night, Avery commented about the location of Faith's tattoo on the back of her neck. Faith only has the one tattoo, the one she and Ella got after graduation and it's on her foot. That triggered it and I knew it wasn't Faith, but I had to go see to believe it."

I look at Mom and see the pain on her face as tears leak out the corner of her eyes and run toward her pillow. Pain caused by my words, reminding her that her daughter who was just yesterday coming out of a coma, is now missing.

"I'm so sorry, Mom. It was bad enough when it was Ella. But—"

"At least Ella's parents will finally have some peace." Mom sniffs, closing her eyes at the thought. Tears flowing freely.

"Yes, but you know they are worried about Faith." I rub my thumb over the back of Mom's hand.

"I know they are. We talked for a long-time last night. Well, Denise did most of the talking, I was a mess staring at Ella lying there." Mom gives a halfhearted laugh which turns in to a sob.

"So, now what?" I ask. "What do we do? Where do we start?"

"I don't know, honey, but you are going to heal, and your memory will come back. Faith is out there; we don't give up." Mom sits up in bed and throws the covers off, still sniffing as she stands up. "I've cried long enough; time to find her."

I get up to follow Mom to the bathroom and stop to still my spinning head as I grab on to the bed post for support when the doorbell rings.

"I'll get it," I say.

"No." Mom rushes out. "You need to go lay down. You shouldn't be up."

"Mom, I'm—"

"Go lay down," Mom orders, face pale and puffy, eyes red. She turns and walks out of the bedroom.

In my room, I crawl back in bed and pull up the covers, Merida by my side, when I hear the front door open.

"Sam," Mom announces.

"Mrs. DeWitt, I just wanted to check on Fiona. I'm so sorry."

"I know you are. That's very kind of you." I hear my mom sniff. "And thank you. I hate to think what might have happened if you hadn't been there to help last night. You are all really lucky to be safe."

"I wish she wouldn't have gone by herself," Sam admits.

"We've already talked about that. Just be there for her. She is in her room."

I hear Sam walking down the hallway, he stops to knock before entering.

"Can I come in?" Sam peeks his head in. He is wearing a Cincinnati Reds baseball hat; his clothes are wrinkled, and his eyes are blood shot. He looks like how I feel.

I nod and wave him in. Not sure how comfortable I am with this since I think I have a boyfriend.

"How ya feelin?" Sam asks standing next to my bed, hands in his front pockets.

"I hurt." I roll my eyes and lay my head back on my propped-up pillows. "You can sit down." I pat the edge of the bed. *He has to know nothing is going to happen. I'm injured, and Mom is here.*

"You gave us all a scare last night," Sam admits, leaning forward, elbows on his knees looking over at me.

"Didn't mean to." I look down and pet Merida who has curled up on my lap to let Sam know she is number one. "I—thank you," I mutter.

"You don't need to thank me. I don't ever want to see you hurt Fi." I want to remind him that he did hurt me but what benefit would that bring?

"How did you end up with Jace anyway?" I ask and look up at him, still petting Mer. "Last time you two were close to each other, you attacked him."

Sam chuckles. "Well, that wasn't planned," Sam says, turning to me. "I mean last night anyway. After you ran past me refusing to talk, I knew something wasn't right. I thought Jace might have done something to hurt you, so I went looking for him. Avery had been looking for him too apparently and when I got there, I heard her explain what you told her. She was worried. She knew something was wrong. Tarin and Simmons' found us about the time we were leaving and followed as Avery filled them in. We jumped in Jace's Tahoe and tried

416

to follow you, but you were gone by the time we got out of the parking lot." Sam looked at me, eyes as dark as storm clouds.

"So Jace called me..." I nod, close my eyes, and lay my head back on the pillow again as fatigue rolls through me. I could sleep for days.

"Yep. And we figured we would catch up to you at the hospital. We all thought you would need our support for whatever was going on, but by the time we got there, we saw you pulling out of the parking lot. We followed you from there. We lost you a few streets from the house, so we drove around until we found your Jeep." Sam drops his head and turns away from me.

"Thank you. I don't know what else to say." I fiddle with the seam of my blanket.

"Not necessary." Sam keeps his eyes on the ground.

"What were you wanting to talk about last night?" I ask hoping to lighten the mood. I wince at the pain in my head and back as I push myself up in bed.

"I—it's nothing. Just forget it. I just wanted to check on you today." Sam watches me with pained eyes, then looks back to the floor.

"I'm glad you did." I reach out for his hand and give it a squeeze, then quickly pull back. It's just such a natural thing to do when I see him upset. To reach out and comfort him.

"Who lives at the end of your street?" Sam asks and nods in the direction of the cul-de-sac. I look to window in that direction, but my curtains are pulled so I can't see anything.

"I don't know. I assume new neighbors, why?" I narrow my eyes wondering what Sam's thoughts are.

"That Charger is straight fire." Sam tilts his head and looks to me. Eyebrows raised.

"The one with blacked out windows?" A chill runs down my spine, my head shoots up a bit too fast and my head is a little woozy.

"Yeah, I've seen it parked there before when I came by—"

"When? When was that?" I sit up and lean toward Sam, ignoring my throbbing head and barely notice I am biting my lip and clutching Mer to my chest.

"Maybe the last time I was over, or the time before that. I didn't really think anything about it then, but I started thinking, 'Why would they park a car like that on the road?'"

"What do you mean?" I lean back and let Mer relax back into my lap, but I keep my fingers in her fur for comfort.

"Well, it's clearly a newer car with several modifications so money has been spent on it. Rims, low profile tires, exhaust, aftermarket hood, after market headlights and taillights. Why would you spend that much

418

money on it to make it Gucci, then leave it on the street to be damaged?"

"Maybe there isn't enough room in the driveway?" I shrug but that sinking feeling in my gut is back.

"Fi, that driveway is as long as yours. You could fit six cars easily."

I think back to when Faith and I would go to that house to play with Kimber and Dara before they moved. The driveway was big, maybe even bigger than ours.

"What did the cops say about Faith when you talked to them at the hospital?" Sam's words snap me back to the present.

"Oh, uh. I told them what happened, how I got to the house and confirmed it was the house they found Ella's car parked in front of. Um, then I told them what I remembered from the night of the accident and who the guy was but all I could give them was Trevion and the description of Ella's friend. I told him about her supposed boyfriend, X. I don't know what that stands for. They are going to check campus records for students with X in the initials. Officer Quincy suspects they are fake names." I pause. Sam hangs his head. "But they are hopeful with the information I gave them that it will give them some knew leads."

"You did good, Fi. Still not happy you went by yourself. You might be the bravest person I know." Sam lets out a small cluck. "Or just really stupid."

"Stupid. It was stupid." I let out a light laugh which hurts my head. Sam keeps his head lowered but lets out a laugh as well.

"Yeah, it was. But leave it to you, Fi, to do something so brave and stupid." Sam shakes his head and avoids looking at me.

"Knock knock." Mom peeks her head in my room. "Fi, I am going to meet your dad at the hospital. If Ella is coming out of the coma, we want to see if she remembers anything—"

"I'm coming." I throw my off my covers off and start to climb out of bed.

"No. Absolutely not. Not today. I will take you into see her tomorrow. Today you need to rest. Sam, it's time for you to go," Mom adds and leaves to give us privacy.

"Yes, Mrs. DeWitt." Sam turns to me. "Keep all the doors locked and call if you need anything."

I nod and sit back in my bed.

"Is Jace coming over?" Sam turns back to me.

"Sam." I roll my eyes. "That's none of your busi—"

"No." Sam shakes his head. "I think it would be smart if you had Jace come over while your parents are gone. There are just too many unanswered questions," Sam sighs. "I just don't think you should be alone."

"I'll ask him when he calls later." I bite my lip and look back to Mer.

"Good." Sam gets up and pulls the covers I threw off back over me. "Bye Fi."

"Bye Sam." I wave and give a weak smile.

I hear Mom at the door with Sam.

"Thanks again, Sam."

"Don't mention it." The front door closes, and Mom walks down the hall.

"Fi, you need to eat something. I left money on the table for you to order food—"

"Mom, can I please go? I really need to see Ella." I want to ask her so many questions if she is up, but my body reminds me I am not ready to do anything yet. I am no help once again.

"Fi, it won't do any good for you to risk doing too much too soon. Besides, she might not be able to communicate yet."

"She can." But I don't think I should tell her what Ella said to me. I need to tell Quincy though.

"Fiona, I understand. We all want answers. But let your dad and me see how she is doing first. We don't want to push her too soon either. I promise, rest today, I will take you to see her tomorrow after your doctor's appointment."

"Fine." I cross my arms and pout my lips for good measure, which gets a laugh combination sob from mom. But deep down, I am relieved and sink back into my bed.

"See, you're already getting back to your normal teenage self." Mom kisses my forehead. "Oh, the investigators talked to your dad at the hospital. They may come by later to ask a few more questions. Do you want us to come home and be with you for that?"

Mom waits by my bed for my answer. I think back over the night in question and wonder if I missed anything. Then I shake my head no.

"I've talked to them before without you and Dad, I'll be fine." I look over to the picture of Ella on my desk still sitting there.

"Okay but call if you change your mind." I nod at my mom's instructions. "Need anything before I go?"

"I'm good. Oh, can I ask Jace over later? If he wants to drive back over here."

"Yes, and I am positive he will drive back over here in a heartbeat. Get some rest, Fi." Mom gives me a weak smile.

"Love you," I call, and Mom blows me a kiss through tears.

I listen to hear the garage door open and close, then get up to use the restroom, but Ella's picture on my desk calls to me. I pick up the picture and flip it over to look at the writing on the back.

12/3/22

53:22

LT 5105

Ella sent this picture to Faith in October. So, what is 12/3/22?

I sit down at my desk, and wince at the pain in my back. I take out my iPad. Damn it. Still dead and no charger. I grab the picture and walk to Faith's room and sit down at her computer.

My heart sinks. *She's gone. She's really gone.*

The computer beeps to life, I pull up the calendar on the screen and scroll back to December. December 3rd was the Saturday before Faith's finals. She came home that weekend to study I remember.

"C'mon, Faith, let's go shopping or something," I begged and *plopped down on her bed.*

"Fi, I can't. I came home to get away from the dorm so I could study in peace!" Faith shouted. "I need to focus. Econ is really hard."

"Ugh." I rolled over and hopped up. "Fine. But if you go out with Ella tonight, I'm going to be pissed."

"She's got plans, remember? I told you, a Christmas party. It's formal and at a Gucci place downtown," Faith said as I left her in her room to study.

At the computer, I close out the calendar and open the internet. Not sure what to search, I type in 5105. The computer screen is filled with tax codes, addresses, all sorts of things.

Thinking of other ideas, I type it in LT 5105. Healthmark Industries LT 5105. I can't image Ella having anything to do with that.

I think about it while staring at the computer screen, tapping on the keypad with my thumb.

I remember the year we went to Myrtle Beach we stayed in room 7321 and the seven meant seventh floor.

What buildings have five floors?

I type in SWU dorms and click on the link for campus housing and scroll through the list of dorms. Nothing starting with the initials LT.

Maybe apartment buildings around campus? Hundreds pop up. I scroll through the list but see no names with initials LT. There is a LS which stands for Logan St. Apartments…*so what else?*

What about hotels?

I search Cincinnati Hotels and a map with 76 hotels pop up, 12 per page. Finally, on page three, LT. Legacy Towers. A really "Gucci place."

I click on the link to the Legacy Towers web page, but I'm interrupted by the doorbell. I hop up from Faith's computer and peek out the window and see Jace's truck in the driveway. I look at the clock and realize two hours have passed.

I swing the door open and smile at Jace. My heart skips a beat.

"Hi." I reach my hand out for his.

"Hi, I tried calling." Jace stays standing at the door.

"Oh, I've been on Faith's computer. I must have left my phone in my room. Come in." I notice how tired he looks.

"I thought we could watch a movie. I know you need to rest." Jace kisses my forehead, then leans in, lifts my chin, and lightly kisses my lips.

I wrap my arms around him, giving Jace a hug and lay my cheek on his chest.

"Thank you again, for saving me last night. And for staying with me. You don't look like you got much sleep." I squeeze him tighter.

"I'm just glad you are okay. Promise you won't do anything that stupid again." Jace puts his hands on my shoulders and steps back forcing me to raise my head up as he stares into my eyes.

"I thought maybe I was brave," I add with a smirk.

"No. No, that wasn't brave." Jace shakes his head. "I mean it was, but no. Don't ever be brave again."

I turn back to the door to shut it and see Officer Buchanan and Quincy pull in the driveway.

"Who's that?" Jace asks stepping to the door and by my side. "The investigators? Didn't you talk to them last night?"

"Yeah, but they said they might come by with a few more questions," I admit, a bit annoyed at their timing but if it helps find Faith.

"Fiona, sorry to bother you again but we've been going over everything and want to try up a few loose ends," Buchanan offers as he sucks in air climbing my front steps. Both Buchanan and Quincy look like shit. They must have been up all night after Mom's call.

I step back and hold open the door, letting the officers in and motion them to the living room.

"We shouldn't be long Fiona." Quincy offers as he walks across the living room and takes a seat on the piano bench. Buchanan looks at a few family pictures on the wall then makes his way to the love seat. I lead Jace to the couch where we are stuck in the middle of the two of them.

"I think I told you everything last night," I offer and look back and forth between the two. My palms growing sweaty. I wipe them on my blue State joggers when Jace reaches out and takes my hand in his, placing his other hand on top. Both of us are sitting on the edge of the couch waiting for the interrogation to begin.

"So, first, everyone collaborated your story about what took place in the house. It sounds like you are pretty lucky to have such great friends." Buchanan nods to Jace. Jace bows his head and squeezes my hand.

"Very lucky." I nod and lean in giving Jace a kiss on the cheek.

"Okay, so let's go back over what you remember from the night of the accident. Not as it came back to you last night, but as you would piece that night back to together as it happened."

I reiterated everything that happened that day, and to the point of Faith and I pulling up to the party. I look to Buchanan who takes a photo of the house out of a folder and places it on the coffee table in front of me.

"Yes, that's it." I nod.

"Great Fiona, what happened next?" Buchanan asks and sits back into the white love seat my mom had to have, insisting Faith and I were old enough to handle a white couch. I still refuse to sit on it.

I walk them through meeting Ella on the front porch, us getting drinks and then sitting on the couch catching up and the guy Ella argued with.

"Did you hear what they were arguing about?" Quincy asks.

"No, it was hushed. But I got the feeling it was about us." I look to Quincy with a little shrug.

"How did he act?" Buchanan turns, ready to write my response.

"Pissed," I say flatly.

"Why do you think it was about you?" Buchanan interrupts, leaning toward me, pen hovering over the paper.

"I'm not sure, but he looked over to us a few times and waived his hand out toward us at one point. Ella looked to us then down to the ground. Like she was afraid." I look down to my hand intertwined in Jace's and feel guilt for not helping her.

"Was he unhappy that she invited you?" Quincy turns to me, still standing.

"I got that feeling but there's something more." I swallow hard. "I found messages on Faith computer the other day between her and Ella. Apparently, Ella had a boyfriend she referred to as X and Faith wanted to meet him. But it didn't sound like the boyfriend wanted to be met."

Buchanan and Quincy look at each other.

"Why didn't you tell us this?" Buchanan's voice booms and I jump.

"She's telling you now." Jace sits up, releases my hand, and puts his arm around me.

"I-I just forgot. Things have been so crazy." I shake my head and feel the all too familiar sting at my eyes. "And I only found the messages a few days ago."

"Okay, okay, so we will need to take a look at Faith's computer when we are done." Quincy lets out a breath, rubs his hand over his face and takes a seat back at the piano bench. "Anything else seem odd at the party?"

"Ah, yeah. Ella and the guy left the room and when she came back, she seemed really..." I look to Buchanan and then Quincy. "Well, she seemed a bit off. Like, she was lit."

"Lit?" Buchanan asks.

"Drunk." Quincy almost rolls his eyes at his partner's question.

"But she said she only had a few beers. There was something else too. Faith started talking to a guy who called himself Trev. 'Short for Trevion,' he said. And I remember when Ella came back, Faith asked Ella if she knew him. Ella acted a bit confused or maybe it was because she was drunk, but I felt like she was taking cues from Trev about how to answer."

"Why do you say that?" Quincy asks and is now leaning forward on his elbows. He raises one hand up and places it on the top of his thigh.

"Faith didn't notice, but when Ella started stammering, I looked to Trev who had this look. Like her was warning her or something; telling her what to say. Or maybe what not to say. Anyway, Ella and I got up to go to the bathroom and when we came back, Faith was gone." Tears pour over my lower lids and Jace hands me a tissue.

"Where were Trev and the other guy Ella was talking to?" Buchanan keeps his eyes on the paper in his small flip notebook.

"When we returned from upstairs, they weren't in the living room either. We started looking through the house and when we entered the kitchen, both Trev and the other guy were talking quietly in the kitchen. When I asked where Faith was, Trev said Faith went to find us in the bathroom."

"But you had just come down from the bathroom and you didn't see her," Quincy says.

"No, we didn't. I remember Ella said, 'We probably just missed her.'"

I shake my head at the memory and wipe my nose with the damp tissue. "It just didn't feel right. Ya know?" I look to both officers.

"So, you went looking for her?" Quincy asks keeping his eyes on me. I nod and fight off a sob. "What did Ella do?" he prompts me.

"I-I don't know. I thought she was following me when I walked out of the kitchen to look for Faith. I went back to the front of the house and stepped out on the front porch, but she wasn't there. I swear I heard her voice." Sobs interrupt my story and take over. I drop my head in my hands. Jace pulls me in to comfort me.

"We are going to do everything we can to find your sister, Fiona." Buchanan's voice softens. "Take a deep breath."

I follow his instructions and let out a huge sigh. Jace gets up and I watch him disappear into the kitchen and hear him open the fridge. He returns a minute later with a bottle of water and twists the lid handing it to me. I take a sip to give me a little more time. I take another deep breath and release.

"Is that when you realized Ella wasn't with you?" Quincy squirms on the wood piano bench.

"Yeah, I walked back into the house, but I didn't see Faith. The room behind the living room was dark. There was a light shining in from the side of the room." I shake my head trying to find my words and fight off a sob. "Something about it was calling to me."

I think back to the night of the accident and the fear I felt, yet I had a need to go into that room. I shiver and take a breath.

"I stepped to the side door in the back room to see what was going on outside when I heard a crunch of metal under my boot. I looked down and saw keys on the wood floor next to the door jam. That's when Ella found me. She scared the crap out of me when she put her

431

hand on my shoulder. I jumped and squealed." I let out a laugh at the memory.

"Once Ella found you, what did you do?" Buchanan asks, keeping his voice soft like he's trying to coax a scared kitten out of hiding.

"I bent over and picked up the keys on the floor. As soon as the light hit them, I saw the blue and white student ID holder. I knew before, but I turned it over and saw the S on the front for State." I swallow hard. "It was Faith's."

"What happened next?" Quincy stands up again.

"I held it up and looked to Ella. She blinked a few times trying to focus, then took it out of my hand to look at it. I heard a door open outside, like a slide door to a van. And I heard Faith's voice yell 'help' but I could only hear the h-e, the rest was muffled like her mouth had been covered up. So, I ran out the side door with Ella right behind me." I stop to get my composure and fight back the dam of sobs about to be released.

"You are doing great, Fiona. I'm right here with you." Jace rubs his hand on my back for reassurance. I close my eyes.

"Two figures in all black and wearing hoodies were wrestling Faith into a van. She was kicking and fighting. Trying to scream," I say fighting through the sobs, sucking in air as hard as I can. Jace pulls me back into him, my cheek on his chest.

432

"They…took...her…" I let out between sobs.

Buchanan and Quincy stay quiet letting Jace comfort me in my time of grief. Time seemed to stand still as the full weight of the situations hits me. My sister was kidnapped. All this time, I knew. I knew what had happened to her. I knew how it happened. I knew why I was driving Faith's car. I knew who was in the car with me when I had the accident. I knew why the accident happened. I knew it wasn't Faith in the coma. I knew I couldn't let them get away with my sister. And here I sit. My sister gone. And I knew.

I have no idea how long Officer Buchanan and Officer Quincy sat while Jace held me in his arms as I face my guilt and grief. I have no idea what time it is or how I still have tears leaking from my eyes. I should be dehydrated at this point. But finally, the heart wrenching sobs slow, and my breathing calms and I look up to find both officers with their elbows on their knees and head hanging. And I realize how hard this must be for them too.

"What else can I answer?" I ask wiping my tears away. I sit up from Jace, but I reach for his hand.

"Just a few more things Fiona—"

"If you feel you are up for it," Quincy interrupts Buchanan but I catch the glare Quincy is giving his partner.

"I-I'm ok. Sorry about that." I shake my head. "I want to help. What else do you need?"

"We are going to have a sketch artist come by first thing in the morning and get the description of this Trev and the other guy we assume might be Ella's boyfriend," Officer Quincy informs. "I know it was dark, but could you tell what color the van was?"

"Ah, yes. White. Like a work van or cargo van." My voice catches and I clear my throat.

"A university van maybe?" Buchanan asks while keeping his head down and pen going.

"Maybe." I shrug. "It all happened so quick. But I don't remember seeing a logo or anything like that."

"Did anything about the two people taking Faith stand out to you? Could you see their face or features?"

"No." I close my eyes and think back to that night and shake my head. "I never saw their faces and the streetlight closest to them was out. But I remember one was average height, about like my dad who is 5'11." I shrug. "I don't really know if that is average or not. The one that came around from the front of the van, I think he was the driver, was taller and thin." I sigh and open my eyes.

"Did you see the license plate?" Jace's voice startles me.

"I don't remember seeing it. By the time we got to Faith's car down the street and turned around, the van was quite a bit in front of us. We were following taillights," I explain, but feel I am forgetting something again.

"We're almost done Fiona. I want to ask you a few questions about the black Charger you called me about," Quincy says and my heart is in my throat. I notice Jace looks over to me.

"Did you find it on the street the night of the party?" I ask rubbing my temples, my head pounding. "Jace, would you go to the kitchen and get me the medicine bottle by the sink?"

Jace nods and stands, but I know he wants to hear about this car.

"Unfortunately, the camera view didn't reach very far. It wasn't in the video feed if it was there," Quincy admits and I hear myself release my breath, my heart sinks. "But we are reaching out to the church to see if they have tapes of other nights, before and after the night of the party."

"Don't give up, Fiona, if the car is connected to Faith, we will find it one way or another." Buchanan nods.

"We are hoping it will pop up on another tape, we will have our guys go over the tapes as soon as we get them. In the meantime, if you see the car, try to get the license place and text it to me." Quincy leans against the wall.

"If this car starts following you, call 911 and go straight to the police station. Explain that you have orders from us to do so." Buchanan nods.

"Can you let us see Faith's computer?" Quincy asks and they follow me to Faith's room.

Jace walks in with my medicine, hands the bottle to me and looks over my shoulder to see the picture of Ella on Faith's computer.

"Do you think the picture has something to do with Faith?" Jace puts his hands in his pockets.

"I'm not ruling anything out at this point." Quincy goes back to the computer and begins printing out the messages.

"Okay, you two. I think we got everything for now." Buchanan looks at me, "If you think of anything else. Call immediately."

"Got it." I nod, my fatigue is taking over.

"I think you need to get some rest," Quincy calls as we walk to the door. Before exiting, Quincy turns back around. "Oh, did you recognize the other person with Ella's friend last night?"

"Trevion," I state and look down to the floor.

"Get some rest, Fiona." Buchanan points to me.

I give a weak smile and a nod, but before Jace can push the door closed, I glance over his shoulder and down the road to the cul-da-sac. I exhale when I see the empty spot on the curb.

"What's up with the black Charger?" Jace pulls me down on the couch next to him and I lean in as he wraps his arm around me. I tell him everything about the car and Jace listens quietly and doesn't say a word, but I can feel him tense from time to time. I shiver at the thought of the car sitting at the end of the road, watching me. I remind myself the car isn't there.

"You cold?" Jace asks and pulls the blanket up around me.

"Just chilled from opening the door," I lie.

"How's your mom doing?" Jace asks as he plays with the ends of my hair.

"She's heartbroken, but she got out of bed and is at the hospital with my dad. She wants to see if Ella is becoming more responsive." I fight off a yawn.

"I can understand. How are you?" Jace places his index figure under my chin and lifts my head up so my eyes meet his.

"Scared." I let out a breath. "And tired. What if we don't find Faith?"

"Don't say that. You have to think positive. The cops have more to go one now thanks to you." Jace kisses my hand and turns slightly helping me settle in. "And with Ella getting better, hopefully she will add more too."

"Let's not talk about it." I yawn. Jace gently kisses my forehead.

"Okay, what movie do you want to watch?" Jace asks as I scroll through the available movies to stream.

"Mom gave me money for food later. Let me know when you are hungry."

We agree on *Top Gun: Maverick* and I let my head rest on Jace's shoulder, I feel safe with him next to me.

My eyes flutter shut. Exhaustion covering me like a blanket. Jace places a gentle kiss on the top of my throbbing head, and I start to drift off in his arms when the doorbell rings.

"Uh, what now?" I roll my eyes as I push away from the couch and my comfy spot against Jace. He follows me to the door.

I turn on the outside light and see a girl wearing a Hoosier's sweatshirt standing at the door.

"OMG! You *have* to be Fiona!" I hear her say as I open the door. "You and Faith look just a like. She told me so much about you." And the beautiful stranger with long Avery like braids steps in and wraps her arms around me for a hug.

My eyes go wide. I pull away from the girl and take a step back.

"I'm sorry. Who are you?" I ask and I feel Jace put his hand on my shoulder.

"I'm Raya. Faith's girlfriend," she says. Then continues when I don't move. "I have been worried sick about her. She hasn't returned

438

any of my calls or texts. I drove to State to find her, but her roommate wasn't there, so I didn't know how else to get ahold of her. I remember her saying her dad's name is Robert and that she grew up in Brookston, so I googled your address."

I stand there my mouth agape with no idea what to do or say.

"I know it's weird for me to just show up like this, but I didn't know what else to do." Raya drags out the word do and bounces nervously to her words. Then I notice the tears forming in her eyes. "*Please* tell me she's okay. I haven't heard from her since the day before Christmas Eve. She texted me when you guys were leaving the mall saying, 'I'll call tomorrow' and she never called. *Please!* Is she here?"

Acknowledgements

First, I have no idea what I am doing as I have never written an acknowledgment page before, let alone a novel. I had this concept for a story but wasn't sure it was worth the time and energy needed to complete it. Or if I could even write it the way I wanted.

I would have given up after chapter eight if not for Michelle, Tonia, Wendi, Angie, and Patty who read the first part of the manuscript and encouraged me to continue. Pam, without you, this book would never have been finished. Your continued support and demand for the next chapter is what prompted me to finish. So, I set up a timeline and outline for the remainder of the book and worked to stay at least one chapter ahead of you. You went a step further by being my support, sounding board and brainstorming partner once I received my development edit notes. Oh! And thank you for being on call 24-7 for grammar questions, ideas, and feedback, and you got me through my melt downs. You believed in this story before I even knew how to finish it. Katie, without your encouraging phone call, this book would not be getting published. You reviewed my outline and read every chapter and guided me on what my next steps should be. Rebekah, you should be a paid editor! Especially for all the help you provided when my editor failed me. And Angela, thank you for offering up all your resources. Your friends at work and your daughter Alyssa. Roz, wow! You are the one who helped me realize that I am a writer, although I am still not convinced. You have been my sounding board, support system, and encourager. Thank you all so much. The amount of support I have had during this process has been amazing. My heart is overflowing.

Of course, I couldn't have done this without the support of my family who have always taught me to stand up for myself and what I believe in. Who have taught me that I am capable of anything and if it is something that I want, to go for it. To my mom, you believed in me even when you probably shouldn't have. Thank you for being there for me, the phone calls, messages, and hugs. And of course, the advice, even when I didn't always listen. To my dad and brother, thank you for teaching me my value even when the world didn't always see it. And to my husband, you have been with me to see so many of my dreams and hopes come true. You believed in me even when I didn't believe in myself. You make me want to be better. Here's to more dreams coming true.

Lastly, to my Pams. You are both my real-life Faith! One of you is my adoptive sister and childhood neighbor and the other was given to me thanks to Aunt Bev and Uncle Tony. Who else is lucky enough to have two VIPs in their life? Very Important Pams!

And lastly, thank you all for taking a chance on Finding Faith.

Made in the USA
Middletown, DE
26 March 2023

27111650R00249